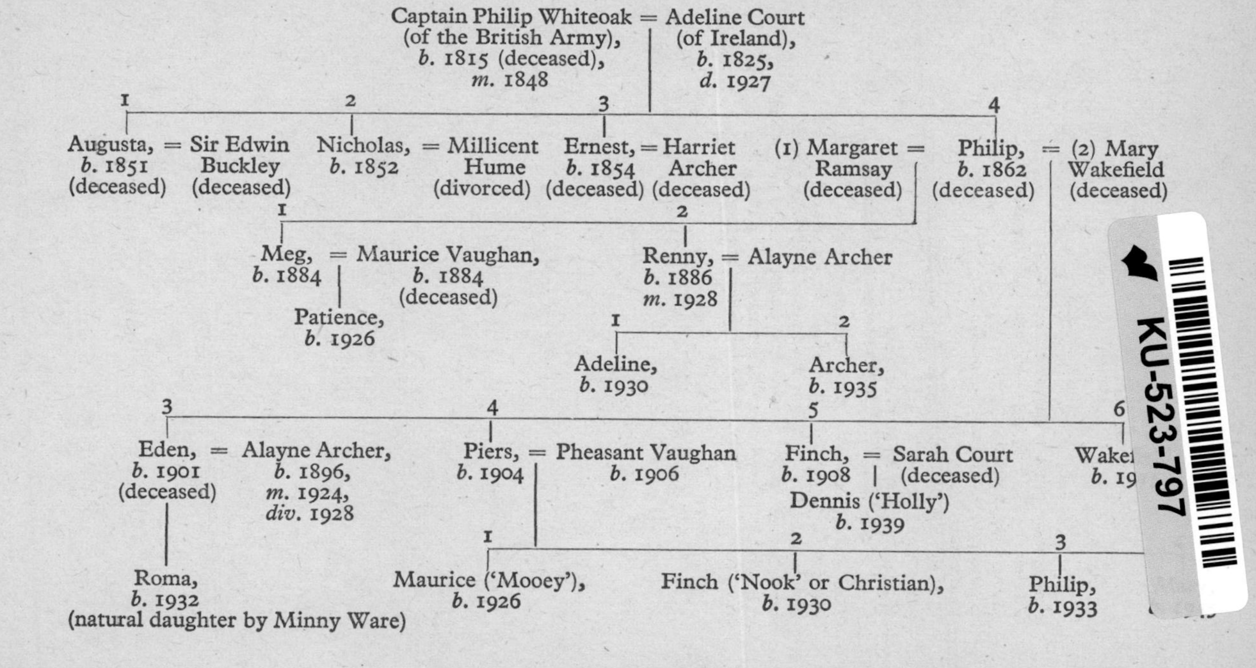
THE WHITEOAK FAMILY
Captain Philip Whiteoak = Adeline Court
(of the British Army),
b. 1815 (deceased),
m. 1848
(of Ireland),
b. 1825,
d. 1927
1
2
3
4
Augusta, = Sir Edwin Buckley
b. 1851
(deceased)
(deceased)
Nicholas, = Millicent Hume
b. 1852
(divorced)
Ernest, = Harriet Archer
b. 1854
(deceased)
(deceased)
(1) Margaret Ramsay
(deceased)
= Philip, = (2) Mary Wakefield
b. 1862
(deceased)
(deceased)
1
2
Meg, = Maurice Vaughan,
b. 1884
b. 1884
(deceased)
Patience,
b. 1926
Renny, = Alayne Archer
b. 1886
m. 1928
1
2
Adeline,
b. 1930
Archer,
b. 1935
3
4
5
6
Eden, = Alayne Archer,
b. 1901
(deceased)
b. 1896,
m. 1924,
div. 1928
Roma,
b. 1932
(natural daughter by Minny Ware)
Piers, = Pheasant Vaughan
b. 1904
b. 1906
1
2
3
Maurice ('Mooey'),
b. 1926
Finch ('Nook' or Christian),
b. 1930
Philip,
b. 1933
Finch, = Sarah Court
b. 1908
(deceased)
Dennis ('Holly')
b. 1939
Wake
b. 19

Variable Winds at Jalna

Mazo de la Roche was born in Toronto and spent her childhood on her father's fruit farm in Ontario. Educated at Toronto University, she disliked city life and decided to live in the country. Her first novel, *Explorers of the Dawn* (1922), attracted little notice, but she achieved fame with *Jalna* (1927), which won the *Atlantic Monthly*'s ten thousand dollar prize, and was followed by a number of sequels forming a family chronicle, which have recently been made into a highly successful television series under the title *The Whiteoaks of Jalna.*

She also wrote a comedy, *Low Life* (1925), several other plays, and a *History of the Port of Quebec* (1944). In 1930 she moved to England and in 1938 she was awarded the Lorne Pierce Medal of the Royal Society of Canada. She died in 1961.

Also by
Mazo de la Roche in Pan Books

The Building of Jalna
Morning at Jalna
Mary Wakefield
Young Renny
Whiteoak Heritage
The Whiteoak Brothers
Jalna
Whiteoaks
Finch's Fortune
The Master of Jalna
Whiteoak Harvest
Wakefield's Course
Return to Jalna
Renny's Daughter
Centenary at Jalna

Mazo de la Roche

Variable Winds at Jalna

Pan Books in association with **Macmillan London**

First published 1955 by Macmillan and Co Ltd
This edition, abridged, published 1958 by Pan Books Ltd,
Cavaye Place, London SW10 9PG
in association with Macmillan London Ltd
11th printing 1979

ISBN 0 330 02168 0
Made and printed in Great Britain by
Cox & Wyman Ltd, London, Reading and Fakenham

I

THE COMING OF THE LOVER

ALAYNE TURNED from the mirror to Renny. "Do I look all right?" she asked, with an odd little smile, as though she deprecated her interest in her appearance at this moment. And she added, "Not that he'll have any eyes for me."

Renny moved back a step to have a better look at her. It had been a distress to him when her beautiful hair, very fair, which she had worn long, had, in the space of a few years, turned silvery white. For a time he had avoided looking at it, as though it were some kind of disfigurement that had descended upon her. Then one day she had suddenly appeared before him with her hair cut short and curled all over her head. He had given her an outraged look—how had she dared have her hair cut without consulting him? Then he had looked again, had been impressed by the charm of her new aspect. He liked it, and, with his eyebrows still expressing outrage, he had given her a grin of approval.

Now he said, "He'll have eyes for you all right. A man usually takes a good look at his future mother-in-law."

She gave a shrug of impatience. "Don't say that, please. This affair may well fade into nothing before he's been here a week."

"Not if I know Adeline."

"Renny, how can you know her, any more than she can know herself? She likes to think she is the reincarnation of your grandmother—a woman of one great love—but remember how young she is. Twenty!"

"Would she know better if she were twenty-five?"

"Certainly."

"Did you?"

Alayne flushed. "You need not have reminded me of that," she said.

"I didn't mean to hurt you. Only to remind you that the great age of twenty-five is not always infallible."

She put a hand on either side of his head, drew it down, and kissed him. She said, "When I met you I could not help myself." She turned then and began briskly to tidy the things on her dressing-table.

He looked at his watch. "The train is due," he said, then added, with a touch of chagrin, "Funny Adeline didn't want me to go with her to meet him."

"I think it was only natural. Those first moments together will be something just for them."

Staring out of the window, Renny said, with his back to her: "Alayne, for some reason I suspect this Fitzturgis. I can't bring myself to like the thought of him."

She made a little ironic sound against her lipstick. "You'd feel just the same about any man Adeline was engaged to."

"No. I deny that. I shouldn't feel like this if it were Maurice."

"Of course you wouldn't. Maurice is her cousin—one of the family. I do believe that if you had your way all the cousins would marry each other. How would it end? With inbreeding. You don't do that with livestock, do you?"

He argued, for the sake of arguing, "There's something in knowing the background of one's son-in-law."

"Well, Adeline has told us quite a lot about him. His mother is a garrulous widow—his sister rather odd—his land unproductive."

"Are you trying to reassure me?" Renny exclaimed.

"It's just my pessimistic way."

"You don't relish this any more than I do!"

She was silent a moment and then answered, "I think Adeline is terribly vulnerable."

"She is made of good stuff," he said.

"Of course she is, but she's very inexperienced; and this Fitzturgis—well, you know what he's been through."

"Married and divorced, you mean."

"Yes."

Renny gave a sudden bark of laughter. He said, "Think how inexperienced I was! And you'd been married and divorced."

He had known before he said this that it would annoy her but had not been able to stop himself. In a tone of the most extreme politeness she said, "I think we had better go downstairs. It will be easier to meet them there, don't you agree?"

"I agree to anything," he returned.

She thought: 'You are in one of your unashamed bad-boy

moods, but you will find no response in me.' She asked, "Is Uncle Nicholas resting?"

"In bed. He wants Fitzturgis brought up to his room before he settles down for the night."

"Dear me—I hope it won't be too much for him."

"Too much! Not a bit of it." It was a part of his protectiveness toward his old uncle that he would not acknowledge the deterioration of his heart. He followed Alayne down the stairs to the drawing room, where tea was laid. He cast an appraising glance about the room. "Everything looks shining," he said, and put his nose into a bowl of roses.

Their son Archer came into the room. He was a tall boy of nearly sixteen, with a high forehead and clear light eyes. He hid his feeling of superiority toward almost everyone else beneath a retiring manner. He never smiled.

Now, looking over the tea table, he remarked in his clear incisive voice, "I suppose we're to starve while Adeline collects the Irishman."

"Surely, Archer," said his mother, "you wouldn't have us begin without our guest." She looked at him dubiously. She had fervently hoped that Archer would be like her father. Now ironically she found him rather too much like her father —an exaggeration of his less attractive qualities, with the gentleness, the politeness, left out, and in their place some disconcerting qualities of the Whiteoaks.

Archer said, "Probably by the time we've seen this Fitzturgis we'll not want our tea." He was a confirmed tea drinker. In a moment of nervous horseplay Renny reached for his son, intending to ruffle his hair, but Archer eluded him, placing the tea table between them.

Wragge, the houseman, appeared in the doorway. After thirty years in Canada his cockney accent still was crisp and confident. He said, particularly addressing Renny, which he invariably did as if no others were present, "I thought you'd like to know, sir, that the train 'as been 'eard to whistle."

"Good," said Renny, looking as though it were the reverse of good. "They'll soon be here."

A step was heard in the hall, and Wragge moved aside to allow Renny's sister, Meg Vaughan, to enter. She was two years older than he, a stout widow of sixty-six, and in great contrast to him, for while her face was smooth and the curve of her lips retained the sweetness of her girlhood, his thin weather-beaten face was strongly lined, marked by endurance and fortitude, and his thick red hair that grew to a point on his forehead showed scarcely a grey hair, while hers was of a fine iron-grey and naturally curly. Her movements were slow, while his had an incisive swiftness. It was the same with their speech.

Now she said, "I simply could not resist dropping in to see the Irish fiancé. How excited Adeline must be!" She waited till Wragge was out of hearing, then added, "If only it might have been Maurice."

"That's just the way I feel," said Renny, putting her into a comfortable chair.

Meg said, noting Alayne's expression, "I know I shouldn't have said that in front of the boy. But you'll forget what Aunty Meg said, won't you, dear?"

"That is '*lex non scripta*'," he returned, dropping into Latin in an irritating way he had. His father once more stretched out a hand to rumple him and again Archer eluded it.

Desultory talk prolonged rather than shortened the period of waiting. Alayne was the first to hear the approaching car. It appeared now on the smoothly raked gravel sweep, and all four peered from the shelter of the window curtains to have their first glimpse of the visitor.

"Oh, he's good-looking," exclaimed Meg in relief, for she attached much importance to looks, "but less tall than I had expected."

"A well-built fellow," said Renny, his appraising glance moving swiftly from Fitzturgis to the glowing face of Adeline. She had waited two years for the coming of this man. That she should be happy in the reunion was what mattered above all else.

Happiness shone from the burnished copper of her hair to her light step as she led the way into the house. The spaniel, the bulldog and the little Cairn terrier greeted the pair noisily in the porch. Fitzturgis bent to pat them and called each by name, for Adeline had so often talked of them and written of them. But, for all her glow of happiness, she was nervously excited too. Her pallor showed it and the swift glance almost of entreaty which she gave the group that now had come into the hall.

"Welcome to Jalna," said Renny, shaking the young Irishman's hand.

Meg, Alayne and Archer in turn greeted him: Meg with warmth; Alayne with calm relief, for she liked his looks better than she had expected; Archer with suspicion.

"Did you have a good crossing?" enquired Meg.

"Almost too good," answered Fitzturgis. "The Atlantic was much smoother than your lake."

"And the railway journey—was it comfortable?"

"Fairly. But very long. And very hot."

Alayne put in, "You must be quite ready for tea." She moved to the tea table, Archer close after her. He felt the teapot. He said, in a stage whisper, "He'd probably prefer whisky."

Fitzturgis answered, "Thank you, but I like tea."

Renny said, "I'll go up with you to your room first."

"Thanks. I should like to wash my hands."

The two men, with a purposeful air, left the room.

"May I have my tea now?" asked Archer. His mother, in desperation, poured it.

"Well," Adeline demanded eagerly, "what do you think of him?"

"He's most attractive," said Meg. "Such a sweet smile. And something a little sad in him too."

"I'm sure I shall like him," Alayne agreed.

Adeline drew a deep sigh of happiness and relief. "I can scarcely believe it's all over," she said. "The waiting, I mean."

"There are worse things than waiting," said Archer.

"Really, you are a pest, Archer," Adeline said hotly. "What can you know about waiting?"

"I know about cold tea," he returned.

Adeline asked of her aunt, "Why didn't Patience come?" Patience was Meg's daughter, an only child, four years older than Adeline. But with her lived also the daughter of her dead brother Eden. To this younger girl, Roma, Meg was as a mother. She now answered for both girls:

"Patience thought it would be confusing for the young man to meet so many of us at once. Roma went off somewhere with her boy-friend."

Adeline said, "It would not have been confusing to have Patience here. I do want her and Mait to meet."

"He'd likely prefer Roma," observed Archer.

"Archer, how can you say such things?" exclaimed Meg, hurt.

"Under a frivolous exterior I conceal a great deal of sagacity," he returned.

"One thing you can't hide is your conceit," said Adeline.

"I don't try," he answered. "I have so much to be conceited about."

Upstairs Maitland Fitzturgis had washed his hands and run a comb through his curly mouse-coloured hair. As he and Renny were passing the closed door of a bedroom Renny said, "In there is my Uncle Nicholas. You'll meet him later. Goes to bed early. He's very old. I hope he takes to you. We set a good deal of store by his opinion here."

"I shall look forward to meeting him."

Hungry though she was, Adeline was too much excited to enjoy her tea. There was her lover at Jalna, sitting among her own people—her mother pouring a second cup of tea for him—her father offering him a cigarette—her Auntie Meg giving him that sweet maternal smile. She was glad that there were not many of the clan present at this first meeting, and yet she was impatient for him to meet them all, to be approved by all and to voice his admiration of them to her. When Meg had gone and they stood alone together in the porch there came her first opportunity to ask:

"Do you like them—him—my father I mean mostly?"

"Very much," Fitzturgis answered warmly. "I like them all."

"Don't you——" She found it difficult to find the words she wanted. "Don't you think he's—rather remarkable-looking?"

"Quite. But it's your mother's looks I admire. She must have been a lovely girl."

"She was. She had beautiful fair hair. She's an American—or was, before she was married to Daddy's brother Eden and divorced—before she and Daddy married."

He answered, almost absent-mindedly, "I know. Maurice, I think, told me when we first met. . . . A nice house, this. I like your trees. How old is the house?"

"It will be a hundred years old before long. It's not very old, I know, in your country. But here it is quite an age. We're giving a party for the house on its centenary. Isn't it wonderful to think that you and I will be here for it—together!"

His answer was to put an arm about her and touch her hair with his lips. "I can't believe in it," he said. "Not yet."

"Soon you will," she said happily. "At this moment nothing seems too good to be true. Everything seems possible. . . . Oh, Maitland, I don't know how I lived through these two years." She looked into his face, on a level with her own, trying to see him as others not emotionally bound to him would see him. She could not, but saw him only through the enamoured eyes of her first love.

His mind returned to what had been told him of her mother's marriage to Eden Whiteoak. "Have you ever seen him?" he asked. "Your mother's first husband?"

"I don't remember him. He died when I was very small. He had a daughter, you know—by another marriage. That's Roma. She lives with Auntie Meg."

"You've something against her, haven't you?" he asked abruptly.

"Goodness, no." Then she added, just as abruptly, "Yes, I have. And you may as well know it. Now, at the beginning, before you meet them all." She took his hand and led him down the steps of the porch, across the lawn and along the path toward the stables. "I'll tell you as we go to see the horses," she said, "and then—no more about it."

He sniffed the sweet-smelling air. "What a lovely spot!" he exclaimed.

Gratified even more than if he had praised her, Adeline said, "*Isn't* it! We're thankful that Jalna isn't near the development schemes. And with five hundred acres we're pretty safe."

"What about Roma?" he asked, as though the subject fascinated him.

"Well, you've just heard about her, haven't you?"

"I've been hearing about her for two years."

She opened her eyes at him. "Really? Not from me, surely."

"Yes. You often mentioned her in your letters. You probably have no idea how often."

"I'm surprised because I didn't know I was a bit interested in Roma. And I wasn't—not till she did this thing to Patience."

"Patience?"

Adeline spoke with some heat now. "Don't pretend, Mait, that you don't know who Patience is."

"There are a good many of you, you know."

They were almost at the stables. Adeline said hurriedly:

"Patience is a darling. We all love her. She's perfectly lovely with animals. Uncle Piers says she's better with an ailing young one than any man."

"She sounds a good sort," said Fitzturgis tranquilly.

"Oh, she is! She's wonderful. Then Roma did this thing to her."

"What?"

"Roma took the boy Patience was in love with."

"Were Patience and the man engaged?"

"Not quite but almost. She adored him. Anyone could see that. And then Roma just reached out and took him. His name is Green."

"H'm . . . what sort of fellow is he?"

Adeline's lip curled in scorn. "Weak as water—but Patience loved him with all her might. . . . Now I've told you let's not talk about it any more."

"Good," he returned tranquilly. His eyes swept over the fine buildings of the stables. "Your horses are well housed," he said.

Adeline's eyes shone in pride. "They have everything," she declared. "We may go without. Not they." She caught his hand in hers. "Do you think you will like living here, Mait?" she asked.

"It would be a strange person who wouldn't," he returned, his fingers tightening on hers. "Why, it's hard to believe that there's a town within a hundred miles. It's hard to believe that yesterday I was in New York."

"And I've never asked you how your family are—your mother and sister!"

"Mother is well. Sylvia is much better."

"And they're going to live in New York?"

"Yes."

One of the doors of the stables opened and a man of about forty-five came out. He hesitated on seeing them, then strode on to meet them, walking with firmness and confidence considering that he had lost a leg in the war. "Oh," Adeline cried eagerly, "here comes Uncle Piers. You will like him." Fitzturgis inspected him with interest as he approached, trying to discover some resemblance to this man's son who lived not far from Fitzturgis in Ireland, but he could discover none. Maurice Whiteoak was as different from his father as he well could be.

"Uncle Piers"—Adeline's voice trembled a little from excitement—"this is Maitland."

"How do you do, Mr Fitzturgis?" Piers said a little stiffly, shaking hands with him.

After a few moments of talk Piers turned back into the stables with them. Two stablemen were bedding down the horses for the night. Adeline was eager to show Fitzturgis her own mare, Bridget, with her first colt, Bridie's Boy. They were in a loose-box together; the son, inheritor of his mother's beauty, stood proudly beside her. Both bent their heads to nuzzle Adeline when she entered the box. The sight of her, with the mare and her colt, made Piers smile at Fitzturgis. "A pretty trio," he said. "A very promising trio," Fitzturgis admiringly agreed.

"Come in," cried Adeline. "She's as kind as can be and so proud of her son."

When Piers Whiteoak stopped his car on his own driveway some time later he saw his wife planting seedlings in the flower border. She sat back on her heels and raised her dark eyes expectantly to his face. "Well," she asked, "did you meet him?"

"Yes, but only for a short while in the stables. Adeline had brought him to see the horses."

"Did you like him?"

"He seems a nice fellow. Likes horses but doesn't know much about them."

"Did he mention Maurice?"

"Yes, though I gather they don't see much of each other."

A silence fell between them, as so often happened when they spoke of their eldest son. Almost two years had passed since they had seen him. In her secret mind Pheasant had accused Piers of being unfair to Maurice. She had never quite forgiven him for sending the boy to Ireland at the whim of an old cousin, Dermot Court, even though that visit had made Maurice Dermot's heir. Maurice's future had been settled for him. He was a well-off, idle young man. Piers envied him his affluence and deplored his idleness.

Pheasant patted the earth about the last of the annual stocks. "I'm late getting them planted," she said. "But then I'm always late getting things done."

"You undertake too much," he said, almost roughly, and, putting his hands beneath her arms, lifted her to her feet. He bent his face to hers and kissed her. He said, "If Adeline and her Irishman get along as well as we do there's no need to worry." She relaxed against his shoulder, forgetting everything but her love for him.

But their loverlike attitudes were an embarrassment to their youngest son Philip, who, returning from a day's fishing, cleared his throat loudly to announce his arrival.

"Hullo, Mum and Dad," he called out. "Are you too busy to see what I've caught?"

His parents separated and strolled toward him. He displayed a catch of gleaming brook trout.

Philip was seventeen. He always had been a handsome boy, but of late the clear fairness of his skin, the sheen of his hair, his heavy-lidded azure eyes, the perfection of his features, all had been intensified. Piers, looking at him now, thought he was, as Pheasant declared, the image of what he had been as a boy, but the truth was that young Philip much more resembled his great-grandfather, Captain Philip Whiteoak.

"I stopped in at Jalna," Philip said, "and left a couple of trout for Uncle Renny's breakfast."

"Good," said Piers, but he spoke without heart. Philip's devotion to Renny was rather irritating to Piers.

Pheasant looked at her son charitably, as she did at all males. She asked, "Did you see Adeline's Irishman?"

"No, but we're all invited there this evening to inspect him."

"Good God!" exclaimed a voice just emerging from the house. "A gathering of the clan to greet the betrothed of the fair daughter of the house! What does he bring as an offering? Six head of lean cattle from the Kerry hills or a litter of starving pigs?"

The owner of the voice, a particularly pleasant one, now appeared. He was the second son, three years older than Philip. He had been christened Finch; but as that name belonged to another of the family, he had been, for some inexplicable reason, called Nooky, later shortened to Nook. He was an art student and already several of his pictures had been shown in small exhibitions.

This was Piers's favourite son. He condoned in Nook what would have seemed intolerable in Maurice. He liked his pictures. He had allowed him to turn the old carriage house into a studio. He looked tolerantly on the paint-stained smock in which Nook now appeared. But he was no longer to be called by any childish nickname. He must have a name of some dignity as signature to his pictures. What of his real name 'Finch'? That was already borne by the uncle for whom he was named. Finch Whiteoak was a concert pianist. His name was well known on this continent and abroad. It would be confusing to have two Finch Whiteoaks in the world of art. But what was Nook to call himself? He had been given only the one Christian name. One Christian name! As he remarked this, on a note of reproach to his parents, he had a sudden idea. "I have it!" he exclaimed. "I shall call myself Christian." And then added, "With your permission, of course." For though Nook always took his own way he took it so politely that Piers and Pheasant were under the impression that he was the most dutiful and considerate of all their children.

So Piers had only remarked, "An odd sort of name for a Whiteoak."

"Surely no odder than Finch," said his son.

"I guess I made a mistake in naming you after my brother," said Piers, "but at the time it seemed a good idea. For one thing he'd lately had a fortune left him."

"That was a pretty good reason, but what was the other?"

"Well, he was and is a decent sort of fellow."

Nook agreed. "I like that reason best. I've always admired Uncle Finch, but I don't believe he'd thank me for setting out to distinguish myself under his name."

"Anyhow," said Pheasant, "he'll scarcely make you his heir when he has a son of his own."

"Just the same," said Piers, "he might do more for Nook, if Nook didn't take another name."

"On the other hand," put in the boy, "he might be induced to pay me for changing it."

Pheasant said, "You wouldn't be disgracing the name if you painted good pictures."

Nook asked, "Has anyone any objection to Christian as a name?"

"It's too much like *Pilgrim's Progress*," said Piers.

"Then there are the kings of Denmark," said his wife, preferring kings to pilgrims. "I think I can get used to it in time."

"Do you object, Dad?" Nook would not go openly against the grain of the family. "Do you think Uncle Renny will object?"

Piers at once became brusque. "It's not for him to say."

"But it would do no harm to ask him," said Pheasant.

"I'm quite willing. I mean I have nothing against Christian. That ought to be enough for Nook."

"And we can still call you Nooky in private, can't we?" Pheasant put her arm about the youth and pressed him to her.

That had been months ago. Now the name Christian had become firmly attached to Nook outside the family and was ceasing to be a joke inside it. Christian himself did not mind being laughed at. What he could not bear were anger and unkind words. He was quick to retaliate in them but as quick to be sorry and to say so.

The artist's smock in which he now appeared somehow accentuated his extreme erectness and thinness. His dark eyes were bright in his fair face.

Pheasant said, "We must be very nice to this Maitland Fitzturgis. His visit here means a great deal to Adeline."

"Visit!" repeated Philip. "I thought he'd come to stay."

"Do you mean as Adeline's husband?" asked Pheasant.

"Yes, I suppose so."

"People don't get married in that offhand way."

"You and Dad eloped, didn't you?"

Piers gave a shout of laughter. He said, "We'd given lots of thought to it. It wasn't offhand."

Philip said, "Adeline and he have been corresponding for two years. Why didn't he come sooner?"

"He had to settle his affairs. Find a purchaser for his property."

Christian asked, "Did he speak of Maurice coming any time soon?"

"Yes," answered Piers. "He hopes to come this summer."

In this family there were the three sons and, as though an afterthought, at the end of the war, a little daughter, Mary. She ran to join the others now with the careless grace of the five-year-old. But there were marks of tears on her cheeks. She had been in one of her own secret places shedding a few private tears. She looked up pathetically into the faces of those about her, as though searching for a friendly one. Piers picked her up and she pressed her pink face to his cheek.

"Whom do you love best?" he asked.

Suddenly smiling, she answered emphatically, "Uncle Renny."

"Well, I like that—after all I do for you!"

He set her on her feet, took her hand, and led her into the house. Skipping happily beside him, Mary chanted, "I love Uncle Renny best—best—best!"

Piers called over his shoulder, "Pheasant—it's time for this child's tea and bed."

Nook returned to his studio, his refuge, the place where he was happiest. He stood before the unfinished picture on the easel—the study of a cloud above a summer field—and regarded it absently. He did not see it clearly because Adeline's vivid face came between him and the canvas. He had a feeling of something like anger toward her for bringing the Irishman on the scene, in the very summer when Maurice was expected home on a visit. Maurice had once confided to Nook that he loved her. It did seem a shame that Fitzturgis should, after two years of what Nook thought of as shilly-shallying, come to claim Adeline. And of what use would he be at Jalna?

"That's what I'd like to know," he said aloud, as he scraped his palette.

A voice behind him asked, "What would you like to know?"

He wheeled and faced his cousin Patience, who had dropped in, as she so often did, on her way home, after her work at Jalna.

"This Maitland Fitzturgis. Of what good will he be at Jalna?"

"Quite a lot, I imagine—to Adeline."

"He can't just come here and sponge on Uncle Renny. There are enough already trying to wrench a living out of Jalna."

Patience laughed good-humouredly. "Oh, Christian, what a horrid description of us!" She came and stood in front of the canvas. "This is lovely. It makes you feel peaceful and as if things don't matter."

He gave her a swift appraising glance. He said, "You have a peaceful look, Patience. Some day, when I'm better at it, I'm going to paint you. You'll make a good subject in those blue overalls, with your short dark hair, grey eyes and your complete lack of . . ." He hesitated, not wanting to hurt her feelings.

"Go on," she urged. "It's fun to be noticed."

"Very well then—I'll say what the newspapers call 'sleek sophistication'."

Patience made a sound of derision. "I never can hope to have that," she said.

"Do you like it?"

"I envy it, Nooky."

"I think it's disgusting."

"You say that, but you probably admire it when you see it."

"I admired Roma before she achieved it. I didn't admire her much, but I quite liked her looks."

"You did three pictures of her last year."

"Look about and see if you can discover them."

Patience looked vaguely about her. "I don't see them."

"No one ever will. They're obliterated."

"I don't understand you," she said. "Roma is admired by almost everyone."

With a frankness which brought colour to her cheeks he said, "I suppose you're thinking of Norman Green."

For a moment she could not speak, then she said in a consciously matter-of-fact voice, "Well, I must be going. I suppose you'll be at the party this evening."

"I suppose so."

"Goodbye, Christian."

"Goodbye, Patience. Love to Auntie Meg."

"*And* Roma?"

"Of course."

The road past the church was quiet. It was quiet when she turned into her own home, through the brown wicket-gate set in the hedge. The front door opened and Meg appeared.

"Oh, here you are, dear!" she exclaimed in her warm, welcoming voice. The two exchanged kisses. "Did you have a good day, Patience?"

Meg looked into her child's face with solicitude. She had not very much liked young Green, but she suffered in seeing Patience deprived of him. She was conscious that Patience had been ready to devote the rest of her life to making Green happy; and if she thought the object of her devotion not worthy of Patience, she never said so. In fact Meg displayed greater tact than ever before in her life. She lived in the house with her daughter and her niece through a crisis that might have left them either not on speaking terms or in open antagonism. But toward both girls Meg retained her attitude of loving calm. Patience was the child of her body, her own child. But to Roma she gave a tender love. Roma was the daughter of her dead brother Eden. Eden had been a poet. He had been what Meg called 'wild', but she had loved him dearly, had nursed him through his last illness. Meg thought of herself as a poor widow bearing the responsibility of those two young lives.

Mother and daughter had just entered the house, hand in hand, when a sports car appeared on the tree-shaded road, then stopped outside the gate.

Meg said, "It's Roma—and *him.*"

Patience turned toward the stairs. "I must clean myself up. What time are we expected at Jalna?"

"Oh, soon after supper. Do put on something pretty, Patience. I must tell Roma. Norman's not getting out of the car."

As though she had not heard, Patience went slowly up the stairs. She turned into her own room just as Roma reached the top of the stairs. Roma sang out "Hullo" in a cheerful voice but did not glance into her cousin's room as she passed. Patience could hear her opening and shutting drawers, running water in the bathroom, then hurrying down the stairs. Not till she heard Roma's steps running toward the gate did she move from her motionless attitude of attention. Now she went slowly to the wide open door of Roma's room and saw the usual disorder—shoes and stockings strewn on the floor; the bed littered with underclothes, hairbrush and writing-pad; the dressing-table strewn with so many odds and ends that Patience wondered how she ever found anything. Yet find what she wanted she did and came out of that room shining with a sleekness Patience never achieved. Her lips curling in disgust, Patience returned to her own room where she kept her possessions in almost military order. She looked dispassionately at her reflection in the glass and thought, 'No wonder Norman likes her best.'

Meg was in the hall as Roma came running down the stairs. She just touched Meg's cheek with hers and said, "Oh, Aunty Meg, I forgot to say I'll not be at home for supper. Norman and I are going to see a friend of his in Mistwell."

Meg put out a hand toward Roma, as though to draw the girl to her, but she was gone, running along the path to join Norman in the car. Meg, from the doorway, called:

"We're invited to Jalna this evening to meet Adeline's

friend from Ireland. I think you should be there, Roma."

Roma consulted with Norman. She called back, "All right, Aunty Meg. I'll come. Bye-bye."

The car moved swiftly down the road, Norman's lacquered head bending to Roma. Meg gave a deep sigh and slowly climbed the stairs. But she arrived soon enough to discover Patience peering out of the window after the car. There were both girls, their minds fixed on the one young man, and he, to Meg's way of thinking, quite undesirable. It seemed hard to Meg that this rift should have come to separate the three in her house. She wanted to love and be loved. Now she went to Patience, put an arm about her. Here were caresses for the asking. Patience hugged her mother almost fiercely and promised to put on her prettiest dress for the evening.

"This is quite an event," Meg said. "Something we've all been looking forward to ever since Adeline's visit to Ireland. Maitland Fitzturgis must be a captivating young man to have fascinated Adeline at their meeting and held her fancy ever since. Now she will marry him. The first marriage among you young cousins, and naturally you will be maid of honour, with Roma as bridesmaid and little Mary as flower-girl. What a pretty affair it will be! You know, we haven't had any pretty weddings in our church. Mine was a small affair with just the family. Renny and Finch married their wives in England. Piers eloped. As for Eden—well, the less said about his connections with women, the better. But he was a poet, and—whatever Piers may say—you can't expect poets to behave like ordinary men."

2

THE WELCOME FOR FITZTURGIS

NICHOLAS HAD made up his mind that he would go downstairs that evening. "I will not," he had said, "meet Adeline's fiancé up in my bed like an old invalid. After all, I'm only ninety-eight. My mother was up and about when she was a hundred. By Jove, I haven't been downstairs in a month. I will go down tonight."

"Good," said Renny. "Shall you come down to dinner or just for a while in the evening?"

"To dinner, certainly. Will you lay out my clothes, like a

good fellow, and be ready to give me an arm when the time comes? I don't want that Irishman to see me being helped down the stairs. Tell Adeline to keep him out of the way."

"I will, Uncle Nick."

When the time came Renny helped him get into his clothes. He had already shaved him and made his hair spruce. When he was dressed he had to rest a bit, before starting the descent. Renny looked down at him with a mixture of admiration and sadness. Time had dealt differently with him than with his mother. Her it had coarsened, brought out wiry hairs on her chin, roughened her voice, given a truculence and daring to her aspect, as though she challenged death itself. But the face of Nicholas had fined down. His features had taken on an almost cameo-like delicacy. Yet sometimes he was surprisingly like the Nicholas of old, and tonight was one of the times.

"Now," he said in his still deep-toned voice, "let us make the descent. Heave me up, Renny. Egad, my leg is stiff!"

Renny's strong arm about his waist, he hobbled to the stairs. For many years he had suffered from gout. Alayne anxiously watched the descent of the two heads, one of them iron-grey that had never turned to white, the other that narrow head with its thatch of dark red hair, the sight of which always had the power to hold her. To Archer—who had appeared, it seemed, from nowhere—it was merely a question as to whether Renny would get the old man down without help. There was no admiration, no sadness, nothing of retrospect in his young mind.

Now they were in the hall and making good progress toward the drawing room.

"Strange," said Archer to Alayne, "how, when people are either very old or very young, they are always wanting to do something they shouldn't do."

"So already you are a student of human nature," smiled Alayne.

"I have so much of it about me."

"But you should not be so critical at your age, Archer."

"It only proves what I say. I want to do what I shouldn't do at my age."

"Don't we all," sighed Alayne.

"It seems to me that when you're not so very young or not so very old the trouble is that you don't want to do what you should do."

"You do make things complicated, Archer."

"They are more interesting that way." He drew aside the curtain of the window at the landing and peeped out. "There is Adeline and her boy-friend. She's keeping him out of the way till Uncle Nicholas is settled in his chair. Somehow I don't think the two of them look well together."

Alayne also peeped out. She said, "I think they look very well together. They look happy too."

"I wonder what it feels like."

"Why, Archer, what a thing to say!"

"Well, happiness seems so positive. I should think it would soon be boring."

Renny passed through the hall carrying a glass of whisky and water to Nicholas. He waved his hand to the two on the landing.

"He's fine," he called up. "I'm just taking him a bit of stimulant."

A little later Adeline brought Fitzturgis to the drawing room and he was formally presented to Nicholas, who grasped him warmly by the hand.

"I'm glad indeed to meet you," he said. "I've waited a long while and began to be afraid I'd not have the opportunity."

Fitzturgis bowed over his hand with a deference pleasing to Nicholas. He sat down on one side of him and Adeline sat on the other. There was a moment of decorous restraint in which Nicholas inspected the visitor. Then—"And how did you leave Ireland?" he asked, looking as though pleased by what he had seen.

"Much the same as usual—fairly content in feeling sorry for herself and blaming England for all her troubles."

"Ah, it's a lovely country. I used often to visit my mother's people there, but it's years since I have seen it. You'll find it quite a change—living in this New World. What happy, happy people we are! Just look, Mr Fitzturgis."

"Maitland, Uncle Nicholas," put in Adeline. "You'll want to be called that by us all, won't you, Mait?"

"I shall indeed."

"Very well—Maitland," Nicholas agreed and held his newspaper spread in front of Fitzturgis. "Now see what a happy people. In all these pictures of politicians, club-women, teenagers—have you teenagers in Ireland?—there is none who is not grinning. The only ones who have seriousness and dignity in our newspaper prints are the very young children who have not yet learned to grin."

"I see," said Fitzturgis. "But are all those people really happy? Do their grins mean anything?"

"I take them at their face value," said Nicholas.

"Archer," put in Adeline, "never smiles."

"I can make him smile," said Renny, and put out a hand toward his son, who eluded it.

Rags sounded the gong. Nicholas, buoyed by the whisky and water, moved, on Renny's arm, quite strongly to the dining room. Adeline whispered to Fitzturgis:

"I do hope you like him. We think he's a grand old man."

"He is indeed. And what remarkable eyes for a man of his age—for a man of any age."

"There's where he got them." She laughed and pointed to the portrait of her great-grandmother that hung above the sideboard.

"And now you are the inheritor," said Fitzturgis, with one of his rare, ardent looks.

Nicholas saw that they were looking at the portrait. He gave a little bow toward it and said, "My mother—a granddaughter of the Marquess of Killiekeggan: and the companion portrait is my father, in the uniform of an officer of Hussars."

Fitzturgis was conscious that the eyes of all were on him, as though to observe the effect of the portraits on him. It was as though they wanted him to understand the influence which these two people, long dead, still exerted on the lives of all at Jalna.

Nicholas was saying, "I should like you to have met my brother. He sat next me at table here. He died—bless my soul, it will be two years in July."

Fitzturgis's face clouded. He was not likely to forget that death, the summons to return to Jalna for the funeral in the very hour when he and Adeline had counted on days of enchantment in London. He said glumly, "I remember."

Renny shot him a look. What had the fellow in his mind?

Nicholas was exhilarated by dining once more downstairs, and with the company as well. He was in a mood for reminiscence rather than for giving his attention to the talk of others. The eyes of Adeline and Fitzturgis met across the table. They were outwardly attentive but inwardly wondering what experience the future would bring, she striving toward its enrichment of her life, he trying to picture himself as part of this scene.

A decanter of burgundy was set on the table. Its glow in the glass produced a brightness to all eyes, and Archer was moved to quote, "'*Dum vivimus vivamus*'."

"I was in England," said Nicholas, "in 1930. That year the Grand National was won by an Irish horse, Shaun Goilin. His dam, Golden Day, was at grass in a paddock in Ireland, and in an adjoining field there were a number of two-year-olds. During the night several of these rascals jumped the fence between and the result was Shaun Goilin. No one ever knew which colt was his sire, but it was a lucky bit of wildness."

"'*Qui capit*——'" began Archer, but Adeline interrupted him.

"For goodness' sake don't be always showing off," she said in a loud whisper.

He gave her an icy look, and Fitzturgis began to wonder if he were going to dislike his future brother-in-law.

"Life," Nicholas was declaring, "can only be understood backward. Now I see so clearly all the mistakes I made and could have avoided."

"I don't think you made many mistakes, Uncle Nick," said Renny.

Nicholas blew under his drooping moustache, emptied his glass and set it sharply on the table. "You young people," he said, "have your lives ahead of you, but I shall soon be extinguished. I don't mind telling you I shall be sorry to leave this world. I find it very interesting. But my marriage turned out badly." He fixed his eyes on Fitzturgis. "Don't let your marriage turn out badly. It's a new experience for you. You don't know what marriage is." Nicholas had quite forgotten that Fitzturgis was a divorcé.

"I was married," said Fitzturgis, looking steadily at him.

"No! Really—dear me, then I shouldn't have said that. Well, well, perhaps it's better for you to have had experience. Not that mine helped me. A little more of the burgundy, please, Renny."

Renny, filling his glass, remarked, "We all are the better for experience. Divorce is of little account in this modern world." He glanced at his wife to see if he had said the wrong thing. Her eyes were on Fitzturgis, sympathetic to his flushed embarrassment.

Nicholas, fortified by more wine, now said to him, "I suppose your wife was an Irishwoman."

"No. An Englishwoman."

"Ah, I remember now! An actress. But I just cannot recall her name."

Fitzturgis burst out, "Must we discuss this now?"

Adeline smiled across the table at him. "I don't mind, Mait." Turning to Nicholas, she said, "Her name is Georgina Lennox. Uncle Nick. She lives in London. She's a friend of Uncle Wakefield's."

"What of Wakefield's play?" asked Nicholas. "Did it come on?"

"It ran for three weeks," said Renny. "I suppose it was a failure, but I thought it was pretty good when he read it to us, didn't you, Alayne?" Wakefield was his youngest brother, to whom he had been a father.

Nicholas turned courteously to Fitzturgis. "I regret," he said, "if I have brought up a subject embarrassing to you. I am a very old man. I say things I shouldn't. But I'm not as bad at that sort of thing as my mother was, am I, Renny?"

"It's all in the family," said Renny. "Maitland will soon be one of us."

Fitzturgis looked slightly rueful, but a smile flickered on his lips. "It's all right," he said.

Alayne's eyes met his. "A newcomer to Jalna," she said, "has certain things to get used to."

"I suppose you too were very much a newcomer once," he said, in a tone which set them apart.

"Twenty-five years ago I was a newcomer."

Archer said, "I suppose I might be called a newcomer since I've been here only fifteen years."

"Very new indeed," said Alayne repressively.

"Yet I got used to things in little or no time. Now nothing surprises me."

Adeline said, "I pity your wife, if ever any girl is crazy enough to marry you."

"No girl will ever get the chance," he said. "I intend to look at life as an observer. I shall leave it to you to propagate our kind."

The conversation was interrupted by the arrival of Piers and his family, who always came early. After the introduction to Fitzturgis they crowded about the table, drawing up chairs as though for a meal. They were given a glass of port, Piers raising his toward Adeline and her fiancé with a little bow and a—"to your future happiness." The two young boys, Philip and Archer, were alike only in their youth—both at the dawn of life—but Philip was as a radiant rosy dawn, while Archer was a pale and frosty one with a penetrating air.

Philip, with a loving look at Renny, said, "Uncle Renny is going to leave Jalna to me, aren't you, Uncle Renny?"

"I might do worse," said the Master of Jalna, with a teasing look at his wife and son.

Archer said imperturbably, "It wouldn't worry me, as I shouldn't know what to do with Jalna if I had it."

Renny looked at him aghast. "You mean to say you wouldn't mind?" he exclaimed.

"Well, I am attached to the place," said Archer, "if that's what you mean, but I am attached to it only because I'm used to it."

"Then I suppose," said Renny, "that you're attached to your mother and me for no more than the same reason."

"I guess that's natural," said Archer. "I guess you're attached to me for the same reason. You'd scarcely have chosen me for a son if you'd been given a choice, would you?"

"Philip," Renny slapped him on the shoulder, "Jalna will be yours."

"We'll hold you to that," said Piers.

Alayne smiled kindly at Philip. "Of course you realize that your uncle was joking," she said.

"No joking about it," insisted Piers. "We'll hold him to it. I call you to witness, Fitzturgis."

"It's too early for me to commit myself," he said. "On either side."

"I call you to witness," repeated Piers, and Philip went round behind Renny's chair and laid an arm about his shoulders.

Pheasant's eyes were on Adeline and Fitzturgis. Romantically she was considering their suitability to each other. 'His is the face of experience,' she thought. 'Adeline's is the face of character. Her face is the warmer, the fierier. His the more sensitive. She will be able to forget herself. He will forget himself—never. Except where his senses are concerned.'

"Well, Pheasant," said Renny. "Will he do?" He smiled at

Fitzturgis. "She's sizing you up. She's of an analytical turn of mind."

"And usually wrong," said Piers. "When she declares someone is trustworthy I hide my wallet."

Nicholas asked, "Where are Meg and the girls?" Then, imitating his ancient mother, added, "I like the young people about me."

"We used," Renny said to Fitzturgis, "to have a tableful in the old days. As well as those you now see we had my three younger brothers—Eden, Finch and Wakefield. Eden died, poor chap; Finch is a pianist, now off on tour; Wakefield is an actor in London."

"Was I here?" asked Archer.

"Your type had not yet been invented," answered his father.

Adeline spoke up: "Aunty Meg and Patience are at the door."

The two alighted from a ten-year-old Ford car and came straight into the dining room. Meg exclaimed with delight on seeing Nicholas at table. Patience was wearing a sleeveless white dress which showed to advantage her shapely brown arms.

"Where is the other one?" demanded Nicholas. "Eden's little girl?"

"Oh, she's off somewhere with her young man," Meg answered, trying to sound bright.

"Who is he? I don't remember him."

"His name is Norman."

"H'm—don't remember him." Nicholas blew through his moustache. "Getting terribly forgetful. Can't remember who the little girl's mother was." He looked to Alayne for help.

She rose. "I think we will go to the drawing room for coffee," she said.

"Drawing room for coffee!" muttered Nicholas, as he was being heaved to his feet. "All these new-fangled ideas."

"We have been doing it for the past twenty-five years," she returned crisply.

He stretched out a trembling hand to pat her shoulder. "You've been wonderful, Alayne."

As Fitzturgis and she passed through the door she said, "You mustn't mind anything Uncle Nicholas says. He is really a dear and quite excited at being downstairs again. Your coming has done him good."

He gave her an admiring look. "I am very happy to be here," he said. "In fact Jalna is just what I expected it to be."

In the porch, two hours later, Adeline isolated Christian. "Tell me," she demanded, "what you think of him. Do you like him?"

"I hated him on sight."

"Oh, Nooky—I am disappointed."

"And I am disappointed in you. I wanted you to marry Maurice."

"There never was anything between Maurice and me."

"Excepting that he loves you."

"He's over all that."

"I hope so. Are Maitland and he friendly?"

"Mait admires Maurice."

Patience now joined them in the porch. She laid an arm about the shoulders of each. She said: "I've been talking to your Irishman, Adeline, and I do like him. He's a bit older than I expected."

"I'm not interested in youths."

"Should you call me a youth?" asked Christian.

"Well, I think you are rather old for your years."

"I wonder what Maitland will think of Roma," Patience said, as though she could not keep her mind off Roma.

"I expect she'll bore him," said Adeline, in happy assurance.

Christian yawned. "As she would bore anyone with brains."

"She and Norman," said Patience, "consider themselves intellectuals."

"You're making me ill," said Christian.

"Perhaps, but I couldn't possibly understand the books they read."

"Do *they* understand them, d'you think? Or do they just carry them about as the badge of the Lodge they belong to?"

Patience knit her brow in puzzlement. "Well, they know the names of the authors and the tables of contents."

Christian shouted with laughter. "I'll bet they do. And Roma is damned proud of being the daughter of a poet. She knows the titles of all Uncle Eden's poems, but has she ever read one of them? I doubt it."

Renny now joined them. He said, "It's time your Uncle

Nicholas went to bed, but he's so enjoying himself I hate to suggest it."

"Bless his heart," said Patience.

A car was glimpsed coming slowly up the drive.

"Our little friend Roma arrives," said Christian.

The car stopped but remained hidden behind the hemlocks. Roma came, trudging crossly along the gravel sweep, her eyes fixed on the group in the porch.

"She has just two expressions," said Christian. "She either smiles or doesn't smile."

"She has just two tones of voice," said Adeline. "She speaks soft and sweet or matter-of-fact and down to earth."

"Hello," called out Roma. "Hello, Uncle Renny." She was the only one of the young Whiteoaks not fond of Renny. Too often he had read her a lesson.

Now he called back, "You are very late."

"Better late than never," she returned.

Christian said low, "She doesn't smile."

To Roma Adeline said, "Come on in and meet Maitland."

All returned to the drawing room. Fitzturgis was devoting himself to Nicholas, who drew Roma to the arm of his chair. "This little girl," he said, "is my nephew Eden's daughter. Eden was a poet—the first of the Whiteoaks to turn to things artistic, though my brother Ernest had quite a bent toward writing and always intended to do a book about Shakespeare but never found the time. Of course you've heard that young Nooky—what is it he calls himself now?"

"Christian," said Roma.

"Ah, yes—Christian, he's turned to painting. And Finch is a concert pianist, and Wakefield is an actor. And there's a young man nearby who writes. What's his name, Roma?"

"Humphrey Bell."

"That's it. And what does he write?"

She answered, as though in a lesson, "Short stories in the American and Canadian magazines. He's done some radio scripts and a little work in television."

"Well, well," said Nicholas. "Before we know it we shall have an artists' colony here in place of the settlement of retired British officers we set out with. Do you think that will be a change for the better, Roma?"

"I haven't thought about it," she returned.

Nicholas's head sank on his breast. He looked unutterably

weary. Adeline came to them. "Say goodnight to Uncle Nicholas, Mait. He's off to bed." She stroked the old man's belligerent crest of hair, then drew Fitzturgis to join the other young people outdoors. They strolled down into the ravine. Roma hesitated, as though not quite knowing what to do, then followed them. At the path that led to the stream they stood in a group talking for a little. Fitzturgis held Adeline's fingers in his.

Indoors Nicholas was being half carried to his room by Renny and Piers. They looked at him with anxiety. They had never seen him look so old.

"How do you feel?" asked Piers, when they had set him in his own big chair. "Pretty tired?"

"No, no, not too tired," he growled, "but ready for my bed. Get me one of my pills, Renny. And you, Piers, my pyjamas." He looked longingly at his bed.

They busied themselves waiting on him, in that room where as little boys they had felt it a privilege just to be admitted; to which he had returned, a traveller, from the mysterious outside world. Now, instead of awe, he moved them to pity and protection. Yet when he was safe in bed, propped up by his pillows, he looked imposing. He was pleased with himself, too, and inclined to take a favourable view of Fitzturgis.

"I like the man," he said. "He appears to be a very agreeable fellow, but I can't somehow picture him at Jalna. Can you, Piers?"

"Not for the life of me," said Piers. And, as though Renny were not present, he went on, "I can't imagine what Renny's going to do with him. He'll be of no use to anyone."

Renny retorted, "You're always complaining that you have too much to do."

"What I need," said Piers, "is another good farm hand, not a gentleman farmer to share the profits."

"I understand from Adeline that he'll do anything."

"You may understand it from her, but has he said so?"

"My God!" exclaimed Renny. "The man has barely arrived."

"He tells me," said Nicholas, "that his brother-in-law has offered him a position in New York."

"What sort of position?"

"He didn't say. Ah, yes, it had something to do with advertising."

Renny frowned. "Adeline would never go to New York. There's plenty for him to do at Jalna."

"Is there plenty of money for the support of another family?" asked Piers.

Renny, looking him full in the eyes, answered, "Yes."

Piers was shaking with internal laughter. He patted his uncle's shoulder. "Goodnight, Uncle Nick. It's been splendid seeing you downstairs again."

When he had gone Nicholas asked, "When is the marriage to take place? I hope it will be fairly soon. I should like to be there."

"It wouldn't go off properly without you, Uncle Nicholas. . . . Shall I put out the light?"

"Yes. I'm pretty tired but glad to have been downstairs. From now on I shall be down every evening."

As the first light was extinguished the face on the pillow was dimmed. With the putting out of the second light the face was gone.

"Are you all right?" asked Renny.

"Fine, thanks."

"Goodnight."

"Goodnight. . . . What are you waiting for?"

"I'm going now." But he lingered till he heard a rhythmic snore.

In the cool night air he crossed the lawn and descended half way down the path to the ravine. From there he could see by the misty moonlight the figures of Adeline and Fitzturgis on the bridge above the stream. He experienced an odd constriction of the heart to see her in this attitude of loving isolation with another man, in the spot where she had so often stood with him. Yet, at the same time, his almost predatory patriarchal nature reached out to draw Fitzturgis into the fold. 'There is plenty for him to do here,' he thought. 'Plenty for us all.'

With these contradictory emotions moving him he went to the stables. He opened the door and entered the straw-scented quietness. How different the effect of the moonlight coming in at these windows! Outdoors it whitened the paths, turned the grass to dark velvet, sought out the mystery of each separate tree. Here it showed the dim shapes of the resting horses, some lying in the straw, others standing. A three-days-old foal lay secure against its dam's side. In the darkness, the warmth, the seclusion, it felt as safe as it had within her body. Even when Renny entered the loose-box it felt no alarm. The mare gave him a low rumble of greeting as he bent to pat her.

"Good girl," he said. "You have a lovely baby. I'm proud of you." And his pride in his horses seemed to enter their consciousness. They moved, and low whickers came from stall and loose-box at the sound of his voice.

3

GETTING ACQUAINTED

FITZTURGIS HAD come to Jalna with mingled feelings of apprehension, self-distrust and remembered love. As an Irishman, the close-knit family life was not new to him. But somehow he could not picture himself as resident son-in-law (so he grimly put it) to the man who figured so largely in Adeline's letters. How deeply in love was he? He could not have said. He realized that there was within himself a desire for almost melancholy retreat from the closest human relations. And the events of his life had strengthened this—his life in these last years with his mother and sister—his sister's mental illness. Yet the remembrance of Adeline in his arms, of her trust in him and her joyous confidence in the future, was a sunshine to burn away these mists of doubt. Standing on the rustic bridge with her, the darkling stream scarcely audible below, he felt a passionate upsurge of desire and a determination to be steadfast in his love.

On the following morning Renny mounted him on a peppery grey gelding and took him on a tour of the estate, showed him the fields with the wheat tall, golden and stately, soon to be reaped; the orchards where Piers was spraying the apple trees; the cherry orchard where pickers were filling their baskets with the glossy red fruit; the old apple orchard, planted by his grandfather, where the fruit would rot unpicked, where the old trees leant to the knee-high grass.

"These apples," said Renny, "are no longer marketable. Their varieties are forgotten, but I say they are better flavoured than the showy sort they sell in the shops today. I'm sure you'll think so." He took it for granted that Fitzturgis would remain at Jalna.

On his part the Irishman was not sorry to dismount at the stable door. The gelding, in his irritable shyings, had shown an invincible desire to throw him, and Fitzturgis had a disagreeable suspicion that Renny had mounted him on this particular horse to test his powers. Well, thank God, he'd stuck on him.

Inside the stable they found the elderly ruddy-faced head groom, Wright, directing a new hand in his work.

"Wright," said Renny, "has been with me for over thirty years. In all that time he has scarcely taken a holiday—unless you call going to the Horse Show in New York a holiday. Eh, Wright?"

"I call it hard work, sir," said Wright, "but it's holiday enough for me." He stood squarely, sizing up Fitzturgis out of his round blue eyes.

Renny went on, "He's been to Ireland, too. It was he who took Maurice over when he was a little fellow."

"And a nice little boy he was," said Wright. "I'd no trouble with him. I guess it was a lucky trip for him, though it seemed hard at the time."

"He's coming here later," said Fitzturgis without warmth. "Home he still calls it."

"I should think he would," exclaimed Renny. "This is always home to all of us."

Wright asked, "Would you like to see the foal, sir?" He led the way to the loose-box where it stood, proud in its infant strength, beside its mother. "It has her head," said Wright, "and its sire's body. I believe it'll be a good one."

"Is the sire well known?" Fitzturgis asked, for something to say.

"I'll say he is," said Wright. "He won the King's Plate once and might have done wonders, but he has one fault. As long as there were fences in front of him he was O.K., but the moment the run-in was reached he lost interest and wanted nothing but to get off the course. His rider could never tell when he might run out to the left."

Renny said to the foal, caressing it, "See to it that you inherit only your dad's virtues."

"That's easier said than done," said Wright. "I think we're all inclined to inherit faults."

"You say that, Wright," laughed Renny. "Yet you call Miss Adeline perfect."

"She's the exception, sir." Wright turned to Fitzturgis and added in his old-fashioned way, "I hope I may make free to congratulate you, sir. I've known the young lady all her life. I carried her about these stables in my arms before she could walk, and she never knew the meaning of fear."

"I agree," said Fitzturgis, "that she's perfect."

In the passage they were joined by Patience, wearing a blue overall, a bottle of liniment in her hand. "I've been rubbing Frigate's leg," she explained. "It's much better this morning." She joined them in an inspection of the stables, showing a pride even in excess of Wright's. Their order, their modern comforts, were indeed something to be proud of, and Fitzturgis said so.

"Where is Adeline?" asked Patience.

"I wanted Mait's strict attention," said Renny, "so I left her at home."

"Uncle Finch is coming," Patience announced. "Mother had a letter from him this morning. Isn't that good news? It's sooner than we expected. The funny thing is that he doesn't want us to prepare for him. He just wants to be left alone."

"What's the matter with him?"

"Nothing, he says. He's just tired and wants to be left alone."

"He couldn't come to a better place," Renny said cheerfully. "You must know"—his eyes were now on Fitzturgis—"we don't bother much about the outer world, aside from the activities of our professions—if one can call the breeding of show horses a profession."

"I do," said Patience, "and a mighty exacting one." She added, not without pride, "I breed dogs too. Fashionable ones. Want to come and see my kennels?"

"A little later," said Renny. "I'd like to show Maitland my office first." He found it difficult to call Fitzturgis by his Christian name, for the Whiteoaks were not accustomed to bandy first names till acquaintance had ripened. In truth he found it hard to feel at complete ease with his guest. He realized, a little wryly, that he might have felt nearer to him if he had not been engaged to Adeline. As he looked at Fitzturgis he could not help thinking, 'Here is the man who will supplant me.'

Now, leading the way into his office, he said, "You would not think that girl had lately had a disappointment in love, would you?"

"Indeed, no. She strikes me as being very serene."

"Oh, she'll get over it," said Renny. "The fact is, she's well rid of him. He seems a poor creature. Unluckily young Roma is now engaged to him. Have a drink?"

"Thanks." Fitzturgis settled himself in the chair facing the shiny desk. His deepset eyes took in the pictures of horses on the walls.

"Later," said Renny, "I'll show you the tack-room and our trophies."

"I'd like that," said Fitzturgis, and added: "Roma's a pretty little thing, isn't she? Innocent and rather wistful-looking."

"She is," agreed Renny. "She's a nice girl at times. At other times I should like to take a stick to her back. Her father, my brother Eden, died a good many years ago. I sometimes wonder what he would have thought of her."

Their drinks in their hands, they regarded each other across the desk in an odd, forced intimacy, having nothing to build on but their love for Adeline, each a little suspicious of the other's love for her. Had Renny the intention of managing their lives for them, Fitzturgis wondered. In his turn Renny wondered whether this Irishman's love were of the enduring sort—whether he would settle down comfortably at Jalna—and also, with concentrated interest, how much money he had. Well, surely a man had a right to know what were his future son-in-law's prospects. He said: "I hope you did well in the sale of your property."

Fitzturgis gave an audible sigh. "Not as well as I'd hoped. Still, there is enough to support my mother and my sister. Later on, my sister hopes to get work in New York."

"You could find no better investment for your money," said Renny, "than the stables at Jalna. I've done very well in the past few years, but I need more capital. There is a good deal of money to be made from show horses and racehorses. I have a friend named Crowdy, who owned just one racehorse but it turned out to be a good one. He not only made a lot of prize money, but he lately sold the horse to a millionaire for a fancy price."

"I warned you," said Fitzturgis, "that I am a poor man. But I look forward to working for Adeline. My brother-in-law can get me a job in New York, in advertising. He thinks I could get the hang of it before long."

"What makes him think so?"

"Well . . . I suppose I have average intelligence."

Renny said, with severity, "I am surprised at your brother-in-law, for I can tell you from the little I've seen of you that you wouldn't do at all."

Fitzturgis looked stubborn. He said, "My brother-in-law ought to know."

"Yes. That is why I'm surprised that he doesn't."

Amber light flickered in the glasses they raised to their lips, as sharp antagonism flickered for an instant in their eyes.

Fitzturgis spoke first, and with warmth. "You must understand, Mr Whiteoak, that I should like to come to Jalna, but I don't want to come as a sham horseman. I know little about show horses. I know nothing of farming in Canada. I don't want you to be disappointed in me, that's all."

"If that's all," exclaimed Renny, "we have nothing to worry about. You'll learn. And let me tell you—if Adeline hasn't—she would never go to New York. She hates city life."

"I know."

"If money is a little scarce we still shall have plenty of room. We used to have a family of ten at Jalna and all very happy."

"Adeline has told me. But—I'm certain of one thing, and that is that when we marry we must have a place of our own. That's something I have set my heart on."

"Has Adeline set her heart on it?"

"Well, as a matter of fact we have not talked of that."

"I see. Then supposing we decide nothing till we find out what she feels."

Fitzturgis broke out, "No matter what she feels, I must have a roof of my own."

"In that case," Renny said cheerfully, "I know the very house for you. Nice small houses are difficult to get, you know. But my sister Meg Vaughan is going to move and I'm sure she'd let you have her house—either to buy or rent—very reasonably. She and Patience are going to live with my brother Finch, who has built himself a house just beyond the ravine. He's built on the site of one that was burned down, and there was so much delay in getting the rubble cleared away and getting a builder to undertake the job and in Finch's not being able to decide on the sort of house he wanted, that it is only now it's ready for him. Now tonight we're going to dinner with Meg, and you'll find out what she thinks about your taking her house. When do you and Adeline want to get married?"

Fitzturgis answered defensively. "We haven't decided on a time yet." Then he added, "So far as I am concerned the sooner the better."

As he returned to the house he had the feeling that his affairs were being taken out of his hands. In a way this suited him, for he was inclined to indolence; he was in a strange country; he was committed to a new and different life. On the other hand he resented what he felt to be the somewhat arrogant tone of the Master of Jalna. He wondered if it was a good combination, this combining of father-in-law and employer in the one person.

Adeline came across the lawn to meet him, carrying roses she had just been cutting. He took her hand and they walked together to a seat that encircled an old silver-birch tree. Then, her eager eyes on his, she asked, "Did you enjoy your morning with Daddy? And what do you think of Jalna?"

"Oh, I like it." He spoke warmly, but he did not go into the details she wanted. They sat silent a space, watching a squirrel dig a hole in the grass, find something to its liking, then deftly extract it and sit up nibbling it.

"The wild things here are so tame," he said; then added, "I had a talk with your father—in his office."

She laughed gaily. "Oh, I wish I'd been there!"

"Why?" he asked abruptly.

"Because you are the two men I love best in all the world. It fascinates me to see your reactions to each other."

"They might not have been altogether pleasing to you," said Fitzturgis. "My ideas are different from what he seemed to expect and I find it hard to understand him."

"Once you do you wouldn't want him different. I think we all feel that way about him—except perhaps Mummy."

"I can imagine she would."

"It's funny you'd feel that—so soon."

Fitzturgis said sombrely, "Your father and I should have arranged everything before I came out."

Her eyebrows flew up. "Why, I thought you and I had. We corresponded for two years."

"What about?" he demanded, seeing his reflection in the dark depths of her eyes, noticing a tiny mole near one of them.

"About how we wished we might be together, and I told you all the news from Jalna."

"And I have made it clear that I am a poor man. I mean that I have nothing to invest. You know that my mother and sister are dependent on me."

She heaved an exaggerated child's sigh. "Of course I do. But don't worry. Daddy always hopes people will have money to invest in the stables, but—if they haven't—it doesn't really matter."

"But I'm not just 'people', Adeline."

"You're too sensitive, Mait. There will be plenty for you to do. Daddy's always wishing Uncle Piers had more time to help with the horses. And he's so generous. He'll give you a good share, you may be sure."

He took her hand and kissed the palm. "You make me feel middle-aged and disillusioned," he said. "But perhaps I'll get over it in the air of Jalna where you all have a sort of born-with-a-silver-spoon-in-the-mouth look and a Victorian confidence in the future."

He told her of Renny's suggestion that they might arrange to have Meg's house and she was delighted. She strained toward the evening when they could inspect it. She said: "It will be splendid for when your people come from New York to visit us. Of course when they come to the wedding they'll stay at Jalna."

"Couldn't we get married without any fuss? Just your family here—and we two?"

Adeline was astonished. "Why, Maitland, don't you want a proper wedding?"

"Not particularly. I hate fuss."

"But don't you want your family to come to see you married?"

"Not particularly. We could go down to New York to see them on our honeymoon."

"Oh, I thought we'd go to one of our lakes in the north or perhaps to Quebec."

"All right, dearest, whatever you want."

At Meg's all was preparation for the dinner party. Patience stayed at home that day and she and her mother became involved in intricate preparations for a meal to rival those at Jalna. Meg felt that when Renny came to her house he must be offered cooking equal to Mrs Wragge's. Patience, with little experience to help her, had a passion for trying new recipes.

The result was that every utensil in the kitchen was in use, and by the time the guests began to arrive they were both in a state of confusion, heat and almost despair. It had been Roma's part to lay the table, but the setting of twelve places about the table, even with the extension leaf added, had been too much for her patience. She showed a flushed face at the kitchen door. "I'd like," she said, "to throw all these dishes and knives and forks on the floor."

"If you were doing what I'm doing," said her cousin, "you might talk. Can't you set the table without getting in a temper?"

"There's no room for twelve. Why can't we have a buffet dinner like other people do?"

Meg called from the pantry, "I never have set my brother down to a buffet dinner, and never shall."

"You don't sit down, you stand," grumbled Roma.

"Not in this house you don't," said Meg.

At this moment Piers and his family arrived, and Pheasant at once took over the setting of the table, Christian drifted away with Roma, Piers undertook the sharpening of the carving-knife, Philip began to mow the lawn and little Mary went into a corner and cried.

By the time the party arrived from Jalna all was in order. They were welcomed by Meg wearing a dark-blue dress with white belt, which somehow made her plump waist appear even plumper; Patience in frilly pink, with not at all the fashionable silhouette; Roma in pale angelic blue. As soon as possible Renny drew his sister aside.

"Meggie," he said, "I have a prospective tenant or buyer for your house."

"Oh, splendid," she cried. "Who is it?"

"Fitzturgis. He is determined that he and Adeline shall have their own house, and I dare say he's right. I haven't been able to find out what means he has, but I guess not very affluent. Still, he should be able to pay a fair price or rent."

"Oh, he must! Of course, if I were not a widow, with two young girls to support, it would not matter so much, but—with times what they are——"

"I know," he said sympathetically, not reminding her that he paid her for Roma's support and that Patience earned her own living.

"I shall love to think of Adeline in this house and that sweet

Irishman too. And with me keeping house for Finch it seems almost too——"

"Too true to be good," said Archer, just entering.

Renny looked with some sternness at his son. "Were you listening?" he demanded.

"I suppose I was," answered Archer. "I find it so hard to draw the line between being not interested enough and being too interested."

"I'll draw it for you," said Renny. "When you come upon two people talking in low tones together that's the time to keep out."

"But wherever I go I find two people talking in low tones. There seems to be no place for me."

There now came a smell of burning from the kitchen and Meg flew to it in panic. However, no mischief had been done and shortly a pair of fine plump capons were placed on the table. Pheasant found her little daughter, comforted her, and the family drew about the table. Renny took up the carving-knife and fork.

He had barely disjointed a wing when there was the sound of a car on the drive. From where she sat Roma could see the arrival. "Do you know what?" she said to Christian, who sat next her. "It's Uncle Nicholas. You'd think he'd know enough to stay home at his age."

Now everyone had discovered him. There was a general standing up and craning of necks, Renny still gripping the carving-knife and fork. He exclaimed:

"The dear old boy said he wanted to come. I told him I thought it would be too much for him. He looked disappointed and now, by the Lord, he's had his own way. Philip and Nooky, you two go and help him in." The boys obeyed.

"Who brought him?" Alayne asked in the voice she used when she was prepared to endure some fresh evidence of family wilfulness.

"Wright. In his own car. Now Wright has got him out. Why—he's walking strongly!"

"Bless his heart," said Meg. "Patience, will you lay a place for him?" She looked hopefully about the already crowded table.

"He had his dinner before we left," said Alayne. "I saw to that."

"I know," Renny agreed. "But he ate very little. He'll be

hungry by now. Archer, you could let Uncle Nick have your place, couldn't you?"

"Mercy!" said Archer. It was his latest favourite in words and he uttered it on a high complaining note.

By this time the old man was in the room, smiling his triumph. "Thought you'd got rid of me, didn't you? But I enjoy a party as well as anyone."

"And we're delighted to have you," cried Meg, going to him and kissing him.

"Now don't trouble about me," said Nicholas. "I'll just sit at this little table and gnaw a bone. How pretty everything looks."

But they troubled a good deal, the boys bringing a comfortable chair, Patience laying a cloth and dishes on the little table, Renny cutting his favourite parts from the chicken.

Little Mary said, "I want to bring flowers for his table." She had to be lifted from her chair; and when she reappeared, with three short-stemmed daisies, a vase must be found for them. Luckily the night was warm and the food not too chilled as Fitzturgis had feared. He listened to, rather than joined in the loud animated talk, now and again meeting Alayne's eyes in an amused interchange. He saw Roma's cool gaze on him and wondered what she was thinking.

After they had had coffee Meg said to him privately: "Renny tells me you are anxious to find a house and that you'd like to consider this. Now would be a good time to go over it."

"Yes, indeed," he smiled; "I'd love to."

Meg led the way and Renny joined them. He said, "Meg and I have known this house all our lives. We used to come here to tea as children. After the first war it was made into a two-family house, but Meg restored it to its original form when she bought it."

In every room Meg had some memory of its past to relate. Adeline, who had been helping Patience, now joined them. "Oh, Mait," she breathed, tucking her hand into his arm, "won't it be lovely?"

At the end of the tour Meg asked, "Do you think you'd like to buy it or rent it?"

"It would suit me better to rent," said Fitzturgis.

"Oh yes," agreed Adeline. "It would suit us better to rent."

Downstairs Patience was saying to Roma. "Do you think

you could give me that fifty dollars you borrowed from me?"

Roma looked faintly surprised. "Yes," she said, "I'll pay it—when I can get hold of some money."

"But, Roma, you said Uncle Nick was making you a present of some quite soon."

"I thought he was."

"Mother would be very annoyed if I told her this."

"Then don't tell her."

"Roma, do you expect to pay me back?"

"Why, yes. Some day." She was bored by the family party. She wanted to get away somewhere with Norman, whose car was waiting for her down the road a little way. But she went dutifully and kissed Nicholas goodnight, lingered a little on the lawn with the three boys, before drifting through the gate into the dusk.

Norman moved a book on psycho-analysis out of the way to make room for her on the seat of his car. "How'd the party go?" he asked.

"Like hell," she said. "Uncle Nick arrived without warning just as we sat down at the table."

"Hmph. How is he?"

"He's all right—the old miser!"

"How's your Aunt Meg behaving?"

"Oh, she's been pretty bitchy for days. I suppose she's tired. But who isn't? I know I am. Patience has been bothering me for the fifty dollars I borrowed. *Fifty dollars!* You'd think it was a *thousand.*"

"Never mind, darling," Norman's arm slid about her. "We'll soon be married and you'll be safe with me, where your family can harm you no more."

Roma did not answer. She could see her reflection in the little looking-glass and she was gazing at it rapt.

4

FINCH'S RETURN

FINCH HAD expected to return alone to Jalna. But in London he had been joined by Maurice, who had come over from Ireland on a sudden impulse to see him before he sailed.

Maurice had been suffering a mood of depression. He had felt himself to be alone, without deep roots either in Ireland or Canada. Most of all he had felt the finality of Fitzturgis's departure. He had never believed that the engagement between him and Adeline would end in marriage. He had expected to see Fitzturgis making spasmodic efforts to sell his property, writing less and less often to Adeline, and at last settling down to an indolent and not unpleasant life on his infertile acres. Then suddenly out of the blue (that is, out of an airmail letter from Pheasant) had come word that Fitzturgis had made a sale, and was leaving with his mother and sister for New York, that Adeline expected to be married in the early fall.

Sitting with Finch over a drink in his London hotel, Maurice had said, "I feel sure I could make Adeline happier than Fitzturgis can. I've always loved her—as long as I can remember. I understand her. The trouble is she takes me for granted. I'm just another cousin."

"How old are you?" asked Finch.

"Twenty-four. And please don't tell me I'll grow out of this because I shan't."

"I was only thinking how faithful you and Fitzturgis have been to Adeline."

"Adeline is the sort of girl men are faithful to."

"I was thinking, too, why not come home with me and give Fitzturgis a run for his money? And what a splendid surprise for your mother. She misses you, Maurice." Finch spoke as in solicitude for Pheasant, but his solicitude was really for Maurice. He had noticed that he was not looking well, that the hand that held the glass trembled, that it was too often refilled. Was the boy just getting over a drinking bout, he wondered, and put the question abruptly: "Do you drink a good deal, Mooey?"

Perhaps it had been the use of the family's abbreviation of his name that had made Maurice answer, with childlike simplicity, "I'm afraid I do, Uncle Finch." And he added, under his breath, "I get lonely and depressed at times."

"Then do come home with me. It's two years since you were there. It's time we had a reunion at Jalna. Wakefield is coming a bit later."

Maurice had not been difficult to persuade and now the two were descending from the aeroplane. They narrowed their eyes against the intense heat and glare of the landing-field. The tall figure of Finch was discovered by Piers, who had come in the car to meet him.

"Hullo," he shouted, then, as soon as it was permitted, pressed forward to shake Finch by the hand. "You're two hours late," he added.

"Here's Maurice, Piers." Finch's tone said, 'Here's a surprise to make up for all the waiting.'

Piers stared at his eldest-born in open-mouthed astonishment for a moment, then his healthy sunburnt face warmed into fatherly welcome.

"Well, I'll be darned," he said. "And won't your mother be delighted! But why didn't you send word?"

"I thought I'd surprise her. But—perhaps I should have sent word."

"It would have been better. Never mind. Let's find your baggage and get out of here."

Piers's car, from standing in the heat of the sun, was like an oven. Finch and Maurice sank into the blistering seat subdued.

"Hot spell," said Piers, explaining.

"I had forgotten," said Maurice, "how hot it can be."

"How is everybody?" asked Finch.

"Fine. Renny couldn't come to meet you. He's off to a sale and taken Fitzturgis with him." Piers chuckled. "Trying to teach him the elements of breeding show horses. I can't make the fellow out. What sort of life does he lead in Ireland, Maurice?"

"Very pleasant, I believe. I don't see much of him. . . . Did Adeline go to the sale too?"

"No. I guess Renny thought that Fitzturgis would have no eyes for the horses if she were there."

They were moving swiftly through the shimmering countryside, where every hour the sun gained in power, the shadows crept closer under the trees, the breeze created by the movement of the car became hotter. Yet Maurice was exhilarated. He was grateful to Finch for having persuaded him to come, and turned toward him to smile his gratitude. But Finch looked suddenly detached, lost in his own thoughts.

Finch was thinking of his new house and how densely it was surrounded by trees. That would be a problem, what trees to cut down. They had stood there so many years. They had surely absorbed through their roots the very essence of those who had lived in the old house which had been burned down.

Those who had lived there and those who had died. Eden had died there. He had looked out on those same trees from his bedroom window when he was ill. Finch's brows drew together in pain as he pictured Eden, in that light blue dressing-gown, standing at the window, looking out at the sombre wintry scene, longing for spring. Why did one remember the sad things about the dead? He should have remembered Eden's gaiety and generosity—remembered him when he was full of life, not declining into death. Finch thought of his dead wife Sarah, not in pain but in wonder at how unreal she had become to him. Even the son she had left him seemed . . . well, he could hardly think of Dennis as unreal. He was an active eleven-year-old, but somehow Finch had never been able to feel close to Dennis, never had wanted to have the child with him. Was it because he felt in Dennis a predatory reaching out toward him that reminded him of Sarah? Was it because there was probably no fatherliness in himself—not as in Renny, who had been as a father to his brothers—a rough and ready one at times but generous and warm-hearted? Finch found in himself no eagerness to see Dennis, who was at a boys' camp somewhere. He had brought him a camera because he knew that was what Dennis wanted, but he had not written to him—had not answered the neat little letter Dennis had sent him. Why had Dennis signed it 'Your aff. and only son'? That was like Sarah—possessive.

Finch leant forward to ask of Piers, "How is Dennis? Have you heard lately?"

"He's all right, I believe. He'll be home soon. Renny only sent him for half the season. He thought you'd want him with you. Your house is ready. You'll have fun furnishing it. Meg is all agog to take it in hand."

The dimple at the corner of Piers's mouth was roguish as he glanced over his shoulder to note the effect of these words on Finch. He looked more imperturbable than he felt. He said, "That's very kind of Meg. However, I don't intend to furnish all the house straight away. I shall go slowly and get the sort of things I'll enjoy living with."

Maurice asked, "If Auntie Meg is letting her house where will she and the two girls live?"

"With Finch, naturally."

"There has been nothing arranged," Finch said in the loud tone that betrayed his nerves.

"Meggie has arranged it all," laughed Piers. "It would never do for you—a poor lone widower, with a child—to struggle with housekeeping when she——"

Finch interrupted, "Nothing is arranged."

"Tell her that. She thinks it is."

They drove on in silence. Then they were in the familiar road, with its spreading trees, and the quiet fields and orchards of Jalna lay on the left. They were in the driveway, that green tunnel that looked cool but still was breathlessly hot. Now they were in front of the house, with the browning grass, the drooping flower borders subservient to the sun.

"We need rain," said Piers and took out his handkerchief and mopped his forehead. Out of some shady corner the dogs gathered themselves, as though this were the last effort of which they were capable, and sent up a concerted bark, which on the part of the spaniel ended in a howl of protest. The front door opened and Alayne stood there, in mauve, her silvery hair elegantly brushed back from her clear-cut cool features.

Finch had always been a favourite of hers, and now she welcomed him. "Why, Finch, what weather we have for you! What heat! Do come in where it's more bearable." Then, seeing Maurice—"My dear, what a lovely surprise! Does your mother expect you? Will you all come in and have a cold drink?"

"How strong?" asked Piers.

"I was thinking of blackcurrant cordial, but, if you like something stronger . . ."

Piers said, "I think we should be getting along. Don't you, Maurice? You're anxious to see your mother, aren't you?" Maurice agreed that he was.

Finch was now out of the car, had saluted Alayne on the cheek and, with Maurice's help, was unloading his luggage. Wragge appeared, with his anxious secretive smile, and took possession of the two lightest of the suitcases. Maurice promised to return later that day and the car disappeared down the drive. Finch stood in the porch, its familiarity, its very insignificance, its sun-warmed stone and brick festooned by vines, drawing him in, dimming the immensity of the flight under bright sky and over dark sea, the confusion of crowds, the concert halls. The dogs pushed their way into the house and threw themselves with grunts on to the coolness of the floor.

"What a day for a sale," Alayne said. "But Renny would go

and would take Maitland with him. The poor man will be melted. He so feels the heat."

They were in the shuttered coolness of the drawing room. Wragge had brought the iced blackcurrant drink; and after enquiring for Nicholas, Finch asked, "How do you like Fitzturgis?"

"Very much." Alayne spoke almost as though in defence of him as though she perhaps were the only one who understood him. "He and I have had some interesting talks. I find him quite unusual."

"Do you think he can make Adeline happy?"

Alayne gave a resigned little shrug. "Who knows? And just what is happiness?"

"I certainly cannot answer that question," said Finch and, sipping his drink, let himself sink into the blank-minded familiarity of the room.

"How is Maurice?" asked Alayne.

"He's still in love with Adeline, if that's what you mean."

Alayne showed surprise, without maternal gratification. "I did not know," she said, "that there was anything serious in his affection for her. I thought it was just cousinly."

"It's quite serious." After a pause Finch added, "He drinks more than is good for him."

"I'm sorry to hear that. Pheasant would be so distressed if she knew."

"I'm hoping he'll go straight while he's at home. He's promised me."

Archer now came into the room. He greeted Finch and heard without surprise that Maurice had accompanied him. He asked, "Do people visit their old home out of duty or for pleasure?"

"It is natural," said Alayne, "to return to one's people."

"Animals don't. You can't imagine a tiger seeking out his parents. He'd know they'd criticize him."

"Domestic animals return to their homes, Archer."

"Yes," he agreed. "I read of a cat that was presented with a medal for returning sixty-eight miles to its home. But what use was the medal to the cat? The only consequence was to make the cat's owner conceited, as though he had done something."

"You'll find," said Finch, "that you'll long for home when you've left it."

"The only thing I long for," said Archer, "is to understand. Uncle Nicholas says you only understand when it's too late."

At this moment Adeline came in, Finch embraced her with affection. "Lovely as ever, Adeline," he said, "and happy. I can see that in your eyes."

Archer examined his sister's eyes. "I don't see any expression in them," he said. "I think eyes are over-rated. It's the mouth that shows whether you are happy. Adeline is grinning, so we know she is happy."

Alayne said to Finch, "He goes on like this at every opportunity. He has such an analytical mind." She spoke half in pride, half in despair of her son.

"When is the wedding to be?" asked Finch. "I want to be here for it, if possible. So does Maurice."

"Is he coming over?" Adeline exclaimed.

"He is here. He came with me."

"How splendid! And Uncle Wake will be here, I hope. We plan to be married in September. Mait's sister Sylvia is coming from New York to visit us and stay for the wedding. You remember her?"

"One could never forget her," said Finch. His mind flew back to that brief meeting. Again he pictured the lovely, wan face, heard the pleasant cadence of her voice. "Is she quite recovered? She'd been ill, hadn't she?"

"Yes. She'd had a shock in the war—seen her husband killed in an air raid. Her nerves were awfully bad, but she's much better. She's hoping to get a job in New York."

"A strange place to choose for nerves," said Finch. "Yet—perhaps a good place—for forgetting."

Archer remembered that Alayne had met her first husband when she was working in a New York publishing house. That afternoon he had the opportunity to speak to Adeline alone and he remarked: "I wonder which husband Mother was happier with—Uncle Eden or Dad."

Adeline gave him a look of disgust. "You do say the most uncomfortable things," she exclaimed.

"Life has to be thought about," he said.

"There's no need for you to think about Uncle Eden, who died before you were born."

"But how closely connected to me! I once heard Dad say that sometimes offspring resemble a former mate. I may resemble Uncle Eden."

"You're disgusting, Archer. Besides, Daddy was talking of animals—not intelligent human beings."

"I don't see anything intelligent in having all your children resemble their sire."

She said, "You certainly don't resemble yours—more's the pity."

"Do you honestly wish I had red hair and dark eyes?"

"Not with your kind of mind."

"Do you consider Dad's mind superior to mine?"

"I do."

"Because it's instinctive rather than analytical?"

Adeline could endure him no longer. Forcibly she tried to eject him from the house into the outdoor heat. This roused the dogs, who set up a loud barking, and during the uproar Renny and Fitzturgis returned from the sale. Renny was in great good humour, having been able to acquire the mare he had set his heart on at what seemed to him a reasonable price, though he had warned Fitzturgis not to mention the amount to the family, with the exception of Adeline, who could be trusted to keep it to herself.

Fitzturgis and Finch shook hands with moderate friendliness, but Renny put his arm about his brother and hugged him. He was delighted to hear that Maurice had come with him.

"As soon as we have had some tea, Finch, we shall go to inspect your house and then on to see Maurice. It will be cooler by that time. Will you come with us, Alayne?"

But Alayne begged off. It was much too hot for her, she said, and she suggested that Fitzturgis also might prefer the coolness of the house. Adeline, however, showed her eagerness to go with Renny and Finch.

"It's not really hot now," she said. "And the new house is in deep shade."

"You'll have to cut down some trees, Finch," said Renny. "But don't do it till I can be with you. I know just which ones to choose." He looked at his watch. "By the time we return the mare will be here. I shall ask Rags to hurry the tea along." He strode to the hall and to the top of the stairs which led to the basement kitchen.

Alayne muttered under her breath, "There is a bell."

But he wanted to tell Wragge of his purchase. He shouted his name down the stairway. Wragge, in shirtsleeves, appeared at the bottom.

"Rags, d'you think your missus could hurry along the tea a bit? We want to go over to the new house."

"It'll be up directly, sir. We're 'aving it iced today, if that will be all right, sir."

"Fine. And, Rags, I bought the mare I've wanted! A regular beauty. Wonderful brood mare—short muscular back—well-let-down hocks—deep through the heart! You'll fall in love with her at sight."

"I bet I shall, sir. I *am* glad for you." He was already pulling on his jacket. His wife said, as he turned back into the kitchen: "Another horse, eh? And a fancy price, I make my guess."

"A lovely brood mare! Ah, 'e knaows wot 'e's about," exclaimed Wragge. "'E 'as vision *and* knowledge."

Noah Binns, now past eighty, a frequent visitor to Mrs Wragge's kitchen and a great consumer of her good cakes, took a deep drink of tea and remarked, "All he lacks is common sense. *That* he ain't never had."

"I'd like to know what you mean?" said Rags truculently.

"It's not common sense to break your bones and spend your money on horses. If there's one animal I despise it's a horse. This is a machine age and I'm glad of it—danged if I ain't. I seen enough of horses and their riders in my youth."

"I ask no better sight," said Rags, "than to see the boss on horseback."

Noah remarked, with concentrated bitterness, "Of all men on horseback, he makes me feel the worst. Yes, my gorge is stirred up when I see him prancing on a horse."

"I guess you don't like him, Mr Binns."

Noah shook his head and wiped his mouth on the back of his hand. "It ain't because I don't like him. He affected me that way when I first saw him mounted. He was only a toddler and his pa was holdin' him steady on a Shetland pony. My gorge rose then."

"Have some more tea," comforted Mrs Wragge.

But he pushed away his cup. "No, thanks." He sighed. "I feel kind of sickly. I guess it's the humility in the atmosphere. Heat and humility. That's what I can't stand. And there's more of it coming."

"I suppose you mean humidity," said Wragge.

"You can call it any fancy name you like. I call it humility. It's a biblical term and it's good enough for me."

The tea-tray was now ready and Wragge carried it up the stairs, at the top of which the dogs were waiting.

The intensity of the heat had lessened, but there was a strange stillness in the air as Renny, Finch, Adeline, Fitzturgis and Archer walked through the ravine and up the steep path to Vaughanlands. The little stream which had been seeking and finding the lake in all these hundred years since Captain Philip Whiteoak had first spanned it here with a rustic bridge now moved languidly past the luxuriant growth that edged it. A pleasant coolness rose from the water. They followed the path across a stubble field where small birds were finding their evening meal. Trees grew so thickly about the house that its whiteness was discernible some time before its design could be guessed, even though a number of trees had been destroyed in the fire which had burned the earlier building. Now this house was seen to be of typical West Coast architecture, all on one floor, with few but very large windows.

"The Vaughan who built the old house must be turning over in his grave," remarked Renny. "It makes me think of the advertising pages in magazines. All it lacks is a shiny new car and a shiny new wife."

Archer remarked, "It seems to me a perfect house for a concert pianist"—Finch looked doubtfully pleased—"and his pathetic child."

"I don't think Dennis is at all pathetic," said Adeline. "You are pathetic because you imagine you know so much and really know so little."

Archer was imperturbable. "All children are pathetic," he said. "And all old people."

"What about those in between?" asked Fitzturgis.

"They are just pitiable."

Finch said, "When I have my piano and my furniture it will look different."

"Shall you get a wife also?" asked Archer.

His father gave him a look and he went and peered in through the largest window.

"That's the music room," said Finch. He had the key of the front door and now unlocked it and they trooped into the house. The sound of their steps and their voices were magnified into a false importance. Adeline and Fitzturgis smiled into each other's eyes, thinking how well they could do with this charming new house.

He said, "I've never seen anything like it. The music room is so large. The others small and cosy. The outdoors seems to come right in at the windows. It seems made for——" He hesitated, searching for a word.

"Us," put in Adeline. "If ever you tire of it, Uncle Finch, we'll take it over."

"It will cost plenty to furnish it," said Renny. "There are some nice old pieces at Jalna I can let you have. Chairs and a cabinet."

"Thanks. I'd love to have them—if Alayne wouldn't mind."

Archer looked thoughtful. "She'd mind very much, I'm pretty sure."

"Why," said Renny, "your mother often remarks that the house has too much furniture."

"It's one thing," said Archer, "to say that, but it's quite another to give the things away."

At this remark everyone but him looked embarrassed.

Finch said, "It would only be temporary. I'd give the things back whenever she wanted."

Archer looked intensely interested. "I've heard her say that if you lend a piece of furniture to anyone it's the hardest thing in the world to get it back again. When they've possessed it for a while they look on it as their own and they resist if you ask for it. Aunty Meg was like that with an occasional table we lent her."

"After all," Renny said, "the furniture belongs to me."

"Would you dare take the occasional table?" asked Archer.

"I have forgotten the incident."

Renny led the way through the echoing house. "It's a tiny place," he said. "Just three bedrooms. I don't see where you all are to sleep."

"All?" repeated Finch, trying to look as though he did not understand.

"Yes. One for you. One for Dennis. That leaves one for Meg and the girls. But Roma will be getting married."

Archer said, "I don't think Aunty Meg will like to share a room with Patience who so often comes in from working in the stable."

"What a marvellous kitchen!" exclaimed Adeline. "And no

basement stairs! No one need mind doing the work in this house. I'd just love it."

"Mercy!" said Archer.

5

MAURICE AT HOME

PHEASANT HELD Maurice tightly in her arms, her eyes searching his face with loving anxiety. "I just can't believe in you . . ." Her voice had both laughter and tears in it. "Are you sure you are here in the flesh?"

"Yes, and with a mosquito bite already."

"Oh, Mooey, darling. . . ."

How sweet the childish name sounded to him! He smiled lovingly down into her eyes. Piers was occupied with the car and let him go into the house alone. The room, with its memories of childhood, engulfed him. It was hard for him to free himself from them, to see his mother clearly. Hardest of all to forget was the goodbye they had said when he had first gone to Ireland. Neither of them would ever forget that. It had left its scar on them.

"I believe you are taller. Have you grown?"

"No."

"But you're thinner. Are you well, Mooey?"

"Perfectly. . . . How pretty you look, Mummy. And the house! Those curtains are new, aren't they?"

"Yes. Fancy your noticing. Are you hungry, dear?"

"No. I'm much too hot. I'd forgotten how hot it can be."

"Your tweeds are so heavy. Do take your jacket off. I'll make you a cold drink."

Piers came in. He gave Pheasant a quick glance as though begging her not to fuss over the boy the moment he arrived. Little Mary came in. She was eating an ice-cream cone.

"Hello, little sister," said Maurice. "Will you come and kiss me?" She turned and fled.

"She's shy," said Piers. "She'll get over it and be as bold as brass—the way they all are."

Pheasant now brought iced drinks on a small tray.

"What is it?" asked Maurice.

"Ginger ale. Don't you like it?"

"Yes, indeed. . . . But—might I have a drop of whisky in mine? The plane flight has left me a bit squeamish."

"Certainly," said Piers, feeling ready for a drink himself. He went to a cupboard and brought out a bottle of Canadian rye.

Maurice looked at the label.

"I haven't any Irish," said Piers, "if that's what you want."

"No, no. This is fine, thanks."

"Take a mouthful from the glass to make room for the whisky." Maurice drank half the glass.

"Say when,' said Piers, looking rather hard at his son.

"You may fill it up." Maurice gave a little laugh. "As I said —I feel a bit squeamish."

Piers filled the glass. He beamed at Maurice.

"I do think he is thinner, don't you, Piers?" Pheasant asked.

"It's a wonder," said Piers, "he isn't getting fat and lazy. What do you do with yourself, Maurice? I mean, how do you pass the time?"

"Oh, the time passes fast enough."

"It's a wonderful thing," Piers went on, "for a young fellow to have an independent fortune. It was lucky for you that you went to visit Cousin Dermot."

"Yes, indeed. Where is Nook? Have I got to call him Christian now?"

"You've got to try. I find it hard."

"I'm quite used to it," said Pheasant, "except that at bed-time I always say 'Goodnight, Nooky'."

"Listen to her," laughed Piers. "She still looks on you boys as though you were five-year-olds."

Little Mary again came in, sidled between Piers's knees and stared large-eyed at Maurice.

"Whom do you think she's like?" asked Pheasant, smiling encouragement at her daughter.

"Certainly not you," said Maurice. "More like Father."

"No," said Piers. "Like my mother. She's named for her, you know. Tell brother your name, pet."

Little Mary, in panic, scrambled on to his knees and hid her face against him. She did not mind the heat from his stalwart body.

"Wait till you see Philip," said Pheasant. "He's grown devastatingly handsome in the past two years."

"He'll outgrow that," said Piers. "I was the same at his age."

Pheasant was silent.

"Wasn't I?" he repeated.

"Why, yes, dear." She spoke in a comforting tone. Then to the little girl she said, "Run to the studio and tell Christian that big brother is here."

Mary gripped Piers and hid her face. Setting her on her feet, he said in a tone of command, "Run along with you."

Mary went out through the kitchen door and across the yard to the studio. She could see Christian there, scraping paint from a palette. The room looked very large, Christian very forbidding in his smock; the smell of the paint was sinister. She stood looking in through the crack of the door and a tear ran down her cheek. The world so large, so full of strange scents and sounds! So many men—and another one come. She could hear Philip's piercing sweet whistle as he crossed the yard. He strode past her without seeing her and went into the studio.

"Do you know what?" he said, in his new man's voice. "Maurice is here. In the house with Mother and Dad, I saw him through the window."

Christian gave an exclamation of surprise, began to pull off his smock, decided to leave it on, and the two passed Mary on their way back to the house. She had not given Christian the message. She had not done as she was told. Tears ran down her cheeks and she scratched a mosquito bite on the back of her neck.

Indoors the three brothers stared at each other, trying to recapture the old familiarity. The two younger always had been together. Maurice was the outsider. They felt that he now considered himself superior to them—in experience of life, in travel, in his position as a young man of means. Philip frankly looked up to him, even while he was inclined to show off in front of him as a citizen of a young, uninhibited, flagrantly rich country.

"And how is poor ould Ireland?" he asked.

"Fine," smiled Maurice. He was in good spirits now. He looked Philip over admiringly.

"I hope you're not homesick for the ould sod," Philip said, eyeing Maurice's clothes with envy.

Christian put in, "Don't mind Philip. It's just his idea of wit."

Pheasant said, "It's wonderful having Mooey home with us, isn't it, boys?"

"Splendid," agreed Piers, wanting to be included. "Where is that little Mary?" he added.

The boys said they had not seen her.

"I'd better find her." Piers rose and went with his slight limp toward the door. "Sometimes she has a little cry all by herself."

In the two years that had passed since Maurice had last seen his brothers Christian had developed mentally more than had Philip. In an odd way he felt himself to be richer in experience than his elder because of his dedication to art. He looked on Maurice as a dilettante in life and himself as an ardent worker. Yet he envied Maurice his experience in travel. They had had a few talks in Maurice's last visit from Ireland which he could not forget. He wanted to place himself again on that footing with his brother—yes, and to leave the light-hearted scatter-brained Philip outside.

At the first opportunity when, in the cool of the evening, they were alone together in the studio Christian brought the talk round to Adeline and her lover. Maurice had been very nice about the pictures, had wanted to buy one, which immediately Christian had given him. Maurice sat on a bench, with it on his knee, as though he would not risk being parted from it. Christian admired his air of detachment that was tempered by a gentle authority.

"I remember your telling me," said Christian, "and I was proud of your confidence, that you loved Adeline. However, I suppose that's all over now."

He saw a bitter smile bend Maurice's lips. "It was always a one-sided affair. Adeline never cared for me. But I'm damned if I can discover what she finds in Fitzturgis. Do Adeline's parents like him?"

"Well, to tell the truth, I think that Aunt Alayne likes him very much and that Uncle Renny has a few doubts. But you know what Uncle Renny is."

"Indeed I don't. I really don't know what any of you are. I'm an outsider, Nooky."

"You'll not be for long. You'll be very much an insider . . . with me, anyway. I want to be your friend . . . if you'll let me."

Christian was frank and a little detached, even when he spoke warmly. Maurice was impulsive—eager to be loved—all too ready to be hurt. Now he exclaimed:

"There's nothing I want so much."

Christian laughed. "Nothing?"

"Nothing that I can attain."

They had lighted cigarettes and they smoked in silence for a space. Outside the wide, open doorway (wide enough to have admitted a carriage in former days) a pair of bats, darker than the night, padded the languid air with silent wings.

"How different this is," said Maurice. "The very smell of the air is different."

"I should like to see Ireland."

"You must come and stay with me. You must come when I go back this time. Could you do that?" There was a sudden eagerness in Maurice's voice. Heretofore he had considered only a visit from his parents, though it was his mother he really wanted. But the flowering into manhood of Christian, the newborn thought—'Here is a brother who may be a friend' —made Maurice reach out toward Christian. He did not realize that he wanted someone to lean on, to cling to—but there was the longing. As a child he had been swept away from all that was familiar to him into a strange country, into a strange house, not like a boy sent to boarding-school among other boys, but into a great lonely house, with an old man. The gentleness, the affection, he had found there had never quite effaced his feeling of insecurity. All his childhood he had felt insecure in his father's affection. Now, in manhood, he had a feeling of resentment, of wariness, toward Piers. But in this tranquil night-time his heart warmed to Christian.

"You must come and stay with me," he repeated.

"I'd love to," said Christian, and added, "It must be nice to have a place of one's own at your age, to invite whoever you like to come and stay with you. Do you often have friends to stay?"

"I've never had anyone—not yet. Except, of course, Adeline and Uncle Finch."

"But what do you *do*? I mean you're not like a chap who paints or writes."

"I find plenty to do. You know I have cottages and land to look after. I have a congenial neighbour—Pat Crawshay. We go fishing and sailing together."

"What a life! And you really want me to go and visit you?"

"I most certainly do."

"Nothing shall stop me," Christian exclaimed. "I'll paint Irish scenery—fall in love with an Irish girl and settle down at your gate. It's just what I've been waiting for."

"And on my part I'd like nothing better. . . . I say, Nook, have you anything to drink in the studio? I don't know what's wrong with me tonight, but I'm dry as hell."

Christian gave him a puzzled look. "But——" he began, then got to his feet. "I don't keep anything to drink here," he said. "I'll fetch something from the house."

"Never mind, never mind," Maurice hastened to say. "It doesn't matter. It's only that I have this damned thirst." But he objected no more as his brother left the studio and went into the darkness.

The lights in the house were out, but a rising moon gleamed against one window in the room where little Mary slept. Christian heard a step and made out the figure of Philip in the hall. He had left off the jacket of his pyjamas and his naked torso showed palely against the dark staircase.

"Gosh, isn't it hot!" he exclaimed, then lowered his voice. "I went to bed but couldn't sleep. What are you and Maurice doing?"

Christian sensed envy in the boy's voice. Here was the younger brother left out of things. To reassure him he said, "We shall be coming up soon. Maurice is tired, but he's sort of restless. He wants a drink."

"Oh . . . I guess I'll come out too. I feel restless and shouldn't mind a drink."

"I'm not having any," Christian said curtly. "Nor you either."

Philip stroked his smooth diaphragm. "I don't really want anything," he said. He followed Christian into the dining room and the light was turned on. "Dad will notice if you take more than a little."

Christian held up the decanter. "Not a great deal in it," he said. "Maurice is used to having as much as he wants when he wants it. He's his own master."

Philip came close and watched with absorption the doling out of half a glass of whisky.

"I guess it will look pretty mean to Maurice not to take out the decanter," he said.

"Damn." Christian poured back the whisky from the glass, returned the stopper to the decanter and grasped it by the neck. "You're right," he said. "We mustn't look mean, but—it strikes me . . ."

"What strikes you?"

"Nothing."
"But you were going to say something."
"Only that you'd better go to bed."
"I was going to the studio with you."
"No, no, Philip. Maurice is tired. He will be coming to bed directly."
There was an elder-brotherly tone in Christian's voice that offended Philip. "OK," he said gruffly, and went back into the hall and up the stairs, two steps at a time, in silent barefoot strides.
Maurice was holding the picture Christian had given him where the light fell on it when Christian re-entered with the decanter. He appeared rapt by the picture, and when Christian set the decanter in front of him gave it a look of faint surprise. "Oh yes," he said. "Something more to drink, eh? A good idea."
He poured himself a drink. A breeze, with the promise of freshness in it, blew through the door.
"I can't tell you," Maurice said, "how strange it is to me to picture Fitzturgis at Jalna, under the same roof with Adeline."
"I suppose it does seem strange."
"Strange—and utterly hateful."
The last word was startling to Christian. He asked, a little embarrassed, "Do you dislike him so much?"
"Not in his own place. He's all right—possibly—where he belongs. But it's not here. . . . You know, Nook——" He sipped his whisky and water and exclaimed, "Aren't you having any? Lord, I don't want to be a pig."
"Thanks, I don't want any." Christian's eyes were on what remained in the bottle, hoping that Piers would not notice how much had been drunk.
"I'm afraid I drink a good deal," Maurice said seriously. "But I intend to cut it out—now."
"We don't have much of it about. Dad is the only one who takes anything stronger than coffee. . . ."
"Uncle Nicholas and Uncle Renny used to like good wine."
"They still do. Brandy helps to keep Uncle Nick alive."
"I'm sure it does," Maurice agreed heartily. "I've been thinking, Nook, that I might buy a little supply of spirits that we could keep in the studio here. It would be convenient if one wanted a drink at the odd time. What about that cupboard? Does it lock? Have you a key?"

"Yes, it locks. We could do that, Maurice."

Christian had a feeling of relief. If Maurice wanted an occasional drink, how much better to have a supply here in the studio than to be dependent on what their father so carefully guarded. He said, "I'll see to it tomorrow. What would you like? A bottle of Scotch?"

Maurice gave a little carefree laugh. "Don't let us be stingy with ourselves," he said. "Get three bottles of Scotch, one of vermouth and one of gin. We might like an occasional cocktail."

"Why, yes," Christian said doubtfully. "The only thing is, I shall have to borrow Dad's permit. In this country it's necessary, you know. He might think it rather a lot."

"I'll get a permit for myself. That will settle it. We'll keep our little secret to ourselves, Nook."

Steps were heard outside, then low voices. The brothers turned toward the doorway to see Adeline and Fitzturgis emerge from the night. She was in a pale yellow dress. She brought the radiance of her content into the studio. Her world was going well with her.

"I couldn't wait till tomorrow to see you, Mooey," she cried. "I made Mait come across the fields. It's a divine night." She ran to Maurice and kissed him on the cheek.

"I did not need any persuasion," said Fitzturgis. He spoke as though with calculated warmth and shook Maurice by the hand.

They gave each other appraising looks, while Christian regarded them both with a detached interest. He saw Fitzturgis glance at the decanter and offered him a drink. It was accepted. He brought a glass from the cupboard.

"Say when," he said as he poured the spirits.

"Just a little," said Fitzturgis, noting the amount in the decanter.

Maurice remarked to him jocularly, "That's not the way we do things in Ireland, is it?"

"And it's not the way we do things here," cried Adeline. She turned to Christian. "Can't you get something from the house?" she asked, her eyes commanding him.

"Nothing more for me," said Fitzturgis.

"Nor me either," added Maurice cheerfully. He strolled to the door, glass in hand, and looked out into the darkness.

"It's getting a bit cooler," he said, then, turning to Fitzturgis, asked, "How do you think you'll endure this climate?"

Adeline answered for him. "He enjoys being warm for a change—don't you, Mait?"

"I enjoy everything," he said, with a possessive look at her.

She went on, "I can't remember being really warm all the while I was staying in Ireland. That huge old house of yours was always cold, Maurice."

"I know, I know. Everything was wrong."

"Mooey, how can you say that? I had a wonderful time."

"I'll wager you had." He spoke in a tone so low that only she could hear. "Once you and Fitzturgis were together again."

She was amused. She could not help being a little gratified. "You are an old silly," she said and put her arm about his shoulders.

A car stopped on the road. Two people alighted from it. They were Roma and her fiancé. She said, "Oh, hullo, everybody. We were passing and saw the light in the studio. We guessed you were having a party. Come on, Norman, and meet Mr Fitzturgis." She pronounced the Irishman's name with a kind of teasing pomposity, as though there were something ridiculous about his being there.

There were introductions. Maurice said, "It's not much of a party. We have nothing to offer you to drink."

"I can soon fix that up," said Norman. "I have several bottles in the car. I bought them for a party I'm giving for a bridegroom-to-be. I'll bring one in." He strode purposefully toward the door.

Half-heartedly the others (with the exception of Roma) sought to dissuade him. He strode off determinedly, his black, too-well-groomed hair gleaming like lacquer. Roma examined the picture on an easel. She avoided Adeline. Her round childish face wore an expression of complete absorption in the painted landscape.

Fitzturgis came to her side. "I want you to tell me," he said, "why you think I'm funny."

"Me?" she said, making wide eyes at him. "I never said so."

"You implied it." He spoke with mock severity.

"I didn't know. I thought I said things straight out."

"What girl does?"

"Adeline. . . . What I was thinking was, it seemed funny to see her engaged."

"I don't see why."

"Well . . . it's always been her father . . . Uncle Renny. . . . She thinks he's perfect."

Fitzturgis looked thoughtful. "Yes," he said. "I've noticed that."

"I dare say it's natural," she went on in her sensible little voice. "All the family sort of look up to him. Not me. He's too overbearing. I won't stand it. I like to go my own way—and let other people go theirs."

"That's a very nice trait," he said warmly.

"Oh, I don't know. It's just the way I feel." Her eyes turned admiringly to Adeline. "Adeline is a strong character," she said. "She's like great-grandmother—the one in the portrait."

"A remarkable likeness," he agreed.

Roma gave a smile that somehow conveyed disparagement. "It's to be hoped," she said, "that Adeline doesn't grow into what that old woman was. A regular old tyrant . . . I never like the thought of her. . . . For goodness' sake don't tell that I said that or they'd all be after me."

"*After* you?"

"Well, I'm a sort of outsider. They all hang together. I don't think it's a good idea for a family to hang together too closely, do you?"

"I do not."

Norman now returned with a bottle of rye. Maurice asked Christian about more glasses and he obediently went to the house for three. He moved very quietly, for fear of disturbing the sleepers upstairs, but in taking the glasses from a pantry shelf he dropped one, and the small tray on which he had placed others tilted. They fell splintering to the floor. They made but a small crash, yet while Christian was still regarding the broken glass in dismay (for he had chosen the best ones) Pheasant appeared in her nightdress.

"See what I've done!" he exclaimed. "I'm sorry."

"Oh, Nooky, why did you have to take the best ones? Whom have you got in the studio?"

He was trying to gather up the fragments in his hands. "Adeline and Fitzturgis. Roma and Norman. They wanted a drink. Norman brought it."

Pheasant found a dustpan and brush. She said, "I hope you won't take more than one drink. And Maurice too. He must be tired. He ought to bc in his bed, poor darling."

Possibly it was the solicitude in the last words that made Christian remark, "Oh, Maurice will drink plenty."

From her kneeling position she raised startled eyes to his. "What do you mean?"

He hastened to say, "Nothing—except that he feels the heat and he's thirsty."

"He ought to be in his bed," she repeated a little crossly. She stood up, the broken glass collected.

"I hope you're not saying that about me." Maurice spoke from the doorway.

"I broke the glasses," was Christian's needless explanation.

"Teacups will do. Anything will do." Maurice put his arm about Pheasant and dropped a kiss on her hair. "Come on out and join us, Mummy. You look sweet in your nightdress."

She looked from one loved face to the other. "All I ask is that you boys will not take much to drink. You know what your father thinks about that."

They chimed in to reassure her and, supplied with fresh glasses, returned to the studio. On the way Maurice said, "Norman seems a decent chap."

"Well, he's always ready to supply drinks. I don't look on him as an interesting addition to the family. However, he is as interesting as Roma is."

"We thought you two had decided to go to bed," Adeline exclaimed when they appeared.

"I'll bet their precious elders were after them," said Roma. She was sharing a drink from Norman's glass, sitting beside him on a bench.

Fitzturgis said, "This is an excellent concoction. Is the formula a secret?"

Norman, with almost religious fervour, named the ingredients and the manner of mixing. He went on to talk of various drinks he had savoured in various night clubs. It was plain that he set great store on his experience of night life, which in truth was very limited. Fitzturgis listened to him with tranquil amusement. Ever and again his deepset eyes rested on Roma, who sat relaxed and silent, with the exception of an occasional interjected remark so banal, so without originality, that he wondered if she spoke seriously. Christian listened with a kind of hypnotized boredom as Norman continued to hold forth. Of those present Maurice was most ready to have his glass refilled. His heavy eyes regarded Fitzturgis with slumbering jealousy and Adeline with melancholy desire. Adeline's spirits soared to wildness. She wanted to dance, to laugh, to sing.

She went to a small radio in a far corner of the studio and turned it on. At the first brutal blare of a band playing an American version of native African music Christian sprang up and ran to her. "Are you mad, Adeline?" he demanded and lowered the tone.

"I believe I am—a little," she laughed. "Why not? We're all of us together again, aren't we?"

"We shall have Dad down here."

"Who cares? I don't." And she called out: "Do you, Maurice?"

"Do I what?"

"Do you care if Uncle Piers comes?"

"I care for nobody but you, Adeline."

"Come and dance then!"

He rose a little uncertainly.

"It's too warm for dancing," said Christian.

"You're afraid Uncle Piers will be disturbed. You know you are," Adeline scoffed.

"Good Lord!" exclaimed Christian in exasperation. "If you are willing to dance in this heat—go ahead! But not with the radio at full blast."

Norman said, "The night is still young. Have another drink."

"Will no one dance with me?" cried Adeline, executing a few steps of a rumba.

"The girl is suffering from frustration," said Roma. "Somebody dance with her."

Maurice, glass in hand, stood uncertainly, the light from the unshaded electric bulb throwing shadows as of illness on his pale face. He stammered, "I will dance with you . . . will dance with you . . . my angel."

"No, no," repeated Christian. "It's too hot."

"Who says it's hot?" exclaimed Roma. She sprang to her feet with a sudden energy, startling after her seeming languor.

The two girls faced each other. They threw their mobile bodies with abandon into the South American dance now played by an orchestra. Norman clapped his palms sharply together in the rhythm of the dance. A somewhat macabre beauty descended on the scene, the four young men appearing as under a spell cast by dancing nymphs.

This continued till the music was broken in on by the voice of the announcer.

Adeline went and sat beside Fitzturgis, who laid an arm lightly about her waist. His air was possessive as he said, "That was beautifully done. You made me forget the heat."

Norman handed another drink to Roma, who accepted it with cool unconcern. He now filled a glass and carried it to Adeline. "This is the last," he said.

"Are you telling me we've drunk all that?"

"We have. Don't worry. There's more where it came from."

"She shouldn't have any more," said Maurice. "I shall drink it for her." He appropriated the glass and sat down at her other side. "You might make a little more room," he complained.

"Move over, Mait." She gave Fitzturgis a little push.

"There is no place here for anyone but us," he said truculently.

"Do you hear that, Mooey?" she said with a reckless laugh.

There seemed to Maurice something insulting in the stress she put on the old pet name. He gave her a look of mingled reproach and anger. He pressed close to her on the bench, so that her body was wedged between him and Fitzturgis. A scowl darkened the face of the latter and he resolutely stiffened himself.

Maurice tossed off his drink. He leant across Adeline to say, "Move along, you blackguard."

The fury in his voice was so unexpected that Adeline sprang up in amazement. The two men were left in possession, facing each other. They looked so ridiculous sitting there that Christian broke into an appreciative chuckle.

"I don't like your vocabulary," Fitzturgis said to Maurice.

He retorted hotly, "And I don't like anything about you. You're an interloper and I wish you'd get to hell out of here."

The next moment he was lying on the floor. Fitzturgis had pushed him off the bench.

Adeline uttered a cry of fright. Christian interposed his body between Fitzturgis and Maurice, who had got to his feet and stood swaying in anger and bewilderment. Norman said, "I guess we'd better break up this party. Come on, Roma."

"What's the use of everybody getting in a stew?" she objected.

Maurice said thickly, "I demand an apology."

"I have been insulted," said Fitzturgis. "And I am ready to defend myself at any time and in any place."

Adeline took him by the arm. "You both have been drinking too much," she said. "I call it a shame to get quarrelsome at our first little party."

"I call it a damned unpleasant party," said Maurice, nursing an elbow. "And if *Mister* Fitzturgis would like any satisfaction from me I'm willing to give it."

"Norman certainly did his part," said Roma.

"Oh, that's all right," said Norman. With an expression of distaste he emptied the last of the last bottle into a glass and drank it.

Roma regarded him with wide-eyed disapproval. "Remember you're driving," she said.

"I flatter myself that I can carry my liquor like a gentleman," he returned.

"Is that the fellow," Maurice asked of Adeline, indicating Norman with a trembling forefinger, "who was once engaged to Patience?"

"If you're going to indulge in personalities," said Roma, "we'll say goodnight."

"Goodnight," Christian said readily.

At Maurice's words Norman had passed out into the night. The bats moved softly about him.

Drops of sweat stood on Fitzturgis's forehead beneath his upright curly hair. He asked Maurice in a growling tone, "Do you want to carry on this discussion?"

Christian interposed, "The party is over. Goodnight, everybody."

Roma asked of Adeline, "Want a lift?"

"Thanks, but we're going to walk."

As Roma passed Fitzturgis she gave him a look that was neither friendly nor unfriendly but like a signal held out.

Fitzturgis followed her departure with studied attention. He thanked Christian punctiliously for his hospitality, then suffered himself to be led away by Adeline. It was so dark that he would have lost his way had not she taken him by the hand. They went down the road and through a farm gate into a field where dark shapes of cows showed in peaceful humps beneath an elm tree. An extraordinarily sweet and pungent scent had been drawn from the field by the heat—the scent of clover and small wild flowers, the scent of the earth in high summer.

The moon had risen and set. The sun was on its fiery way, but there was still an hour before its coming.

Fitzturgis was dizzy, not from the intoxication of the spirits he had drunk but from the languor of the heat and the isolation with Adeline. In the darkness of the field he took her in his arms and pressed her to him, murmuring incoherent terms of endearment and desire.

There was a sensuality in his approach to her that was new and startling. With a swift and violent movement she pushed him from her.

"No," she said, and repeated, "No."

"Why, Adeline," he exclaimed, half laughing, half hurt, "don't you love me?"

She moved lightly along the narrow path, leaving him to the darkness.

"Very well, then," he said, "you don't love me."

Her voice came back to him. "I do."

"Then—what's the matter?"

"I don't like to be touched."

"But, my darling . . ."

"Not in that way."

He plunged after her into the darkness, as into a well. He caught her and drew her again to him. Again his passion repelled her. She struck him, and, disengaging herself, fled along the path. He found his way after her as best he could. They passed by the wood and the orchard without speaking. At last the house, with a light burning in the hall, was before them. They separated silently for their own rooms.

6

FINCH'S HOUSE

"NOW THIS little occasional table," said Meg, "is one that I've always loved. We must take it to the new house."

"Yes," agreed Finch, trying to recall something he had been told about the little table.

"And this what-not . . ." she continued. "This dear old what-not is a piece I shall never want to part with. Still—the question is, where to put it. I do wish there were more corners in your house. The what-not must have a corner. Then I have three corner cupboards. I wish you had built an extra room to the house while you were about it."

They were in the living room of Meg's house and Finch's eyes were still on the occasional table.

"That table," he said, "doesn't it belong to Alayne?"

"Alayne?" she cried. "Why, Finch—whatever do you mean? Alayne doesn't own anything."

"What I meant was," he hastened to say, "I had remembered it at Jalna."

"Certainly," she agreed, "it used to be at Jalna. But it was lent—I should say *given* to me when I needed an extra table, years ago."

"I intend to buy a good deal of furniture," said Finch firmly. "The sort that will suit my sort of house. I have my own ideas, you know."

"Of course, dear. But you would be ruined if you set out to buy furniture for a house. Now, as to my piano. You remember the old piano at Vaughanlands you used to go to practise on when you were a boy because the noise of the scales worried Granny?"

"I do indeed," he said. "But I'm going to buy a piano."

"Buy a piano! With a perfectly good piano—almost an antique—at your disposal? You'll be telling me next that you don't want any of my furniture."

"I'd like the occasional table," he said.

Meg sat down plump on an over-stuffed Victorian lady's chair. "You mean that it is all you want?"

"Yes."

"But whatever shall I do with all my things?"

"Why not sell them? This is a good time for selling."

"But supposing you married again? Where should I be?"

"That's one contingency you need not consider," he said.

The idea of a sale and the cash produced by it was not unpleasant to Meg. She mused on the thought for a space, then jumped up and threw her arms about Finch. "I'll do it," she cried. "I'll go to you with only the occasional table."

Weeks of cheerful interest followed for Finch. Alayne, of whose good taste he had the highest opinion, threw herself with almost passionate interest into the furnishing of the new house. Together they visited the city stores. They attended an auction sale of the contents of a luxurious house, and later had dinner together at a restaurant. Finch had bought a car, and as they drove back to Jalna Alayne felt that she had not for years so much enjoyed herself. The companionship of Finch was congenial to her. She marvelled at the change in him, from a lanky, sullen and shy boy, to this distinguished-looking man. Yet when he turned his long light eyes to her with a questioning look or gave her his wide feckless smile he was the same Finch. She flattered herself that she had been a not feeble instrument in his development. It was she who had persuaded Renny to give him piano lessons. After one of these excursions when they had left the highway and were moving quietly along the country road that led to Jalna she said, "How swiftly the years fly! I have been thinking of when you first began to play the piano."

"It seems long ago to me. I can scarcely remember the time before that."

She was astonished. "I picture you," she said, "with very clear recollections of childhood and adolescence."

"They're all jumbled," he muttered. "Confused and rather painful memories. But—I must have been a young beast as a boy. I wonder you took so much trouble over me. For you did, you know. I shall never forget that."

"I refuse to listen when you talk such nonsense," she said. "You were a sensitive boy who was not understood by his family. I merely had the intelligence to see what you might become. I am very proud of you, Finch. You are a fine artist. You have fame."

He gave a short laugh. "It sounds first rate," he said.

"But who is satisfied?" she exclaimed. "No artist surely. Neither are we others."

"But you are happily married, Alayne. A happy marriage is something I cannot look back on."

"You will marry again."

"Never."

"But, Finch, picture Dennis with a new mother, waiting for you in your own house when you return from a tour." She was not so much painting a pretty picture for him as probing his feelings with feminine curiosity.

She was sympathetic, but he was not laying himself open to sympathy. He said, in a matter-of-fact tone, "I am pleased with my house as it is."

"I am so glad of that. Because I don't really want you married. I want to be able to walk across the ravine to find you sitting at your piano. I want you to go on playing, just as though I were not there."

"Meggie will be there," he said. "And Patience. Had you forgotten that?"

"Merciful heaven, I had!" she exclaimed. "But is it really settled? Can't you get out of it?"

This was putting the matter harshly. "I guess," he said, "that I am lucky to have two such women to come and keep house for me—and Dennis."

He added his son's name as though in an afterthought. Alayne, always puzzled by his attitude toward Dennis, said in a questioning tone, "He is a very interesting boy." She dared not give voice to what she felt about those two female relatives pushing (as she considered) their way into this citadel of his which should be sacred to his music and his privacy.

"I scarcely know him," he returned tersely.

"And sound as though you don't want to," she cried. "Really, Finch, you are impossible. Dennis will be eleven next Christmas. He is a thoughtful boy, a little backward in his studies, a little precocious in his attitude toward life."

"Doubtless I shall see more of him in future," said Finch. "Gosh, the way the youngsters are growing up. Piers's boys—young men! Adeline and Roma both engaged! Tell me, Alayne, what do you feel about your future son-in-law as the weeks go on?"

"He wears well," she said firmly. "And he fits into life at Jalna better than at first I guessed he would. He really *tries*. And I imagine it's not easy for him. I gather that he is used to doing just as he pleases, *when* he pleases. Now he will rise at six to help Piers in the orchards or on the farm. He is learning about horses from Renny, who says he is a nervous rider and always will be." She added, in a tone scarcely audible, "I am not sure that he is *quite* happy."

"He certainly ought to be," said Finch. "Engaged to a girl like Adeline. Anyone can see how deeply in love she is."

"She is little more than a child. Can one be truly in love at her age?"

"More truly I should say than later," said Finch. "Later it's harder to forget one's self—and all that lies behind. Adeline has no past."

Alayne spoke with almost impersonal gentleness. "We can

only hope for the happiness of her future. She is a dear girl."

These excursions to the city were made with a certain amount of secrecy. It would not do for Meg to discover that Alayne was assisting Finch in his choice of furniture for his house. Almost opportunely it seemed, Meg was suffering from a rash of poison ivy on her face and did not wish to be seen in public. Now Finch turned the car through the gateway of Vaughanlands, along the drive that sloped downward to where the house stood.

Alighting from the car, Finch stood to gaze, with that concentrated attention one gives to one's own new house. He did not yet love it but felt pride of possession mounting in him. There was as yet no soul in the house. It was but a shell. Nothing had happened in it. No vine or leaf of vine or smallest tendril of vine had darkened one inch of it. It was as purely white as the new-laid egg of a Leghorn pullet.

"Shall you keep the name Vaughanlands?" asked Alayne.

"Well—I have not thought about it. Must the house have a name? Very well, I'll keep the name. Unless you can think of a better."

"Uncle Nicholas—indeed all the family—would like to stick to Vaughanlands, I feel sure." They went indoors. The smell of newness greeted them. "Oh," she exclaimed, "how fresh it is! It makes Jalna appear really fusty. Finch, you are going to love it. And *there* stands the piano! How splendid it looks in the almost empty room!" She stopped in front of the occasional table with a thoughtful air.

"Meg is selling her things," Finch said, "with the exception of the few I want. . . . That little table came from Jalna. But that was so long ago."

"Not so very long ago," said Alayne, stroking the table with the affection of a lover. "I don't know why Renny lent it to Meg in the first place. I have always admired it."

"Would you like to have it back again?" Finch asked eagerly. "Because if you would——"

"No, no, no—that might annoy Meg."

"But—if it was only lent to her . . ."

"That is all it was. Just lent."

"Then, Alayne, let me give it back. Look here, I'll take it straight out to the car."

"I don't wish to annoy anyone," she said wistfully, "but I have missed this little table."

Finch was already on his way to the car with it. When he returned she was wandering from room to room. In each she had some happy suggestion to make, some commendation of what had been done. He drove her to Jalna, carried the occasional table into the house for her, escaped, without being seen, and returned, to find Christian awaiting him. He was seated at the piano, picking out a tune with one hand. He swung round to greet Finch.

"I hope you don't mind, Uncle Finch," he said. "I found all the lights on and thought I'd like to try the new piano. It's magnificent. It must be splendid to be able to play as you do. It's hard, isn't it, that life is so short a fellow has time to do only one thing well? And is lucky if he achieves that. As for me, I should like to be a painter, play the piano, the violin and the flute, and write novels."

"I know," said Finch. "I once wanted to be an actor."

"Did you really? Like Uncle Wake, eh? I didn't know that. I can't imagine your being anything but what you are. Uncle Finch, what does it feel like to be reunited with your family? After each tour I suppose you find quite a change in us young ones. Are you pleased by these changes or do you think the family is deteriorating?"

"Oh, never that," said Finch. "I admire you all. It's wonderful to see you young cousins developing. Adeline and Roma turning into women."

"Adeline the very spit of great-grandmother," laughed Christian, "and feeling very cock-a-hoop about it. Roma feeling herself the image of her poet father and conceited about that."

"Roma is not in the least like Eden. She is like her mother, Minny Ware, though she lacks the jolly generosity of Minny —or so it seems to me."

"There's nothing very jolly or generous about Roma," said Christian thoughtfully. "But she must be a sweet little thing. All her friends say so." He added in a lower tone, "There is one among us cousins I am worried about, Uncle Finch."

"Yes?" Finch's expression, so suddenly concerned, brought a smile of reassurance from the young man.

"It's not that I'm *terribly* worried. But it's a bit of a problem for me. It's about Maurice. You know he drinks too much?"

"I thought that—in London—and on the voyage out. He's still at it, is he?"

"He bought a supply. It seemed quite a lot to me. He kept it in the cupboard in my studio. Mother and Dad didn't know. Please don't mention it to Dad or Uncle Renny. But I felt I had to tell you. I need the advice of one of you older ones."

"I certainly will not tell," said Finch. "How much does he drink?"

"I actually don't know. He finished the first lot—with the help of Roma and Norman and two of their friends. Now he has a second supply. He likes company, but—if he has none—he'll drink alone."

"Alone, eh?"

"Yes, alone. So far I've been able to conceal it from Mother and Dad, though she suspects. Last night I had to help him up to his room. I'm awfully fond of Maurice, but—he's making things beastly difficult."

"Does he see much of Fitzturgis?"

"Very little. On his first night at home we had a little party—Adeline and Fitzturgis were there, and Maurice was disagreeable to him—actually insulting. But, you understand, he was tight. Fitzturgis pushed Maurice off a bench. They've scarcely spoken since."

"I'll see Maurice. I'll do what I can. It's a shame that he should behave like this."

"What I'm afraid of is there'll be a regular bust-up with Dad. Maurice has invited me to go back to Ireland with him on a visit, but Dad would never let me go if he found out that Maurice is a hard drinker."

Finch did not answer. His mind had flown back to a night when he himself was eighteen years old. He had left his studies and stolen into the bedroom occupied by Piers and Pheasant to see if he could find a cigarette to smoke. His nerves had been torturing him. Maurice had been asleep in his cradle. Finch remembered bending over him in curiosity. He had gone weak with tenderness as he gazed down at that baby slumber—at the round, baby fist curled beneath the flower-petal cheek. He had kissed the baby repeatedly in an almost ecstatic yearning. And now the baby was a man—Maurice—a 'hard drinker'.

"He and I," Christian was saying, "have become very good friends in the past weeks. I don't want anything—not anything—to come between us."

"I'll have a talk with him. . . . What do you think, Christian, of his feelings toward Adeline?"

"He loves her. I have no doubt of it. I think that is at the bottom of his trouble, poor fellow . . ."

When Christian had gone the last light was fading. Behind the trees to the westward where the great window of the living room faced, little red-gold sparklets of the afterglow danced between the leaves. It was a little past midsummer. The glorious energetic period of growth was slackening into the period of ripening. Finch was deeply conscious of this feeling of repose in the land. He wanted to draw it into his own house, into his own breast. At that moment he wanted, above all things, his house to himself. He wanted to get acquainted with it—to go from room to room, looking out of each window in turn, returning always to the music room and to the piano. But not yet could he bring himself to touch the keys. Before that moment there must be the agreement of peace between his spirit and his hands.

He took off his jacket and went and hung it in the clothes cupboard of his bedroom. It was the first garment he had hung there and he contemplated it almost in wonder. He gave the mattress of the bed a thump with his fist to test its resilience. He wished he might sleep there tonight—in the house alone.

The silence was almost palpable. As the sun disappeared, a fresh breeze stirred the new curtains at the window. Alayne had chosen them. At the time Finch had been a little doubtful of the choice, but now he saw that no other colour, no other pattern would have pleased him as did these. No other bedroom was yet furnished, and he felt that he would have liked them to remain empty—to live there in delicious isolation, alone. He wished—and made a wry face at himself for the wish—that Meg and the two girls would stay where they were. To be alone in this house with his piano—to give himself up to composing. He knew he had better work in him than had yet been put to paper. To be alone.

He remembered how as a boy he had thought it would be the very height of felicity to have a room of one's own. Piers had been a tyrannical sharer of room and bed. Piers had found a good deal of amusement in baiting him.

He remembered bedrooms he had shared with his wife Sarah, and he stretched his arms ceilingward, stretched all his body to its utmost, in his relief to be free. No other woman—no other marriage—not for him. The piano his woman. Music his mistress. The trees his audience. . . . He looked at his watch. He should be moving along to Jalna. He had a mind to spend the night here alone, to play the piano for the first time in this dear house of his.

But how to send word that he was not coming? If only he had a telephone installed. He would have to go to Jalna and tell them. But he would return here—and *alone*. He would spend the night alone with his piano . . . in the house alone. This was what he had been straining toward—to be alone!

From the wood beyond Jalna a whip-poor-will began to call. In mindless energy it threw its cruel command into the dusk. *Whip-poor-will . . . Whip-poor-will.* From his earliest days Finch had loved and feared this bird's song. Piers had told him in mischief that it cried *Whip-poor-Finch*, and for a long while he had believed that. Now he stood listening in the darkening room till there was silence again.

A small, remarkably sweet boy's voice came from the doorway. "Did you hear the whip-poor-will?" it said.

He wheeled and saw his son.

"Did you hear it?" repeated the boy. "I counted thirty-one times it did the call without taking breath."

"Once," said Finch, "I counted more than two hundred times."

"Gee whiz!" Dennis gave his high-pitched treble laugh. He then stood irresolute, as though not sure of his welcome. Finch wondered if he should embrace the boy—give him a hug and a kiss. The Whiteoaks were a demonstrative family. Renny was never embarrassed by kissing his brothers. Yet Finch could not make up his mind to move across the room to the side of his son—to draw him close—after almost a year's separation. . . . Was it that some essence of Sarah clung about the boy—emanated from him? Was it that Sarah had been so possessive toward Dennis that she had created a barrier Finch could not overcome? Another shadow fell. Again the whip-poor-will began to call.

"There he goes," exclaimed Dennis and counted the calls aloud. "One—two—three—four—five——"

Finch went to the clothes cupboard and took his jacket from the hook. Dennis at once stopped counting and followed. He said, "So this is where you keep your clothes? Is that all you have? What a nice house! I'd better turn on the light." Without waiting for permission he switched on the light and the room shone forth in all its newness. "What a pretty lamp!" said Dennis. "What a nice room!" He stood transfixed a moment in admiration and was himself revealed as small for his age, of compact build, with clear-cut features, straight fair hair and greenish eyes—eyes like Sarah's. But Sarah's hair had been black.

"Which is my room?" asked Dennis. He spoke with an almost quizzical air, as though he already knew and was tempting Finch to subterfuge.

"The small room at the back."

Dennis repeated, on a note of disappointment, "The small room at the back."

"The others are for Meg and the girls."

"But I thought we were going to live here—you and me . . . alone together."

His clear eyes, that looked shallow as a bird's, rested, as it were, accusingly on Finch's face, which now had a look of great weariness. Finch asked abruptly, "Why are you home from camp so soon?"

"But it's not soon. Uncle Renny sent me for only half the season because you were coming home. Wasn't that good?"

"Splendid," said Finch heavily.

Dennis seemed to have taken possession of the house. He went from room to room, turning on all the lights, moving as though to music, moving as though he had never been tired in his life.

"Why is my room not furnished?" he demanded.

"I haven't got round to that yet."

"Yours is the only bedroom furnished, isn't it?"

"It is."

A shadow crossed the little boy's face. It was as though he said, "That's being selfish, isn't it?"

Finch thought, 'Oh, to be rid of him—rid of everybody—to be alone.' The crawling, creeping pain that had troubled him toward the end of his tour now again struck the back of his neck, his temples. He pressed a middle finger and thumb to them. He went to the window of the living room, and looked out into the darkness. Dennis pressed down treble keys of the piano and it cried out as though in anguish.

"Don't!" exclaimed Finch roughly. "Come away from there."

Dennis hung his head, his lips quivering. Then he came

and slipped his hand into Finch's with a proprietary air. What a small firm hand—like Sarah's.

Finch asked quietly, "Will you be afraid to go back to Jalna in the dark?"

"No. For I shall have you."

Finch gently returned Dennis's hand to him. He said, "What I meant was, I wish you would go home."

"This is home," interrupted Dennis.

"I know—I know. . . . I wish you would go to Jalna and tell Aunty Alayne that I have decided to spend the night here. Tell them that I am quite all right but I am going to sleep here. I shall be there for breakfast."

"But they're having some supper pretty soon."

"I can do without that. Do you mind going?"

"No, I don't mind."

"Good. Now what are you to say?"

"I'm to say you are staying here but you'll be there for breakfast. Goodnight." He vanished as quickly as he had come.

It seemed too good to be true. Finch went from room to room, turning off the lights—all but the one in his bedroom. He looked longingly at the bed. But not yet could he lie in it. He discovered that his mouth was very dry. But the water was not yet available in the house. He must just forget his thirst. He would play something of Haydn's and find tranquillity.

But when he laid his hands on the keys they were helpless. The keys were frozen—immovable. He rested his elbows on the keyboard and his head on his hands. He gave himself up to the quiet of the night.

After a time he went and lay down on his bed. Physically he began to be at ease. He stretched his body to its fullest length and threw out his arms. An immense relief enveloped him to think that he had been able to send that message by Dennis. He was thankful that Dennis had come, and still more thankful that he had gone. . . . Taken the message. He began to feel drowsy. . . .

He was roused by the sound of quick footsteps on the flagstones of the terrace. He heard them enter at the open door. He held his breath, listening. . . . Then came the sound of a crash—not heavy, but as of a small body falling on the floor of the music room, and simultaneously the rattle of dishes. Finch sprang up. It was very dark in the music room. In his confusion he forgot where the electric switch was. He fumbled along the wall, dazed.

The clear treble voice of Dennis came out of the darkness.

"It was a surprise," he said, "but I fell."

"A surprise," muttered Finch. "A surprise. What the devil are you up to?" Suddenly he found the electric switch. Two floor lamps and several wall lights brightly discovered the scene. Dennis lay sprawled on the floor. A hamper beside him had burst open and its contents discharged—sandwiches, fruit, broken dishes, a Thermos bottle.

Dennis lay on his back, softly beating the floor with his fists. Tears were in his eyes. "I'm disappointed," he said. "It was to be a lovely surprise for you. I gave the message and Mrs Wragge packed the hamper. Aunty said so. And here are your pyjamas and here are mine. We've moved in."

Finch picked up the Thermos bottle.

"What's in this?" he asked, his mouth parched.

"Coffee. With cream in it. There's sugar in this little bag. And here are scones and butter and black cherries and cheese and—gee whiz—the cups are broken!"

"I have plenty of dishes here," said Finch. He went to the pantry and filled a large cup with coffee. It seemed to him the best he ever had tasted. It put new life into him. He could hear Dennis moving about gathering up the contents of the hamper. He came and asked, "Where shall we have our picnic?"

"Anywhere you like," said Finch.

"I choose the kitchen, then. It's a pretty little kitchen." He began deftly to lay the table. He drew up two chairs. "Are you hungry?" he asked.

"I believe I am." This was true. Finch suddenly found himself very hungry. He drank a second cup of coffee and looked over the little spread on the table with interest.

"Coffee should be taken last—not first," Dennis said with some severity.

"I know, but I was very thirsty."

"It's nice to have your own way sometimes," said Dennis.

They sat facing each other across the small table. Mrs Wragge had been generous, but soon they made a clean sweep of the food and had poured the last cups of coffee. They had eaten in silence, Dennis with outward composure, though inwardly a little shy, a little puzzled by this strange father.

Suddenly he asked, "What should I call you?"

Finch's mind was far away. With a start he repeated, "*Call* me? What do you mean, *call* me?"

"Well, I generally just say *you*. But what do you like to be called—Father—Daddy—Papa—Pop?" At the last he gave his high laugh and said again, "Pop."

"Certainly not that," said Finch, "if you value your skin."

"What then?"

"Daddy, I think. You're still a small boy."

Inexplicably Dennis jumped up, ran round the table to Finch and hugged him. "May I stay here with you tonight?" he whispered close into Finch's ear. "I have my pyjamas, you know." His arms tightened. "Please, please, let me stay. I'll be as quiet as a mouse."

Finch looked at his watch. It was ten o'clock, long past the boy's bedtime. He looked very small and pale.

"Very well," Finch said gruffly. "To bed with you, then, and keep yourself small."

Somehow he had become resigned to the boy's presence. A blessed peace had descended on his nerves. He felt healthily tired. He knew that he could sleep. He moved quietly about the rooms, making things tidy for the night. He lighted another cigarette and sat by the open window of the music room, looking out into the gentle darkness. Tomorrow he would have solitude—seclusion.

7

MAURICE

THERE WERE moments when Maurice half regretted this visit home. At these times he wondered whether the pleasure of being again under the same roof with his mother and Christian compensated for the pain of seeing Adeline and Fitzturgis together as so obviously lovers. He longed to remove Adeline physically out of reach of Fitzturgis; yet when, as it occasionally happened, he found himself alone with her he became almost speechless, behaving, as she thought, like a sulky boy. A boy . . . that was what he really longed to be. He had not felt ready for manhood when Dermot Court died and left him in possession of his estate. Maurice had clung to his position in that house, of a cherished boy dreaming of a distant future, living in a present where there was no responsibility. Now here in Canada he felt himself to be once again under Piers's discipline. He could not forget his childhood fear of his father. He thought of his mother as suffering under Piers's arbitrary domination, yet he could see how Piers about the house meekly did as Pheasant told him.

Young Philip looked on Maurice as something of a curiosity. A brother and no brother—a visitor, yet one of the family—one of the family, yet an outsider, because he owned a place in Ireland to which he would before long return. A few presents and the evidence of means which lay behind them, these produced respect in Philip, but he envied no one. That autumn he was entering the Royal Military College as a cadet. He was to make the army his career. There would be another Captain Philip Whiteoak! One hope which he lovingly harboured was that Renny should make him heir to Jalna. Why not? Of what use would land and a large house and a stable full of horses be to Archer? All Archer would require for content were a small apartment and plenty of books.

Philip had twice helped Christian steer Maurice to his room past the bedroom where their parents slept. He had seen his mother give a swift, pained look at Maurice, as though she guessed what her sons so carefully sought to hide from her. Maurice was such gay company when he was sober and in good spirits. When he had drunk even a little too much, his every word and movement was crowned by a melancholy intensity.

Philip now stood in the open door of the studio where he could see Maurice turning over some sketches Christian had made during the past spring, examining them intently and yet, strangely, seeming scarcely to see them. Piers and Pheasant, taking little Mary with them, were away for the day. Christian was away on some affair of his own. Maurice was in possession of the studio. Philip saw that an almost empty glass was on a table beside him. He saw the glass emptied, then Maurice turned and saw him.

"Ah, hullo, Philip," he said. "Going fishing?"

"I've just come back. No luck. Would you like a game of tennis?"

"Too hot. Get Fitzturgis to play with you."

Philip gave a crow of amusement. "Him! He feels the heat worse than you. Besides, he is off with Uncle Renny and two horse dealers to a sale. You should have seen him yesterday on the three-year-old Sligo. He's a bit of a devil. They're hoping to sell him to a man who has made a pot of money and is going in for horses and fox-hunting. Well, Sligo gave Maitland such a tumble as you never saw—right over his head. I thought his neck would be broken, but he's up and around today, his wrist bandaged. Dad says he'll never be much good with horses, or farming either. He's just not interested."

"Poor devil, I feel for him. Where is Adeline?"

"She and Uncle Finch have driven to town to meet Maitland's sister. She's coming on a visit, you know. Staying on for the wedding."

"Yes, so I've heard," Maurice went to the cupboard and took out a bottle of Scotch. Philip watched fascinated: He wondered if Maurice were going to get tight.

"It's a strange thing," said Maurice, settling down to his glass, "to see Adeline—so bright and beautiful—about to make so undistinguished a match. She might have had anyone. Don't you agree?"

"I've never thought about it."

"Do you ever think?" Maurice spoke with some severity.

"Well—I have plenty to think of without troubling my head over her."

"What—for instance?"

"I can't tell you offhand—but I think a good deal."

"Do you ever think about girls?"

Philip gave an embarrassed laugh. "Sometimes. Not seriously. There's no particular girl."

"Do you realize, Philip, what a handsome fellow you are?"

"I only know that I look like great-grandfather."

"He had a happy life—serene and contented—married to the woman he loved." Maurice drank a third of his glass. "Not like me, Philip. I must stand by and see Adeline hitched up with that blasted Fitzturgis."

Never before had Maurice spoken so to Philip. The boy was flattered by being treated as an equal but could find no adequate return but a large-eyed look of sympathy, a compressing of his pouting lips, several nods of the head.

"Sometimes I wonder," said Maurice, his eyes filling with tears, "if I can bear to be here for the wedding."

"Why—you wouldn't go away, would you?"

"Who would really mind? Be honest. Tell me that, Philip."

"We'd all be sorry. We'd be terribly sorry."

Maurice drew a deep sigh. "I like to think so. Perhaps you and Christian and Mother——"

Philip interrupted: "But he's going back with you, isn't he? To Ireland, I mean."

"Why, yes, so he is. I guess we must be here for the wedding. But I'd a damned sight sooner go." Maurice emptied his glass and sat in melancholy contemplation of an unfinished picture on an easel. "Very charming but very immature," he murmured. "Don't tell Christian I said that.... Praise, praise, that's what they want."

Philip did not know whether to go or stay. As he lingered undecided, Patience appeared in the doorway accompanied by a large, very curly, brown poodle. As she stood there in her blue overalls, the brightness of the summer garden behind her, the poodle in its soft graceful prancing attitude by her side, she appeared to Maurice as the embodiment of the season. He could not think of her as anything but serene—yet somewhere in the back of his mind was the recollection of unhappiness. He groped for this, while she stood with an enquiring smile on her sun-browned face, then he remembered she had been jilted. Poor girl! And by that hollow, lacquered excuse for a man—Norman!

"Hullo, Patty," he said. "Come in and have a drink."

She released the poodle and entered. It preceded her with a soft gambolling motion and a look of human intelligence and inhuman gaiety in its eyes.

"A drink," repeated Patience. "I was just going home for tea."

"Your day's work done. The very hour for a cocktail. Go into the house, Philip, and bring the cocktail-shaker and ice."

"No, thanks." She came and sat down near him. "I want my tea and Becky wants hers."

Philip said, "Well, I'll be off. I promised to be at the stables when Uncle Renny came back."

"He's back now," said Patience.

"Gosh! How did Misther Fitzturgis come through the day?"

"He's cheerful. Perhaps a bit pensive."

Maurice growled. "What the hell has he to be *pensive* about?"

Philip gave Patience a roguish look, as though to say, 'Here's a man with a grievance.' For a moment he romped with the poodle, then was gone.

"If you won't have a cocktail," said Maurice, "let me give you a whisky and soda."

"Thanks, but I don't drink."

"Good girl." After a moment he added, "I wish I didn't."

She said, with a direct look into his eyes, "Why not stop it, then?"

His own gaze faltered. "That's not easy to do, Patty," he said, "once you've begun."

She struck herself on her knee with her brown hand. "Just say to yourself, 'I won't', and stick to it. You've character, surely."

"I get depressed," he said. "I don't belong anywhere. I'm not necessary to anyone."

"What about your parents—your brothers?"

"You're not trying to make me believe I'm necessary to my father or to Christian and Philip, are you?"

"But to your mother you are. You are her favourite son."

His face lighted with the smile he had kept from boyhood, a smile that showed his vulnerability. He said, "Mummy's a darling and—well, there's something special between us—we've *suffered* together. To tell the truth, that consciousness of suffering is always with us when we are together—both holding us together and apart." After a silence he added, as though to bolster his belief in himself, "Philip says they would miss me if I were to leave before the wedding."

"But, Mooey"—she was almost too astonished for speech—"that's what you came over for—to be at Adeline's wedding."

"I did not," he declared with violence. "It was my time for a visit and it simply coincided with this wedding. Do you suppose that I would cross the ocean to see Adeline married to a man I detest? And—he detests me. Were you here that night when we almost came to blows?"

"No, but I heard of it."

"Who told you?"

"Roma. She said it was a scene typical of two badly adjusted people."

"Good God—what a mind she has! How do you endure living with her?"

"I shan't be much longer."

"Oh yes, she's getting married—to *Norman*."

The contempt in his voice brought a flame to Patience's cheeks. She bent to caress the poodle that had settled between her knees and was searching her face with cold analytical intelligence.

"I forgot," Maurice said. "You liked him once."

"I still like him," she returned gently. "I couldn't stop liking him because he changed his mind."

"Perhaps not. But you could despise him for his bad taste."

"Roma is very pretty. I'm not in the least pretty."

"You're better than merely pretty. You have looks that will endure."

She gave him a teasing glance. She said, "I suppose you would value Adeline just as much if she looked like me?"

"She would not be Adeline without that face, that hair, those eyes."

"There you go—loving her for her looks!"

"Did I ever say I loved her?"

"Somebody said so. . . . You know what the family is . . . in on everyone's business."

"I think that's terribly irritating."

Patience returned stoutly, "I like it—because they all really love one. . . . Roma resents it."

"Why do you always bring Roma into things?"

"I guess because I'm not able to keep her out."

"Patience, you are so understanding. Can you tell me what the real Adeline is? Is she just a flawless young animal, with nothing in her head? Or is she a woman doomed to tragedy?"

Patience saw that his glass was empty. She said gently, "Mooey, I wish you'd promise me to give up this drinking. It's bad enough in company, but to sit here alone . . . it's all wrong."

He demanded, "What did I say to make you take that tone?"

"I think you are not quite sober."

"But don't you agree that it's a tragedy for Adeline to give herself to Fitzturgis? Oh God, it makes me sick."

He went to the cupboard and took out a bottle of French brandy. The poodle trotted softly beside him, peered into the cupboard, half entered it.

Patience said, "Becky, don't! Maurice, don't!"

He said, "You use exactly the same tone to me as to this poodle. Is thy servant a dog?"

She went to him and put the bottle back on the shelf. "Please, don't," she said. "You're too good for this sort of thing. Will you trust me with the key? I'll lock up for a bit, if you agree."

"No, no, Patience, you can be sure I shan't drink any more today. . . . One little drink tomorrow, and the next day—none. I'm in dead earnest."

"But you are not really sober."

"Perfectly sober. Put me to any test you like. Shall I stand on one leg? Walk along a crack in the floor? Repeat the alphabet backward?"

He stood before her, looking rather like the scion of some banished royal family. Or perhaps an earnest young actor studying a part. At that moment there was born in her a desire to serve him, to protect him, from the world and from himself. She contrasted his elegantly shaped head, his rumpled locks, with Norman's, which were the very model for advertisements of hair cream. At that moment the thought of Norman became less painful to her and slightly distasteful.

"You and I," she said, "both have suffered."

He came and took her hand. "We have indeed," he said, though he did not for a moment consider that her suffering could equal his.

"We will help each other," she said in a comforting voice.

"I wish I knew some way of helping you, Patience. You've been so sweet to me."

"You can help me," she said in a tone between coaxing and command, "by cutting out this drinking—above all, this solitary drinking."

"I will." He spoke fervently, as though in a religious service. "I swear I will."

"Oh, I'm so glad, Maurice. I have been worried about you. Christian has been worried."

"No need to be worried any longer," he said. "I'm determined to stop drinking—except with the greatest moderation. Just a drink in a sociable way with others. Never alone."

"I'm so glad," she repeated.

There came the sound of a motor, then little Mary's voice.

"I must be off," Patience said. "Are you sure it would not be better for me to lock the cupboard and take the key?"

"Positive. I shall be a rock for firmness. Look. I'll lock it. There. And I'll give the key to Christian."

"Splendid. You've made me feel ever so much better. . . . Come, Becky."

Maurice stood in the doorway watching them disappear down the road. He felt a new bond between himself and Patience. He had been treated as badly by Adeline as Patience had been treated by Norman. In this moment of melancholy he was convinced that Adeline had once loved him.

He heard small footsteps running. He hid himself behind the door as Mary ran into the studio. She was calling, "Maurice, come to tea! Mummy says you're to come! I'm to bring you to tea!"

She stood in the middle of the great empty room, a tiny figure. She looked fearfully about her—at the pictures ranged about the walls; at a life-size charcoal drawing of a human skeleton. She knew she should have given the message to Maurice, but how could she? He was not there. Maurice stood silent till she trotted off. Then he found the key of the cupboard and poured himself another drink.

He tried to picture Adeline, to concentrate all his faculties on the calling up of the beloved image. But he could not extricate her face from the confused shadows of his imagination. If only he could remember Adeline's eyes . . . those eyes that mocked his pain. He would drink till he could remember what he chose—forget what he chose. Yes—forget, and promises be damned!

Time passed and he sat there, his legs outstretched, his hands limp, his mouth open emitting slow heavy breaths. It was beginning to rain, and Pheasant, having put her little daughter to bed, stepped inside, for she liked the feel of this room, its aloofness from the house, a room where something was being created by the hand of an artist. She did not know how Christian's pictures would be judged by the world, if indeed they would be thought worthy of judgment. But to her they were wonderful, amazing. Christian, in his artist's smock, was a miracle, as he was in his first baby clothes.

She was close beside Maurice before she saw him. She looked down in astonishment at the lounging figure, and he raised his heavy eyes to hers.

"Why, Maurice!" she exclaimed. "You here?"

"Yes," he said heavily.

"Where were you when Mary came to call you?"

"Here."

"Maurice—you've been drinking!" She bent over him in solicitude. He put out a hand to catch hers and hold it to his breast.

The first spatter of rain had become a determined shower, its vertical lines descending with ringing clarity on the roof of the studio. Pheasant wondered whether she should leave her boy here till Christian's return or take him now into the house through the rain. In any case Piers must not see him. She decided that he should go without delay.

"Maurice," she said, speaking more firmly than her tremulous heart warranted, "your father has gone to Jalna to enquire after a cow that has just calved. I want you to be safely in bed when he returns. Do you understand?"

"Yes, I do," he returned with sudden hot anger. "I'm to scuttle out of the way in deadly fear of my old man. But I'm not afraid. To hell with——"

He did not finish. He was on his feet, reeling toward the door. There he stopped. "W-why," he said thickly, "it's raining." He turned back, as though to venture out in the rain were impossible.

Half laughing but on the verge of tears, Pheasant caught him by the arm and steadied him. "Come," she said. "The rain will do you good." She steered him through the door and along the streaming path to the house. Though the distance was so short, both were wet through when they arrived. Up the stairs she propelled him, he clinging to the banister. At the top they heard Mary calling. She had been woken by the sound of the rain gurgling in the eaves and dreaded a thunderclap.

"I must go to her," Pheasant said, pushing Maurice into his room and closing the door on him. He went, feeling deserted, ill-used. He muttered, "One squeak from young Mary and I'm nothing." He moved forward unsteadily in the darkness. He tripped over a stool and fell with a resounding crash. Little Mary, hearing Maurice's fall, called out in panic for her mother. Above the drum of the rain came the sound of a motor. Piers had arrived, and with him Christian, whom he had overtaken on the road. Maurice uttered a groan. Pheasant turned on the light and bent over him.

"Mooey, are you hurt?"

He covered his face with his hands. "No. I don't know. Let me alone." Anger flared in his voice. "Why can't I be left alone?"

Piers's voice came from below. "What's the matter up there? Why doesn't someone go to Mary?"

She, hearing his voice, instead of being comforted, cried in greater panic. Pheasant, closing the door on her eldest, hastened to her youngest. In the passage she met Philip. She caught him by the arm and begged: "Go to Maurice. Quickly. Keep the door shut. Don't let Daddy know."

He had been interrupted in listening to a war play on the radio and was a little cross. He stood, with knitted brow and pouting lips, staring at the prostrate form of his brother.

"Want any help?" he asked.

"No. Lemme alone." The words came thickly. He wanted to sleep. Nothing else but that.

"Dad's back."

"I don't give a damn."

"Wouldn't you like to go to bed?"

Maurice uncovered his face to give Philip a look of reproach. "Isn't it possible," he growled, "for me to have a lil peash? Tha's all I ask. A lil peash."

"But you can't lie there all night."

"Can't I? Wait and shee."

Christian now came into the room. Philip turned to him with relief. "He's tight," he explained, as though with that figure on the floor an explanation could be necessary.

"Put out light," said Maurice. "Hurts my eyes."

Christian squatted on his heels beside him. He said, "Look here, old fellow, you simply must get to bed. Let us help you." He turned to Philip. "Take his other arm. Up you come!" They heaved him, first to a sitting position, then to his feet. They stood on either side of him, holding him up.

He looked doubtfully at the bed. "Don' wanna go to bed," he said. "Jus' wan' you fellows to get out." Suddenly he was truculent. "Bring that blackguard Fitzturgis here. I'd like a word with him."

"Tomorrow," soothed Christian. "I'll bring him tomorrow."

They could hear Piers's voice from the stairway. "Hullo! Where is everybody?"

Then Pheasant calling, "I'll be right down. I've been shutting the windows." She put her head into Maurice's room. "Is he all right?" she asked.

"Right as rain," answered Maurice and lay down on the bed.

8

THE SISTER

SYLVIA FLEMING was met at the railway station by Adeline and Finch. She had looked about her anxiously, for, although her health was again normal, she felt a tremor of nerves in this throng of strangers, in this strange city.

Then she was discovered by Adeline, heard her name called and, wheeling, was facc to facc with thc young girl and with Finch.

"Splendid," cried Adeline. "I began to be frightened." She embraced Sylvia, then released her to Finch. She had a proprietary air toward Sylvia. She looked on her as already a sister.

"You remember my Uncle Finch, don't you? You met him once in Ireland, and he wasn't very pleased with me that day, was he?"

She rattled on, asking questions, not waiting for an answer. At last they were able to disentangle themselves from the crowd, retrieve Sylvia's luggage from the customs and put it into Finch's new car. This car he regarded with pride and a little wonderment. Strangely enough he never could get used to owning things. As Adeline was impulsively possessive, so he was reluctantly so. Whether in material possessions or in human relations, it was his nature to stand back, partly in shyness, partly in a kind of self-protective aloofness.

Now it was Adeline who drew Sylvia's notice to the excellence of the new car, to the glimpses of lake or farm. Possessively she searched Sylvia's face for resemblance to Maitland. Saw how her skin was more delicate, her hair fairer, her lips more consciously self-controlled, her eyes less steady. She wondered if Finch had noticed how Sylvia had improved in looks. She was quite lovely.

Finch was conscious only that Sylvia had the same effect on him that she'd had in Ireland. His brief encounter with her there had left the imprint on his memory of the fair crisply curling hair, the large blue eyes, the pointed chin, the extreme thinness. Her hands looked almost emaciated.

When the car drew up before Jalna, Adeline said, not having spoken as they passed through the green tunnel of the balsams and hemlock that bordered the drive, because always she felt that that was a dramatic moment, "Here we are!"

She turned to see the effect of the disclosure on Sylvia—as though she had shown her in the brief glimpse the whole florid history of the family—as though she had put in motion the entire set of Whiteoaks, to display to this newcomer, who so soon would be almost one of them, all their individuality, charm and waywardness.

What Sylvia saw was a solid-looking brick house, with a stone porch, so enveloped in a Virginia creeper that its colour of a faded red could only here and there be glimpsed. And though the windows were open to the summer air, the curtains were drawn, as if those who lived under that roof would not willingly invite the intruding gaze of even the birds. There were plenty of those about who scarcely took the trouble to fly more than a few yards away as the three alighted from the car and Adeline said, "Welcome to Jalna."

It had been explained to Sylvia that Renny and Fitzturgis had gone to a place some distance away on important business. She was rather pleased to meet the family in relays. Now there were present only Alayne and Archer to greet her.

He said, after the first interchange was over, "We used to be a large family, you know."

"We still are," Alayne said, almost apologetically, "but not all under the one roof. There are nearby three other houses where members of the family live."

"I don't quite live in mine yet," said Finch.

Sylvia said, "I think it's better not to have too many in the one house—I mean all mingling together as one family. Unless, of course, a very united family, as I know yours is."

"How do you know?" asked Archer.

"Adeline has told me."

"I don't feel united with anyone," said Archer.

Adeline gave him a quelling look. "You are, whether you like it or not," she said. She then ordered him to help her carry Sylvia's luggage upstairs. As they passed Nicholas's room they saw Roma sitting there with him. In the room prepared for Sylvia Archer asked, "What is Roma doing there, I wonder?"

"Up to some of her tricks, I'll bet. Probably she's after money."

"But she sat with him yesterday, too."

"Then it's more money."

"He'd never give her money twice—so near together. There's something sinister in it."

"Goodness, you're suspicious."

"I'm observant. I've observed how it bores Roma to be with Uncle Nick. Now I enjoy being with him, yet he never gives me money."

"You're not a large-eyed appealing young girl."

"Neither am I an orphan. There's something in being an orphan."

He spoke musingly and Adeline did not hear him. She was absorbed in the appointments of the room over which she had taken much thought. She felt that all must be welcoming and beautiful for Maitland's sister. Consequently she had filled every available vase with flowers. In this room there was a small grate, on the mantelshelf of which she had arranged six vases, large and small, of flowers of all colours. This was to say nothing of two large earthen jars filled with sunflowers in front of the empty grate, the grate itself replenished with ferns. Vases of pansies, sweet peas, roses and nasturtiums were on the dressing-table and window sill.

Archer regarded these decorations pessimistically. "Is this Sylvia going to stay here long?" he asked.

"As far as I am concerned," she returned, "Sylvia may stay for ever."

"Mercy!" said Archer.

Meanwhile downstairs it had been arranged that Finch was to drive Sylvia and Adeline to inspect the new house. Only the last touches had to be added and he was soon to remove to it. Sylvia was not tired and was, she said, all eagerness to see it. Adeline wanted Fitzturgis to be present when they went on a tour of Jalna.

The front door of the new house stood open. The wholesome Finnish woman who was to work for Finch by the day was polishing windows. He said, a little apologetically, to Sylvia, "It's really not worth coming to see. It's very small. But I'm rather proud of it. For some time I've wanted a place of my own near to Jalna."

Sylvia exclaimed in admiration. Never had she seen a house like this—small indeed, but with such large windows looking out into what seemed a forest of stately trees. And inside, everything so new, so fresh and spotless.

"It's adorable," she said. "How I love new houses, new furniture. I'm accustomed to things old and fusty. This has a different smell."

"Jalna is not new," said Adeline, "but it's not fusty."

"There is something so happy about a new house," Sylvia continued. "No memories to torment one."

"You begin to collect memories from the very day you move in," said Adeline. "As for this one—memories will be coming right up through the floor because it is built where an old house stood."

"Don't," said Finch. "I'd rather not think of that."

Sylvia knew his wife had died. Now she asked, "Have you children?"

He looked vague, then said, "Yes. A small boy."

"Is he like you?" Now she looked him full in the face, wondering what sort of small boy he had been. The face of the man was so sensitive, so marked by experience, she could not picture him as a child.

Adeline said, "Dennis isn't at all like Uncle Finch. He's not even musical."

"What a pity! Not inheriting that talent, I mean. It's wonderful to be talented."

"Have you heard Uncle Finch play?"

"I'm sorry to say, no. I've been in Ireland since the war, and before that . . ."

"Tell the truth," said Finch. "You'd never heard of me."

"Oh, but I had."

"Well," said Adeline, "you will have the opportunity now. Have you played since you came home, Uncle Finch? Surely you have on this gorgeous piano." She wanted to show him off, show the piano off.

He stood staring at it, drinking in the beauty of its form in sensuous anticipation. Even in its silence it dominated the house.

Adeline put an arm round each of the others. "What fun we three shall have together!" she said. "And Mait, too, naturally. Oh, I can scarcely believe that the long time of waiting is over. All happy things seem to be happening at once."

"When is the wedding to be?" Sylvia asked.

"In a month." A shadow crossed her face. "We are to have a double wedding. I didn't much want that, but Aunt Meg and Daddy think it is best. And it will certainly save money. A double wedding. Roma and Norman. Maitland and me." Now she smiled gaily, picturing the four of them, marching triumphant down the aisle. Then she remembered how Finch and Sylvia both had lost their mates. Her eyes grew misty in sympathy and she kissed first one of them and then the other.

She flew off then to investigate a step she heard, thinking it might be Fitzturgis. Finch said, "Adeline's so completely happy, it makes one afraid for her."

"I am afraid for her," said Sylvia.

"You mean no one should take such felicity for granted?"

"I suppose I mean that it's safer to expect trouble."

"Adeline has it in her to make a man happy."

"I love her," said Sylvia, "more than any woman I have ever met—if you can call her a woman. She's really still a child."

Adeline returned then, having discovered Dennis outside. She led him to Sylvia. "This is Uncle Finch's cross, Sylvia. Dennis, this lady is going to be your cousin. She is Maitland's sister."

"How do you do?" said Dennis, offering his square child's hand. Then he added, "They're back."

"Maitland and Daddy? Why didn't they come over here? Do they know Sylvia has arrived?"

"Yes. They're having a drink." He took a turn up and down the room with an air of possession. He asked of Sylvia, "Do you like this room?" He looked up and down and around it, as though he had designed it, built the house. "I live here," he said. "Want to see my room?" He was so small, so young, that they had to look at him—as at a kitten, a puppy. He went and touched one note on the piano. "This piano," he said to Sylvia, "is a concert grand. My father is going to play on it. Would you like to hear him play?" He spoke as though at his bidding Finch would sit down at the instrument and perform. Yet he cast an uncertain sidewise glance at Finch, as if to anticipate dismissal.

He had it in a quick gesture. He went to the window and stood in an attitude of unconcern looking out at the tall old trees in their dense summer foliage, their greenness unrelieved by the bright colours of flower border or flowering shrub. In the fire that had destroyed the earlier house all these had been burned and the rubble of builders had choked the roots.

Finch drove them back to Jalna. Dennis came with them, but Finch returned to his bungalow. "You'd better stay here," he had said to the child and had added: "I must be alone. You understand—alone."

On the way upstairs they discovered Fitzturgis and Roma sitting together on the window seat of the landing. They did not hear the two girls approaching till they were half way up the stairs. Fitzturgis got to his feet, with a half-apologetic smile for Adeline and a "Hullo, my dear," to his sister. He kissed her cheek.

Roma slid from the seat and stood with childish unconcern, waiting to be introduced. When this had been done, with a certain abruptness, by Adeline, she turned to Fitzturgis. "You are back sooner than I expected. Did you know Sylvia had arrived?"

"The business was soon settled. Your father bought the horse," he replied to the first question, and to the second, "Yes. I was told you and Finch had gone to meet her."

Adeline looked at him steadily. She said, "I am taking Sylvia to the stables to see the horses. Do you want to come?"

"Horses!" he ejaculated. "Good Lord—I've had enough of horses for one day."

"Very well." She turned away. "Come along, Sylvia." She darted up the remaining stairs, temper in every movement of her lithe body.

Sylvia followed, a smile of amusement lighting her pale face. In her room Adeline asked, "Can I help you to unpack?"

"Thanks, but I shall just change into other shoes and unpack later. I haven't much to unpack."

"You'll not need a lot of clothes here. We lead a country life. Why do you suppose Maitland wouldn't come? Even if he has seen enough horses, he's seen nothing of me today, and you not for weeks."

"He's a lazy dog. Surely you have discovered that, Adeline."

Adeline said, with passion, "I don't want to drag him about where he doesn't want to go, but—to think he'd prefer . . ." She could not finish the sentence but bit her lip in anger.

"Look here," said Sylvia, "if you're going to start off by taking Maitland too seriously—why, I pity you."

"Whom should I take seriously if not the man I'm going to marry?"

"What I mean is, you must take him as you find him."

Adeline's eyes flashed. "Well, I find him very irritating at the moment."

Sylvia had now changed into sturdy shoes. "I'm ready," she said, and added, "Your cousin is very pretty, isn't she?"

"I suppose so. I haven't thought about her looks. To tell the truth, she hasn't interested me. Now Patience—wait till you meet Patience!"

Fitzturgis and Roma were sitting on the window seat, but he now rose and said, "Well, I see you're ready. So am I."

"You stay here and rest. Sylvia and I are quite happy by ourselves. Aren't we, Sylvia?"

Adeline tossed her mane of hair, burnished to red by the sun, caught Sylvia's hand, and the two ran down the stairs. Roma blew a column of smoke down her nostrils. "Now you've done it," she said.

"Done what?"

"Put Adeline's back up. It doesn't take much."

As though asking for comfort he said, "All I remarked was that I'd seen enough of horses."

"Oh, she'll soon get over it. She's very sweet really. Just a bit spoilt."

"I can see that her father dotes on her."

"And she on him! I love that word. *Dote*. I wish someone doted on me."

"Norman shows every sign of doting."

"Please don't bring Norman into this conversation."

"I thought girls always liked to talk of the chaps they're engaged to."

"I talk enough of Norman when I'm with Norman. His plans, his propositions. The big things he's going to do."

"Don't we all like to talk of ourselves?"

"Not me."

"I wish you would."

"I'm not interesting."

"You're very interesting to me."

"I wish I could believe you. But perhaps you're one of those fellows who think anything in a skirt is fascinating."

"Have I given you that impression?"

"Oh, I don't know. When I'm with you I'm always thinking I'd like to fight with you."

Fitzturgis gave her an amused, a speculative look. She met

it with daring and the warm yet challenging smile she had inherited from her mother.

"This place, this family, are getting me down," she said. "I'd like to go a thousand miles away. Or five hundred would do—perhaps New York."

Alayne came into the hall below, looked up at the sound of their voices, then, with an air of not having seen them, returned to the library.

"She hates me," said Roma. "Firstly because of something I did when I was a child. Secondly for being who I am. I'm the daughter of her first husband, you know, and I guess she hated him. He ran off and left her and I don't blame him. I'd do the same if I were her husband."

Abruptly she said she must be going. They went down the stairs together. She departed, and Fitzturgis turned into the library, where Alayne was selecting a book from the shelves. When first she had come to Jalna there had been few books there—mostly romantic novels of the mid-nineteenth century, belonging to old Mrs Whiteoak, and books on the breeding of show horses, histories of the Grand National and other great racing events, books on farming and the rearing of farm stock. Byron and Moore, old Adeline's favourites, had been the only poets represented. To these Alayne had added many volumes of poetry, old and new, novels, works of philosophy, history, essays. It had been necessary to build new shelves to accommodate the books she had collected. It was not only in the library that her influence during the years of her marriage to Renny had been exercised. How many struggles, both silent and vocal, had taken place in the basement kitchen between her and the Wragges! There was the subject of the refrigerator. Should fruit be kept where its scent would taint butter and milk? Should the refrigerator be kept religiously clean or was a wiping with a dish-cloth now and again enough? Should mouldy scraps be allowed to accumulate in the breadbox? Should the good old English dinner service be put into a fiercely hot oven to warm? Should the dogs be allowed to lick the platters? Well—dogs had been licking platters in that kitchen for seventy-five years before ever she had entered it!

By Alayne (and she had paid for this out of her own purse) a proper heating system had been installed to take the place of the huge old stove in the hall and the numerous fireplaces that had caused so much work. Certain renovations had been opposed by the Master of Jalna, yet carried through by Alayne. But there were others which he would not endure. Several ornate and ugly pieces of mid-Victorian furniture which she considered out of place beside the fine old Chippendale, Renny tenaciously clung to and would not have banished.

He refused to have the Virginia creeper that draped the house kept in decent restraint. It seemed to Alayne that the rugged vine, whose stock was thick as a man's arm, laughed at her—laughed and sent out fresh tendrils to take possession of every spot where a vine could cling. It seemed to her that the long yellow velour curtains at the windows of dining room and library with which Renny refused to part laughed at her. As they heavily undulated in the warm summer breeze they seemed to say, 'We shall hang here when you are gone.' In truth she sometimes felt that the very essence of the house was antagonistic to her, and this was her mood when Fitzturgis now came into the room. He stood in the doorway, smiling a little, and said, "I'm interrupting you. I'll go."

"No, no—please come in." There was no one whom she would have welcomed at that moment but Fitzturgis. There was in him some quality that appealed to her sense of aloneness, as though they two, under certain circumstances, might be in the same boat together. She was many years older than he, but when she was with him she felt almost his contemporary. He had experience of the world outside that circle which she still at times found stifling. There was in him, she thought, a potential intellectuality which she longed to cultivate. There was in him a dark, underlying something she could not or would not have named that puzzled yet attracted her. Already there had grown between them an understanding that required no words.

Now she said, feeling it to be the proper thing to say, "I like your sister so much."

"It's very kind of you to have her here," he said.

She went on more warmly, "I can see how fond Adeline is of her. It is a good beginning."

He said with a rueful smile, "I'm in Adeline's black books."

"Goodness—am I to know why?"

"It's because I said I'd seen enough of horses for today. They've gone to the stables."

Alayne gave an almost imperceptible shrug. "Adeline is so like her father."

"I wish," he said boldly, "that she were just a little like you."

She smiled into his eyes. "I should not wish anyone to be like me. Least of all a Whiteoak."

He came and stood beside her. "You find plenty," he said, "to amuse you—in all these books."

"They have been more than amusement. Almost life itself."

He had looked on her as happily married, but now he wondered. He was conscious of her interest in him and was flattered by it, warmed by it. He knew that Renny had not that day been quite pleased with him. Adeline had been openly displeased. Sylvia, in passing, had given him one of her scornful little smiles. He felt himself to be the bad boy of the family and reached out toward Alayne's sympathy. What a lovely woman she was! The lines in her face were of experience, of character, he thought, rather than age. What had she found in that hard-riding, overbearing husband of hers to attract her? Surely the dead poet would have been more in her line.

She took a volume of essays from the shelves and recommended it to him. As the book passed from her graceful hands to his their hands touched and they exchanged a glance which was to him intriguing but to her profoundly moving. She told herself how glad she was that she was to have Fitzturgis as her future son-in-law, yet a perverse pity for herself and for him ran tremblingly through all her nerves. Not since the days of her frustrated passion for Renny had she felt like this toward any man. Not that this present emotion was comparable in intensity, but it was enough to shake her, to make her call herself a fool.

The front door stood wide open, and as Fitzturgis finally left the library and Alayne a fresh breeze was sweeping the hall. Archer, coming in from outdoors, met Fitzturgis in the hall. Archer's fine fair hair was blown upright. A flicker of something that was almost a smile passed across his lips. He remarked, without preliminary, "I don't wish to deprecate the intellect, but occasionally I find myself longing for the tough life. Funny, isn't it?"

"Very," said Fitzturgis. "I hope you are able to gratify this longing."

"No. That's the worst of it. I simply don't know how."

"Why don't you confide in your father? He might help you."

"Mercy!" said Archer. "He is the last person I'd confide in."

Fitzturgis stood fondling the cluster of grapes and their leaves carved on the newel post at the foot of the stairs. "How smooth this is," he said, "as though it has been much handled."

"A French-Canadian wood-carver came all the way from Quebec to carve that a hundred years ago. Do you consider that our family has improved or degenerated?"

"Ask me that in ten years," said Fitzturgis.

"We'll scarcely both be here in ten years."

"Where are you thinking of going?" asked Fitzturgis.

Archer, slowly ascending the stairs, said over his shoulder, "Oh, I guess *I* shall still be hanging around."

He had barely disappeared when Dennis came sliding down the banister. Arriving at the bottom, he laid himself over the carven grapes. He gave a slanting look at Fitzturgis out of his greenish eyes. He said, "Your sister has been to see our new house—the house where I live with my father."

"So I've heard."

"My father," said Dennis, "is a famous pianist. My mother played on the violin, but she got killed in a motor accident. I was there. Did you ever see anyone killed?" Now he sat upright, his hands on the bunch of grapes.

"Lots," said Fitzturgis.

"Where?" Dennis looked sceptical.

"In the war."

"That's nothing," laughed Dennis. "That's what they go to war *for*."

"You're an odd sort of boy," said Fitzturgis.

"I resemble my father. He was an odd sort of boy. Aunty Meg says how proud they were of him. My father and I do everything together. When he's on a tour he writes to me every week. He wrote and asked me to leave the summer camp early so he shouldn't miss any of my company. He's a widower. I'm his only child."

He now slid off the banister, walked rather stiffly past Fitzturgis out on to the lawn. He lay flat on his back on the grass. He plucked handfuls of it and scattered it over his pale handsome little face. When Fitzturgis spoke to him he did not answer.

The Irishman went upstairs, and when he heard his sister

come to her room he followed her. Casually they embraced, then she held him off, and with a smile half affectionate, half mocking, scanned his face.

"Good," she said. "You are standing the racket pretty well."

"Racket?" he frowned. "What do you mean, *racket*?"

"I mean the turbulence—the living between hawk and buzzard of your life here, the working with Renny and Piers Whiteoak. I've met them both this afternoon."

"My past life," he said, "has not been exactly tranquil."

"No one will be better pleased than I," she returned, "if you fit in here."

"But you doubt it, eh? I hope you're not doubtful of my love for Adeline."

"Indeed I am not, but . . ."

"But what, for the love of God?"

"There are other places beside Jalna."

"Are you suggesting *escape*? For me, Sylvia?"

"For you both." She said this quietly and simply.

"Look here," he exclaimed in exasperation. "You arrived just a few hours ago, yet you take for granted that you understand everything—understand us better than we understand ourselves."

"Anyhow," she said, "you can't say that that's just like me, for I have never interfered in your affairs."

"No," he returned with heat, "we have both been far too harassed by your affairs to think of mine."

She put out her hand to touch his. Her eyes filled with tears. She said, "Don't imagine I forget all you've been to me . . . all we've been through together."

"Anything I have done for you," he said, with a break in his voice, "I have done because I wanted to."

"I know. . . . You may not believe me, but sometimes I actually *writhe* to think of what I've put you through because of my damned nerves."

He dropped a kiss on top of her head. "You're all right now, Sylvia. We're beginning a new life."

"That's just it," she exclaimed. "A new life—and I don't want us to begin by making mistakes."

"Well, you are making a mistake," he said lightly, "if you think everything is not OK between Adeline and me."

"I didn't mean that. I know you love and trust each other. . . . But it's this place. These people."

"For God's sake, don't be so serious. That's the trouble with you, Sylvia. You take things too seriously."

"Very well." She laid herself down on a hard little sofa in a corner of the room. "We'll not speak of this again. . . . Oh, how tired I am!"

"That's right," he said. "Rest yourself before you must dress." He lingered a moment, looking down at her, then left the room.

Adeline was on the window seat where he had sat with Roma. He put an arm about her and asked, "Where can we be alone?"

"Here," she said, and drew the long velour curtains in front of them.

He clasped her to him. "I adore you," he whispered, "and always shall. No one else in the world matters."

As they kissed, there was deep silence in the house, except for the croak the grandfather clock gave before it struck.

"Can you say the same?" he asked.

"A lot of people matter to me," she said, "but you have the power to make me suffer."

"May I be cursed," he said, "if ever I make you suffer."

Now the clock struck, solemnly, benignly, as though it had them all under its watchful care.

9

THE OCCASIONAL TABLE

SEVERAL HAPPENINGS of importance to those at Jalna took place within the two following days. Adeline and Renny conducted Sylvia on a tour of the estate. As in any well-conducted tour, they pointed out to her every object of interest in orchard, farm and woodland. Here was the hut where a queer old character named Fiddling Jock had lived before Jalna was built. Here was the pine wood where stood the primeval trees, sheltered, secure from the axe. Here, over-grown by grass, was the 'old orchard', the saplings brought from England by Captain Whiteoak. Some of the trees were dead but were the support of a tangle of the wild grape, the wild cucumber, the wild rose. ("Look out, Sylvia—there's poison ivy!") But some trees, moss-trunked, half reclining, still bore fruit. ("And what a flavour, Sylvia! None of the new varieties can equal them.") This was a sanctuary for birds and bees. ("Look out, Sylvia—there's a snake! Ah, it's only a little garter snake—and it won't harm you.") And here was the orchard of today, kept in apple-pie order by Piers.

Father and daughter vied with each other in showing Sylvia the sights. Never had they had such an enthusiastic visitor. Joy in the place made her spirits feel on holiday. These two, with their red hair and dark eyes, had the power to make her forget the thoughts that dragged her down, to turn a fresh page in life.

That same day Finch moved to his own house. He went alone, for Dennis's room was not yet furnished. Meg and the two girls were to remain in her house till after the double wedding. Already preparation for this stirred the air. Two trousseaux were being made. Renny was to pay for Roma's. Meg, an exquisite seamstress, was making pretty things for her. Alayne and Adeline visited the shops together.

The third happening was a family dinner party at Jalna for Fitzturgis and Sylvia. To this came all the clan. The dining table was extended to its greatest length. There was much polishing of silver by Wragge, much baking by Mrs Wragge. Indeed, so enthusiastic was she in preparing food for the occasion that there was scarcely a spot in the kitchen which had not its sprinkling of flour. The higher Mrs Wragge's mood, the more she cast flour over her domain. The double wedding now in prospect raised her spirits to their loftiest pitch. In consequence, even the face of the kitchen clock had its smudge of flour. Mrs Wragge would never forget her own wedding, the glory of her passage up the aisle of the church, leaning on Renny Whiteoak's arm. The bridegroom, waiting at the chancel steps, signified little to her. The ceremony could not have taken place without him, but it was the fact that *she* was the bride, that *she* was given away by the Master of Jalna, which had lent the day its wonder. Now as she scattered flour like flowers in honour of this pre-wedding party, her thoughts were all for the two girls. She had not a single one to spare for Norman or Fitzturgis.

It was a lovely evening, with that touch of tenderness in the air of a summer soon to leave. The french windows of the drawing room stood open. The moon had not yet risen. The lawn and trees beyond it were only discovered by the lights from the house. The women, in pale flimsy dresses, with long full skirts and necklines low enough for the display of beauty, were drinking coffee. The men had remained a little longer in the dining room, with the exception of Archer, who wandered in and out through the french windows, finding himself unwanted by either party. Dennis, after dinner, had been sent to bed. Young Philip, at seventeen, remained with the men and none thought to question his doing so.

Fitzturgis remarked, as he had already done, the boy's resemblance to the portrait of his great-grandfather.

"Let's not speak of that," said Philip, rising glass in hand and standing beneath the portrait.

"And why not?" asked Fitzturgis.

"Because it's a sore point between Uncle Renny and me. Either his son should have been the spit of the portrait or I should have been his son—I'm not sure which."

"One thing is certain," said Nicholas, "my father lives again in Philip."

"Time will change all that," said Fitzturgis. "Your father, sir, could not live on in Philip, in the world of today. Where could you match that look of complete well-being and composure in any modern face?"

"Have I got it?" asked Philip.

Fitzturgis scrutinized his face and answered, "Yes."

"Then I'll keep it," said Philip. "See if I don't."

Nicholas, his eyes on the portrait, remarked, "My father had many a fine run to hounds before he went to India. I remember his telling how he rode fifty miles in one day on the same horse. But the queerest thing he told me about fox-hunting was something he'd seen when a boy. He saw a huntsman and three hounds coming into a village street and a fox dead beat a few yards ahead. The huntsman was calling out, 'Hoick!' The fox lay down in the main street and the hounds, as exhausted as he was, quite powerless to tackle him, just lay down beside him."

"Would you say those were the days, Uncle Nicholas?" asked Christian.

"All days are the days when you're young," answered Nicholas.

Nevertheless, as Renny took his arm to assist him when they rose to leave the room, it was remarkable how these two men, one very old, the other past middle age, overshadowed, in their essence, in the vitality of their very natures, the young ones, especially the very modern Norman.

When they reached the drawing room Fitzturgis went straight to where Alayne sat and dropped to the sofa beside her. She gave a swift glance to Renny and another to Adeline, to see if they had noticed. His coming to her seemed to her so pointed that she felt if she had been in the place of those two she would have been jealously conscious of it. Renny was indeed looking at them with a puzzled expression, but Adeline, being chaffed by Christian, apparently was not watchful of her lover.

When Alayne had finished with her duties of coffee-pouring she turned to Fitzturgis and said, "Now that you see all the clan together I hope you are not too much intimidated."

"I have seldom felt more so," he answered in his rather abrupt manner. "That's why I come to you for protection."

Alayne gave a gay little laugh. "You could not do worse," she said, "for I have never been able to protect myself." She felt exhilarated, there was no denying it.

"If you are not one of the clan after all these years," he said, "can I ever hope to be?"

"I am sure you can."

"And may I always come to you for understanding?"

"If you feel you need it."

"I have never had it from any woman," he answered.

"Nor I," she said, with an almost provocative look, "from any man."

His hand rested for an instant on hers, as it lay on a fold of her dress. "I shall make it my business," he said, "to understand you."

Renny's voice, raised hilariously, as he recounted some ridiculous incident of the day's doings, now dominated the rest of the room. The two on the sofa gave him a look more critical than sympathetic. Roma now appeared beside them, coffee-cup in hand.

"May I have some more, Aunty Alayne?" she asked in a small voice.

Fitzturgis had risen, and now, as she made no move to return to her seat beside her fiancé, moved aside to offer his place on the sofa. She shook her head. "No," she said. "I'll just sit down here, if I may." She dropped, with youthful ease, to the rug at their feet and added, "I'd like to hear some sensible conversation. They're being absolutely crazy over there."

Fitzturgis said, "Surely at your age you are not craving sensible conversation."

She raised large eyes from the level of his knee. "Why not?" she asked.

"Well, it's your right to be wild—crazy, as you call it—before you settle down to life in earnest."

"I must be prepared," she said.

"Isn't she absurd!" Fitzturgis said to Alayne, with an almost tender smile for the girl's simplicity.

Alayne did not answer. Roma's coming had shattered a moment of something more than charm, a moment of such sympathetic intercourse as she seldom enjoyed except with Finch, and his company lacked the almost dangerous appeal of the Irishman's.

Meg now swam across their vision, dressed in voluminous white, like a vessel in full sail. She came to anchor beside the occasional table. She laid her plump hand on it "This little table," she said, "this little table that I've always adored—how, in the name of goodness, did it get here?"

With an effort Finch said, "Well, to tell the truth, Meggie, I brought it."

"Then you don't like it," she cried, "not after my giving it to you for your new house!"

"But I do like it," he protested, "very much indeed."

She ignored this and went on, "You scorned all my furniture openly but this. You advised me to sell my furniture. I have been arranging to sell it—to come to you with only this little occasional table; and now—I find it here."

"Why," put in Renny, "I didn't notice that it had been returned."

"Returned!" she cried. "I don't know what you mean by returned. It's been mine for years and years."

"I don't know how you make that out," said Piers. "I've always understood that it was one of the pieces brought out from England by Grandfather."

"You're right," said Nicholas. "It was."

"Naturally," said Meg. "I can't pretend that I brought it out from England a hundred years ago, but I do know that Renny gave it——"

"Lent it," he interrupted.

"That is perfectly ridiculous," she said, her colour rising. "You gave it to me because I badly needed an occasional table and this one had been relegated to the attic or somewhere——"

Alayne now spoke in a consciously polite tone, "It was never out of this room," she said.

"I beg your pardon," Meg returned. "Humbly I beg your pardon. But if this occasional table could speak it would rise up on its hind legs and deny that."

All eyes were on the table, as though none would be surprised if it rose (on whichever legs were its hindmost) and declared where it was on such and such a night.

"Meg is right," said Nicholas, and he gave the table top a slap. "It was I, myself, who somehow managed to knock the table over. Two of the dogs had got into a fight and I was separating them. One leg of the table was cracked and it was carried to the attic to await repairs."

"And there it waited five years," said Meg. "Do you deny that, Alayne?"

"No," returned Alayne bitterly.

"Then, when I needed a little occasional table, Renny said, 'There's that old one in the attic that needs repairing. I'll give——' "

"*Lend*," he interrupted.

"That's better," said Nicholas. "I don't like my mother's belongings scattered over the countryside."

Now Meg was truly hurt. "Uncle Nicholas," she cried, "surely you would not call my little drawing room, where every article is cared for, polished, and loved for its past associations, the countryside!"

"I don't know what you're driving at," growled Nicholas.

"She is saying," said Piers, "that she intends to have the table, by fair means or foul."

"How perfectly ridiculous," she cried. "I have put forward no claim that is not just. Renny gave me the table. I took it to Finch's house——"

"Why?" asked Nicholas.

"Because, Uncle Nick, dear, I am going to live there."

"Why?" repeated Nicholas.

Meg looked about her in despair. "Will you please tell him, Finch," she said in a desperate tone.

Finch mumbled, "I guess I need a woman to look after me, Uncle Nicholas."

Nicholas looked doggish. "Get a wife," he said. "Where's that pretty young widow who was visiting here?"

Sylvia was sitting just behind him. Renny, Piers and Pheasant, their sons, all broke into laughter. But Piers almost instantly became serious again. "One thing is certain," he said. "I never have had any of Gran's things either given or lent me."

Meg's eyes opened wide in wonder to think he could be so forgetful of favours. "What about that beautiful old dressing-table and wash-stand with marble tops? I presume you haven't sold them."

"Lord, no," laughed Piers. "One could scarcely give them away today."

"They were bought right here, in Ontario," added Pheasant.

"Jacques and Hayes, that was the name of the maker," Nicholas said brightly.

"Fancy his remembering that," exclaimed Meg in appreciation.

"I'm not in my dotage yet," he returned crossly.

Meg went and sat on the arm of his chair and stroked his thick grey hair. "Not one of us has a better brain than you, Uncle Nicholas. And I think it is for you to decide who is to have the occasional table." She drew his head to the beguiling softness of her bosom.

He said, as everybody knew he would, "I think you should have the table, Meggie. It will be my present to the new house." He smiled round him benignly. Archer, under his breath, said, "Mercy!"

Later Nicholas expressed a wish for a game of backgammon. Meg was his opponent and in such good spirits that she was delighted to be beaten. Renny, Piers, Pheasant and Alayne settled down to bridge. The others drifted outdoors. . . . Enveloped in the rich darkness, the full moon glimmering low among the trees but as yet casting no shadow, the air enticing with the scent of nicotiana, the grass moist from the first evening dew, the wan orchestra of locusts losing not one beat in their melancholy recitative which, while vibrant with life, spoke only of death, those who drifted outdoors wondered that any could bear to remain in.

Maurice took Adeline's hand, openly as though she belonged to him, and led her into the dim tunnel of the driveway. "Surely," he said, "you can't deny me a word alone with you—now that everything is so finally settled between you and Fitzturgis. In a little while I shall have no right to ask for even that."

"I want us always to be able to talk together as good friends," she said gently. She still left her hand in his. "What is it you want to say to me?" she asked.

"As soon as I'm alone with you I forget what I intended to say. It doesn't matter."

"Think hard and it will come back to you."

"I can't think. . . . It's only when I am alone that I can properly think. What I mean is, I understand things better then."

"I wish," she said, "that you wouldn't try to understand. Just take things calmly as they come."

"What I want you to tell me"—his voice shook a little—"is why you cannot care for me. What is wrong with me? There must be something wrong."

"I care for you a great deal, as a cousin——"

He flung her hand from him.

"You are my favourite cousin," she said, "except perhaps Christian."

"Christian! Good Lord—you surprise me."

"I admire Christian."

"You love Fitzturgis. You admire Christian. And you neither love nor admire me."

"Sometimes I do both. Not always."

"I suppose I should be thankful for the crumbs you throw me." He tried to see her face in the shaft of moonlight that now entered the drive as they neared the gate. He knew that face so well. The curve of the nostril, the line of chin and lip were so clear, yet never could he feel secure in the knowledge of her features. Changefully they eluded him, took on one expression after another, like a face seen through a moving veil.

They reached the gate and stood talking in desultory snatches before they retraced their steps. He had a faint feeling of satisfaction in the thought that Fitzturgis must be wondering why they had gone off together.

Fitzturgis did wonder but with a certain grim amusement at Maurice's expense. Obviously Maurice was snatching at anything he could get. It did not matter. Yet mingled with his amusement Fitzturgis felt a moment's hot anger.

The anger passed as he found himself at Roma's side, strolling across the open lawn toward the ravine. She looked so cool, so innocently self-possessed, in that low-cut dinner dress, with those smooth fair locks.

"Did you ever hear such a lot of nonsense," she said, "about an old table?"

"It was fun listening," he returned.

She gave her abrupt laugh. "Well, you'll very soon find yourself in the thick of these discussions."

"I couldn't," he said positively. "Material things don't matter to me."

"They will. You'll get just like the others. Why, they'd quarrel about which way a doorknob turns."

He looked down at her with detached curiosity. "You're an odd sort of girl, Roma."

"It would be strange if I weren't."

"Just what do you mean by that?"

She plucked the flower from a day lily, smelled it, then threw it on the grass. His curiosity was no longer detached. As though to try her, he said, "You'll be happier when you're married."

"Don't!" she exclaimed almost violently.

They had reached the brink of the ravine. On the rustic bridge, in the moonlight, they could just make out the figures of Finch and Sylvia. They could hear the faint rippling of the stream.

"Shall we go down?" he asked.

"No," she said. "I'd rather be here with you—for a moment. I've got to pull myself out of this mood. But you needn't stay. . . . Go and rescue Adeline from that playboy Maurice."

Fitzturgis said seriously, "When I first met Maurice he liked me."

"When I first met Norman," she said, "I liked him."

"And what has poor Norman done now?" asked Fitzturgis.

"Just been himself. His ambition is to become an executive. Bah!"

The contempt she put into the last syllable was remarkable.

"What quality do you admire in a man?" he asked.

"I can't tell you. You ought to know."

Adeline and Maurice now emerged from the drive, through a break in the trees, and began crossing the lawn toward them.

Patience had at this time gone off by herself. She had felt herself unwanted by any of the others. She had gone round the house to the side entrance and sat down on the doorstep. She folded her hands on her knees and laid her forehead on her hands. Under her breath she whistled a little inaudible tune to comfort herself.

"I'm always surprised," Finch was saying to Sylvia, "by the smallness of this little bridge and stream when I return home after a long absence. I used to look on it as quite a torrent when I was small. I used to think the stream was playing a tune. I thought it had a special message for me. And I'd try to understand it and repeat the tune on the piano. . . . Once, when I was a boy, I came upon my brother Eden—the one that died—crying here. I never knew what about. . . . I remember his reading some of his poems aloud, sitting on this bridge. There'd been a fog and the boards were still damp. Do you find it damp down here now?"

"After Ireland," she said, "nowhere seems damp."

"I like Ireland. You'll find it a great change to live in New York."

"At the present time I am hating it," she said in an expressionless tone.

"Oh," he said, and waited for her to explain why.

She did not, but continued after a moment, "It fascinates me to visit strange places. I invariably think I'd like to live there. Just now I am thinking how delightful it must be to live at Jalna."

"It is," he said with boyish earnestness. "When I am away on a tour I am always longing for the day when I return. You will laugh at me, but even a scene like that about the occasional table will have a kind of heart-warming pull, though at the time I may be damned uncomfortable."

"Do you mind my asking which you think has the better right to the table?"

"Well," he said judicially, "the table really belongs to Renny, and Alayne is Renny's wife, but Meg has possessed it for years. She hasn't much that was my grandmother's. She's cared for it and polished it and taken pride in it. Alayne had forgotten all about it till she saw it in my house."

"I quite agree. Your sister should have it."

"Both Alayne and Meg," said Finch, "are what one would call high-minded women. I'm just a blundering man, but I couldn't struggle over an occasional table."

"I like them both so much."

"I'm glad of that," he said warmly, and added after a silence,

"You know, I can't recall any painful scenes between myself and either of them. That's a great thing to look back on, isn't it?"

The moon was now casting its light on the bridge. Turning to Finch, Sylvia could see his face clearly. She had thought of him as an artist, absorbed in his own life, successful as a concert pianist. But now she saw his vulnerability, the marks left by the suffering of a nature too sensitive for the harsh encounters of life.

He was conscious of the gentle compassion of her face that was still in shadow. He smiled, as if to disclaim his need for compassion. He said, "Do you know what I should like to do? I'd like to go to my house and see it in this light. The moon is full and it will be shining right in at the large window. Would you come with me? It's not far. I think you'd like the walk."

"I'd love to go," she said, and felt a quick glow of pride at his asking her.

They returned to the house to tell that they were leaving.

"Do you mind?" Sylvia asked, bending over Alayne as she sat at the card table.

"Do go," said Alayne. "It's a divine night for a walk. How sensible you are."

"It's the first time I have been told that."

In the porch Sylvia and Finch found Meg waiting with the occasional table. "Uncle Nicholas has gone to bed," she said. "I saw you come in—heard you say you are going to Vaughanlands—and quietly carried the table out here, without being noticed by anyone. Now what I want you to do, Finch, is to take it back with you and so put an end to any dissension on the subject."

"But, Meggie," he said, "wouldn't tomorrow do?"

"You brought it to Jalna, unknown to me." The tone of her voice now became high-flown. "It is only fair that you should take it back unknown to Alayne."

"All right," he grumbled, and shouldered the table.

Now the two were trudging—for their romantic moonlit walk had come to that—along the country road.

"Is it heavy?" asked Sylvia. "Could I help?"

"It's nothing. . . . As a matter of fact I am quite pleased to have the table again."

They walked on in silence, their shadows distinct on the

white road, Finch's grotesque because of the occasional table. The air was vibrant with the shrilling of the locusts.

"What a strange feeling they give one," said Sylvia, "as though there were no time to spare."

"There isn't," said Finch.

She said, with regret rather than bitterness, "And I have wasted so much of my time."

As Finch turned this over in his mind, considering what to say to her, she added, "I wasted some of my time in a nervous breakdown. Had you heard?"

"Yes."

"It was horrible. I try to forget it."

"I know what nerves are. I've gone through hell with mine."

She stopped stock still to look at him. "It's hard to believe," she said. "You seem so steady."

"So do you!"

"You appear rather cool and detached."

"So do you."

"We seem to be good dissemblers," she said. "Perhaps we are just hiding from ourselves."

"The moral is," said Finch, "that we must get better acquainted." He spoke with sudden gaiety, and, finding the table cumbersome in his arms, he raised it and placed its underpart on the top of his head. His shadow thus became a grotesque monster moving beside the perfect silhouette of hers, as though in menace.

"Anyone meeting us," said Sylvia, "would take us to be a couple evicted from their home, you carrying our one piece of furniture on your head."

"Our shadows," he said, "the straight white road, that orchestra of locusts, seem symbolic. Surely it means something. Have you any idea what?"

"I have only one idea and it is that I'm in love with this place."

Finch, in his strange head-dress, began to caper; his shadow, wildly formed, prancing beside hers. But soon there were no shadows. They were in a wooded grove and before long stood on the terrace of his house. Moonlight lay on the stones. The front door stood open. Finch set down the table and led Sylvia into the music room. He stood entranced. Surely it was unique.

"Do you like it?" he demanded. "Please say you like it." The moonlight on his face was what held her.

"I do," she answered earnestly. "I think it's the most adorable house I have ever seen."

"Oh, I say," he exclaimed in gratification. "That's too much. I didn't expect that."

He was unexpectedly boyish, she thought. There was something almost theatrical in his exclamation, as though the acquisition of this little house were something spectacular. But then perhaps he was one of those to whom all life is spectacular. She envied him that.

He led her to the mantelshelf, where stood a porcelain figure of a Chinese goddess.

"That's the goddess Kuan Yin," he said. "She's my greatest treasure. My grandmother gave her to me when I was nineteen. Gran was a hundred."

"No wonder you cherish it."

"I used to steal out of the house at night," he said, "when I was supposed to be studying and go to the church to play on the organ. One night Gran heard me when I came in and called me into her room. You know where it is—right behind the staircase."

"Adeline's room. When she showed it me, what do you suppose she said? She said that if ever she were going to have a baby she would not go to a hospital but would have it right there in that bed."

"That's like Adeline. I hope she does."

"Tell me more."

"Well, after that," he went on, "I used to go to her room every night—after I'd played in the church. I'd bring sherry from the dining room and we'd talk and talk. In those nights I discovered what she must have been when she was younger. I guess it was bad for her to lose her sleep and all that, but—it was wonderful for me." He took the porcelain figure from the shelf and held it tenderly in his hand as though in that contact he re-created those scenes of the past. "She would sit propped up on her pillows, her eyes shining below her nightcap, and talk of her past—and my future."

"That would be a great thing for you."

He set the figure again on the mantelshelf and turned, as though deliberately, away from it.

"Not so much then, as later," he said. "You see, she died,

and . . . she left me all her money. Nothing seemed to matter for a while . . . but now, twenty-five years later, I remember so clearly things she said to me then." He went and stood by the piano, the tips of his fingers just touching the keys.

"Shall I play?" he asked.

"Please do."

He turned on the light of a lamp. She sat where she could see his face as he played.

"A little Bach first," he said. "Then some Beethoven, eh?"

Sylvia smiled and nodded. To speak, she felt, would be to shatter the entrancement of the moment. She sat, still as the statue of Kuan Yin, while he played. Sometimes the intricacies of the Bach stole her senses. She could not see the player. At other times she scarcely heard the music but was conscious only of the flying hands. Their isolation appeared so complete to her that the house they had left seemed far away. All her present life seemed far away. Her illness an evil dream. Strangely her thoughts moved back to the time of her marriage. She thought of it calmly. For the first time she recalled the time of her husband's death—recalled it with calmness. It, too, was a dream—a tragic dream.

She became conscious after a time that Finch was no longer playing Bach but Beethoven. He appeared oblivious to her presence, and she was glad of that. . . . Her imagination now turned back to the time of her girlhood in Ireland, to the time when she had felt safe, protected, when her father and mother and brother had stood between her and all that was troubling in life. She saw herself as a long-legged tow-headed girl surrounded by primroses, bluebells, misty hills and happy peasants. How wonderful Maitland had been, how wonderful it all had been! She smiled at the ridiculousness of it. . . .

An hour had passed and Finch still was playing. But now he remembered her presence. His hands rested on the keys and he asked, "Tired?"

"Tired—no, rested! Please go on."

"Something of Brahms?"

"Yes. And after that—Mozart."

"I warn you, when I play Mozart I never know when to stop."

"I shall be here—enjoying it—if you play all night. . . . If my plumage ever has been ruffled, at the present moment it is as smooth as silk."

He gave her a glance of appreciation, both for what she said and for how she looked sitting there. He went on playing.

The moon was gone. When, between pieces, there was a pause, the silence seemed palpable, like a silver shape, standing in the open doorway. Then, after a little, the trill of the locusts became faintly audible, grew in its tiny but persistent volume, never missing a syllable, till it was again drowned in the music.

All the pent-up desire for the piano was now loosed in Finch. The felicity he had pictured had been to play in solitude, in that house. But now he found himself playing to Sylvia, sometimes unconscious of her presence, at others acutely aware of it, as though in her he had discovered the listener perfect above all others. They lost all consciousness of time.

At last, pale but bright-eyed, he rose and came to her. He sat down beside her, looking anxiously into her face. "I've been an egotistical brute," he said. "You must be terribly tired."

"I have not felt so truly rested in years."

"It has been . . . I can't tell you what it has meant to me, having you here . . . just ourselves." He added, with something of an effort, "That last thing I played—did you notice it?"

"I thought it was enchanting."

"It's something I've been jotting down at odd times. I hadn't played it through till tonight. I played it very badly."

"And it was your own?"

"Yes. A gavotte."

"I wish I had known it was yours. Will you play it again for me?"

"Yes. But not tonight."

"What time is it?"

"I'm afraid to tell you."

"I see that the moon is gone. It must be terribly late."

"I'll take you back in my car, but not till I've made you some coffee."

She sprang up. "Let me help." They went together to the kitchen. As if they were children playing at housekeeping they got the cups and saucers, the cream, boiled the kettle. When the tray was laid Finch carried it to the music room and Sylvia brought the occasional table.

"The very thing," he exclaimed, setting the tray on it with a triumphant air.

"I'm so glad it was decided we should have it." There was something in the plural pronoun that struck them both like the striking of a bell. They were silent a space, as though listening to its echo in their hearts. Then, quietly, as though not to disturb someone who slept, he placed chairs by the little table, and almost formally they seated themselves. They smiled into each other's eyes across the cups.

"Is it right?" she asked anxiously, for she had made the coffee.

"It's just as I like it," he said, and looked deep into her eyes.

They talked a little but could not afterward have told what they talked of. And then it happened that, standing by the window, with the dark night outside, she found herself in his arms, with her head on his breast.

"I love you," he was saying. "I realize now that I've loved you from the first."

"But you couldn't."

"But I did."

"Oh, my dear."

"Sylvia." His lips discovered the reluctant passion of hers. She tried not to show that she loved him, but she could not help herself.

"We must marry," he said after a little. "You will marry me, won't you?"

"I don't think I ought."

He held her from him to look in her face. "But why not?"

She hid her face against him. "I cannot tell you—not now."

But he persisted. "Is it because . . . " He fumbled for words. "Because of your . . . illness?"

"No, no. I am well enough."

"Tell me just one thing. Do you love any other man?"

"There's no one but you."

"My dearest—that's enough for me tonight. But no—one thing more! There's nothing that could make it impossible for us to marry, is there?"

"Not for me. Possibly for you." She withdrew from him and went to the window as though for air. "Don't ask me now." A shadow of unhappiness darkened her face.

"I'll not ask you," he said. "Tell me when you feel that you can." He tried to look as though resigned to waiting, but he was passionately impatient, for he desired all to be settled in that very hour.

As in relief she exclaimed, "Someone is coming. I hear a car."

"Damn!" he muttered, and followed her to the window. He pressed his forehead to the cool pane.

The light from the car blazed against the trees. It stopped and Renny got out. He strode to the house. The two went into the hall to meet him.

"I've been sent by my wife to rescue you," he said, looking hard at Sylvia. "She refuses to go to bed till you come. The others left some time ago. It's almost morning." He laid the blame, if blame there were, at Alayne's door. In truth it was he who was determined to discover what kept Sylvia so late.

"It's all my fault," said Finch. "I've been playing the piano."

"All this while?"

"All this while."

"No wonder Mrs Fleming looks——" He had been going to say tired, but, scrutinizing her, weariness was certainly not apparent.

As he hesitated she could not resist asking, "Well—what do I look?"

He gave her a mischievous grin. "As though you'd just been kissed," he said.

Sylvia uttered a gasp that was half a laugh and half a cry of dismay.

"Don't mind," said Renny. "It's very becoming."

They came into the music room. Almost apologetically Finch said, "We had coffee."

"For the second time tonight!" Renny's eyebrows flew up. "No wonder you are wakeful." He stood contemplating the occasional table.

"Meggie thought we'd better bring it," said Finch.

"That table," observed Renny, "is really mine."

"I know."

"And, as Uncle Nick says, I don't think that Gran would like her possessions scattered over the countryside."

Finch stood, biting his thumb. "What the dickens . . ." he muttered; and repeated, "What the dickens . . ."

"Now I'll tell you what I'll do," said Renny. "I'll lend you the table, as I lent it to Meg, and say no more about it. The table remains here."

"Thanks," murmured Finch.

There was nothing more to be said. He followed Renny and Sylvia to the car, and when Renny's back was turned he raised her hand to his lips.

In the car, during the brief drive, she resolutely talked of music—a subject which, she guessed, was subduing to the Master of Jalna.

10

BROTHER AND SISTER

SYLVIA AND Renny parted in the hall, he descending to the basement, she mounting the stairs. The door of Renny's room stood open, and she glimpsed the shape of a dog stretched on the foot of the bed. A deep rumbling snore came from the room of the old uncle. The clock struck four.

A pencil of light showed beneath Fitzturgis's door. She went straight to it and softly tapped with the tips of her fingers. Almost instantly the door was flung open and he stood there, in shirt and trousers, a look of something approaching apprehension on his face.

"I knew it was you," he said.

"And were afraid?" She came into the room. "Poor Maitland! I've put you through too much." She softly closed the door.

He scanned her pale face. "I was not afraid," he said, "but —there's nothing wrong, is there?"

The thoughts of both flew back to nights in Ireland, when, in the illness of her mind, she had struggled with him, been forcibly restrained by him.

"So much is wrong," she said, "that I think I shall have to go." She sank to the side of the bed and covered her face with her hands.

He sat down beside her and put his arm about her. "Oh, help me, help me," she sobbed against his shoulder. "Oh, what have I done?"

"Now," he said, in his tone of command, "let's have no more of this lamenting. Tell me what has happened."

"Finch Whiteoak," she managed to get out, "is in love with me."

He pressed his arm about her and said, "That doesn't sound

very terrible to me. It's rather sudden, but why should you feel it a calamity?"

"Because—oh, Mait, it's so ghastly—he's asked me to marry him and—I want to. But I can't—not after that affair with Galbraith."

"My dear child, he need not be told anything of that. It's past and done with."

"I should hate myself if I deceived Finch. I haven't been an admirable person, but I have been above-board. I've got my own idea of myself and I must live up to it—to the end."

"Tell him then."

"I can't." A shudder passed through her.

He took a cigarette from the bedside table, lighted it and put it between her lips. "You'll make yourself ill again," he said, "if you go on like this."

Still shuddering, she puffed at the cigarette. Then—"Oh, why did I meet Galbraith!" she cried.

"Keep your voice down," he said, and added, with a certain hardness of tone, "You appeared to think a lot of him. You were scarcely ever apart on board ship. And afterwards, in New York."

"I know. But now the thought of him is distasteful."

"Perhaps Finch would become distasteful—if you lived with him."

"Never." She spoke with passion. "It's utterly different—my feeling for him. I never loved Galbraith."

"He certainly was—and still is—mad about you."

"He had the power to give me a feeling of something like—I won't say the word love—even a spurious kind—in connection with him—but a feeling of being *enamoured*. Oh, God, how I wish I'd never done it!"

"You were swept away."

"No, no," she denied. "I did it in cold blood. I thought I was being sensible."

"And so you were," he said. "You made an experiment. You are free. You have met a man you want to marry. You are a fool if you don't."

"I will not deceive him. Not in any way."

"You and I," Fitzturgis said almost tenderly, "have known trouble. I believe we have a right to reach out and grasp good luck wherever we find it. If it happens to be in the shape of someone who loves us—so much the better."

"I will not deceive Finch," she repeated. "There is something so good in him—so pure. . . ." She scanned her brother's face, fearing a smile of derision, the chill of cynicism, but his eyes reflected her earnestness.

"I know," he said.

"I have spoilt everything," she said.

He had so often seen her despairing. He braced himself to endure this.

"Go to bed," she said, "and forget me." She turned as though to leave. "As for me, I shall not close my eyes tonight."

He made a dramatic gesture toward the window. "Indeed you will not," he said, "for the night is gone."

She looked and saw a paleness in the east. A small bird began to sing.

"Sylvia," Fitzturgis said suddenly, "would you be willing for me to explain to Finch Whiteoak?" In a peculiar way he felt himself better able to grapple with her problems than with his own.

She turned her face, wan in the increasing light, to his.

"Oh, Mait, I should bless you for it. Then—if need be, I could leave without seeing him again."

"You have some sleeping pills," he said. "Take one. Try to get some rest."

She cried in a ferment, "Adeline has arranged a picnic for today. A picnic!"

"She would," he said grimly. "Well, lie down and relax if you can. Is Finch to be at the picnic?"

"Yes."

"I'll have a talk with him first. . . . That will be picnic enough for him."

"If I thought you were joking," she said, "I should hate you."

"I have seldom felt less like joking." He laid his hand on her arm and steered her back to her own room.

Five hours later, with the picnic in the offing, Fitzturgis walked through the morning freshness of the ravine to Finch's house. His expression was resolute. If Sylvia were determined to make a sacrifice of herself he would help her out with it; but beneath his hardy exterior he concealed considerable foreboding as to what the effect of this interview might have on her nerves if Finch should turn his back on her.

He found him just finishing his breakfast and refused his

invitation to drink a cup of coffee. Finch looked surprised by this morning call. They went to the paved terrace and stood smoking and remarking the luxuriant growth of the season. Then Fitzturgis said: "I've come to see you because of what happened last night between my sister and you."

"Yes?" Finch stared at him, trying to guess what was coming.

"Sylvia, as you must know, had a bad nervous breakdown after the war. She saw her husband killed in a London raid. She should have been taken care of after that, but she went right on working—till she went to pieces. She had a bad time of it—for a long while."

Hot colour flooded Finch's face. He knew what was coming! This thick-set, insensate brute was going to tell him that Sylvia must not marry—that her mental balance was too precarious—that he, as her brother, must forbid it. . . . But Fitzturgis went on:

"There is nothing I should like so much as a happy marriage for Sylvia. Her health is good. There is *nothing* wrong with her. There's no man I had rather see her marry than you."

"Then what's the trouble?" asked Finch. "Out with it, for God's sake."

"There was an incident," said Fitzturgis, "in Sylvia's life—a quite recent affair—that she thinks you should be told of."

"Why shouldn't she tell me of it herself?"

"She is too sensitive or—she thinks you have too much moral sensibility—to hear it from her. . . . Oh, I don't know. . . . What does a woman really think?"

"Will you be good enough to tell me," Finch said calmly, "what all this is about?"

"It's about a chap named Galbraith—a newspaper man whom we met on shipboard. He fell in love with Sylvia. He asked her to marry him, as soon as he got his divorce which was pending. Sylvia liked Galbraith. Very much indeed. She saw him every day after we arrived in New York. My older sister and my brother-in-law urged her to accept him. . . . She did accept him. But not in marriage. . . . She was afraid of marriage—till she could be absolutely certain of her feelings. And there was another thing. Since her illness Sylvia has never taken life for granted. All she has taken for granted is that there will be suffering. But she will get over that, I'm positive. Give her the right man—the right marriage—and she'll be as sound as ever."

"And—this Galbraith—he wasn't the right man?"

Finch, the flush still reddening his forehead, spoke in a cool, detached tone.

"He was not."

"You are telling me, I suppose, that she lived with him. How long did she live with him?"

"Oh, it was just a matter of a few weeks. Possibly less. Actually I don't know. There is one thing I want you to understand. Sylvia is a moral woman. I am her brother. I can truthfully say I've never met a more virtuous one."

"What do you mean by saying she takes suffering for granted?"

"Well, she'd been through a hell of a time. Her nerves had gone to pieces. She had to find out how they would behave before she settled down. She wanted to make sure that she wasn't going to saddle Galbraith with a wife who was liable to breakdowns .... I know I've put this badly. I wish to God Sylvia could have told you herself."

"It seems to me you've put it very well," said Finch thoughtfully. Then he asked, "And how did the experiment turn out?"

"Sylvia simply discovered that she did not care enough for Galbraith to marry him."

"And now she is ready to experiment with me," said Finch.

"If you can call marriage an experiment—yes."

"Well, I'm afraid I am not willing." As Finch spoke the colour receded first from his forehead, then from his long, lean cheeks, lastly from his lips, giving them a drained look.

"You don't want to go on with this?" asked Fitzturgis.

"No."

Fitzturgis felt as though he had made a considerable journey by the time he had returned to Jalna. His steps lagged as he mounted the stairs. He was deeply disappointed in the outcome of the interview with Finch. He dreaded the effect of what he must tell her, on Sylvia. It had been arranged she should wait for him in her room.

Now he tapped on the door. She opened it at once, saying, "I saw you coming. What did he say?"

There was no need for him to speak. His face told the tale. He said, however, "I'm surprised and disappointed. I could not have believed he was so narrow-minded, so intolerant.

I think perhaps if you had gone to him yourself it would have been better. In the first place he doesn't like me. It was harder to take from me."

She stood twisting her fingers together. Her face was undefended before him. He scanned it, feature by feature. Even more than pity he was feeling anxiety for her power of self-control.

She eased that by saying, "It is no more than I expected. Don't worry. I shall get over this."

"What about the picnic?"

"I'll be there," she answered with a faint smile.

"You're a good girl," he said, and stepped inside the door and kissed her.

Downstairs Adeline was waiting for him. She caught him round the waist and whirled him in an impromptu dance. Rather she tried to whirl him and then stood stock-still staring at him.

"What is the matter?" she demanded.

"Nothing."

"No work for anyone today and a lovely picnic! Aren't you pleased?"

"I'm delighted."

"But you look positively glum."

"It's the heat."

"Surely you don't call this hot! No—something is wrong."

"Well, to tell you the truth," he said, "Sylvia is a bit upset. She had bad news. I can't tell you, but please be especially nice to her, will you?"

"Of course I shall. . . . But we are one family now. I think we should share our troubles."

"This is something she cannot share."

"Except with you?"

"Yes."

"Perhaps the day will come when I shall be as close to her as you are."

To Adeline he appeared to draw back. "That could hardly be possible," he said.

Alayne, coming up from the basement kitchen, now joined them. She said, "The hampers are ready. Whose idea was it to have a picnic right on top of a dinner party?"

"Mine," said Adeline.

II

AGAIN THAT NIGHT

WHEN, AFTER dinner, Maurice and Adeline had returned from their stroll along the drive she had joined Roma and Fitzturgis but he had returned to the house. He entered at the front door and could see groups on either side, in the drawing room and in the library. The dining room was empty. The table had been cleared, but there were decanters and clean glasses on the sideboard. Maurice stood gazing, as though in admiration or perhaps indecision, at the imprisoned sparkle in the amber depths of a particular decanter.

He picked it up and poured himself a drink. He took but one sip and then stood, with eyes raised reflectively to the portrait of his great-grandfather hanging above the sideboard. His expression was one of good-humoured boldness. He had not lived to be old and weak but had died quite suddenly from the kick of a horse—died in that room just across the hall where Adeline now slept, where Fitzturgis looked forward to sleeping with her. Again Maurice took a sip of the Scotch.

What would Great-grandfather have thought of Fitzturgis, he wondered. Any man who was Adeline's kin, who had her welfare at heart, would have a low opinion of him. Whether or not Captain Whiteoak would have had a high opinion of himself Maurice did not consider. He drank his glass of Scotch and poured himself another, feeling deeply in accord with that pictured officer in the uniform of a Hussar.

Rags came in with a tray of clean glasses to put in the cabinet. He looked weary and gave a noticeable sigh as he remarked, "Everything went off nicely, I 'ope, sir."

"Very nicely," said Maurice amiably.

"There's nothing like a nice family party, I always s'y."

"You ought to know," Maurice said. "You have had plenty of experience."

"I have that, sir. More than thirty years I've worked in this 'ouse."

"That's a long while to stick in one job."

"You're right, sir. It is a long while. When I came 'ere the old lady was alive and none of you young ones was born. I didn't know nothink about domestic service, but I thought a lot of Mr Whiteoak, and I still think a lot of him. . . . I'll be sorry to leave."

"Surely you are not leaving, Rags."

"Not permanent, I 'ope. But my missus and me, we're taking a year off. We're going to London."

"If you spend a year there you'll never come back," exclaimed Maurice in consternation. He could not picture Jalna without the Wragges.

"We 'ave saved a bit. We may start a small pub on our own."

"You'll never come back," reiterated Maurice.

"That's as may be, sir," said Rags with a lofty air.

"Does my uncle know this?"

"I told 'im this morning. 'You'll be back,' 'e says. 'You couldn't stay away from me,' 'e says. 'Besides,' 'e says, 'your wife 'as become pure Ontario. She talks Ontario. She thinks Ontario. You'll come back.' " He gave Maurice a searching look. "If you 'ad your choice, sir, would you live over there in the Old Land or over 'ere in the New?"

"I think that life over there suits me best."

Rags' eyes were on the glass in Maurice's hand. "You get a bit depressed over here, do you, sir?"

Maurice emptied the glass. "A bit depressed, yes."

"But you mustn't be depressed, sir. Not with two weddings coming on."

"Neither of them is mine, Rags."

"I don't want to put my opinion forward," said Rags, "but what I should 'ave liked to see was a match between you and Miss Adeline."

"Well—she's getting the man of her choice."

"She don't"—Rags made a grimace of scepticism—"know what's good for her. W'y don't you take things into your own hands before it's too late?" He stood staring at Maurice, giving him the uncomfortable feeling that he was sorry for him. Then a great yawn of weariness opened the little man's mouth, made his eyes water. He murmured some sort of apology and disappeared. Maurice was glad to be left alone. He turned off the light, the better to secure his privacy. He sat sipping the whisky, listening to the voices that came from the other rooms. A feeling of benign peace settled over him like sheltering wings.

He was not aware how long he had sat there, when Philip came into the room. He had been wandering about, not quite belonging anywhere—not with the players at the card tables, not with the young lovers beneath the trees, not with Christian and Patience engaged in earnest conversation in the porch.

"Hullo," said Philip. "I didn't know you were here, Maurice."

"I came here to be alone," said Maurice pleasantly.

"Oh. Would you like me to go?"

"Stay or go. It's all one to me."

"Thanks." Philip sat down on a straight-backed chair facing Maurice. After a little he remarked, "It's nice in here."

"What do you mean—nice in here?"

"Well, I don't care to play cards and I don't want to spoon. I like sitting here with you."

"Who is spooning?"

"Oh, the engaged couples."

"Have you *seen* them?"

"Seen them spooning?" A mischievous devil in him made Philip answer, "Not Roma and Norman."

"The others then—were they spooning?"

Philip began to laugh. "Don't ask me," he laughed.

Maurice gave a groan. His peace was shattered, and the sharp sword of jealousy pierced his heart. His dignity, his reticence were gone. He allowed tears to wet his cheeks. But he was clear-headed enough to realize that he could not walk steadily to the sideboard. He said, "Bring that decanter, Philip, the one on the left, and pour me a glass."

The boy turned on the light. He looked curiously down into Maurice's face as he filled his glass. He was sorry for Maurice. As he saw him holding the glass with shaky hand to his lips he wished he could do something for him.

Maurice drew the back of his hand across his eyes. After the Scotch he felt firmer, steadier. A feeling of pure anger ran through his nerves—justifiable anger. This was centred on two people, his father and Fitzturgis. The long-time, half-conscious resentment toward Piers merged with the resentment toward Fitzturgis. He had a desire to show them that he was as good a man as either.

"How long have I been here?" he asked.

"Quite a time, I should guess," said Philip, eyeing him judicially.

"Where are Adeline and Fitzturgis?"

"They have just come into the drawing room."

"Where is Dad?"

"He's there."

Maurice drank the last drops from the glass, set it carefully on the table and rose, with the air of a large, solid, mature man, rather than a very young, very slender one. Philip watched him with a good deal of apprehension as he walked firmly through the door into the drawing room.

Adeline and Fitzturgis were standing by the card table watching the finish of a game. Maurice came and stood between them, putting his arm about Adeline's waist, and at the same time giving Fitzturgis an almost threatening look.

Adeline smiled teasingly into his flushed face. It was more than he could endure. His arm tightened about her. He said, "Adeline and I have settled everything tonight. We're going to be married."

"Shut up," said Piers out of the side of his mouth, and went on stolidly with his play.

For a moment Maurice looked dashed, but he still clasped Adeline to him. "You are an old silly," she said. She laid her hand against his cheek, but whether as a caress or to hold him off it was impossible to say. Fitzturgis deliberately moved away from them and went and stood in an open french window.

The game was finished, in a victory for Pheasant and Renny.

Piers rose and went to Maurice's side. He said in an undertone, "Don't act like a damned fool."

Maurice ignored this. He said, "Tell them the good news, Adeline. Don't be shy, my darling." He caught the hand that was on his cheek and covered it with kisses.

"Really," exclaimed Meg, "I think Mooey is behaving very badly. Why don't you take him home, Piers?"

Piers took his son by the arm. "Come, come," he said, almost soothingly, "that is no way to act."

Maurice looked at him as though seeing him for the first time. "What's that you say?" he asked in an indistinct voice.

Piers tightened his grip on his arm. "I say you are to come home." And he continued in reproof to Adeline, "You could have prevented this."

"I'd like to know how," she said saucily.

"Adeline!" exclaimed Alayne, ashamed for her daughter.

Both turned their eyes toward Fitzturgis, Alayne in apology

and sympathy, as if they two had an understanding between them—Adeline with a teasing smile.

Pheasant came to Maurice and took him by the lapels of his jacket. She said, raising her face to his, "Don't be so naughty, darling. You're making everyone angry."

Maurice spoke in a suddenly clear voice, "I won't go till Adeline admits that we're engaged."

Pheasant turned away. "The thing to do," she said, "is to pay no attention to him. He is just being silly."

"This is beyond silliness," said Piers. "He's making a nuisance of himself."

Suddenly Maurice shook himself free and faced them like a young animal at bay. "Let me be, will you!" he shouted. "I'll say what I choose and be damned to you."

Patience pushed past Philip and went into the hall. She wondered if she were going to be sick.

"All this comes," said Meg, "of sending the poor boy away to Ireland where he never had any proper training and where they are addicted to strong drink."

"And try to take it like gentlemen," said Fitzturgis.

Maurice, with calculated steadiness, moved across the room and faced him. "Please repeat that," he said, with the politeness of a man about to draw his sword.

Fitzturgis turned away and went through the french window on to the lawn.

"Sneak!" Maurice threw after him.

Renny, who during all this had remained at the card table letting the cards drip through his fingers, as though oblivious to what happened, now sprang up. He went to Maurice and put an arm about him. "Goodnight, old man," he said. "It's been so nice having you. You must come again. Hullo, Nooky. Bring round the car."

Christian darted out while Renny steered Maurice into the hall. Patience was there and gave him her kind smile. "Goodnight," she said.

"Goodnight, Patience." Then, remembering his manners, he added, "And thanks for a lovely party."

The car was at the door. Piers and Pheasant were saying goodbye to Alayne, being distant toward Meg. Piers gave Adeline a pinch and said, "You minx." Pheasant kissed Alayne, whispering, "We're so apologetic. I do hope you are not angry with Mooey. You know, he has always loved Adeline."

Alayne said, "Adeline was as much to blame."

Now Renny had steered Maurice into the car. He sat between his parents, who both looked ready to disown him. The two younger sons were in the front seat. The drive was short and passed in complete silence. Maurice's chin was sunk on his breast. When the car stopped in front of the door he looked dazed and made no attempt to alight with the others.

"Pull yourself together and get out," Piers said peremptorily.

"Shall I help him?" asked Philip.

"I don't require any help," said Maurice and scrambled out. He stalked ahead of his mother into the house.

"What's become of your manners?" demanded Piers, his angry face close to Maurice's beneath the hall light that deepened the shadows about eye and nostril.

"Sorry," muttered Maurice. "I didn't see."

"No, you didn't see," shouted Piers, suddenly furious, "because you are too damned drunk to see. I was thoroughly ashamed of you. So was your mother. You made an ass of yourself. If you hadn't the guts to win Adeline why do you try to push in now, when everything is settled between her and Fitzturgis? He, at least, behaved like a gentleman."

"You never could see anything good in me," Maurice shouted in his turn. "You've always treated me badly and now you insult me."

"Get to your bed, you young fool!"

"Get out of my way!"

Piers caught him by the shoulders and violently shook him. Maurice grappled with him. Piers's artificial leg gave way. He crashed to the floor. Pheasant gave a cry of terror. Christian and Philip helped him to his feet. Neither leg was broken, but he was paler than they had ever seen him.

"Maurice didn't mean to, did you, Maurice?" wailed Pheasant.

"*Maurice* didn't mean to!" growled Piers. "What are you saying? I knocked *myself* off my feet shaking *him* and I've a mind to give him a thrashing that he'll never forget."

Christian said in a low voice to Piers, "Maurice doesn't know what he's doing, Dad. I'll help him upstairs." In a moment the three brothers were mounting the stairs. Piers and Pheasant were alone in the hall.

"Are you hurt?" she repeated.

"No." But he looked a little shaken.

"I guess it's a good thing," she said, "that Mooey's visit is nearly over."

Piers answered curtly, "I shall certainly be glad to see him go."

12

A VARIETY OF SCENES

PATIENCE HAD left her lonely seat on the door-sill of the side entrance and wandered along a sandy path that skirted the orchards and led to where the vegetables flourished. It was a season of rich growth. Beyond the vegetable garden a field had been given over to tomato plants. Hundreds upon hundreds of tomatoes gleamed, red and smooth as silk, along the pungent vines.

Patience saw the form of a man bending among the vines, filling a basket with the fruit. Coming closer she saw that it was Humphrey Bell, a young man who lived alone in a house beyond the ravine. This house belonged to Renny Whiteoak. Humphrey Bell was a writer of short stories, who earned just enough to keep soul and body together. Soul was pure-minded, to judge by the look in his eyes. Body also was attractive, except for the extreme paleness of his hair and eyelashes. In the moonlight these looked almost white, but his eyes were of a charming harebell blue.

"Hullo," called out Patience. "Getting some tomatoes?"

He straightened himself. "Yes, and I'm not the thief I look. Your uncle told me to help myself." He displayed the basket half full of tomatoes. "I really have taken more than I need. That's the way when one gets something for nothing."

"I'll help you," said Patience. "Let's get plums from that tree." Without waiting for his reply she began to gather the plums. He stood admiring the grace of her arms as she reached upward, where was the finest fruit.

Then—"You're looking unusually elegant," he said, "for loitering in a vegetable garden."

"We are having a family dinner party for Adeline's fiancé and his sister."

Humphrey said in his rather diffident way, "And you—I'd expect you to be in the middle of things—the life of the party."

Patience laughed almost scornfully. "Me? Goodness, no. They'll not miss me. As a matter of fact, the party is rather scattered. The young people have paired off and are strolling about in the moonlight."

Bell considered this. Then, with a kind of diffident boldness, he said, "Then I consider myself lucky that you've paired off with me—in the vegetable garden."

"It doesn't sound very romantic," she said.

"You make it so." He was so shy that after he had said this he quite furiously gathered plums till the basket was almost full.

After a somewhat embarrassed silence she asked, "How are you getting on with your writing?"

"Not very well, as to acceptances. As to my own feelings, better and better."

"You mean," she said, "that you yourself like what you write?"

"Yes, I do." He spoke with tranquil conviction. "And even though the editors don't agree with me I can't help feeling that the day will come when they will." Recklessly he bit into a plum. "Anyhow, between selling a few stories and pilfering fruit and vegetables from my rich neighbours I manage to get along very well."

"And you don't mind living alone?"

"If I had exactly the right person to live with me I should like that, but as I haven't . . ." He gave a resigned shrug.

"I envy your not needing people. I'm terribly dependent."

He looked surprised. "I shouldn't have expected that. I think of you as very independent."

"If you think of me at all," she said, "which I very much doubt."

"Now your cousin Roma——" he went on.

Patience interrupted, "She's the most self-sufficient being I ever have known."

"Perhaps Roma is like me—surrounded by people she imagines. They are very satisfactory companions."

"Roma is all for hard fact."

"Perhaps she has more imagination than you think."

"I dare say you're right." They turned and walked together in the direction whence he had come, he carrying his basket, she giving him now and again a glance of curiosity. When they reached the grassy verge where he would turn homeward, she could not, though she tried to stop herself, resist saying, "I suppose you've never been in love."

"What makes you suppose that?"

"Well . . . I guess you can invent just the right sort of person. Flesh and blood don't matter."

"You're wrong. You're quite wrong," he said decidedly. "I was in love. Pretty desperately." He looked so cheerful that she had no sense of having hurt him.

"*Was?*" she echoed.

"I recovered from it some time ago. Luckily I had made no advances, so the young lady never had the faintest suspicions."

Patience thought, 'Who on earth could it have been? Roma perhaps? I wonder if it might have been me . . .' She searched his face for some confirmation of this, but there was something in his pale colouring that made it inscrutable.

Not able to stop herself, she said, "It might have been Adeline."

"Yes," he agreed, without embarrassment, "and it might have been Adeline's mother or your aunt. But I am not going to tell you, so there's no use in your looking at me in that charmingly enquiring way." He began to talk of plans he had made for the future, and before long Patience returned to the house.

When she and Roma were undressing for bed Meg made cocoa and brought it to the girls.

"This will help you to sleep," she said. "There's nothing like a hot nourishing drink after a party. The night has turned cool."

"Thanks," said Roma, "but I never need anything to make me sleep. I sleep like a log."

"Ah, I wish I did," said Meg with a yawn. "When I think of the sleepless nights I have spent I wonder I am not as thin as a stick."

Her daughter gave her a look of tender solicitude; her niece one of cool disbelief. All three sipped their cocoa. Pink with the comfort of it, Roma remarked: "What a fool Maurice made of himself tonight!"

"Any psychologist would tell you," said Meg, "that the poor boy is the victim of his upbringing."

"I wish I'd been such a victim," returned Roma.

"Sent away from home, when you were only a child, to live in a huge old house with a very old man!"

"Yes—and fall heir to his money. It would have just suited me."

"I should have died of homesickness," said Patience.

"I dare say." Roma stepped out of her dress and stood like a child in her slip, her hair soft about her short white neck.

Later, in Meg's bedroom, Patience said to her mother, "What do you suppose Humphrey Bell told me tonight?"

"Humphrey Bell—why, he wasn't at the party."

"I met him, in the tomato patch."

"Patience! How could you go wandering in the tomato patch with your pretty dress on?"

"I forgot."

"Well, what did he tell you?"

"He told me that he has let a part of his house. We'd been speaking of his living alone and he'd said he liked it. Then he told me that money is so tight with him that he has let the greater part of his house to the Chases. I know Mr Chase. He's a friend of Uncle Renny's. He's been married just lately to a widow, a Mrs Lebraux. She and her first husband had once lived in that very house. They were friends of Uncle Renny's too."

"Dear me," said Meg, "that is strange. I knew Mrs Lebraux slightly. Alayne disliked her, and, I'm afraid, had some reason for her dislike. Your Uncle Renny used to go there a great deal."

"You mean," said Patience, "that he went there more often than Aunty Alayne approved of?"

"I'm afraid so. But I shouldn't be talking like this. Still there's no use in my trying to hide the fact that Alayne is a frantically jealous woman. I grant he has given her some cause for jealousy. He's one of those men who just naturally attract other women. One thing is certain: that woman won't be welcome as a neighbour to poor Alayne."

"Oh." Patience looked deeply thoughtful, then said, "But all that must have been over years and years ago."

"Things are never over with wives," said Meg.

At Jalna Renny, Alayne and Archer were left in the drawing room. She was tired and was about to kiss Archer goodnight when he said, "We are to have the Chases as neighbours."

"What Chases?" asked Renny. "I know only one Chase and he's unmarried."

"That horsy Chase who used to come here occasionally?" Alayne asked.

"Yes. He's the only Chase I know. He seemed a confirmed bachelor."

"Patience tells me," said Archer, "that Humphrey Bell has let part of his house to a couple named Chase. She and her first husband once lived in that same house and bred foxes."

"It's unbelievable," said Renny. "I can't picture old Chase as married. Old Chase—why, if ever a man despised women he did." Renny tried to speak with unconcern, but Archer, who was extremely sensitive to the moods of his parents, noted his embarrassment. He gave his mother a penetrating look.

Alayne said, "I cannot imagine a less attractive pair."

"You can't, eh?" said Renny.

"No, I cannot."

A chilly silence fell between them. Then Renny remarked, "Chase is quite a good-looking fellow, and he's clever too. He's a very clever lawyer though his interests are now chiefly in racehorses."

"So I have gathered from his conversation."

While this chilly interchange was being carried on, the minds of both were fixed on the woman whom the horse fancier had lately married. 'Clara,' thought Renny. 'Clara married again! How many years is it since I've seen her? What is she like now?' His mind dwelt for a moment on that amorous episode of the past. Then, with an inward chuckle, he pictured her and Chase together.

'That dreadful time,' thought Alayne, 'when because of her I almost hated him, is far in the past. I must not let any recollection of it trouble me.'

Archer remarked, "How nice it is when all the people are gone."

Alayne looked at the ormolu clock on the mantelshelf. "I wish," she said, "that Sylvia would come. I can't think what is keeping her so long at Vaughanlands."

"Shall I go and find out?" asked Archer.

"Goodness, no." Alayne came and put her arm about him. He did not soften under her caressing touch but turned his head to scrutinize her face.

"I shall go myself," said Renny, "and bring her back, but not for a while. Finch is probably playing for her."

"Mercy!" said Archer.

The Wragges, man and wife, had been asleep in bed for hours, but Alayne, for something to complain about, since her heart felt suddenly heavy, dragged forth their images, and said, "I thought Wragge was terribly slow in waiting at table tonight. And he so tilted the soup plates that I was afraid my soup would land in my lap."

"I didn't notice," said Renny.

"I don't see how you could fail to notice," she went on. "By the time he had served those at the farther end the soup of those first served was cold."

"I noticed," said Archer. "Mine was."

"As for Cook," Alayne continued, "she grows more and more extravagant. She spoils half her dishes by too many eggs, too much butter, too much sugar. Tonight the meringues were sickeningly sweet."

"Were they?" said Renny cheerfully. "I didn't notice."

"I did," said Archer. "Mine were."

"The worst of her is," Alayne continued, "that she won't pay any attention when I try to reason with her. She simply looks the other way or changes the subject."

Renny gave Alayne the grin so like his grandmother's.

"You won't have to put up with her much longer," he said. "They're leaving."

She looked unbelievingly at him. Surely he was joking—being teasing and inconsiderate, just when she needed a little sympathy.

"Yes," he repeated. "They're leaving. Right after the weddings. Rags told me this morning."

"Mercy!" said Archer.

Alayne sat down. For a moment she was too dazed to speak. Then she asked in a hoarse voice, "Why did you not tell me this before?"

"I thought it would be upsetting to you, but to judge by the way you feel toward them you'll be glad to see them go."

"Don't be cruel," cried Alayne. "You know quite well that I simply can't get on without the Wragges. I may complain of them a little—once in a great while—but to run this big old house, with its basement kitchen and all its inconveniences, with the sort of domestic help one gets nowadays—well, I don't see how I can."

Archer slipped out of the room. Renny put his arms about Alayne and drew her head to his breast. "Don't worry, darling," he said. "The Wragges are only going home for a year. I'm sure they'll come back. We shall get along somehow. I'll look after

Uncle Nick. If it comes to the worst Adeline can cook the meals. Fitzturgis can wash the dishes and carry the coals. You can keep us all in order. It will be quite a picnic."

"Picnic," wailed Alayne. "We are to have a picnic this very day! I must go to my bed and get what rest I can, even though I shall not sleep a wink."

13

NICHOLAS DEPARTS

THE PICNIC did not take place. The thoughts of the family were shocked into a very different channel by the sudden serious illness of Nicholas. When, as usual, he had his breakfast in bed he was not feeling well. In mid-morning he suffered great pain in his leg. The family doctor diagnosed the case as one of coronary thrombosis. In little more than an hour two nurses were in the house. It had taken on the atmosphere of a hospital.

Nicholas had protested that he did not want to go to one of those institutions, and Renny upheld him in this, though no member of the family abhorred the sight of those uniformed women in the house as did he. His concern, his grief, over his uncle were written on his weather-beaten face. He could scarcely bear to stay in the room with him. He could scarcely bear to remain away. At mealtimes, during the days that followed, he would eat in brooding silence, except possibly to exclaim, "Can't anybody think of something cheerful to say?" Yet when Alayne, Adeline or Fitzturgis essayed to be animated, he would look at them in melancholy surprise, as though he wondered how they could bring themselves to do it. He persuaded Meg to come to Jalna and to remain till either Nicholas had recovered or the worst had happened. He urged Piers and Finch to be constantly at hand. He ordered Archer to be ready to run at top speed to summon him from his office in the stables if necessary.

"Good God!" exclaimed Fitzturgis to Sylvia when they were sitting in the cobweb-hung summerhouse. "How long does he expect the old gentleman to live? He is ninety-eight. He has had his day, and a long one too."

"I look on Renny Whiteoak as a romantic," said Sylvia.

"I think he is dedicated to the romantic past of the family. And I think the dear old uncle somehow typifies it for him."

"Is Uncle Nicholas going to recover?"

"Alayne Whiteoak thinks not. She thinks it is only a matter of days. The doctors are not hopeful."

Fitzturgis said gloomily, "What a time to choose for dying! It's upset everything."

"When can the wedding take place?"

He returned irritably, "How can I tell? Adeline won't even discuss it. The poor girl is like the rest of us—weighed down by her father's mood. On my part, I like him less and less."

"I realize that."

"I hope," he said anxiously, "that I haven't shown it."

"Don't worry. You've been beautifully behaved. To tell the truth, I don't think that any of the family notices our behaviour. They are too occupied by this calamity. It's as though the foundations of their life shook."

"Imagine getting worked up because a man of nearly a hundred is dying!"

"He is an old pet," said Sylvia, with sudden tears in her eyes, "and I know just how they feel."

"It's just that they can't see themselves without him."

On one of his better days Nicholas said to Renny, who was sitting close beside him, his head bent to hear that voice which so lately had been strong and sonorous:

"What I have saved will be yours, Renny. I wish it were more. You've been so good to me."

"No, no, Uncle Nick—you mustn't talk like this. You're getting better." Renny patted him gently on the breast, as though he would impart some of his own vitality into the failing parts beneath.

Nicholas gave a smile of great sadness but with a touch of his old sardonic humour. He said, "It's time I went, Renny. I don't think Mama would have liked me to rival her in age."

Renny patted him the harder. "But you're not tired of life, Uncle Nick."

"No . . . not tired of life . . . I've had a good life . . . but very . . . very tired . . ." He closed his eyes.

Two days later he died. All were aware the end was coming. Renny and Alayne were in the room with him. He was conscious, though dimly so. As they moved about, for they were restless, tense from waiting, he did not notice. The nurse was in the kitchen eating her lunch.

A golden sunshine enveloped the house. There was no slightest breeze. The pigeons sat motionless on the roof. Above Renny's consciousness that Nicholas was about to die was the vivid consciousness that old Adeline was present in the house. He could feel her strong presence in the room.

Nicholas spoke in a small voice, not opening his eyes. "Mama . . . Papa . . ." he said, "hold my hands."

They knelt on either side of the bed, holding his hands. . . . Now he was gone.

Wakefield Whiteoak was in New York when news of the illness of Nicholas reached him. He was acting in a play that had had a success in London. It ran for only three performances in New York. This great disappointment to the company and financial loss to the backers of the play was regarded by Renny as a fitting coincidence, since it made it possible for Wakefield to come to Jalna. He had arrived the night before, in time to see Nicholas alive—to be kissed and welcomed by him.

"How did the play go?" Nicholas had whispered.

"Fine," Wake had answered. "A great success."

"Splendid."

Wakefield was thankful that he had given Nicholas that tiny offering of pleasure. From his boyhood he had felt pride when his resemblance to Nicholas was remarked. He always would lack the massive look of Nicholas. But his thick waving hair, his luminous dark eyes, his nose—a distinguishing mark of his grandmother's family—these he had in common with Nicholas. He had inherited, too, his uncle's love of spending money and a spirit that could be mocking but was more often warmly affectionate.

On the morning of the funeral there was a gentle rain, but after lunch it had cleared and bright sunlight shone on the flower-covered coffin as it was carried from the house. In it lay the gaunt old man who had first been carried into that house in his mother's arms—a lusty crowing baby—who thousands of times had run up and down its stairs, in and out through its doors. Through its rooms he had moved slowly, leaning on his stick, an old man, suffering from gout. From his life abroad he had always returned there and the house had beamed its welcome.

The entire family went to the service at the church, even to little Mary. She who so often retired into a quiet corner by herself to shed a few tears, now sat in dry-eyed wonder among the grown-ups, some of whom she perceived were crying. Pheasant could scarcely restrain her sobs as she remembered how Nicholas had once given her a lovely doll when she was a little girl.

Lying in his coffin at the chancel steps there was no doubt about it, Nicholas was as distinguished-looking a man as you might see in a year's travel. All marks of suffering had left his face, which wore the look of a wilful and individualistic Victorian gentleman. Renny had been tempted to leave the ring with the large green stone which he always wore on his hand, but Nicholas had wanted Renny to have it.

When they came out of the church into the churchyard, rain was once more falling, but it was a gentle rain and Mr Fennel looked unperturbed as his head and his surplice grew wet at the graveside. Little Mary, holding tightly to her father's hand, leant forward to peep down into the grave.

14

THE BEQUESTS

THOUGH NICHOLAS, in the flesh, had departed, he had left his mark, the flavour of his strongly masculine individuality, in the rooms he had frequented. There, in the drawing room, was that deep, comfortable chair, so snug to sink into but difficult to heave yourself out of when you were a heavy old man with gout. The arms of the chair were broadened and flattened by the pressure of his hands. There was the recollection of him seated at the piano, playing from his favourite Mendelssohn, the firelight luminous on his face. There, in the library, was his chair by the fireplace, his pipe, rather strong-smelling, and the tin canister where he kept his tobacco. There was his place at the dining table, marked by his heavy silver napkin-ring against which reclined the silver figure of a lady in Grecian costume.

Above all, there was his own room, filled with his own belongings—his piano, on which always stood a decanter with some Scotch whisky in it and a siphon of soda, and in later years a bottle or two of medicine. It often was the receptacle, too, of books and magazines, catalogues of horse shows brought to him by his nephews, copies of *Punch* and *Country Life*, a box of cigars. On the walls pictures that had hung there for seventy years and more. Scattered about were photographs of nieces, nephews, and babies which might be either. In the wardrobe were the clothes he had worn so well; in its English leather case his silk hat which he had last worn at his brother's funeral two years ago. And there was the bed!

Renny stood looking at it, Nicholas's watch in his hand. He had just wound it, and now it ticked in almost distracted haste, it seemed, as though to make up for the days when it had been silent. Piers had been given Uncle Ernest's handsome wrist watch. Renny himself carried his father's watch. Nicholas had, some days before his death, told Renny that he wanted him to have this watch which had belonged to Captain Whiteoak. Renny stood, his eyes fixed on the bed; the watch, its finely chased gold case warmed by his hand. He had an idea which had come to him because of a boy's merry whistle that rose from the lawn below. He knew the whistling as young Philip's, and he now went to the window and called him in his peculiarly peremptory way.

"Come up here, Philip," he said, "to Uncle Nick's room."

Philip thought, 'Now what the dickens have I done?' Yet he was not really apprehensive, for in these past weeks he had been leading an exemplary life and his relations with his uncle were almost always affectionate. He leaped up the stairs, but when he reached the top he walked decorously to the doorway where Renny now stood, watch in hand.

He said, "Come in here, Philip," and led him into the room and closed the door behind them. Philip gave a quick look about him, then raised his blue eyes to Renny's face.

"It all looks so natural," said Renny, "you'd expect to see him here, wouldn't you?"

"Yes," agreed Philip a little uncomfortably.

"This room," said Renny, "will be kept—just as he left it. You may come in here sometimes and sit down and remember him."

"Oh—thanks."

"Uncle Ernest's room has been given to Fitzturgis," Renny continued with a frown. "I should like to have kept it as it was, but as he and his sister both are here . . ."

"Of course," agreed Philip, then added, "Dad doesn't think Mait will ever be much help with horses."

"That's neither here nor there," said Renny curtly.

He still held the watch in his hand. "You recognize this watch?" he asked. "It belonged to your great-grandfather, who left it to his eldest son, Uncle Nicholas."

"About the first thing I remember when I was a tiny kid," said Philip, "was Uncle Nicholas showing me his watch—letting me listen to its ticking. I badly wanted to hold it in my own hands, and once, on my birthday, I think it was, he let me."

"You remember that!" exclaimed Renny, touched. "Well—it is now to be yours. I have a feeling that you more than any of the other boys will appreciate it." He put the watch into Philip's hand. "You're too young yet to carry this sort of watch, but I want you to wind it carefully every night. Never forget."

"I'll not forget. Thanks ever so much, Uncle Renny." Philip, deeply impressed, stretched out his muscular hand to grasp his uncle's. They looked into each other's eyes with affection.

Archer put his head in at the door to tell Renny that he was wanted on the telephone.

"I'll be back," Renny said to Philip as he followed his son. Archer had a remarkable curiosity toward telephone conversations, usually listening to them from a convenient doorway, ready to drift away when the receiver was hung up.

Now he heard his father say, "Hullo! Hullo, old man. . . . It's some time since you've been to see me. . . . What is this I hear about you? . . . You're the last man I'd have expected. . . . Ha! Well—it comes to us all. . . . Yes, I remember her very well—give her my respects. . . . Tell her I'm looking forward to having her as a neighbour. . . . Yes—Bell is a very nice fellow. . . . You couldn't do better."

There was a silence as Renny listened to a lengthy recital at the other end of the line. Archer stood outside the door, his high white forehead laid against the wall.

Upstairs, in Nicholas's bedroom, Philip passed the time by examining some of the old gentleman's belongings. He peeped into a *papier mâché* box where there was a collection of cravat pins, cuff-links and studs, a tiny gold pencil and a woman's ring. Philip tried this on his little finger, wondering whose it had been. He then looked into the wardrobe, saw the leather hat-box, opened it and took out the silk hat which he had always admired on the leonine head of his great-uncle. He ran his cuff round it to smooth the silken nap. He then placed it on his own fair head and went and stood in front of the pier-glass in an attitude the most elegant he could command. He had seen a walking-stick with an ivory handle in the wardrobe and he now added it to his costume.

Now he straightened his shoulders and stood in military fashion. Now he lackadaisically drooped, with the ivory top of the walking-stick in his lips. Now he removed the hat and bowed low over the hand of an imaginary lady. Now he put the walking-stick under his arm and tilted the hat at a rakish angle. He took a skipping step.

This last was too much for the watcher who had, unnoticed, appeared in the doorway. Renny exclaimed: "You young rascal! I've a mind to take that stick to your back." But somehow his expression was not so stern as his words. His eyes were bright with amusement.

Philip drooped in front of him. "I didn't mean . . ." he got out. "I mean I didn't know . . ."

"You're trying to tell me you didn't know you were prancing about with Uncle Nick's hat on your silly young head?"

"Oh—not *prancing*, Uncle Renny! Just trying to see how I looked in it."

"Well, let me tell you that you look a young ass. Put it away—in its box."

Philip meekly returned the hat to the wardrobe, while glancing guardedly over his shoulder, for he feared punishment from the rear. In the same meek spirit he was about to leave the room, forgetting to take the watch with him.

"So," exclaimed Renny, "you think so little of the watch that you are leaving it behind!"

Philip wheeled, scarlet-cheeked, to retrieve it. "I don't know what I'm doing," he said. "Everything is so confused these days."

Renny put an arm about him and gave him a hug. "It's all right," he said. "Now get along with you. I've a thousand things to do."

Downstairs Philip displayed the watch to Archer. He showed no envy. "I'm glad," he said, "that it wasn't given to me. It's responsibility without pleasure. You can't carry the watch, yet you've got to wind it. Now if it was an electric clock that wouldn't need winding . . ."

"I shall enjoy keeping it going," said Philip.

Archer sighed. "I'm long past the age," he said, "when I thought tick-tock had a meaning."

That same day, in the afternoon, Nicholas's will was read. Meg, Renny and Alayne, Piers and Pheasant, Finch and Wakefield gathered in the library. Mr Patton, the family lawyer, had read old Mrs Whiteoak's will to the assembled family twenty-three years ago. By it she had bequeathed her fortune to the boy Finch. This was a very different affair, for the bulk of what had supplied Nicholas with his income came from the estate of his sister, Lady Buckley, who had died in Devon in 1931. She had left the income from all she possessed to her two brothers, the principal to be divided at their death equally among her nephews and her niece. This principal had been firmly invested, and now gave a legacy of somewhat over sixteen thousand dollars to each of the five heirs.

But Nicholas had lived economically in his later years, a contrast to the extravagance of his earlier. From his income he had saved a quite substantial sum, enough for several bequests which he hoped would come as pleasant surprises, as indeed they did. To the Wragges, man and wife, he had left five hundred dollars each, 'In appreciation of their years of faithful service'. To his nieces by marriage, Alayne and Pheasant, two thousand dollars each. To Patience and Adeline an equal amount. To Roma, who had not benefited by Lady Buckley's will, since at the time of Lady Buckley's death she had not known of Roma's existence, he had bequeathed five thousand dollars. Nicholas knew how tenderly his sister had loved Eden and that she would have desired that Eden's daughter should inherit something from her estate. The remainder of what Nicholas had saved was to go to Renny. This amounted to more than ten thousand dollars.

No one of the family grudged him this. All knew of his devotion to Nicholas and of his generosity to his uncles. Meg was honestly glad of it and of the bequest to Roma, but she saw no reason why Nicholas should have remembered Alayne and Pheasant. She remarked this to Piers.

"Alayne and Pheasant," she said, "naturally will benefit by the legacies to Renny and you. Besides, Alayne must still have some of the money left her by her aunt, and Pheasant has a rich young son who adores her."

"Maurice's money will do Pheasant no good," he returned.

"Do her no good!" she repeated. "Why, only the other day he bought her that perfectly charming black dress for the funeral."

Piers looked at her huffily. "If Maurice," he said, "wishes to buy a new dress for his mother, that is nobody's business but theirs."

Meg continued, as though Piers had not spoken, "Uncle Nicholas would have thought it very strange, could he have known, that his niece by marriage should have a lovely new dress for his funeral, while his very own niece should have worn that faded old mauve dress which has been laundered time and again."

"Uncle Nick has other things to worry about beside your clothes."

"Are you suggesting," Meg cried, aghast, "that our dear good uncle, who never harmed anyone, is in some awful place like Purgatory?"

"I am not."

"Then what have you in mind?"

"Well—I suppose a man appears before his Maker."

"Not till the Judgment Day. . . . In the meantime, Piers, it would be much better for you to refrain from theosophical discussions."

"Theosophical?" he questioned.

"Very well—theoretical," she corrected herself.

"Mercy!" exclaimed Archer, who had just joined them.

"Your aunt," Piers said, "means theological."

"When you are grown up," Meg said to Archer, "never let yourself be drawn into an argument with your Uncle Piers."

"Listening to you," said Archer, "I feel terribly old."

Renny now joined them. He put an arm about Meg and said, "Could you imagine a kinder will than Uncle Nick's? He thought of everyone. As for his legacy to me—it was magnificent." There was a moisture on his thick dark lashes.

"You deserve all he left you," said Piers heartily.

"Yes, indeed," cried Meg, not to be outdone. Then she asked, "Is Alayne pleased by his bequest to her? But probably she will scarcely notice it. She already has such ample means."

"Alayne ample means! Why, my dear girl, Alayne has not

very much left of her aunt's money. She has spent a good deal on this house at various times. And on her children."

"Me?" put in Archer. "I don't remember anything spent on me."

"Your mother," said Renny, "intends paying for your university education and for several years abroad."

"I shall take scholarships," said the boy without gratitude.

Roma could be seen pirouetting up and down the hall. Renny called her. She came into the drawing room bright-eyed.

"I hope you understand, dear," said Meg, "that this lovely legacy comes to you because of your dear father."

"It's the first thing he ever did for you, isn't it, Roma?" said Piers.

"Piers, how can you say such things!" exclaimed Meg. "Eden died too young to have time for doing all he would have liked to do."

"A new edition of his poems is to be published," said Roma with pride.

"I know," said Renny. "Naturally, as I am his executor and your guardian."

Roma wanted to hear the good news again. She was stirred and exhilarated by the double good-fortune, but her face remained almost expressionless.

Renny fixed his eyes on Piers, as though to command his appreciation. "Eden's publishers," he said, "wrote to me from New York, saying they would like to bring out a volume containing all of Eden's poems. You remember he had three thin little books published. This will be a quite respectable size."

Meg continued, with tears in her eyes, "The publishers asked if he left any unpublished poems that they might include. So I gathered up all his papers and took them to Finch. He will know."

"Well," said Piers, "it's to be hoped the book sells—for Roma's sake."

"You're quite an important little person, aren't you, dear?" Meg put an affectionate arm about the girl.

Roma drew away—but she was pleased. She went out on to the lawn, where she saw Adeline and Fitzturgis sitting on the hammock beneath the mulberry tree. Adeline greeted her with "Congratulations on a wonderful wedding present."

Roma dropped to the grass beside the hammock. "After all," she said, "it was my right."
"So that's the way you look at it."
"I'm grateful to Uncle Nick—if that's what you're thinking of—but, after all, my father's share is coming to me." She picked up a mulberry from the grass and sniffed it, her eyes on Fitzturgis.
He returned her look, rather as an opponent might measure his strength against hers. He remarked in an impersonal tone to Adeline, "Your cousin is a young lady who takes things as they come, without fuss or flurry."
"Oh, she'll take things," said Adeline, laughing.
"You sit on the hammock," Fitzturgis said to Roma. "Those berries will stain your frock."
"*Frock!*" she scoffed. "You do sound Victorian."
"What should you call it?" he asked, considering the faded blue dress.
"An old rag," she answered. But she accepted the seat he offered beside Adeline and he now sat on the grass. The two girls looked down on his closely curling hair as though they would like to do something to it.
"Roma and I," said Adeline, after a pause, "have all our good clothes put away in our trousseaux."
"If we go on the way we're going," said Roma, "we can use them on our golden-wedding anniversary."
"The anniversary of what might have been," said Fitzturgis. He was contemplating the feet of the two girls—Adeline's, long, narrow, shapely, in white canvas sandals—Roma's, shorter, wider, bare in her sandals, the toenails enamelled red.
Adeline said, "We can soon get on with our weddings now. I've asked Mummy and she thinks in a couple of weeks. Of course, they'll have to be very quiet."
Roma tossed up two mulberries and caught them.
"I may as well tell you," she said, "that I have broken off my engagement to Norman."
The affianced pair stared at her bewildered. Roma gave a little laugh of amusement. "You look as though something important had happened," she said.
"I'll bet it's important to Norman," said Adeline. Looking very like her father, she demanded, "Roma, I want you to tell me this—did you break off your engagement before or after the legacy?"

Roma replied with simple, childlike sincerity, "Norman doesn't interest me any longer."

"That is not answering my question."

Still sincerely Roma went on, "I've felt differently about him for some time. He seems shallow. He seems dull. He hardly ever smiles any more."

"Answer my question," repeated Adeline.

"I don't mind telling," said Roma. "I broke it off before. But I knew that Uncle Nicholas was leaving me money. He told me, a few days before he died. I was alone with him for a few minutes and he told me."

"So it's all over between you and Norman," said Fitzturgis.

"Yes. It's all over."

"I congratulate you," said Fitzturgis.

"Now," exclaimed Adeline, "it won't be a double wedding after all!"

"No," said Roma. "You can go right ahead without me."

Dennis came from the direction of Vaughanlands and joined them. He squatted on his heels and said, "My father is going to order furniture for my bedroom right away. Then I shall go and live with him. He wants me there with him." His greenish eyes shone beneath the blond fringe of his hair. "And I'm to inherit a lot of money, too, when I'm twenty-one."

"Sez you," observed Roma.

"But it's true. He is," said Adeline. "It comes from his mother."

"What luck!" Roma sighed in envy. "How long have you known this, Dennis?"

"I heard my father and Uncle Renny talking of it this morning. I shall be able to do anything I want. I'll buy a steam yacht, a racing car, and an island, and give them all to my father."

Fitzturgis asked, "Where is your father?" Certainly Finch had made himself scarce since their last interview. And Sylvia, poor girl, had seldom left her room, even was talking of returning to New York before the wedding.

"He has gone to Humphrey Bell's. He told me to meet him there." Now Dennis left them as swiftly and quietly as he had joined them. He passed through the little gate which led to the path into the ravine and stood a moment looking back at the group on the lawn, wondering what they were saying. Well, he had given them a surprise, shown them how important he was and what a lot his father thought of him. He trotted down the path, crossed the bridge, and mounted the opposite steep, with an air of bravado. His lips were compressed, his eyes coldly steady. He felt that he could look any man in the face.

But when he had passed through the bit of woodland and reached Humphrey Bell's house a change came over him. There was no sign of life about the small house, but an empty packing-case stood on the verandah with some pieces of rather shabby luggage. Dennis stole up and examined these. On one trunk was a label with the name—Inigo Chase. Another, rather battered trunk, had C. Lebraux painted on it.

The door opened and Humphrey Bell appeared.

"Oh, hullo," he said. "Do you want to see me?"

"No, thanks. I'm looking for my father. He asked me to meet him here."

"Good. Come right in." Humphrey Bell led him into his living room, and Finch was discovered, smoking a pipe by the open window. He said: "I saw you coming, Dennis. Why did you follow me here?"

Suddenly deflated, left without an idea in his head, Dennis murmured, "I don't know."

Finch remarked in a complaining tone to Bell, "I don't know what to make of him. He has the most extraordinary way of popping up at odd times—of looking as though he'd something important to say, and—having nothing to say."

Bell asked Dennis, on a jocular note, "Come now. What important thing have you to say? Out with it."

Dennis hung his head. "Nothing," he murmured. He looked at the two men, beings of a world mysterious to him, of whose language he felt himself ignorant.

Finch's pipe had gone out. Now, lighting it, he said between puffs, "My younger brother Wakefield was a precocious kid—always pushing in and trying to make himself appear impressive. But he was clever. This one . . ." Finch did not finish the sentence. He regarded his son with a puzzled frown. Dennis sat on a stool, his hands clasped between his knees.

From above came the sounds of furniture being moved about, voices loudly talking.

"I hope," said Finch, "they're not going to be noisy up there. That would be a nuisance for you."

"They assure me they go early to bed. I do my writing late at night. Anyhow, I was forced to take someone into my house, and these people seem to be rather pleasant. I think I shall like them."

"I used to know Mrs Chase and her daughter," said Finch.

"So she told me. The daughter is a nun. Mrs Chase thinks a lot of your family. She says they were mighty good to her."

"It seems very strange to have her as a neighbour again," said Finch.

"Think of me," said Bell, "in a horsy atmosphere. I don't know one end of a horse from the other."

"You can count on her to mind her own business. She's had a lot of trouble, but she inflicts her troubles on no one."

Mrs Chase now appeared at the door. She was a strongly made woman just past sixty. She was wearing slacks and a grey pullover. Her short hair, once fair, was mixed with white in such an odd fashion that in some lights it appeared as quite white, while in others it seemed blonde. Her face was in keeping with the oddity of her hair, for at times it looked tired and a little battered, but at others it showed a zest for life that time could not vanquish. It was the older face which she now presented.

"Oh, God," she said, leaning against the frame of the door, "why did I come back to this house! Never stir up old memories, Mr Bell. Let them lie mouldering where they belong." Then she saw Finch and came to him with outstretched hand. "Finch Whiteoak!" she exclaimed. "How wonderful to see you again! And what a distinguished man you've become. I have two of your piano records. I like to listen to them because it makes me proud to recall how I knew you when you were a boy."

"Thanks." Finch gripped her hand in his strong nervous fingers. "You haven't changed at all. Excepting your name. You've got married. I remember Mr Chase. Is he as keen as ever about horses?"

"He thinks of nothing else."

"Evidently he thought about you."

"A little." She now saw Dennis. "Who is the little boy?" she asked.

"That's Dennis," said Finch, as though surprised to find him still there.

"And whose boy are you?" she asked, with her friendly smile.

"His," answered Dennis, indicating Finch, with a possessive nod of the head. "We live together, in a new house."

"He has a way," said Finch, "of following me about."

"And quite rightly," she returned. "I'd follow you about if you were my father. Isn't it wonderful, Dennis, to have such a brilliant father?"

"Is he?" asked Dennis. "I thought he just played on the piano."

Clara was looking absently through the window into the trees. She seemed to be making up her mind as to what she would say next. But it was Finch who spoke.

"We have lately lost my Uncle Nicholas," he said, as though imparting a piece of heavy news.

"Oh, I'm sorry," she said. "What a distinguished-looking old gentleman! I always admired him."

Dennis said, in his clear treble, "He left Uncle Renny a great deal of money. No one else got nearly as much."

Finch strode across the room and took him by the collar. "Out you go," he said, and put Dennis out through the door. When he returned he said, "That youngster has a disgusting habit of boasting—I can't imagine why."

"I think it's quite natural at that age," said Bell.

Mrs Chase's face was alight with interest. "I can't think of any better news," she exclaimed. "Your brother has always been so generous to others—it's time he had a break." She turned to her husband, who had come downstairs and now joined them. He was a sallow-faced thin man, with an habitually disgruntled expression. But it also was an intelligent face, and he could tell a humorous story with good effect. He was not sorry that he had married, but he was greatly surprised at himself and continued to be surprised by this woman's presence in his life, while she now was as accustomed to him as to an old shoe. He remembered Finch and they shook hands.

"I have wonderful news," his wife told him. "Renny Whiteoak's uncle has left him a lot of money."

Finch thought this remark was in rather bad taste. Mr Chase greeted it with pessimism. "He'll soon find ways of getting rid of it," he said. "I always have wondered how he managed to keep Jalna going, with such an expensive family and so many men about the stables. Has he been doing pretty well with his show horses?"

"Fairly well," said Finch with some reserve.

"I have been two years in the West," said Chase. "I'm out of touch with everyone here. We got married in the West," and he nodded toward his wife. "She followed me out there—to marry me."

"Liar," exclaimed Mrs Chase. "I'd never heard of you till I met you in Calgary."

"Well, I'm delighted to know of this legacy," said Chase. "And so will my friend Crowdy be. You remember Mr Crowdy?"

"I do indeed." Finch remembered how Alayne had disliked these two horsy friends of Renny's. He had a feeling, too, that she did not like Mrs Chase. Well, it did not very much matter. They were not people who would intrude. But he wondered how Humphrey Bell would be able to put up with the loud-voiced pair and their friends.

Chase now exclaimed, "Here comes the Master of Jalna. Gosh, I'm glad to see him."

Clara Chase watched his approach through narrowed eyes as though at a bright light. "He's not at all changed," she said. She saw him bare-headed, his hair still thick, growing to a point on the forehead, red in the sunlight. She saw him lithe, narrow of hip, his back showing the droop of the horseman. She saw him as the man she had loved above all others in life. Now he was in the room and her hand was in his. She saw in his eyes a look half mischievous, half tender.

"Clara!" he exclaimed; then, shaking hands with Chase, he added, "You could have knocked me down with a feather when I heard the news."

"Well," said Chase, "we went about together till we'd said everything there was to say. We'd got used to each other, so we thought we might as well be married." While making these prosaic remarks he was at the same moment giving a fond look to his wife.

"It's wonderful luck," said Renny, "having you two as neighbours." He looked at them impartially.

"Thanks," said Chase; "and, speaking of luck, our congratulations to you. Your brother tells us you've had money left you."

Renny frowned. "Did he tell you the reason for it?"

"He did," said Clara Chase, "and I was terribly sorry to hear it. One never sees the like of your uncle nowadays. How is the other uncle?"

"Dead, too."
"How sad . . . but they were pretty old, weren't they?"
"They were. It doesn't make it any easier."
"You are a long-lived family."
"It'll be my turn next."
"In about forty years," said Chase.

The newcomers and Renny continued to talk. Finch wandered about the room. Bell began to doubt his own right to be there. The Whiteoaks, the Chases, seemed to have taken possession. He busied himself with the papers on his writing table, as a hint to them to depart, but with the exception of Finch they appeared not to notice. He came to Bell's side, and, taking the picture of a woman that Bell had cut from a magazine he asked, "Who is she?"

"Nancy Mitford."

"Never heard of her, but I like her looks. What does she do?"

"Writes books I dote on," answered Bell.

"She's rather beautiful and rather wicked, I should guess," said Finch, holding the picture at arm's length to view it.

Hearing this talk of a woman, Renny at once joined them.

"It's Nancy Mitford," said Finch. "She writes books that Humphrey dotes on."

"I know about her," said Renny, with an approving look at the pictured face. "Alayne admires her too."

"I think," said Clara Chase, "we'd better go upstairs. I have things to do and Mr Bell will want to get on with his writing." She appeared to feel that the moment he was alone he could get on with it. 'Just like a machine, when you press a button,' he thought bitterly, as he listened to three pairs of feet mount the uncarpeted stairs and move about overhead. Finch had already left and disappeared in the direction of his own house—Dennis, unseen, following him at a short distance.

Upstairs Renny exclaimed, "You have very nice quarters here. I had forgotten what pleasant rooms these are."

"It's my furniture," said Chase. "Bell hadn't a stick of furniture up here." He stalked about the rooms with a proprietary air.

"What a charming young man Mr Bell is," said Clara Chase; and she added in a low voice, as she and Renny were left together while her husband went to mix a drink, "That room below is where Antoine died. Do you remember?"

"I never could forget, Clara," he said, "or forget how brave you were."

"Or what a friend you were." She caught his hand in hers and pressed it.

Chase soon came back, carrying a tray with glasses. "An old-fashioned," he said. "Is that OK?"

"Fine," said Renny, raising his glass. "Well—here's to happy days and many of them."

"Thanks," murmured the lately married pair. They linked arms and swayed a little, as though about to dance. Renny eyed them in mild appreciation of their union. Certain amorous recollections he had of Clara came to him with clarity as the drink was consumed.

She, now looking steadily at Chase, asked him, "Dare I tell Renny what is in our minds?"

Chase answered, "Why not? He can do as he likes about it."

"What's the mystery?" demanded Renny.

"There is no mystery. Simply a plain fact. We have discovered a wonderful horse and he's for sale."

"A horse! A show horse?"

"He is a racehorse," said Chase solemnly. "A two-year-old. He has already done quite well, but—he is capable of anything —if he is properly trained. If I had the money I should pay the price and consider that I had a bargain."

"What is the price?"

"He can be bought for twelve thousand dollars."

Renny laughed outright. "I have no money to spend on racehorses."

"You have twelve thousand."

His wife added fervently, "If I had that much and nothing more I'd not be afraid to buy him."

"I have no facilities for training a racehorse," said Renny.

"You once won the Grand National."

"I know, but—this I dare not risk."

"Why?" demanded Clara Chase.

"Well—as I have said, I have no trainer at my disposal. Also it would be a terrible risk. I might lose all that my uncle left me."

"You couldn't," said Chase. "This horse could always be sold for as much as you had paid for him."

"What if he didn't turn out well? Didn't win anything important?"

"But he would win!" cried Clara Chase. "Mr Crowdy says he's got a fine future. You'll agree that Mr Crowdy is one of the best judges of horseflesh in the country."

Chase added, "Some Americans are interested in him."

Renny took a sharp turn about the room. Then—"Where can this marvel be seen?"

"At the stables of a man named Turner. He's an amateur—lately interested in racing. He has got into financial difficulties and needs cash."

"H'm. Where was he bred? The horse, I mean."

"In Alberta. There is no horse of great note among his forebears, but they were a good stock, with plenty of stamina. It won't cost you anything to look at him."

Clara Chase exclaimed, in sudden panic, "I think Renny is right. He shouldn't risk it."

That was enough to confirm him in his desire to inspect the horse. A half hour later he was returning through the ravine to his own house, a meeting with Crowdy arranged.

15

THE EAST WIND

HE NOTICED, as he reached the level of the lawn, above the steepness of the path from the ravine, that a fresh cool wind had sprung up and that it was blowing majestic white clouds about the sky. Beside the porch he stopped to examine the web of a spider which he had been noticing for a week or more. Each evening it showed some damage of the day where blundering bee or diminutive cyclone had struck it. Yet each morning found it precisely repaired, fresh from the spinner's toil. What troubled Renny was the bad luck of the old spinner. Renny himself had known bad luck and he had a feeling of sympathy for the spider, in whose web he never had seen a single fly. There he squatted patiently in the centre, as though with chin sunk on breast, arms folded, eyes observant. But only a bit of dandelion fluff had been trapped by the web. Nothing to eat—nothing to eat.

Renny examined the stones of the porch, hoping he might discover a fly. Yes—there was one, sunning itself on a leaf of the Virginia creeper. With a sweep of the hand he caught it and tossed it into the web. It was caught—it struggled—it was gone—leaving a rent in the shining web. But the old spider never moved. He sat humped, imperturbable, waiting. The fly buzzed overhead.

Roma came out of the house, looking sweet-faced and anxious.

"Uncle Renny," she said, raising her candid gaze to his, "I've something to tell you. I've broken off my engagement to Norman."

He looked neither pleased nor displeased.

"Broken it off, eh?" he said. "What happened? A quarrel?"

"No. I was just tired of him."

"I don't wonder. Have you anyone else in mind?"

"N-no. Not exactly."

"There's no hurry for you to marry," he said, his eyes on the spider's web. "You're very young."

"Yes," she agreed, and came close and slipped her hand on to his arm. Marks of affection came seldom from her and he was pleased. He smiled down on her.

"I never liked Norman," he said, "and I want to like the chaps you girls marry. It's more comfortable."

"You do like Mait Fitzturgis, don't you?"

"Well enough," he answered guardedly.

She gave her suddenly sarcastic smile. "Well enough—for what?"

"Oh, I suppose, to endure."

"I guess we all have to endure each other, eh?" she said, still smiling. Then she added, "I suppose you think he isn't good enough for Adeline. But then, no one would be good enough for her—would he?"

"I wish you girls would get your minds off matrimony," he said testily. He lighted a cigarette but did not offer one to Roma. She stood looking after him as he turned away. Then she noticed the spider's web. She picked a small tendril from the Virginia creeper and poked it into the centre of the web. She moved the tendril round and round till she had gathered up the web, then she tossed it away among the shrubs.

A few moments later Fitzturgis came from the direction of the stables. He wore riding breeches, and a flush of annoyance was on his cheeks.

"Got a cigarette to spare?" she asked on a note of cold familiarity. He produced a packet and lighted one for her.

"Your hand is shaking," she said, and looked at him across the tiny flame. "More trouble with father-in-law?"

Fitzturgis inhaled, then expelled the smoke in deliberate calm. He avoided looking at Roma.

She went on, "He was just telling me that he thought he could endure you."

"He said that?"

"Well, you see, he adores Adeline."

Chagrin deepened his colour. He muttered, "So do I."

"I'll say you do," she exclaimed, "or you wouldn't be here."

He gave her a troubled look. "You think I'm not suited to this life, Roma?" He seemed to ask for reassurances.

"About as well as I am. I'm thankful that Uncle Nicholas left me money straight away, with no strings to it."

"What shall you do?" he asked, his intent eyes on her.

"Go to New York. Look about me. Travel a bit—perhaps just get a job. Change, that's what I'm after."

They smoked in silence for a space. Roma was the first to speak. She said, "I like being with you. I'd like to be with you all the time."

He gave an embarrassed laugh. "I'm afraid you would be disappointed in me. I'm not a comfortable person."

"Who is—when you get to know them?"

Again they smoked in silence.

Meanwhile the Master of Jalna had met his daughter on the way to the stables.

"I'm looking for Maitland," she explained.

Renny caught her by the arm. "Come into my office," he said. "I have something to tell you." He led her into the austere little room that smelt of liniment and Windsor soap, and shut and locked the door behind them. Adeline looked a little anxiously into his face, saw that it was ornamented by an hilarious grin, and herself smiled.

He said, "I've had a very interesting talk with the Chases, who have rented a part of Humphrey Bell's house."

"I've heard of them," she said eagerly. "Was it about a horse?"

"It was. Adeline, you remember how I once won the Grand National?"

"Oh, Daddy, it was glorious—the happiest day of my life! And that lovely horse—Johnny the Bird. Why did you sell him, Daddy?"

"I needed the money. There was the war——"

"You went to the war. And you've never since had such a stroke of luck! What a pity!"

Renny said, "I have never since owned a racehorse, but, by Judas—I've a mind to have a look at one I have just heard of."

"From the Chases?"

"Yes. They say he's a wonder—on any sort of track. They'd heard about the legacy from Uncle Nicholas and they think I should be safe in investing part of it in this horse. Chase is one of the best judges of horses I ever have known. And Mr Crowdy agrees that this horse has a great future. Now, Adeline, not a word of this to your mother or to anyone."

"Never a word! Oh, Daddy"—she threw her arms about his neck—"promise that you will take me to see him. I couldn't bear not to go."

"Of course I'll take you to see him."

Suddenly serious, she asked, "Daddy, is he *very* expensive?"

Renny could not resist the impulse to tell her. He wanted to see her open wide her eyes in astonishment, to discover whether she would give her approval to such a venture. But there was nothing she would not risk to be one with him. She did indeed open her eyes in sheer amazement but in the same moment she laughed with delight. "Oh, marvellous," she cried. "Why, that's the sort of price very rich men pay! But—if Mr Crowdy and Mr Chase say the horse is worth it—I'll bet he is. And I'm absolutely sure Uncle Nicholas would approve."

She could have said nothing more pleasing to Renny. He beamed at her. "But remember," he said, "it's a secret."

The following day they two and the Chases set out for the stables where the racehorse was to be seen, and were met there by Mr Crowdy. He was a heavily built man and Nature had endowed him with an expression of great sagacity which had been an invaluable asset to him. He had a curious habit of stretching out the palm of his left hand when he was about to make a statement of importance, and, with the forefinger of his right hand, making mysterious signs on it, as of the writing on the wall. Now, standing outside the loose-box of the racehorse, along with Renny, Adeline and Chase (the owner having retired to a little distance), he fixed his eyes on his extended palm, drew some cryptic design on it, then said in his husky voice:

"You can't go wrong in making this deal."

"It's a lot of money to risk," said Renny.

"I wish I could take the risk."

Chase put in, "You have seen his record. A good one for so young a horse. Wait till you see him in action."

The fine big chestnut colt looked out at them with mild interest. He mouthed his thick velvety lips as though he had an agreeable taste in his mouth.

Renny said, "He looks more like a big overgrown baby than a racehorse."

"True," agreed Mr Crowdy solemnly. "True. That's how he looks."

"How can Mr Turner ask so much for him," demanded Adeline, "when he's had so few important wins?"

"In both instances he beat the favourite," said Crowdy. "One on a hard dry track, the other on a muddy one."

"We'll live to see him sire some winners," said Chase.

Soon they saw the colt in action, ridden by a groom. There was a further consultation. Adeline was on tiptoe with excitement. With all the magnetic power in her, she drew Renny on to buy the colt. "Uncle Nick would want you to," she whispered. "I know he would."

He would think it over, he told them, make up his mind by tomorrow. His mind, however, was made up for him by the entrance of an American who had come to see the colt. The price seemed not to shock the American. He nonchalantly considered it, then said, "I've a good mind to buy this fellow. He looks as though he'd plenty of stamina. His record's fine for so young a horse." He made these remarks to Renny, not knowing that he too was a prospective buyer.

Messrs Crowdy and Chase, overhearing this, gave Renny such looks of passionate pleading that what resistance he still fostered melted under their fire. Added to this he felt springing up between him and the colt that promise of trust and good-fellowship which is sometimes born between horse and man at first sight. He gave the owner a nod. The deal was settled.

Back at Jalna Adeline ran from the stables to where she saw Fitzturgis strolling along the drive and called out, "Such news! We've bought a racehorse."

"Well, there's nothing very new about that, is there?" he asked without enthusiasm.

"*New?*" she cried. "*New?* Why, it's terrifically new. We

haven't owned a racehorse for years and years. Ours are show horses—hunters—steeplechasers. But this colt is a *wonder*, darling. Everybody says so. His name is East Wind and there's an east wind blowing! A lucky omen!"

Fitzturgis took her hand in a peremptory gesture.

"The only wind that interests me," he said, "is the wind that will blow us to the altar."

"Oh, Mait, what a lovely thing to say!" She laid her bright head on his shoulder, but only for a moment. Then she raised it and looked searchingly into his eyes. "But surely," she said, "you are excited by our owning a racehorse."

"I shall try to be. Tell me more about him."

Adeline poured out the tale of the colt's wins, his exceeding promise, ending by saying, "Wasn't it lucky that we had this money from Uncle Nicholas? Otherwise we never could have bought him."

"Did he cost a lot?"

So proud of the purchase was Adeline, so magical did it appear to her that the Jalna stables were to possess this equine wonder, that, without a second thought, she broke her promise to Renny. She said, "Guess."

"A thousand dollars."

"Oh, Mait, what do you think we were buying? A work-horse? More!"

"Two thousand."

"Multiply that by six!" She looked triumphant.

He was aghast. "Good Lord," he exclaimed. "That's about half your uncle's legacy."

"And why not?" she said defiantly. "It couldn't be put to better use. But you mustn't tell anybody. I remember now that I promised not to tell."

But Fitzturgis did tell. At the first opportunity he followed Alayne into the library and closed the door after him. She gave him a welcoming and enquiring look.

"Have you heard?" he asked.

"I have heard nothing new," she smiled, thinking how much she liked his looks.

"I suppose I should not tell this," he said, "but I feel bound to—in the hope that you may be able to do something about it. But—perhaps you won't mind."

She said nothing, just waited.

"Adeline has been telling me," he said, "that her father has agreed to pay twelve thousand dollars for that colt they went to see. Of course, it's none of my business."

"I didn't know. I never hear of these things till they are accomplished." Now her lips were set in anger. "Oh, how could he? It's nothing short of insane."

"I've seen too many fortunes lost on the racetrack," he said. "I hate to think of your having such a loss."

"I don't suppose it will affect me one way or the other," she said. "If the money didn't go into a racehorse it would be spent on the stables." She added, with a kind of breathless sharpness in her voice, "My husband lives for his horses."

Fitzturgis made a sympathetic sound. He dared not trust himself to speak, for at that moment he lumped Renny and his daughter together as stubborn devotees of a senseless pursuit.

Alayne gave a little laugh. "I comfort myself with one thought," she said. "I had rather he were absorbed in horse-flesh than in big business. I should find that unbearable."

"At least he'd have something to show for it," Fitzturgis said curtly.

"Not the perfect health he enjoys."

"I do admire his physique," said Fitzturgis with sincerity. "He's as thin and muscular as a man of twenty-five."

"He has scarcely a grey hair," she exclaimed, "and look at me!"

"Your hair is beautiful," he said tenderly. "At the moment of our meeting I noticed it and I thought—how beautiful!"

She looked up into his eyes from where she sat at her writing table. For some reason her heart quickened its beat. She felt happy in his presence.

When he had gone and she heard Renny's step in the hall she went out and faced him. He gave her a keen look, for there was something in her bearing that put him on his guard.

"So," she said, "you have bought a racehorse."

"Why, yes . . . who told you?"

"Maitland. He had it from Adeline." There was nothing in Alayne's face to encourage him. Still he broke out:

"Alayne, you ought to see him. The most promising colt you ever laid eyes on. I'm sure you'll never regret that I bought him."

She said stiffly, "I hope you won't regret the fantastic price you're paying for him."

"I suppose Mait told you that, too?"

"Yes."

"I don't see how the hell he found out.... Oh yes—Adeline!" His lips showed his chagrin. "I told her to tell no one."

"I suppose she was too delighted to keep it to herself. But it doesn't matter. I can't do anything to stop you. Poor Uncle Nicholas—I wonder what he would feel if he could know how his money is being thrown away!"

"It is not being thrown away," he said defiantly. "It's being invested—to what I believe is the best advantage."

Alayne shrugged her shoulders in despair.

The spaniel came to the door and looked in at them, then turned and went out again. It was as though the sight of them together was too much for him.

Renny caressed the carved cluster of grapes that decorated the newel post, then said deliberately, "I should know better than to expect sympathy from you in any venture of mine."

"If only they were of a different sort," she exclaimed.

"You knew what I was when you married me."

"Surely," she said, speaking calmly, determined not to quarrel, "surely we may expect to develop through life."

"God only knows," he said, "what you expected me to develop into, but I'm afraid you'll have to put up with me as I am."

The spaniel was waiting outside for him. Together they went toward the stables.

Renny saw Adeline leaning on the gate of a field behind the paddock watching a dozen of the show horses at pasture. He took her not gently by the nape and said, "You're a fine one, aren't you, to keep a secret?"

She screwed round her head to look at him. "Me? What have I done?"

"You told that precious Irishman of yours what I'm paying for the colt and he went straight to your mother with the news."

Adeline was for a moment struck dumb. Then she got out. "No—surely not! Oh, Daddy!"

"In future," he said, "I shall know better than to confide in you."

She could not speak. Two large tears rolled down her cheeks. He released her neck and crammed both hands in his pockets. He began to whistle 'A hundred pipers and a' '.

Adeline left him and almost ran, her tears half blinding her, to where she saw Fitzturgis leaving the stables in company with Wright, the head groom.

"Did you want me, miss?" asked Wright, who was familiar with her signs of distress or temper, and thought her perfect in all.

"No, no, Wright—go to your tea. Thanks."

"Very well, miss. . . . You're sure there's nothing I can do?"

"Well, Wright," she exclaimed hotly, "if you can teach Mr Fitzturgis how to keep his word—I shall be very glad."

Much embarrassed, Wright mumbled, "Hm-mph—I guess you're the one to teach him that, miss." He turned and hurried to his flat above the garage.

Fitzturgis gave Adeline a look of astonishment, of outrage. "Will you please explain what you mean," he demanded, "by that remark?"

"You know very well." Her eyes blazed into his. "You told Mummy what Daddy paid for the colt and—you'd promised faithfully."

"You ordered me not to tell. I never promised. I thought that your mother ought to know."

"Why the hell should she know?"

"I thought she might have some influence to prevent him."

"She has none. Anyway, you broke your word!"

"It was you who broke yours. You promised your father not to tell."

"But that was different."

"Why?"

She knit her brows. "Well, men are supposed to be strong and silent. Women aren't."

"Are you in the habit," he asked coldly, "of airing your private affairs in front of stablemen?"

"Wright's different. He's more like a friend."

"Well—I think it's in very bad taste."

"Honour comes before taste."

"You're impossible!" he exclaimed angrily.

"And you're incredible!" They flung off in opposite directions.

He met Roma coming slowly along the drive in Meg's car. She called out, "I'm going to the lake for a swim. Would you and Adeline care to come?"

"I'd like very much to go. I can't answer for Adeline. She's—not here."

Roma looked at him steadily. "Dare you come without her?"

"I don't think she'd mind. As a matter of fact we've been having words."

"Lovely," said Roma, and he ran upstairs to change into his bathing suit.

16

THIS WAY AND THAT

FINCH'S PRIDE and pleasure in his new house might have been to his heart's content but for two reasons, embodied in two people—one of whom he tried to love and could not quite succeed; the other whom he tried to stop loving and was equally unsuccessful. He could not force any real warmth of paternal affection into his feelings toward Dennis. No one had criticized this lack in him, if indeed it had been observed. But he tried to explain it to himself, for he was, since he had moved into this house, sometimes almost painfully aware that he was not the sort of father a boy could confide in or warmly love. And Dennis had no mother. . . . The mother. Ah, perhaps that was the reason! There was something in Dennis that brought back the memory of Sarah—the clinging cold passion of her love that had been like seaweed dragging down the swimmer to his death. Sarah's greenish eyes had shone on Finch from beneath bands of hair black as jet. Dennis's looked up from under a fringe of pale gold, yet they were Sarah's eyes. There was something ruthless in the clinging of the child's small, firmly knit hands, as there had been in his mother's. His hands were so like Sarah's. And lately he talked of taking lessons on the violin, which Sarah had played with considerable talent. The thought of a schoolboy's scraping away on a fiddle in this house was intolerable to Finch. Later on, yes, if the desire persisted—not now.

Finch had delayed in buying furniture for Dennis's room. The holidays were drawing to an end. Soon Dennis would be going back to school. Better wait till the Christmas holidays and have the room complete as a surprise then. But onc morning Finch discovered Dennis asleep on the floor of the verandah with a ragged old sofa cushion under his head.

He woke when Finch opened the door and explained, "I

thought, as this is my home, I'd better sleep here, even if I have no bed."

Finch felt a pang of shame and that day went to town and bought furniture suitable for a boy's room. He enjoyed buying it and did not spare expense. Today it was set in place and Finch pictured the delight in the little boy's face when he beheld it.

While he stood there wondering what sort of pictures to hang on the walls he heard a step and Maurice stood in the doorway looking in at him.

"Sure, it's a sweet little place you have here," he observed in the Irish accents it sometimes pleased him to affect. "I didn't know this little room was here at all."

"It wasn't furnished. I've just had it done for Dennis. It's right that he should live with me, you know."

"Oh Lord," said Maurice, "I was hoping it was for me."

"For you?" Finch took in Maurice's youthfully battered look, the melancholy bend to his lips. "What's the matter, Maurice?"

"I don't get on well with my father. He thinks I'm a bad example to his well-behaved younger sons. I must get out of the house—for a time, at any rate. It's too uncomfortable, and it's making Mummy miserable."

"Why not go to Jalna for a bit?"

Maurice said, with bitter emphasis, "I'd stay where I am rather than be under the same roof with Fitzturgis."

Finch looked at him, puzzled as to what he should do. He did not want to disappoint Dennis, but Maurice was his favourite among all the young people, they had become close friends during Finch's visit to Ireland—he had stayed in Maurice's house. How could he refuse him hospitality now? He said, "Certainly you must come here. But it's a pity that you and Piers aren't congenial."

"Well, I can't blame him, but—I just can't endure it. Thanks for taking me in, Uncle Finch. . . . By the way, have you a drop of whisky you could spare? I've a terrible thirst."

Finch brought out a bottle of rye and Maurice poured himself a drink. He settled himself in a deep chair with it, his hand curved fondly about the glass, a look of content on his lips.

"I've never thought to hate anyone," he said, "but I believe I do hate Fitzturgis."

"Oh no you don't. You'd not want to see him suffer."

"I should indeed. I hope that Adeline will make life hell for him." He zestfully added, after he had taken some of the whisky, "She is likely to do that—more power to her."

"When is the wedding to be?" asked Finch. "Surely they will hurry it on, before the Wragges leave."

"Yes, they will. Lord, I believe I shall go away. It would be too depressing to see that ceremony. Still—I'd not want them to think I couldn't bear it. A drink, Uncle Finch?"

"I believe I shall."

Maurice poured it for him, then, looking about remarked. "How cosy it is here! But what you need is a lovely woman to share it."

"Music is marriage for me."

"Ah, how lucky you are! God, how I wish I had a talent. I could be happy. I'd ask nothing more."

"I'm happy here," said Finch in a pensive tone. "Listen to the stillness, Maurice. I'm really secluded."

"It's beautiful," said Maurice, listening.

The only sound was the singing of a locust. Hidden in the grass, this long green insect, in passionate devotion to the music he was making, poured out his fervour. Another locust answered. They sang. They challenged. They sang. They sought out each other for combat.

"There is a woman," said Finch, "whom I love."

"I believe I can guess."

"Who then?"

"Sylvia Fleming."

"You're right. But have I been so transparent?"

Maurice made a characteristic gesture, as though reaching out to touch Finch. "I think I know better than the others do, Uncle Finch. And I like her tremendously—as much as I dislike her brother. Is it all settled?"

"It's all off," Finch returned gloomily.

"But surely she wouldn't reject you?"

"I'm not such a prize as that. . . . Still—she would have me if——" He broke off. "I can't tell you, Maurice. I shouldn't have mentioned it. Please forget what I've said."

"Very well," said Maurice, "if that's what you want. But it's a pity. Have another drink, Uncle Finch."

"No, thanks."

Finch went to the large window that seemed to bring the outdoors into the room, and stared out in silence for a space.

The two locusts had joined in a falsetto duet, challenging, insulting each other. Maurice contemplated the glass he held lovingly in the curve of his hand. He said, "I'm terribly sorry that an affair of the heart should go wrong for you, Uncle Finch, because Mummy has told me . . ." He hesitated.

"Told you what?" Finch wheeled to face him.

"Well—that you weren't altogether happy in your marriage. You were divorced, weren't you?"

"I was hellishly unhappy . . . Mind you, it was more my fault than Sarah's. I think I'm not cut out for marriage. I guess Sylvia is well rid of me."

"Uncle Finch," Maurice exclaimed in hot defence, "any girl who gets you will be damned lucky."

"No one will get me now. Sylvia makes other women seem like a desert to me. She may say nothing, but I'm conscious of her through my whole being."

"I feel just like that about Adeline."

"You couldn't," said Finch. "Adeline is scarcely grown up. She's had no experience of life."

"I've loved her since she was a child. I don't know how it is, but she gives me finer things to think about than anyone else."

"I shouldn't have spoken as I did," said Finch. "I'm sure you have a great love for Adeline, and God knows it has persisted, without much encouragement."

"With no encouragement. I have to swallow the hard fact that she doesn't care a hoot about me."

"She has shown damned poor judgment in her choice," said Finch. "But there—it is not a matter of judgment."

Now there was complete silence, for the male locusts had ceased to sing, having met in deadly combat.

The silence was at last broken by Finch's saying, "If a woman you wanted to marry told you something about herself which you felt you might recall—almost certainly would recall—with damage to your feeling for her—what would be your reaction? Would you want to go on with the affair?"

"If I love a girl," said Maurice, "I love her. Nothing she has done can make any difference. If she's committed a murder it will make no difference."

"You are so theatrical, Maurice. I'm thinking of something much less startling but something that might live on in the imagination." Finch's face darkened at the vision evoked by what Fitzturgis had told him.

"I'm just a good lover," said Maurice. "If I give my heart—I give it."

Dennis appeared, looking in at the window. He had on a torn shirt and somehow managed to have the look of a waif.

"Hullo, Dennis dear," called out Maurice. "Come in and tell your troubles to Cousin Maurice. He's in a most genial frame of mind."

Dennis came through the door into the room.

"I have only one trouble," he said. "I want to come home to live with my father."

"Well, now," laughed Maurice, "I am the very opposite. My great trouble is that I *am* living at home with my father. Take my advice, Dennis, and shun your father's roof. Fathers are hard to get on with, believe me."

"Just the same," said Dennis, "I want to live with mine."

"And so you may"—Finch spoke with forced geniality—"after Maurice has paid me a visit. Your room will be waiting for you. You may go and have a look at it, if you choose."

When he had gone Maurice said, "I hope he won't mind my coming to stay with you."

"Oh, he won't mind," said Finch. He had an uneasy feeling that he welcomed a visit from Maurice partly because it would postpone Dennis's descent on him.

The little boy again appeared. He asked, "How long will Maurice stay?"

"Mind your manners," Finch said with some severity.

"I only meant that I like my room."

"I promise," said Maurice, "not to make a long visit."

"Did your father put you out?" asked Dennis.

"He did," said Maurice solemnly. "Neck and crop."

"I don't mind sleeping on the floor," said Dennis, "or on the verandah."

"Please don't be so persistent." A vivid recollection of Sarah trying to force her way into his bedroom darkened Finch's mind.

"Or," pursued Dennis, "I could sleep in the garage. I shouldn't mind that."

Finch sprang up, took him by the arm and swept him through the door. Outside he said, "Dennis, listen to me. I want no more of this nonsense. When I'm ready for you I'll send for you. Now make yourself scarce."

When he returned to Maurice it was as though there had

been no interruption. They settled down to talk round and round the subject nearest Finch's heart but never quite touching it.

17

ROUGH WEATHER

After Adeline had left Fitzturgis she was divided between a wish to run back to him with more reproaches for what she thought had been dishonourable in him and a cool reviewing of all that had been said, though she doubted her ability to keep cool. She longed to make him understand how disloyal he had been to Renny and herself—to rub it in—to make him grovel, if only for a moment. She felt an impetuous unreasoning anger toward her mother. Why should Fitzturgis have gone to her with his tale? Adeline remembered how those two always appeared to be hand in glove.

She ran along the path that led to the woods. She beheld in front of her the dimness of the ancient pine wood which first was abandoned by the sun. She knew that if she entered there she would give herself up to her emotion. The solitude would be more than she could bear. No, she would not go away among the sombre pines. She would hold to the last of the day's golden light. She had heard her father remark that the days were growing shorter. Now his face came before her, aquiline, stern, with a look of contempt on the lips. The face of Fitzturgis rose before her, darkened by anger. Surely if anger were to flame, hers was the right . . . but they must not let the sun go down upon their wrath. . . . She felt rather proud of herself for remembering something religious at this time. She pictured the sun's going down behind the pines. She pictured her wrath cooling in the last rays—then completely extinguished as twilight drew near. She made up her mind that she would go straight to Fitzturgis—show him a benign forgiveness—make him, by her own magnanimity, ashamed of his stubborn weakness.

She turned and ran back to the house. Archer had just come into the porch, a copy of the *Odyssey* in his hand.

"Have you seen Maitland?" she asked, trying to appear unflurried.

"Maitland," he repeated musingly. "Y-yes, I believe I did. Let me think. . . ." His high white brow was as untroubled as a mountain peak in January. "I believe that he went in the direction of the lake."

"Walking?"

"Oh no. He was in Aunty Meg's car."

"Aunty Meg's car! Well—I'll be darned!"

"And another thing," said Archer. "He was wearing a bathing suit—dark blue, with a tear in the seat."

"Archer, will you do me a favour? I'm rather tired. Will you go to the stable and saddle Bridget and bring her here? I've something important to tell Mait."

"Gladly," agreed Archer. The book still in his hand, he set off at a trot for the stables.

Adeline was now all impatience to seek out Fitzturgis. Her heart ached with passionate longing to take him again into favour. More closely than ever would they be united in their love. She would hurry forward the wedding and they would live happily at Jalna ever after. She ran into her room, threw off her clothes, scattering them on the floor in her haste—in truth Alayne had never been able to teach her tidiness—put on her bathing things, and over them drew on riding breeches and jacket. When she returned to the porch, the mare, with Archer mounted, his book clamped to his side, was trotting toward the house.

"Thanks, Archie." She beamed at him. "You were quick. Tell Mother I'll not be long."

"Bridget's not at all pleased, I may tell you. She'd just had her oats put in front of her." Archer dismounted, and the roan mare, with every sign of temper, made as though to return to the stables.

But Adeline was now in the saddle and spoke soothingly to her. "You'll have a carrot, old dear, when we come back, and three lumps of sugar."

"I've just remembered," said Archer, his eyes on the tree-tops, "that Maitland was not alone."

Adeline pulled the mare about to face him. So full of temper was the mare that its feet appeared scarcely to touch the ground. So astonished Adeline that their combined vitality admirably suggested a question mark.

"Not *alone*?" she exclaimed.

"No. I think it was Roma who was with him."

Archer watched horse and rider disappear behind the balsams and hemlocks. He sat down on the lowest step, the *Odyssey* on his knees; then, hearing the sound of galloping hoofs from the road, he exclaimed in heartfelt tones, "Mercy!"

Persons who have committed acts of violence sometimes declare that they 'saw red'. Adeline did not see red, but a combination of bright colours did indeed dance before her eyes. At other times she saw nothing. Only instinct guided her along the roads and through the lane that led to the lake. Long before the lake could be seen she heard its waves tumbling on the sandy beach. The mare was not pleased by anything she saw or heard. When the greenish-blue expanse of the lake was spread in front of her, she drew back as though she never before had viewed it. No more was Adeline pleased by what she saw. There in the rolling greenish waves were Roma and Fitzturgis, holding hands, bobbing up and down like silly children! They were laughing, like children who had escaped from authority.

Adeline dismounted and tied the mare to a tree. When she had secured her and again turned to the lake she saw that Fitzturgis had breasted the waves outward for a short distance. He turned then and flung himself on them, was for an instant submerged, then borne buoyantly to the shore. Roma reclined on the lake as on a rocking-chair. She wore an expression of bliss. She loved the water and was a better swimmer than Adeline.

Fitzturgis lay for a little on the sand. He looked like a drowned man cast up by the waves. For a passionate moment Adeline was impelled to fly to him, to gather him into her arms. But he gathered himself up and leaped through the gleaming green waves to Roma's side. He stood looking down at her, his back to Adeline. A greater wave came and washed her as though inevitably straight into his arms.

She flung her arms about his neck. He clasped her to him. Adeline saw their two faces pressed together. She gave a cry of rage and pain. She snatched up a handful of small stones and ran to the lake's edge. With all her strength she hurled them at the embraced pair.

"Villains! Villains!" she shouted. "Take that and that!" She gathered up more of the shingle and flung it at them.

Fitzturgis, after his first consternation, placed his body in protection of Roma. Adeline saw a trickle of blood on his cheek. He called out something, frowning over his shoulder at her, but she could not hear the words. She bent to pick up more stones, but now he was at her side.

"Adeline," he cried, "are you quite mad?"

"I wish I were. Better mad than be sane and see what I've seen."

"It was nothing. It had no meaning."

"Perhaps not to you! Oh—don't talk to me—it's all over—it's finished between us!"

"Adeline!" He stood before her, dripping from the lake, the colour drained from his face. "You can't mean it," he went on. "You don't know what you are saying."

Roma now came out of the lake and approached them. She stood quiescent, looking from one face to the other, rather as a spectator than as one involved in so passionate a crisis. Fitzturgis turned to her. "Tell Adeline," he said, "that there has been nothing between us—nothing more than she saw."

Roma smiled. "There's been nothing," she said.

"You're damned good at this game." Adeline cast a look of scorn at the childish figure in the sky-blue bathing suit. "It's the one thing you are good at—little bitch!" She flung away and plodded through the heavy sand to the mare.

Fitzturgis followed her. "If you throw me over because of this," he said, his voice coming roughly, "I shall know that you had already ceased to care for me."

"Isn't it enough?" she cried. "Can I believe in your love? I've been noticing a difference in you. This is the end." She untied the mare and scrambled to the saddle.

"The trouble is," he said hotly, in an accumulation of resentment, "that your only real love is for your father."

"Didn't I show real love for you in Ireland? Wasn't I a faithful lover for years? It is you who have never loved me. I see it. I feel it. You've been half hearted ever since you came here. You never have belonged."

"You want me to go? Is that what you're telling me?"

"Yes," she said in a strangled voice. "I want you to go." She loosed the rein, and the mare, mad to be back in her stall, with the full manger before her and her stable companion reaching round the partition to nuzzle her, gave a squeal of joy and galloped along the lane.

Patience was standing on the rustic bridge looking down at the stream when she heard someone running down the steep path. She saw it was Adeline, descending in helter-skelter fashion. She ran on to the bridge, almost colliding with Patience, and not till that moment aware of her.

"Goodness," exclaimed Patience. "You *are* in a rush." Then she saw Adeline's face and demanded, "Whatever is the matter?" She barred the way as Adeline would have fled across the bridge.

"Let me pass!" Adeline cried, then without warning flung herself on Patience's breast.

Patience put both arms about her. She said comfortingly, "There, there, darling—tell Patience what's the matter."

"I can't," gasped Adeline, "I can't," and dropped to the floor of the bridge in an abandoned heap.

Now Patience was really frightened. "Please, Adeline," she begged. "Tell me. Whatever has happened?"

Against her cousin's shoulder Adeline got out, "It's Mait—Mait and Roma——"

At that name Patience was shaken out of her protective calm. "Roma," she repeated, "Roma."

Adeline sat up straight and looked into her eyes. "Yes—Roma. . . . I know how it feels now, Patience . . . I heard they had gone to bathe, and I followed them on Bridget to the lake. I saw the car in the lane. Then I saw them. . . . They were out in the waves . . . hugging in the most disgusting way and giving each other *lascivious* looks! I thought I had known what it was to feel fury but never had till that moment."

"What did you do?"

"You remember what they did in ancient times to those caught in adultery?"

"They stoned them."

"That's what I did!"

"No—Adeline, you couldn't."

"I did. I took handfuls of stones and threw them with all my might. I wounded him—his face was bleeding."

Patience sat silent, picturing the scene with the satisfaction in primitive violence which quite gentle women frequently show.

"He tried to explain," went on Adeline, "but I wouldn't listen. I told him all was over between us and rode away."

Patience's poodle now appeared, coming out of the stream where she had been cooling. She chose a spot close to the girls and gave herself a thorough shaking.

"Don't quite drown us, sweet," Patience admonished.

Adeline exclaimed tragically, "Here we sit, you and I—two forlorn women—in the same boat—abandoned!"

Patience added, bitterly, "Done in by that same Delilah. I wonder what she has that we haven't."

"Mait is a very different man from Norman," said Adeline with a certain coolness.

"Well . . . they're both gone."

There was a mournful silence, broken only by the poodle drying herself on the boards of the bridge.

Humphrey Bell now came to the top of the path that led to the bridge from its opposite side. The poodle recognized him as a friend and pranced up the steep to greet him. But Adeline exclaimed, "I can't meet him. I'm going." She fled up the path toward the house.

Patience was undecided as to whether she should follow, remain where she was, pretending not to have seen Bell, or seek his sympathetic understanding of this hour's happenings. The poodle decided it for her. She stood by Bell's side, loudly urging Patience to come up and join them. When she did the poodle ran to meet her, nibbled her ankles, worried the cuffs of her slacks and generally did what she could to impede the progress she had so earnestly urged.

"I hope," said Bell, "that I didn't frighten Adeline away."

"Oh no. She was going anyhow."

"I had a feeling that she ran when she saw me."

"Oh no. She was running anyhow."

"It's rather warm for running."

Patience raised her face to the tree-tops. "It blows like rain," she said.

"Yes, it's an east wind," agreed Bell. He added shyly, "I hope there is nothing wrong."

"There's something terribly wrong," she said tersely. "Adeline has broken off her engagement to Maitland."

"You astound me!" exclaimed Bell. "I thought they were . . . Good Lord, it's the last thing I expected to hear."

"Those are the very things that happen," Patience said sombrely.

"I'm glad"—he looked at her with questioning rather than seriousness in his blue eyes—"that I care for nobody and nobody cares for me."

"You have your writing," she said. "You are safe. You are immune."

"Comparatively," he agreed. "Not quite."

The rain that had been threatening now began gently, almost imperceptibly, to fall. Neither of them noticed it. They could at the moment think of nothing to say.

When Adeline reached the house she examined the gravel sweep to discover whether there were signs of the arrival of the car from the lake. There were not. Inside, the house appeared deserted. She hastened out of the house and to the stable. Evening was coming on. The horses in their boxes were quietly, dreamily munching. Everywhere was clean straw. She went to her father's office and opened the door without knocking. He looked up surprised. She cast herself on him as though she were ten years old, not twenty. The impact caused him to grunt, but he clasped her to him and vigorously patted her on the back. "There—there," he comforted. "Don't feel so badly. Anyone is liable to make mistakes."

She burrowed her face against his neck.

"I'm not feeling badly about that," she said, "but about Mait. *There* was my mistake!"

"What's this?" he demanded, putting her from him and scanning her distressed face. She sought again to burrow into the comfort of him, but he held her off.

"What's this?" he repeated. "Explain."

For a moment she could not speak. Then she brought forth all her self-control and said in a shaking voice. "I've broken off my engagement. It's all over between me and Maitland."

With a supreme effort he drew his brows together in a frown, compressed his lips, concealed the pleasurable—the grateful—astonishment he felt at these words.

"Yes?" he said quietly. "How did it come about?"

"We'd quarrelled." She, too, now spoke quietly. "You can guess about what."

"Yes? And then?" He put his hand up to stroke, in a brief caress, the hair that clung to her forehead.

"We separated. I went for a walk. I had to be alone. When I came back Archer told me that Mait had motored with Roma to the lake. I followed them there on Bridget."

Struck afresh by the pang of her discovery, Adeline got to her feet and stood facing Renny, her back to the door.

"They were there, in the lake, bathing," she said, now speaking quickly to finish the tale. "He took Roma in his arms and held her—and kissed her. She kissed him back. They were like lovers."

"What did you do?" Renny asked sharply.

"I——" Adeline closed her eyes, then opened them wide. "I stoned them."

"Stoned them," he repeated in amazement. "Do you mean you actually *threw stones*?"

"Yes."

"And hit them?"

"Yes."

"Hard enough to hurt?"

"There was blood on his face."

Renny gave a bark of laughter. "By Judas," he exclaimed, "I wish I had been there to see! What did he do?"

"He came up to me—out of the water. He tried . . . to explain, but . . . I told him all was over between us and rode away."

"You did well. I'm proud of you."

Adeline swallowed the sob that rose from the very centre of her being. Renny picked up a paper-knife and balanced it on his hand, hiding the triumph in his eyes.

"It is well," he said, "that you found him out before you married him. If he could play fast and loose before marriage—well, there's no knowing what he might be up to later."

"What had I better do now?" She gave a look of bewilderment about the little room.

"I shall go back with you to the house. It's almost dinner-time. You can go straight to your room. I shall want an interview with the young man, but it will be brief. . . . Now you can see, my pet, that this fellow is not what you thought he was. He's not what I hoped he was. I'll not say what I think of him except that when my daughter marries I want her to marry a man worthy of her."

Renny rose and went swiftly to Adeline. He took her in his arms and held her close to him. Again Adeline clung to him, absorbed strength from the feel, the very smell of him. Never had they been more united. She was painfully tearing her spirit from the bondage that for two years had possessed it. She did not realize that these same bonds had for some time been weakening.

"My darling," Renny repeated, kissing her in a fervour of protective love. "My darling . . . my little pet."

"It's hard," she said, "to lose him to Roma."

"Don't let that trouble you." Gently he stroked her hair. "If it had not been Roma it would have been someone else. He hasn't it in him to be faithful. She was merely at hand. . . . Forget him, my dearest; put him out of your mind. . . . Happy days are coming—for us two!"

Fitzturgis had knocked on the door of Sylvia's room. She was not there. He heard from Archer that she had gone to the summerhouse. This latticed retreat had been in a state of ruin twenty-five years ago, but still it remained standing. It was in deep shadow from morning to night. It was rotting, it was the home of earwigs, spiders and field mice. Sylvia had discovered it, and in these days of bewilderment and indecision she sometimes hid herself in its seclusion.

Now she heard approaching steps and peering through the clustering wild grape vine that covered the summerhouse she saw her brother coming quickly toward her. When he stood in the doorway she saw the greenish pallor of his face and wondered whether it might be tinged by the shadow of the vine. Yet in a moment she realized that his colour was evidence of deep emotion.

"What has happened now?" she asked, as one accustomed to expect unhappy things.

He stood looking sombrely in at her. "What a disgusting spot!" he exclaimed, then added, "Just the right sort of place for the news I have. It's all over between Adeline and me."

"But how can it be?"

"We had a disagreement. Some pretty hot words. On her part she seemed to set out to anger me. I was overheated in my temper and in my body. Roma happened to be going to the lake to bathe . . . I went with her. Adeline followed us there. . . . She caught us . . . well, Roma was in my arms. . . . Adeline made a pretty scene. She actually threw stones at us." He threw up his hand in a gesture of mingled excitement and self-protection. "For Christ's sake don't say it's no more than you expected, Sylvia! I can't bear that."

"It's beyond words of mine," she cried. "I could not have pictured your doing such an imbecile thing. Surely you haven't lost your head over that bit of fluff."

"Can't you understand?" He scowled in exasperation. "It was the impulse of a moment. It signified nothing."

"And everything is spoilt," she exclaimed in distress. "What is wrong with us, Maitland? Can we bring only unhappiness—to ourselves and to others?"

"Well," he said gloomily, "it appears to be all up with us here. In your case you should not have sent me to Finch. You should have gone to him yourself. You might have told your story in a way which would have made you all the more desirable to him."

She felt he was dragging in her case that she might be in the same boat with himself. She said humbly, "No way I could have put it would have made Finch see what I did in any but a horrible light."

"Who the hell do these Whiteoaks think they are!" he exclaimed. "Have they lived such puritanical lives?"

"Finch is just naturally good," she said. "He's fastidious. It makes him unconsciously cruel. As for Adeline—she's had everything her own way. To please her you'd have to be all she's imagined you to be. She's talked to me of you. You should have heard her. God, what a pedestal she'd put you on!"

He said bitterly—"Well, I've come off it with a crash. I've been toppling for some time. I'll bet that her father and her Uncle Piers have never lost an opportunity to put in a word against me."

"Perhaps it's better, Maitland," she said, "that Adeline and you should separate before it's too late. You're not happy here. Tell the truth—you've been trying to make yourself over into a different person. And as long as I've known you, darling, I've known that nothing can change you."

"I would make myself into what they want me to be—for Adeline's sake," he said stubbornly.

"It's no use. You can't. I know you better than you know yourself. We're defeated. Let's go back to New York and start all over again."

He came into the summerhouse, bent over her and kissed her. "You're a brave girl, Sylvia," he said.

Steps were heard drawing near. Sylvia, peering through lattice and wild grape, exclaimed, "Renny's coming. Is he looking for you, I wonder. Oh, Maitland, perhaps you can patch things up. He'd understand."

"He'll take damned good care not to understand."

Fitzturgis strode from the summerhouse and came to meet

Renny with an air more defiant than propitiatory. The rain was coming down softly.

"Come into the drive," Renny said. "The trees will shelter us." They moved in unison as though for a ceremony.

When they were in the drive Renny halted and said, "Well, Fitzturgis, you've turned out no better and no worse than I expected."

"Just what did you expect?" asked Fitzturgis.

Renny gave him a look which showed a kind of liking for him or rather what might have been liking had Fitzturgis been anyone but the object of Adeline's, as he thought, misplaced affection. He now added to the look, "I felt from the first that you two were not suited."

Fitzturgis had not been prepared for anything so mild as this. Withering comment on his lack of honour, determination to make this the object of violent invective, this he had expected. But here was Renny looking at him almost kindly, stroking his left eyebrow as he said:

"Adeline, I must tell you, is the very reincarnation of my grandmother. You may have noticed the portrait of her as a young woman, hanging in the dining room."

As this portrait and its companion—that of Captain Whiteoak—were the most noticeable objects in the dining room, and as the attention of Fitzturgis had been drawn to the resemblance between the two Adelines on the first day of his arrival, he answered a little testily, "I have noticed the picture."

Renny continued, "There is in the drawing room another portrait of my grandmother, one painted in Ireland when she was a child."

"I have seen that too," said Fitzturgis, wondering what the devil the man was driving at.

"Would you say the likeness is remarkable?" Renny asked.

"The features appear to be identical," agreed Fitzturgis.

"And so is the spirit," Renny exclaimed with enthusiasm. "Proud spirits, both of them! And unlikely to forgive a hurt to their pride."

So *that* was it!

Fitzturgis said, "Mr Whiteoak, I want you to believe that my love for Adeline has never wavered. You can understand surely how a man . . ."

"Indeed I can." Renny spoke almost warmly. "But Adeline can't. She'll never forgive you, I promise you that."

"I gave Roma no more than a passing caress," said Fitzturgis. "It signified nothing. Cannot Adeline be brought to believe that?"

"You could not have made a worse choice for that passing caress. Roma is in Adeline's black books because she has already broken up the engagement between Patience and young Green. No—I know my daughter. She'll never forget or forgive the hurt to her pride. I think you know very well that she won't. I fancy she made her feelings clear."

"She threw stones at us," said Fitzturgis. Unconsciously he put his hand to the bit of adhesive plaster on his cheek.

Renny regarded him almost solicitously. "Well," he said, "that was a bit extreme. But Adeline is extreme in her emotions. Certainly she had an infatuation for you. She declared that, like her great-grandmother, she would have only one great love in her life. But her great-grandmother had several lesser loves before settling down to the great one. And so will Adeline, I expect. . . . I realized before you had been here a fortnight that you never were cut out for this life. I know you have tried. You have tried damned hard."

"You were never pleased with me."

"How could I be? I have been more worried than I can tell you. I've seen you and Adeline preparing to take a disastrous step. I've seen nothing but trouble ahead."

"I will try," said Fitzturgis, "for Adeline's forgiveness——"

"You'll never get it."

"My God, that's impossible to believe! If she had been there, in the lake, bathing with us, it might have happened. Roma was swept into my arms by a wave. I kissed her. That was all."

"I quite understand," Renny said mildly. "But Adeline can't and never will. You might have a talk with her. . . ."

"You agree to that?"

"My dear fellow, I am human. I have had temptations. I know what it is to be weak, but—fortunately for me—I have a gentle, old-fashioned, forgiving wife. Adeline is none of these. But—you can try. And if she should bring herself to forgive you, and you are willing to stay on here—to begin all over again——"

"It would never do," broke in Fitzturgis. "We should have to go somewhere else. Possibly New York. No—not there—I realize that she would not be happy in a city."

"I'm glad you understand her so well," Renny said blandly.

In some way this attitude of kindliness cast a deeper gloom over Fitzturgis. He drew a heavy sigh which was echoed by the sighing of the hemlocks and spruces beneath the rain.

"I must tell you," he said, "that I am grateful for the way you have taken this, and I still think that Adeline and I may make it up."

"I'm willing for you to have a try," and somewhat enigmatically the Master of Jalna added, "if you can manage it."

It was almost dark under the heavy-boughed trees. The rain was coming down harder. Fitzturgis said, "I've left my sister waiting in the summerhouse. I must go to her."

"In the summerhouse, eh? A nice old place—or would be, if it were in repair. I really must see to that."

They separated, and Renny strode to the house. In the hall he found Piers waiting for him.

"I've just dropped in to tell you," said Piers, "that Maurice has gone to stay with Finch. Things have not been very pleasant between us—I can't put up with his drinking, and it's a bad example to the younger boys. So far as I am concerned I'm glad that he should go, but it has hurt Pheasant, and I wish you would tell him so—tell him he must come back and try to behave himself. His visit——"

Renny interrupted, "Yes, yes, we can attend to that later. But here is wonderful news, Piers. Adeline has caught Fitzturgis and Roma in the act of kissing—in the lake bathing, mind you—she's broken off her engagement to him!" In the exhilaration of the moment Renny threw his arms about his brother and pressed him into the execution of some triumphant dance steps down the hall. Piers, however, was concerned for his artificial leg and planted himself firmly just outside Adeline's door.

"She's in there," whispered Renny, "and what I want you to do is to take her home with you and keep her there till he's out of the way. He's all out to have another try for her forgiveness. I'm running no risks."

Piers whispered hoarsely, "It's the best news I've heard in many a day. And it's just like Roma—God bless her."

"There's not a minute to spare."

"I'm your man. Bring Adeline along. My car is outside."

"Drive it to the side door."

Renny tapped on the panel of Adeline's door. Twice he tapped before a muffled voice asked, "Who's there?"

He did not answer but went softly into the room. She lay stretched on the bed, her face pressed into the pillow, but when he spoke she put out her hand to him.

He took the hand and bent over her. "Adeline," he said, "you'd rather not meet Fitzturgis again, I'm sure."

She sat up and raised her troubled eyes to his. "Have you been talking to him?" she asked.

"Yes. I've told him that I quite agree with you in breaking off the engagement."

"What did he say?"

"I think he understands that it's hopeless. But—you would find it very embarrassing to meet him at table. I want to save you that, my pet. . . . Now look here. Uncle Piers is at the door with his car. He wants to take you to his house. Everything will be much easier for you. It will be more comfortable all round. Come." He half lifted her from the bed. She was confused, willing to be led. He took her through the side door, outside which Piers was waiting in the rain. Like a sick person she was supported by the brothers, half lifted into the car. It moved off.

Renny blew out his breath in relief. He returned to the hall and closed the door of Adeline's room. He heard the voices of Sylvia and Fitzturgis in the porch and darted up the stairs to avoid them. He knocked on the door of Alayne's room. "It's me, Renny," he said.

She opened the door and stood there looking so cool, so fresh that he spent a moment in admiring her before he spoke. Then he said, "I have some good news for you, Alayne."

His idea of good news did not always agree with hers. Therefore when he came in and closed the door behind him she awaited what he had to say with a degree of uncertainty.

"Yes?" She gave him a look of cool enquiry.

"I'm getting rid of Fitzturgis." For some reason which he could not have defined he used the tone in which he might have informed her of the dismissal of a groom. Possibly he was remembering how she and Fitzturgis seemed naturally to come together in a room.

She could not at the first take in his meaning. She stared, bewildered. Then she said, "But you couldn't . . . I don't understand. . . . Do you mean that you and he have quarrelled?"

"No, indeed," he ejaculated, as though thankfully. "I simply mean that the engagement is off. Adeline is free."

"But why?" she cried. "What has happened?"

"Adeline discovered him and Roma in a compromising situation, so—she broke off her engagement to him."

"Roma," repeated Alayne. A painful colour flooded her face and neck.

"Yes," he said. "There was nothing else for Adeline to do."

"I suppose not," Alayne agreed faintly. "Where is Adeline?"

"She's gone to spend the night with Pheasant and Piers. He'd dropped in most conveniently."

"Is Adeline very much upset?"

"Naturally she's a bit upset. What woman wouldn't be?"

"And you tell me you have seen him since—talked with him?"

"Yes."

She put her hand to her throat, as though to help her to get out the words. "And . . . what does he appear to feel?"

"He's very much ashamed. What man wouldn't be! He realizes that it's all over between them. I think he'll be leaving quite soon. He and I are parting quite civilly. I think it's best, don't you?"

"Yes. I'm sure it's best."

"Alayne, what do you feel about this?"

"I—I'm staggered, but . . ." She hesitated, to moisten her dry lips.

"But what?"

"Well, I never thought that Adeline and he were suited to each other."

"I quite agree. They would have been a very badly matched pair." He took her in his arms and kissed her. "Not a bit like us."

Alayne felt extraordinarily shaken. She grasped Renny's arms in her two hands, as though to dispossess herself of any wild and weak thoughts, to hold herself strong by his strength.

The air reverberated to the sound of the dinner gong. Nowadays Alayne seldom heard it without thinking, 'Soon the Wragges will be leaving. Gongs will be a thing of the past.' But this evening it brought the one thought, 'How can I bear to meet Maitland after what has happened?'

"I think I shall not go down," she said.

"I know just how you feel." He patted her on the back. "But I think you must—for Sylvia's sake. That poor girl isn't herself these days. Possibly she suspects something between her brother and Roma. God knows he has managed to pull the wool over my eyes."

Alayne longed to have a few moments to herself while she finished dressing, but Renny remained with her and they descended the stairs together. Fitzturgis, Sylvia and Archer were in the porch but now joined them. Fitzturgis avoided meeting Alayne's eyes. He gave a swift glance to the dinner table noting that no place had been laid for Adeline.

Renny said to him in an undertone before taking his own place, "Adeline has gone away for the time being. I thought it was best to let her go. We shall be more comfortable without her, I think."

At the thought of comfort at that meal Fitzturgis gave a sardonic smile.

In reverent hush, as for a corpse in the house, Rags waited at table. Somehow tonight he looked wan and old. Alayne pulled herself together. She and Sylvia talked in high excited tones about an anthology of poetry they had been reading, about recipes for blackberry cordial, about which varieties of dahlias they best liked. Now and again Renny joined in with some facetious remark. Fitzturgis was almost silent. When silence fell, Archer, with uncanny tact, held forth in a monologue on his opinion of a scientific broadcast he had heard concerning the weather variations of the past season.

"I wish," he said, "that we might have television. Some of the discussions on it are very interesting."

"Television," repeated Alayne, to whom the word conjured up visions of repulsive faces and still more repulsive sounds. "Oh, surely not, Archer."

"I am too old to be harmed by it," he said, "and too young to be revolted."

"Also," said Alayne, "the cost is prohibitive."

Archer turned to give an appraising look at his father, who, in response, winked at him.

The meal was somehow finished with, everyone moved out of doors. The rain had ceased and the air was incomparably fresh and sweet. Renny looked at his watch. "I must go to the stables for a few minutes," he said. "Wright is a little anxious about one of the brood mares."

As he moved in that direction Fitzturgis followed him. He said, as he overtook him, "My sister and I are planning to return to New York by the morning train. I had hoped to see Adeline again, but—she has made it plain that she doesn't want to see me. I think I ought to go, don't you?"

There was a note of appeal in his voice, as though his longing to see Adeline must be subdued to what her father thought was right. Yet, even as he said the words, he felt stirring in him a restiveness, a desire to free himself from the bonds that clamped him to this place, to this long-legged, red-headed man who faced him. If only he might have taken Adeline away with him. . . . But how often she had said to him, "I could be happy nowhere but at Jalna."

Renny agreed, not too readily but as though with proper consideration. He would arrange, he said, to have the car on hand whenever Fitzturgis required it. He added, suddenly descending from dignity to something like a grin, "Well, from having a double wedding in view, we have nothing and are even losing our servants!"

In return, Fitzturgis achieved a rather grim smile. He turned back toward the house and found Alayne standing alone in the porch. He joined her, quite unable to control the embarrassment, the shame on his face. Alayne forced her eyes to meet his which were fixed on her with a look almost tragic.

He exclaimed, "Mrs Whiteoak, what must you think of me? The worst, I'm afraid."

Alayne was indeed less stung by his fault than by what her own feelings for him had been. She had so warmly accepted him into the family circle, not so much as Adeline's fiancé, but as a new member congenial to herself who had in him something almost lover-like in his attitude to her. Now a word which had been a favourite of her mother's, in the expression of contempt, came into her mind—the word *odious*—but whether it came as applied to Fitzturgis or to herself she did not know or try to discover. She was unhappy enough without analysis of the situation.

Fitzturgis put one foot on the bottom step and, raising his eyes to hers, said, "There seems nothing left for me to do but put on a hang-dog look and skulk away—as a man who had the bad taste to make love to another girl while engaged. . . ."

"Don't," Alayne interrupted. "Please, don't. . . ."

"You have been so perfectly charming to me," he got out. "I shall never forget that."

She coloured deeply. She could find nothing to say.

Archer appeared, a railway time-table in his hand.

"There is no choice of trains," he said. "You could not catch the evening train. I have marked the hour when the morning train leaves. You asked for this, didn't you?"

"I did," said Fitzturgis. "Thanks. I suppose I had better do my packing tonight."

"Can I help in any way?" Archer enquired almost affably. He was one of those people who always are glad to see visitors depart.

18

RENNY'S BIRTHDAY

A NIGHT, a day, and another night had passed, yet Adeline still remained in Piers's house. Pheasant had shown her such a sweet sympathy, not in words but in an enfolding warmth of heart; Piers and his sons had so splendidly behaved as though nothing were wrong; little Mary had trotted after her and confided in her, so like a little angel, that Adeline's outraged feelings, her anger and soreness of heart, began to be a little eased.

On this second morning she saw Patience and the poodle coming along the path to the door. The poodle was carrying a small basket in its mouth and looked so ridiculously like a china poodle of Victorian days that Adeline had to smile and felt it strange to discover herself smiling.

"We've brought you a present," called out Patience.

After some persuasion the poodle consented to relinquish the basket, for it felt that it was giving up considerable prestige in doing so. From the basket Patience produced a late fledgling wrapped in a bit of flannel.

"Wright found it chilled through," said Patience. "It must have flies caught for it. At the moment it's absolutely stuffed, but it will soon be hungry again." The two girls sat down on the steps of the porch, guarding the fledgling. They sat talking in confidential tones of this and that but always keeping from the subject nearest their hearts, till suddenly Patience said,

"When are you going home?"

"I hadn't thought about it."

"You know that he and his sister have left?"

"Yes. Did they say goodbye to you, Patience?"

"No. They left a sort of general goodbye. Sylvia said she would write. It's all rather a miserable ending to the summer, don't you think?"

"I shall never feel the same again."

"The only person," said Patience, "who has come through this summer unscathed is Roma."

"She must be triumphant, after two such killings."

"I avoid her. I begged Mummy to keep off the subject, but she tackled Roma when they two were alone. Roma simply looked at her, cool as a cucumber, and said she'd done nothing. It isn't her fault, she says, if men like her."

"The viper!"

"Uncle Renny came and had a talk with her."

"Oh, I wish he hadn't. She'll be more and more pleased with herself."

"I scarcely think Uncle Renny talked to her about *that* sort of thing. He told Mummy he wanted to find out what Roma would like to do. She told him she's yearning to go to New York and take a course in something—dress-designing, I think it is. Well, she has the money to pay her way. None of us will weep to see her go—God knows."

"It's been tough on you," said Adeline, "having her always in the house with you."

"Oh, I haven't particularly minded," Patience said tranquilly, "not till she took Norman away from me, and I don't much mind that now. . . . The truth is, Adeline, that I've found someone I care for—more than ever I did for Norman."

"Humphrey Bell?"

"Yes. . . . He doesn't know that I care for him, and he's said nothing to me, but it goes to show that one can recover—that one does not die of a broken heart."

"My heart isn't broken," Adeline said fiercely. "It's had a hell of a jolt, but it's not broken." She gave a sudden wild laugh as she remembered the scene by the lake shore. "Oh, Patience, if only you had been there to see me stoning them!" But, even as she laughed, tears sprang to her eyes.

The voice of Christian called to them from the doorway of his studio. "Oh, girls, come and see!"

The girls slowly rose, Patience carrying the basket with the fledgling. Adeline said vehemently, "Never again shall I trust any man."

"You're quite right," said Patience. "I may love them, but I'll never trust them."

"Hard words," exclaimed Christian, who had overheard. "Surely you'll make an exception in my favour." Adeline threw him a fiery look. Was he daring to be waggish at a time like this?

Christian felt himself to be immeasurably more mature than the two girls. He felt that his experience as an artist had given a breadth, a depth, unknown to them in their affairs of the heart. On the other hand, Patience considered herself as by far the most mature. She was in years the eldest. She had early been left fatherless, with a mother who leaned on her, while they had been sheltered by the dominating presence of Renny and Piers. She had a steady job while they were dependent. As for Adeline, she looked on the other two as little more than children who had experienced nothing of the devastating emotions experienced by herself. And when they entered the studio, there was Maurice, thinking of himself as a weary man of the world, considering the other three as little more conversant with real life than the fledgling that Patience now presented to him. He set it on his forefinger and surveyed it pityingly. He was, in fact, already a little drunk.

"Poor creature!" he said. "Pushed from the nest. Its family not caring a damn what happens to it. I know just how it feels."

"The point is," said Patience, "not to let it starve. Do you think you could find a worm for it, Mooey?"

Maurice moved rather uncertainly to the door. "I'll find a worm," he said, "if it's the last thing I do."

Just outside the door he came face to face with Piers.

"What's that you have?" demanded Piers.

"Oh," said Maurice, and before he could stop himself added, "Someone told me you had gone into town."

"So that's why you came—thinking I was out of the way."

"No—no—really I can't remember what it was I thought."

Piers fixed him with a stern eye. "Well, I think you have behaved very badly. You must know how you hurt your mother by going off in a temper to stay with Finch."

"I was not in a temper. I went because I felt that my presence was irritating to you."

"It was your drinking that irritated me. Have you no self-control? Do you intend deliberately to hurt your mother?"

"No," Maurice said loudly. "It was to spare her feelings that I left."

"Well—you are to come back."

"No, no. I can't do that."

"Then go into the house now and tell her I want you back. That's only fair to me."

"All right. I'll do that." And he added, in a muffled tone, "Sorry, Dad." He moved uncertainly toward the house.

"Good God!" exclaimed Piers. "You've been drinking already at this hour!"

Maurice had forgotten the fledgling. It fluttered, half fell to the ground, from where the poodle deftly picked it up and returned it unscathed to Patience.

Those in the studio pretended they had heard nothing of what had passed between Piers and Maurice. This last exclamation from Piers they could not ignore.

"Isn't it awful?" said Patience. "I knew he had. Poor Mooey!"

"I don't pity him." Adeline spoke in the manner of her father. "He deserves to have a stick taken to his back."

Christian began to mix some paint on his palette. He said, "How can you know what his feelings are?"

"I ought to know, for he's always telling me about them."

Piers, for a moment, thought he would not allow Maurice to go to Pheasant as he was, but decided, with a grim smile, "Let her see her darling tight—in the middle of the morning. Perhaps she'll understand better how I feel."

He brought out his car and drove to Vaughanlands. He heard the piano, saw Dennis sitting on the bottom step of the porch.

"Hullo," he greeted the little boy. "You keeping out of the way?"

"Yes," Dennis stood up in a defensive attitude. "My father is composing. I don't think he'd want a visitor."

"I'm not an ordinary visitor. He leaves you on guard, eh? How do you like living here, Dennis?"

"Well, I don't actually live here. Not all the while. But as soon as Maurice goes I shall."

"Good. Well, I'm going in to see what I can do about it. You wait out here, Dennis."

Piers went quietly into the music room where Finch was seated at the piano. Now he took his hands from the keys and began to write notes. Sheets of paper with other notes were scattered on floor and piano. Finch looked supremely happy. Even when he raised his eyes and met the somewhat quizzical gaze of Piers his look of happiness did not fade.

"Having lots of fun, eh?" asked Piers.

Finch drew a deep breath. "Yes," he said. "Lots of fun . . . I've done a piece I'd like you to hear. It's been in my head for some time and now it's written down. Like to hear it?"

Piers was immensely flattered. Never before had Finch confided, as it were, a composition to him.

"Fire away," he said. "I'd love to hear it."

Finch turned again to the piano. When he had played the gay and tuneful piece to the end Piers exclaimed, "It's the best thing you've done!" Then, realizing that this was not the right thing to say, since the composition was of a light nature, he amended, "I should say it suits me better. Most of your stuff is a bit too serious for me."

"This came to me one night when I had been playing to someone. . . . I rather think it was to Sylvia Fleming. . . . She'd gone, but . . . well, there was this thing in my head."

"You should dedicate it to her," said Piers.

"Oh no . . . I couldn't do that. . . . Please don't repeat what I said to anyone . . . not to anyone. . . . What's she doing with herself these days?"

Piers's blue eyes became prominent and somehow bluer. There was both astonishment and laughter behind them. "Don't you really know?" he demanded.

"I don't. Why should I know? What are you driving at?"

"My dear fellow, she's in New York."

Finch had turned on the piano seat to face Piers. Now he turned his back to him and asked, "When did she go?"

"Yesterday morning. She and Fitzturgis both."

"It's unbelievable." Again he turned to face Piers.

"On the contrary," laughed Piers, "it's quite natural. Our dear little Roma got after him and the poor guy hadn't a chance. Adeline has broken off their engagement. He and his sister have gone back to New York. I don't know when I've been so pleased about anything."

"It's contemptible of Sylvia," exclaimed Finch, "to go

away without saying goodbye. Why," he added in excitement, "we were friends—dear friends!"

"The best thing for you to do is to put the thought of her out of your mind. For my part I hope we have seen the last of the Fitzturgis family."

A step was heard, an indolent step, and Maurice came into the room. When he saw Piers he drew back, as though he would retreat, but Piers enquired casually, "Well, did you see your mother?"

"Yes. She agrees to my staying with Uncle Finch for a bit—if he wants me."

"Of course I want you," said Finch.

"Did your mother remark your condition?" Piers asked with a teasing smile.

"She saw nothing in it to remark." Maurice frowned darkly and sank into the most comfortable chair.

Piers said, addressing Finch, "Try to keep him sober—if you can."

Finch sat with his elbows on the music rack and his head on his hands. He did not hear what was being said. The memory of that mysterious and lovely night when he had played to Sylvia shut him off from all else. She should not have gone without saying goodbye to him. He realized now that he wanted to play the new composition to her.

Piers was leaving. He said, "I hope you don't forget that Renny's birthday is tomorrow. We're expected to dinner—all of us. There'll be mixed feeling at the celebration. Uncle Nicholas gone. Yet—there is his money to be pleased about. Adeline's engagement off. Yet—Fitzturgis gone. That's something to make a fellow cheerful."

"I agree with you on that score," said Maurice.

Outside Dennis accompanied Piers to his car.

"You said," the little boy spoke accusingly, "that you were going to do something about Maurice."

"Oh yes—you'd like him to vacate your room, wouldn't you?"

"Yes. I want to live here with my father."

"What about coming to stay with me for a bit?"

Dennis considered this, then said, "Thanks. But I think I shall wait about here till Maurice goes."

"Very well. But come along and have lunch with us."

"Thanks. But I think my father will expect me for lunch."

"Remind him to buy a present for Uncle Renny."

"I'd better see him about it now."

Piers picked him up and put him inside the car.

"You'll come along with me," he said.

"Thanks," said Dennis, "but I think my father——"
The car was now on its way.

Renny's birthday dinner party included all the family, even to its youngest member, little Mary. Fifteen sat down to table—Renny, Alayne, their son and daughter; Meg, her daughter and Roma; Piers, Pheasant, their three sons and daughter; Finch and his son. It was the first family party from which Nicholas was absent. It had been necessary for Wakefield to remain in New York for a time, but he had sent a telegram of congratulation and expected to return to Jalna for a visit.

Adeline had come home that afternoon. It seemed to her that she had been absent for a long while, that she had crossed a gulf, that she was a different being from the girl who had discovered Roma and Fitzturgis on the lake shore. Yet—now that the feel and smell of Jalna were enfolding her—how natural, how *strangely* natural, it all was!

On that first day Alayne had gone to her. She had not gone with a rich maternal show of sympathy, as though Adeline were her wounded ewe lamb. That would have been altogether too much for the girl to bear. But Alayne had talked to her of the splendid show of life—of the freshness of what lay ahead. Mother and daughter had drawn very close together.

Both wondered whether Roma would have the courage to come to the birthday party. Roma did come, along with Meg and Patience. She came as one of the family, without embarrassment, carrying a new necktie and a tin of his favourite tobacco, both daintily wrapped, as presents to Renny. She offered them to him and, at the same time, her round cheek for a kiss.

He kissed her. "Well, well," he said. "So *you're* here."

"Yes, Uncle Renny. I couldn't think of anything more original for your birthday, so I've brought you these."

"Thanks very much. I'm sure they're just what I've wanted."

All the presents were laid, in their wrappings, on the library table, to be opened after dinner.

"What a pity Wakefield isn't here," said Meg, as they gathered about the table.

"Wakefield and Uncle Nick—both greatly missed," said

Renny, then added with a sigh, "But Wakefield will come again." His eyes turned to the place where Nicholas had been accustomed to sit. Piers, now occupying it, felt slightly embarrassed.

The roast lamb, with mint sauce, young peas and new potatoes, was delicious. So were the ice-cream and the huge birthday cake, ablaze with candles. That was Mrs Wragge's final effort in this line before departure. On its top was a horseman, mounted on a racing horse, and surrounding it were the words, in coloured icing: Good luck to you and to East Wind. There had been much discussion as to the number of candles for the cake. Adeline, whose idea it was, wanted the sixty-odd candles of his years, but as there was scarcely space for such a number a round dozen had been settled on.

Renny's gratification when the blazing cake was set in front of him was so reminiscent of his grandmother, old Adeline; the arch grin with which he turned to those about the board, before he summoned his breath for the extinguishing of the candles, was so like to hers, that those who remembered her must exchange a glance of recognition. With one triumphant blast he blew out all the candles.

"I must keep the little horse for luck," he said. "It's a beauty."

"I bought that," said Adeline, and her mind flew back to the day when she and Fitzturgis had gone to the town in search of it. How long ago it seemed.

When little Mary perceived the ruin of the cake, as it was cut into pieces, when she saw the size of the slice laid on her plate by Renny, she took a corner of her napkin and wiped away her tears. Her father picked her up and set her on his knees.

"What's the matter?" he whispered.

"Too much cake," she whispered back. "Too much horse. Too many men."

After dinner all crowded into the library for the ceremony of unwrapping the presents. Renny was satisfactorily grateful for socks, neckties, shirts and bedroom slippers. There was a spaniel in bronze as a paperweight, from Finch. Churchill's latest book from Alayne. A small painting of the house, in summer sunshine, from Christian. All these gifts delighted him, though it required imagination on this sultry August evening to picture the pleasure of wearing the heavy woollen underwear given him by Meg. But she had bought it as a bargain and assuredly winter would come. He clasped the massive garments against his chest and kissed her. "Just what I need," he declared. "The moths have been eating mine!" As Alayne prided herself on the fact that, after years of struggle, she had rid Jalna of moths and buffalo bugs that had feasted there before her coming, she found this hard to bear, but then, there was so much she had had to bear! She did not contradict him.

Archer's present was in an envelope, and for a moment Renny knit his brows in puzzlement. Then he discovered that it was the receipt for a payment of ten dollars on a television set. . . . On the enclosure card Archer had written, 'I hope you will be able to carry on from here.'

"What is it?" demanded a dozen voices.

Renny hugged his son and gave him a resounding kiss. "That is our secret," he returned.

Later, when they were scattered on the lawn with cool drinks, Meg drew Renny and Alayne aside.

"What are we going to do about Roma?" she asked in a tone that combined mystery and foreboding.

"She wants to take a course in something or other—modelling, designing—I don't really know," said Renny.

"Fashion designing," said Meg. "And New York, is the place for that, and that is where she wants to go. It would be a comfort to me to see her depart. Since the affair of young Green she and Patience aren't—well, you can imagine how Patience feels."

"I can indeed."

"Patience is a dear sweet girl," said Alayne.

Meg gave her sister-in-law a loving look. Praise of Patience was very pleasant to her.

"Thank you," she said simply, then added in a forthright tone, "Roma will never settle down here now that she has this money. Something has got to be done about her."

Alayne had been looking thoughtful. Now she said, "I have an idea. I will get into touch with my old friend, Rosamund Trent, and ask her advice. She has lived in New York all her life. She will know what opportunities there are. She will give us just the advice we need."

"Splendid," said Meg.

Renny frowned. "It seems strange that these girls can't get on together."

"There will always be trouble where Roma is," said Meg.

Renny saw Roma, where she was standing with a group of the young people, and called to her. "Roma, come here!" She moved slowly across the dew-wet grass to them.

This evening was the first time that she had encountered Adeline since the violent scene by the lake. At table they had been seated at a distance from each other, but on the lawn they came face to face. A brightness of rage kindled in Adeline's eyes. For very little, she felt, she would have caught Roma in her fierce hands and beaten her. But Roma looked large-eyed and sad, as though puzzled to know what all this was about. Patience, with little Mary by the hand, came and stood beside them, with a troubled smile, as though she would guard all three.

The young male cousins, who had formed themselves into another group, consisting of Piers's three sons, Renny's son, and Finch's, now moved to join the girls. So, in the light of an enormous harvest moon that had just risen above the tree-tops, the nine cousins were in front of the house. The house, which had the look of sinking into its clustering vine, as though for the comfort of a night's repose, now might have been imagined to rouse itself, to take a good look at the new generation of Whiteoaks displayed before it. How did these compare, it might have considered, with those who had reached maturity—with Meg, Renny, Piers, Finch and Wakefield? How did they compare with those whose gravestones, in the churchyard, this same harvest moon emblazoned? They will do, the old house appeared to say, they will do.

Renny's voice, calling to Roma, drew her from her cousins.

"Roma," Renny said, looking down at her with rather a puzzled expression, "why do you want to go to New York?"

"Doesn't everyone?" she asked, with a cool glance, about half way up his height.

"My God!" he exclaimed, and burst out laughing.

"For a visit," said Meg, "that's natural. But you want to stay?"

"I want to learn something."

"You can learn all you need to know in Canada," said Renny.

"You can't be so expert in fashions."

"I think Roma is right." Alayne spoke with unusual warmth toward Roma. "For the particular line she wants to take up there's no place like New York."

"She can't go alone," said Renny, weakening.

"I have been thinking that I might go with her. As I have said, I can get the best advice from my friend Rosamund Trent, and can arrange for a boarding-place—the sort of place suitable for a young girl."

Roma said nothing but looked in acquiescence from one face to the other while they discussed plans.

"One great obstacle," said Alayne, "is that the Wragges are leaving so soon. I should be here."

"Don't worry yourself on that score." Renny gave her a reassuring pat on the back. "We shall manage. There's no dear old uncle to be waited on now. And our visitors are gone."

"I should engage a cook before I leave, but you could not be expected to take her in hand—nor could Adeline."

"Don't worry," said Meg. "I'll come and help. We shall get along famously." She saw Finch wandering about, with an iced drink in his hand, and went to join him.

"Finch, dear," she said in her warm motherly voice, "we have just been arranging for Alayne to take Roma to New York. The child is determined to go. Perhaps you've heard."

"Yes. I've heard."

"Her going will leave only Patience and me to live with you."

"Yes. That's true."

"Finch, what is puzzling me is why you don't have those empty bedrooms furnished. Surely there's a reason."

"I have a room ready for Dennis."

"I know, and you have Mooey occupying it, which is annoying to his parents, for naturally they want their own son at home, and hard on poor little Dennis, who longs to be with you—just as I long to be with you."

"I know." He took a mouthful of the cooling drink. "I know, and I'll arrange it all—in time."

Meg spoke with an older sister's firmness. "Your habit of procrastination is growing on you, Finch. Indecision and procrastination—when you have so much need of resolution and promptness, haven't you?"

"I have," he agreed, "and I'll get those rooms finished very soon."

"I'd gladly bring my own furniture, but, as you say—though I cannot quite agree with you—it's rather large and Victorian for your type of house—though you do seem to like my little occasional table."

"It's a very useful little table," he said eagerly.

"I think"—there was a hint of reproach in her voice—"that it is something more than merely useful."

"It's beautiful," he hastened to add.

19

DEPARTURES

During the following fortnight there was a bustle of preparation at Jalna. The Wragges were preparing for their prolonged holiday in England. Alayne was putting Archer's clothes in order for school and making arrangements for taking Roma to New York. Never before had she and Roma travelled together. Now they were drawn into an odd, uneasy intimacy. The girl would come to Jalna at all sorts of hours to ask Alayne's advice about this or that. Adeline took care to keep out of the way when Roma was in the house.

The day came when Archer and Dennis left for school. Philip left for the Royal Military College. On top of this came the almost unbelievable departure of the Wragges, though they declared that a return to Canada was probable within a year. Two days later Alayne and Roma left for New York.

Renny and Piers went with them to the train. It was Roma's first long journey from home, but she looked cooler and less flurried than Alayne. Alayne pictured a succession of household tragedies in her absence, even while she despised herself for having become no more than a housewife. If only the Wragges had been in charge as of old!

When the train pulled out from the station and she and Roma found themselves facing each other in their compartment, their hand luggage beside them, Alayne had a sense of unreality. How strange it was that she should be taking Roma to New York—where she and Roma's father had first met. That had been twenty-six years ago. Eden . . . how brilliantly good-looking he had been . . . how devastatingly attractive to her. She had been swept into marriage by that attraction, as a becalmed sailing boat by a wind from the north. But what a short while it had lasted. Her passion for Renny had been its undoing.

She tried to trace a resemblance to Eden in the young face opposite. But there was nothing to remind her of Eden and she was glad of that. Let his image remain untouched.

Every time their eyes met, Roma gave her a confident friendly look. 'Just as though we were new acquaintances,' thought Alayne, 'and liked one another and had no past behind us at Jalna.' They chatted cheerfully as they undressed together.

Renny and Piers talked little as they drove homeward. Renny was a consistently erratic and nervous driver. Now and again an exclamation of warning or of protest would be forced from Piers, but when they reached the quiet of their country road he relaxed and remarked in a meditative tone, "Things have taken an odd turn, haven't they?"

"They have. Nothing is like it was at the beginning of summer." But though he spoke even more seriously than Piers, his expression was resigned. "I have important things to see to," he said. "I must engage a trainer for the colt. I've heard of a first-rate man who is free. He's expensive, but if you're going to do a thing you might as well do it properly, eh?"

Piers said nothing but gave him an amused, a very understanding look.

"The trainer is named Kelly. My friends Crowdy and Chase are bringing him to Jalna tomorrow morning. It's pretty certain that I shall engage him."

"Well, let's hope this turns out well. You run the risk of losing a lot of money." And Piers could not resist adding, "It's a good thing Alayne is out of the way."

"Alayne never interferes," Renny returned stiffly.

"She knows it's no damned use," laughed Piers.

They were now nearing Jalna. Renny asked, "Shall I drive you home or will you come in and take pot luck with Adeline and me?"

"I promised to be home. Pheasant has some special dish. We had better pick Adeline up and the two of you come to us."

"Thanks. Another time." After a little he exclaimed: "I hope Roma behaves herself in New York. God, I'm grateful to her! If it hadn't been for her I might have had Fitzturgis on my hands for the rest of my days."

"He'd never have stuck it out here."
"But he might have taken Adeline away with him."
"Someone else will do that, you may be sure."
"Not if I can prevent it."
"Do you know," said Piers, "I should rather hate to be your son-in-law."
"Let Adeline marry the right sort of fellow and he'll find me easy to get on with."
"I wish," said Piers, "that young Philip were older and that he and Adeline might marry. What a pair! Our grandparents right over again."
"The trouble is that girls seem to have such poor judgment. . . . I've seen that happen time and again in my life."
"Well," Piers spoke with some warmth, "I don't see anything wrong in Pheasant's choice."
"It's turned out all right," said Renny cryptically.
There was a somewhat prickly silence till they were passing Vaughanlands. Then Renny remarked, "I can't get used to the sight of that modern little house. The old house, while it had no distinction, was a landmark. It had meaning for us. This house has none."
"It has plenty for Finch."
"Meg is longing to go and look after him."
"He doesn't want her. No more than he wants Dennis. He prefers my tippling son. Finch is a queer fellow."
Soon Piers was set down at his own gate and Renny turned the car in the direction of Jalna.
How strangely empty the house was! Doors and windows stood open, and the cool quietness of the evening had moved in, as though to take possession. The window curtains were gently drawing and withdrawing with a soft flapping sound. There was no sign of Adeline or of the dogs. Empty rooms everywhere. Nicholas's room closed in, silent, secluded. Renny had a sense of foreboding. Never could he remember having been alone in the house.
Suddenly from the basement came the sound of the dogs' barking. He ran down the stairs, down the basement stairs, into the kitchen. Here indeed was life and animation. Adeline was there, an apron tied about her middle, a pucker of anxiety on her forehead. The dogs were there, watching her every movement, getting in her way, acutely conscious of a change in the order of things.

"I thought you'd be hungry," she said. "I thought I'd scramble eggs and make some coffee."

"I'm devilish hungry. I hope you are too."

"I'm starving. Funny, it's the first time I've been hungry since . . . ." She did not finish the sentence.

"Good girl," he said.

He watched her moving about the kitchen, so light, so strong, so restored to him, as it were, from peril. He whistled softly as he beat the eggs. They sizzled in the frying-pan. Adeline was making coffee. "Funny," she remarked, "how you seem to know just how things should be done, till you try to do them yourself. I wonder how much coffee to a person."

"Two tablespoons."

"How long should it stew?"

"About ten minutes."

"Good. Will you have tomatoes with your eggs?"

"Yes. And olive oil on them."

"Would you like some sliced peaches and cream?"

"I certainly should. Come and have a look at the eggs. They're nice and fluffy."

Together they bent over the sizzling eggs. The coffee bubbled in the pot. The dogs were almost beside themselves with anxiety.

"Oh, Daddy," cried Adeline, "I should have heated a covered dish for the eggs! They'll be cold by the time I have set the table and carried them up to the dining room. Where is the large tray? Where is the butter? The eggs are burning! The coffee is boiling over! Where does Rags keep things? *Dogs*—get out of the way! Oh, Daddy!" Quite suddenly she was distraught. She walked in a circle, the frying-pan in her hand.

Renny had seen meals prepared under greater difficulties than this. He said decisively, "No need to worry. We'll eat down here in the kitchen."

She opened her eyes wide. "Oh, heavenly! I'll run up and get a tablecloth."

"We'll not need one. Dish up the eggs."

"Better and better!" She laughed in relief.

A generous helping was served on the two plates. Father and daughter drew up the chairs which for so many years had seated the Wragges. They filled their mouths with scrambled eggs and hot buttered toast. The aroma of the bubbling coffee blessed the air.

"If your mother could see us!" exclaimed Renny.

"She'd not believe her own eyes."

"It goes to show," he said, "that conventions are only on the surface."

"Not with Mummy."

"Not with her—God bless her." Then he added with great seriousness, "You have a wonderful mother, Adeline. We should—both of us—appreciate what an effort she made in taking Roma to New York. Particularly at a time like this."

"Oh, I do appreciate it. Still, it's nice for Mummy to get away sometimes—from everything."

"It certainly is." He spoke with a heartiness that suggested the possible benefit to those left behind, of being for a time left to their own devices.

Adeline now produced a basket of large ripe tomatoes and a basket of richly tinted peaches. Each selected the most appealing tomato, sliced it, smothered it in olive oil. It was the same with the peaches. Greedily they chose the biggest and most richly coloured, sliced and smothered them in cream. Adeline produced Mrs Wragge's final achievement, a pan of currant buns. The meal was, in truth, a picnic. Neither did it lack conversation. This was centred on the colt, the difficulties to be faced in his training, the brilliant possibilities of his future. The possibility of failure was never mentioned.

They sat long over the meal, each with an abundant pleasure in the nearness of the other. It was as though they had been long separated and come together again. The dogs, in sudden good manners, awaited docilely till their turn came. The fact that they had been already well fed that day meant nothing to Adeline. Each was given some of the scrambled eggs, a little bread and butter, and a piece of cake. Surfeited, they stretched themselves on the floor to sleep.

With expedition the remaining food was put in the larder. So well had the dogs licked the plates that they needed little scraping. Plenty of hot water, a foaming mass of soapsuds and Adeline's ideal of cleanliness was fulfilled. With a pipe in his mouth, Renny dried the dishes. From outdoors came the sounds of night. The lonely cry of a screech-owl made the kitchen seem all the cosier. The insistent orchestra of locusts spun out these last fragile hours of summer. The smell of cool dew-drenched earth came in at the window, subduing the scents of the kitchen.

The passionate emotions of recent days had taken something from Adeline's strength. She was tired. She sat herself on Renny's knees when he relaxed in Rags' armchair and laid her head on his shoulder.

"Listen to those insects," he said. "Hysterical chatter-chatter. Like a women's club."

"Have you ever been in a women's club, Daddy?"

"Yes, once. I forget where."

"But you like women, don't you?"

"I do indeed."

"I don't."

"Not like women! Think of your mother and Aunty Meg and Patience and Pheasant."

"Think of Roma."

"Put all that behind you, darling."

"I have put it behind me. . . . I thought I never could, but . . . oh, Daddy, you are so sweet to me. . . . There's no one in the world like you. Never, never shall I want to leave you."

He held her close to him. His dark gaze rested on her face, the closed eyes, the parted lips. His heart swelled to think that she was his—restored to him—Fitzturgis gone.

The kitchen clock struck one. Drowsily she opened her eyes. "What time is it?"

"Time you were in your bed." He became suddenly matter-of-fact. "There's plenty to do tomorrow. No—today. Come." He set her on her feet. She yawned. The dogs rose, stretched, yawned, looked expectant. "Bed, you rascals." Renny gave each in turn an encouraging pat.

All climbed the basement stairs. Chill night air was pouring into the house. Renny shut and locked the front door but had not troubled to lock the others. He said, "You'll need an extra quilt tonight. It's turned cool."

"Yes," she agreed. "But I wonder if I shall sleep. Just us two alone. It's never happened before."

The bulldog announced his intention of sleeping on Adeline's bed. "He'll keep you warm," said Renny. He and the other dogs disappeared up the stairs to his room. Soon all were asleep.

A new order of things now set in, or rather a new gipsy-like disorder of things. Things were done or not done, when or how the fancy of these two so congenial spirits decreed.

Meg and Pheasant came with offers to help with the work, but Adeline declared that she needed no help beyond that of the woman who came two days a week from the village to scrub floors and do the washing and ironing. Sometimes Adeline liked to imagine that she and Renny were shipwrecked on an island. But this island was not a desert. It was inhabited by horses, dogs, grooms, and the tenants of Humphrey Bell's flat.

It was a temptation to Clara Chase to join her husband and Mr Crowdy at the stables, along with Renny and Adeline. All five would crowd into the car and drive to the track where the colt was being trained. The new trainer, Kelly, was a small thin man, experienced, non-committal, unsociable. But the colt himself was friendly, self-confident. He had good forelegs made to race, and strong hocks.

As once Clara had put her heart into the breeding of foxes, so now she gave her mind to the activities connected with the showing and racing of horses. Though she was contentedly married to Chase she never could forget her brief but passionate association with Renny. The thought of renewing that relationship or even recalling it to him never entered her mind; and once when in a moment of exhilaration after a promising performance by the colt he caught her hand, looked into her eyes, exclaiming, "There is no one like you, Clara," she had withdrawn her hand and remained at home for two days.

But she could not long remain away. At home there was nothing to do. Jalna was a hive of activity. On every hand there was something to interest one who found country life congenial. Scarcely a day passed when the Whiteoaks did not congratulate themselves on the heartening fact that Jalna was miles away from the beauty-destroying building developments which afflicted much of the countryside.

Here Clara could wander to the apple orchard and see the glowing mounds of ripe fruit, talk with Piers of its storage or shipping. There was a boy trundling a barrow of defective or over-ripe apples toward the piggery! There were the fat healthy pigs munching the apples, their little eyes twinkling with delight, the sweet juice trickling down their throats—never reckoning how soon those throats would be cut. There was a man ploughing a ten-acre field, turning up the rich sandy loam! There were pale-plumaged gulls, come all the way from the lake to walk in the furrows—to pick up the fat worms. There were the turkeys making procession in the aisles of the blackberry canes, devouring the late neglected berries—sweetest of all—gobbling serenely beneath the harebell-blue sky—never noticing the black cloud of Thanksgiving Day ever nearer. There was the meadow where the foals, in empty-headed abandon, kicked up their heels! There was the paddock where Renny, Pheasant and Adeline schooled the show horses. Clara's eyes were held longest by Pheasant, who seemed a part of the cobby little mare she rode, and there, peering between the palings, was Pheasant's small daughter holding in her hand three late buttercups which no one would admire.

"Oh, what lovely flowers!" Clara exclaimed. She had appeared suddenly. To Mary she loomed large and strange.

"May I see?" asked Clara, kneeling to be on the proper level. She took one of the flowers and held it beneath the little girl's chin. "You do!" she cried. "You do like butter."

Mary smiled, pleased with herself, proud to like butter.

"Now see if I like butter." Clara held the flower beneath her own chin.

"You too!" Mary laughed in glee. There was something in this woman that gave the little girl confidence. They marched off, hand in hand.

The centre, the lodestar of these days of early autumn, was the colt East Wind. He stood big, not elegant but full of brawn, in his loose-box. He looked a great overgrown fellow, full of promise, beaming with confidence. Renny would plait his mane, playing with it as though it were the lovelocks of his beloved. He would say to him, "All my hopes are in you, boy. . . . Win for me! Win for me!"

Word came from Alayne that all was going well in New York. She was staying with her friend Rosamund Trent, who had found just the right sort of house for Roma to live in. The girl was already enrolled in a class in a school of designing. She was happier, more responsive than Alayne had ever known her. Alayne herself was well.

The weather in New York was perfect. She had several delightful invitations from old friends. She hoped to see a few of the new plays, but if all were not going smoothly at home she would return by the next train. She would even fly. She was anxious to hear whether any promise of domestic help had come from the agencies.

In reply Renny wrote:

My dearest Alayne,

I am delighted to get such good news from you. What a little wonder you are! You just take things in hand when they seem in a hopeless muddle and set them straight. I can't tell you how glad I am that you are getting some pleasure out of this affair that started off so miserably. It will probably do Roma good to be away from home for a time, and I guess that Meg and Patience are not sorry to be rid of her. Meg is very anxious to rent her house and go to live with Finch. But he is rather a queer bird, as you know, and is in no hurry to furnish rooms for them. Maurice is still staying with him. It is really surprising how Adeline faces up to the housework, and is pretty efficient too. I think it is good for her—helps to take her mind off her disappointment in Fitzturgis. If you meet that gentleman tell him that my opinion of him remains of the lowest.

The colt is shaping up wonderfully and I think you will live to see the day when you will congratulate me on the purchase. Kelly, the trainer, is a very well-behaved fellow and is living with Wright and his wife over the garage. Now, my darling girl, I want you to enjoy yourself with your friends and don't worry about us. Everything is going smoothly. You'd really be surprised. Adeline sends her love with mine and will write.

Yours ever,
Renny.

Adeline did write to Alayne, and Pheasant also, both assuring her that things were going well and that she was not to be anxious.

But something happened which would have caused her acute anxiety had she known of it. She had been absent less than a week when an operation for appendicitis was performed on Archer in a hospital in the town not far from his school. Renny had gone there to be near his son, and Meg had accompanied him. He had a primitive horror and distrust of hospitals. Meg's presence was a comfort to him.

In ten days Archer was sufficiently recovered to return to Jalna for recuperation. He looked little the worse for his ordeal, as he was always without colour, but he had to be put to bed and waited on as an invalid for a time. Here again Meg's comforting presence was a blessing to all. She made custards and junkets for the boy. She did not worry over dirt or disorder. Indeed she had a mischievous pleasure in tolerating conditions which would have been repellent to Alayne. The butter, for instance, which Alayne insisted should be kept in a tightly closed container in the refrigerator, now was often exposed carelessly on a kitchen shelf. Contents of saucepans boiled over on to the stove. The bulldog had long cherished an ambition to gnaw his bone in the middle of the kitchen floor. This Mrs Wragge had forbidden and stiffened her order with a broom-handle. But now Bill brought his enormous knuckle-bone and, with snufflings and grindings, worked his will on it. The spaniel Sport had long been dissatisfied with his bed and now solidly established himself on the sofa in the library, and, as this was his season for shedding his coat, his hairs were everywhere. The little Cairn terrier was in a continual state of excitement. With the acute intelligence of his breed he realized that things were not as they should be, but all his runnings here and there, all his barking, could not set them right.

The weather was perfect and in the stables all went well. East Wind watched with good-humoured interest all the activities of which he was the centre. He was never excited but seemed to know what was expected of him and to be certain he could do it. Though his body was somewhat heavy, he had a beautiful head that rose like a flame from his great shoulders.

When Archer was able to come downstairs Renny and Adeline sat on either side of him reporting with enthusiasm on the colt's progress. He was entered for the most important of the autumn races.

"There's nothing he can't do," cried Adeline. "If I were a man I'd like to ride him myself."

Archer gave her a disparaging look. "Mercy!" he said.

But one evening when he and Renny were alone together he asked, "When is Mummy coming home?"

"Very soon, I expect. But I've told her to stay as long as she is enjoying herself. She is seeing all the new plays. Naturally I haven't told her of your operation. That would have brought her home on the next train. She badly needs a change."

"I am wondering," said Archer, "whether we might have the television put in before she comes. You will remember that I have already paid an instalment on a set. On your birthday I gave you the receipt."

"By Judas, I had forgotten! There's been so much going on. But do you think we need it?"

Archer fixed him with his penetrating blue gaze. "There are discussions on it," he said, "of great educational value. Our headmaster says that so much future education is to be visual that we cannot overestimate its importance. And there are other features besides the educational ones. There is *football* and there are *fights*."

Archer looked touchingly white and weak. He had risen to his feet. Now he put both arms about his father's muscular body and gave it a feeble hug. His lips parted in an expression of peculiar sweetness. It was his nearest approach to a smile.

To hear these last words from the lips of his son gave Renny a real pleasure. After all, the poor little beggar had been through a hard time. He might have died. He returned Archer's hug with almost painful warmth.

"We'll do it," he said. "I'll see about it tomorrow."

A few days later a peculiar sight might have been observed in front of the old house. A truck carrying two men and a number of rods, wiring, tools and a ladder drew up. The men alighted and soon were on the top of the house. Inside and out it took them a good many hours to install the television set. But finally the work was completed and an ornament was added to the roof that would have filled its original owners with wonder. Some new sort of lightning rod, they would have guessed. But never in their most delirious imaginings would they have pictured the fantastic things that were projected on to the screen in the library. Yet their descendant, Archer Whiteoak, watched the grotesque, the inane, the stupidly revolting pictures with no more than a flicker on his pale face. He listened to noises called music which would have caused those same grandparents of his to clap their hands over their ears in horror, and never turned a hair.

As ill-luck would have it, the woman who came from the village to work contracted a serious cold and was not able to come. Adeline found herself with such an accumulation of work on her hands as she could not hope to cope with. She was really tired. She was in a temper. She thought it time that Archer should no longer demand to be waited on as an invalid. With a somewhat grudging efficiency she placed the things for his evening meal on a tray. Her feet were aching from the brick-paved floor and she frowned as she remembered the flight of stairs to be climbed.

Renny now clattered down them, the dogs at his heels,

impatient for their food. A cigarette hung from the corner of his mouth and he wore the happy-go-lucky expression usual to him in these days.

"It's raining," he said. "Like cats and dogs."

"Archer's tray," Adeline said, indicating it with a bandaged thumb. She was always suffering from a cut or burn.

"What's the matter?" he asked solicitously.

"Nothing." She tried to smile.

"I know," he exclaimed. "The work is getting too much for you. I'll carry up this tray."

"It was all right till Archer came."

"I have an idea." Balancing Archer's tray on his palm, he said with enthusiasm, "Crowdy and the Chases are taking shelter in the porch. I'll ask Mrs Chase to give you a hand with the work. She'd be delighted, I know."

"No. I can manage."

But Adeline liked Clara Chase, and when she appeared, descending the stairs into the kitchen, she welcomed her with a smile. It was a marvel to Adeline to see how order rose out of confusion, what good-humoured efficiency could bring to pass in a kitchen.

It was not long before the three men appeared, each eager to help with the work. From the larder Renny produced lamb chops. Chase rolled up his sleeves and prepared the vegetables. Mr Crowdy, who had a delicate wife, turned out to be an expert chef. Not only did he broil the chops to a turn but made a delicious chocolate soufflé for a sweet and concocted a perfect salad. The dogs, in order to avoid being stepped on, took refuge on the stairway. Before long Archer appeared and seated himself on a step near the top, looking on the activities below with the air of a scientist observing the habits of insects. Mr Crowdy, after a long admiring look at him, drew Renny into the pantry and remarked portentously, "A noble scion of a noble house."

"A clever boy," said Renny, "and better on a horse than you'd expect by the looks of him."

"He'll go far," prophesied Mr Crowdy. He made a comic figure, with his crimson face rising above one of Mrs Wragge's aprons tied beneath his several chins.

Chase, whipping up mashed potatoes with cream, announced that they were ready and that he was starving. Clara Chase offered each of the dogs a dog biscuit. The bulldog turned up his nose still farther and walked away. The spaniel, with a reproachful look, accepted his, but soon hid it in the coal cellar. The polite little Cairn nibbled his, then put out what he had nibbled on to the floor. All three trooped upstairs with the dinner and ranged themselves about Renny's chair.

Shortly before this, Finch and Maurice had appeared on the scene. They had disclaimed any intention of sharing the meal, but when more chops were produced, when they beheld what Mr Crowdy had concocted, when Renny brought out some bottles of excellent hock, they were easily persuaded. He was, in truth, in his element. Outdoors it was wet and cold. Indoors it was brightly lighted and warm. At the table sat eight congenial spirits, for at this moment even Archer was congenial. The talk was of horses.

Clara Chase hesitated to sit down at that table where she was not invited when the mistress of the house was at home, but Adeline would hear of no denial. She liked Clara more and more. It appeared to require no effort on Clara's part to understand both Renny and his daughter. To her they seemed admirable, generous-hearted and lovable. She wished that Adeline might have been her own daughter. Looking at Archer, she felt both protective and humble—protective because of his pale looks, humble because of his coldly intellectual mien. She did not guess that there was some quality in her that made Archer (because he was newly convalescent) want to put his head on her shoulder and brought the whine of childhood into his voice when he addressed her.

Adeline, seated at the end of the table facing Renny, looked askance at her brother. "You've had your tray," she muttered. "Aren't you satisfied?"

"I've been starved too long," said Archer.

"Good man," exclaimed Renny and put a lamb chop on the invalid's plate. "That," he said, "will put strength into you."

The meal progressed, and always the talk was of horses. Even Maurice, who had never very much liked them, joined in the talk and made the most of what he knew about Irish horses. He was in agreement with everything Adeline said. His admiration, his love for her, shone from him. His eyes, whenever they met hers, sought to hold them. Soon he was to return to Ireland. If only he might return with hope in his heart?

"Never have I loved any horse," Renny was saying, "as I

loved my mare Cora. She was as intelligent as she was beautiful."

"The first time I ever saw you," said Chase, "you were riding her at the Horse Show. I thought I had never seen man and horse in such accord. It was a symphony for the eye."

"I was there," said Crowdy, "and never saw a better performance." He went on to tell, somewhat incoherently, of some of his experiences at shows. Usually a rather silent man, he was tonight inspired to talk.

"My favourite," said Adeline, "is Spartan. Wright and I are partners in him. We got him in exchange for an organ that had been my great-aunt's *and* the hundred dollars Wright put in. He's won lots of prizes."

"I know him," said Crowdy. "A fine bold horse."

Clara Chase put in, "It's this racer that excites me. He's magnificent. I can't get him out of my head."

"He'll win," said Crowdy. "He is born to win—you can see it in the set of his head. And what a chest and what legs! You'll never be sorry you bought him."

"I hope not," said Renny, suddenly serious, thinking of his wife.

When they had drunk their coffee Adeline was for leaving the dishes till the morning, but Clara Chase would not hear of that. Her husband, Finch and Maurice cleared the table, carried the dishes down to the kitchen. She washed and Adeline dried them. The kitchen was left in not too great disorder. The dogs, replete, lay stretched asleep.

The rain had long ceased when the Chases and Mr Crowdy took their leave. Renny, Finch and Archer were still watching the television screen. Maurice followed Adeline into her bedroom, that room across the hall from the dining room that had been her great-grandmother's.

"I'm going to bed," she said inhospitably.

"You must be tired." His voice was warm with sympathy.

"Between riding and housework I've a right to be." She began vigorously to brush her hair, which, catching the light, swept in ruddy waves about her temples.

"I know you look on me as hopelessly lazy and quite worthless," he said.

"Lazy certainly. Worthless—well, that's nonsense."

He came close to her and looked in the mirror at their reflections. "If only you could love me a little, Adeline."

She tilted her head towards his. "Don't we make a pretty picture?" she asked.

He needed no more encouragement than that. His arms were about her. He said, "No one but you can save me. I'll stop drinking tomorrow—if only you'll say you care for me."

"And if I don't?"

"Then—there is nothing to stop me."

She drew herself away and faced him. "Mooey," she said, "you ought to be ashamed of yourself. We all love you. All the family. You own a fine place in Ireland. You have so much to be good for."

"I know. But it's you I want and always have wanted. You know that, Adeline. I've been faithful, haven't I?"

"This is a bad time," she said, almost fiercely, "to talk to me of love."

"There never is a right time with you," he said bitterly.

"If I thought——" Her eyes glowed in her earnestness.

"Yes—yes?"

"If I thought you'd go back to Ireland and drink yourself into the grave I'd be absolutely sick with you."

"And you'd not try to help me?"

"What I say is—help yourself! Give up drinking for the rest of your visit here. Show what will-power you have."

"Adeline"—he could not keep his voice steady, he was so eager—"if I do that—will you promise——"

"I promise nothing—except—well, I should think of you in a very different way."

"That's all I ask—just that you should think of me in a different way. . . . You never have thought of me as I really am, you know."

"Nobody thinks of anybody as they really are, I guess."

"I agree," he said. "On my part I idealize you—while you think of me as worse than I really am."

"That's right," she cried. "Pity yourself!"

"I am to be pitied," he said seriously.

That somehow touched her. She smiled at him in the glass. "You old silly," she said. "I do like you."

"Adeline, I'll do anything for you."

She was moved by a sudden feeling of her power for good. "Do this for me then. Promise to give up drinking. I mean a real solemn promise."

"I will." He was all eagerness to show his devotion, his

strength. "I promise. You'll see that I won't fail. I do love you so, darling."

She did not want to hear that word. No love for her. She took up the scissors from the dressing-table. "This hair of mine grows like all possessed." She snipped off a lock from behind her ear.

"No, no," begged Maurice. "Please."

"It's too long."

"So is mine."

"You're picturesque, Mooey. You can't help it. You just are."

"Let's exchange locks of hair—the way they used to do in the old days." He captured her ruddy lock and placed it in a notebook in his pocket. "We'll seal our promise, shall we?"

He bent his head to the scissors. Adeline had just severed a dark lock when Finch appeared in the doorway.

"Don't let me interrupt," he said, giving them a look of amused curiosity. "Playing at barber-shop?"

"No," returned Adeline with composure. "Just tidying up for tomorrow. It's Sunday. When I've finished this I must go and put Archer to bed."

Shortly afterward Finch and Maurice left.

In New York Roma had had a letter from Meg telling her of Archer's operation. Meg had neglected to warn her that this news should be kept secret. That very evening Roma, usually most uncommunicative of beings, had dinner with Alayne and Rosamund Trent. Casting about in her mind for some subject of conversation she casually remarked that Archer had had his appendix out. The next day Alayne took a plane for Canada. She had a feeling that something very frightening was being kept from her. She was determined to know the worst at once, and she had a morbid desire to take Renny by surprise, in retaliation. Before leaving Jalna she had made him promise to let her know if anything went wrong. And this was how he had kept his promise!

She had come from the airport in a taxicab. Now it stopped outside the door. The driver carried her luggage into the porch. She paid him and he drove off. Those inside the house could not hear her approach because of a noise of cheering. Obviously this came from the radio. Alayne had a feeling of deep relief. Her boy could not be so ill as she had feared.

The sound of the radio came from the library. Alayne left

the porch and went to the french window and looked in. She kept in the shelter of the leaves that the light from within might not fall on her face and discover her to those in the room.

She need not have feared. The library had but two occupants and their backs were turned to the window. The room was dimly lighted; still, she could make out the figures of Renny and Archer. They sat close beside each other. Renny's arm lay affectionately across the back of Archer's chair. The attention of both was riveted on a brightly lighted television screen. The screen was also clearly visible to Alayne. She did not know what she had expected to see there. Certainly not the two heaving masses of muscle that twisted and writhed in apparent agony. As for the bloodthirsty yells of the spectators, when the bout now neared its climax, they froze Alayne's blood. She stood petrified in loathing.

Now the wrestlers writhed locked together. One was apparently about to gouge out the eye of the other, who at the same time was twisting his ear. The referee tried to separate them. There was a hideous upheaval. Then one was hurled through the ropes while the gross victor twisted his swollen features into a grin at the wild cheering.

Alayne heard herself give a little moan of dismay. She had been prepared to find Archer weak, in bed, suffering. But to find him sitting by his father's side—both of them obviously enthralled by that disgusting spectacle on the screen!

Two minutes later she stood in the doorway of the library facing them. They stared at her a space in silence, scarcely believing the evidence of their eyes. Then Renny turned off the television and a stunning silence fell, broken by Archer's exclamation of—"Mercy!" The rare colour flooded his face.

Then Renny got out, "Why, Alayne, what a lovely surprise!"

"Yes—a surprise," she repeated. "A great surprise."

The three stood staring at each other. The rain was now beating on the windows. Wind was rocking the trees. Somewhere in the distance equinoctial gales were gathering themselves together for attack.

"I had heard," said Alayne, "that Archer was very ill."

The sound of her voice woke Sport, the spaniel. He bundled himself off the sofa and, giving her a deprecating grin as he passed, went into the hall.

"I *was* ill," said Archer. "I had an operation. I'm still weak. Father persuaded me to come down and have a look at his TV."

Alayne gave them both a cold look. She went into the hall, from there to the porch, and began to pull her luggage about. Renny followed her. "You mustn't be out here," he said. "I'll carry your bags upstairs."

She leant, as though in despair, against one of the pillars of the porch. "I had better not have come home." Her voice trembled.

He looked at her, ready for a quarrel.

"I'd like to know why," he demanded.

"Neither you nor Archer needs me—not with that thing in the house."

"It's done him good. Taken his mind off himself."

"What has it given him?" she cried. "A disgusting exhibition of brute strength. He looks terrible."

"Nonsense. He's looking better every day. Who told you he'd been ill?"

"Meg wrote to Roma. You had promised me—promised me faithfully—to let me know if anything went wrong."

"I wanted you to enjoy yourself."

"Enjoy myself! While my child was undergoing a critical operation."

"It was not critical. He was not at any time in danger."

"You had promised! But I might have known. . . ."

"Well, I like that! Are you implying that a promise from me means nothing?"

"I think it is subject to your convenience."

"Well, you always have been inclined to think the worst of me." He loaded himself with her bags and mounted the stairs with them, she following.

Archer, who had been listening just inside the door, now with great agility darted into the library. When he heard his parents moving about in the room above he slowly went up to his own. Adeline was there, turning down his bed.

"Have you seen Mummy?" he asked.

"Just for a moment. Hurry up and hop in." She wore her dressing-gown and looked tired.

"You've forgotten my Ovaltine," he said. He had worn flannel trousers and jacket over his pyjamas. He now cast them on to the floor and got into bed.

"I had not forgotten it." She produced a Thermos bottle and poured him a glass of the hot drink. She asked, "What did Mummy say about the TV set?"

"She didn't understand. There was a wrestling match on."

"No wonder she didn't understand. They're horrible."

"Adeline."

"Well?"

"My feet are cold. Could I have the hot-water bottle?" She hurled herself on the bed, at his feet. "I'm half dead," she said. "I simply can't go down to the kitchen again. Warm your feet on me."

He sat up enjoying his Ovaltine. He snuggled his feet against her.

"I've been thinking about Mummy," he said. "She'll likely be hungry after the trip. Tell her to come up and see me."

"Oh Lord, I'd forgotten!" Adeline, dazed by weariness, rolled to her feet. She went down the stairs holding to the banister. Outside Alayne's door she called. "Mummy, I'm going to bring you something to eat. What would you like?"

Alayne opened the door. She did not look at all tired, Adeline thought—just flushed and wrought-up. Renny was not there.

In a restrained voice Alayne answered, "I should very much like a cup of coffee and a little thin bread and butter and a small salad and possibly a little cold meat, if you have any that's nice and tender. I was too much upset to eat anything on the plane. Do you mind? I don't want to be a trouble, dear." As Adeline left her Alayne could not help thinking what an ungracious manner the girl had—not sullen, just preoccupied and ungracious.

As Adeline passed the door of the library she saw Dennis, who was home for the mid-term weekend, sitting there, in his pyjamas, in front of the TV screen. The spaniel was once again on the sofa. She was roused from her weariness to exclaim, "Well, I'll be darned! Who said you might be up at this hour?"

"I couldn't sleep," he said. "I'm subject to insomnia, like my father."

"I wish I were." She yawned, her eyes watered.

Down in the pantry she doggedly assembled the things for Alayne's tray. . . . It looked quite appetizing, she thought, when it was ready. While she waited for the kettle to boil she sat down by the table and laid her head on her arm. Half an hour later Alayne found her there, the kettle burnt to a crisp. The air in the kitchen was blue with smoke.

Alayne's nerves were at breaking point, and she let it be known that they were. Adeline woke and burst into tears. The Cairn terrier stood on the stairway steadily barking. All three felt themselves to be victims of the most dire set of circumstances imaginable.

In the midst of this scene Renny came into the kitchen from the stable where he had been summoned by Wright. He wore a rubber cape dripping with rain.

"What the dickens is the matter?" he demanded.

"This house!" said Alayne. "Whichever way I turn—sick children—burning kettles—barking dogs! Never shall I go away again."

"Stop your crying," Renny said to Adeline, "and come and see the lovely little foal that's just arrived."

"Are you aware of the hour?" Alayne was at white heat. "It is a quarter to twelve! You cannot ask this child to go to the stables at such an hour."

He ignored this. He was examining the bottom of the tea-kettle. "A pretty mess. And I'm wanting to make a warm mash for the mare. Is there no other kettle?"

Adeline sprang up as though she never had so much as heard of weariness. She extracted a large saucepan from a cupboard and offered it to him. "I'm not tired, Mummy," she said. "I want to go." Eagerly she put water to boil.

"Go then," said Alayne. "I can't control anything or anybody in this house."

"Poor little woman." Renny patted her absently on the back.

"Don't touch me," she cried. "Can no one stop that dog barking?"

Archer now appeared on the stairs. The little Cairn ran to welcome him extravagantly. Archer said, "My feet have been cold for ages. Adeline said she would bring the hot-water bottle."

"There's a lovely little foal just arrived," Renny told him.

"Good." Archer came on down into the kitchen. Alayne with anguish observed his delicate looks.

"Who is the tray for?" asked Archer.

"It's for Mummy," said Adeline. "I'll carry it up to the dining room," she promised Alayne, "as soon as the coffee is made."

Dennis now descended the stairs.

"My feet are cold," repeated Archer.

"I don't see how they can be as cold as mine," said Dennis, "for mine are freezing."

"Your feet are bare," said Alayne, noticing his beautifully shaped small feet. "Have you no bedroom slippers?"

"The dogs took them." He stood on the brick floor curling up his toes.

The water boiled. The coffee was made. Adeline mounted the stairs with the heavy tray. Alayne followed supporting Archer. Dennis came last, carrying the terrier.

"May I have something to eat from your tray, Aunty Alayne?" he asked. "I'm hungry and my feet are cold."

"You may indeed. There is twice what I could eat." She led Archer to the library and tucked him up on the sofa, beneath the 'afghan' which for many years had comforted Nicholas's knees. She yearned over her boy, painfully considering how he had deteriorated both physically and mentally during her absence.

Adeline had returned to the kitchen and now reappeared with a hot-water bottle, which she placed at Archer's feet. Alayne brought him a cup of coffee. This was something like comfort, he thought, and he almost smiled.

"Is there anything else I can do, Mummy?" Adeline asked with a benign look.

"My feet are freezing," said Dennis.

She swept him on to the foot of the sofa and drew the afghan over him. "Put your feet on the bottle too," she advised. He caught her hand and held it against his cheek. He was too clinging, she thought, and detached herself. She went out through the side door from the hall and ran into the rain toward the stables. Bright lights were burning there. Renny met her and took her to where the new-born foal lay in clean straw in a loose-box.

In the library the music of Mozart was being played by an orchestra seen on the screen. Alayne, hungrily eating a chicken sandwich, drinking coffee, looked into the faces of the two young boys. How innocent, how beautiful they were as they listened. When the piece came to its lovely ending she asked, "Do you like Mozart?"

Swallowing the last bite of his sandwich, Dennis answered, "Yes, because he was a great composer and my father is a great pianist."

"But not for the way the music makes you feel?"

"Oh yes, for that too. It makes me feel happy."
"And you, Archer?"
"Everything is OK," he said, "now that you are home."

20

HUMPHREY BELL AND PATIENCE

HUMPHREY BELL walked twice round the house, looked at it appraisingly from several angles, as though he were a prospective purchaser. What he was in reality doing was simply trying to make up his mind to go to the front door and knock on it. While he was standing irresolute the door opened and Finch came out. When he saw Bell he came straight to him, smiling.

"Hullo," he said, "I didn't hear you knock."

"I didn't knock very loudly. In fact, I'm not at all sure that I did knock. I was passing and I thought I'd just drop in, and if you were about . . ."

"I'm always about. I'm so full of conceit about this little house that I can't tear myself away from it. Come in, and I'll show you over it." As they went into the house he caught Bell by the arm in brotherly fashion. "Isn't this Indian Summer weather fine? It makes you forget how horrible our climate can be."

"I rather like weather—of all sorts," said Bell.

"I think too much about it, I know. When I'm on tour I play well or badly according to the weather."

"I don't believe that. That time you played in New Brunswick the weather was filthy, yet you played magnificently."

"Ah, that was the night I suggested your coming here. I've often wondered whether it's turned out well for you."

"Well—absolutely. I don't want to be anywhere else. I'm happy—that is, I should be—if——"

"I know, I know," said Finch absently. "Now I'd like to show you my little modern kitchen. I've more gadgets. . . ." With concentrated interest he demonstrated their efficiency. He led the way through the other rooms. "This room," he said, "has been occupied by my nephew Maurice. He left yesterday. He is to be at home for a bit before returning to Ireland."

"I admire him," said Bell. "He seems to me the most enviable chap I've ever met. He has good looks—of a kind you don't often see—he has a unique sort of position—independent means—a romantic old place in Ireland—a congenial family—and—the most charming manners. He has everything. Does he perhaps drink a little too much?"

"He did drink, like a fish. But he's much better. It's amazing how he has changed."

Finch insisted on Bell's staying to lunch with him. The Finnish maid was an excellent cook. As they were drinking coffee Finch said, "Now tell me about yourself. How goes your work?"

A look of sensitive withdrawal quivered on Bell's small face. For a moment it seemed as though he could not bring himself to answer, then he got out, "Not too badly. I've written a novel."

"A novel," Finch shouted. "Well, this is news. And it's finished, you say?"

"Yes. It's finished. To tell the truth"—he looked almost shamefaced—"it's been accepted by a publisher."

"Have you been working on it long? When is it to be published?"

"For over a year. . . . Next spring."

"I'm delighted," said Finch. He spoke truthfully. To know that something had been created was wonderful to him. He felt that Humphrey Bell had an elusive and subtle mind. He had read some of his short stories and liked them. But Bell was so shy that he hesitated to ask questions.

Without being asked, Bell said, "It's the story of a man who wanted to be good and do good but unfortunately he had a nature that brought out the evil in other people."

"It sounds rather grim."

"It *is* grim," said Bell tranquilly.

Finch brought out a decanter of French liqueur. They drank to the success of the novel. It was plain that Bell had something on his mind, and after some desultory talk and several long silences he brought himself to speak of it.

"I suppose a girl could hardly do worse for herself," he said, "than by marrying a man who had written his first novel."

"A good deal depends on the novel—and the man."

"I know. And the novel probably wouldn't be a success

and the man wouldn't be of any use for any other life. Talk of marriage as a lottery. . . ."

It was difficult for Bell in his extreme fairness to express black gloom, but he made a certain appearance of it.

"Money isn't terribly important where there's love and understanding." Finch was sure that Bell needed encouragement, was really asking for it, yet he had a desire to protect him, so he added, "However, women are sometimes very different. . . after marriage."

"This one couldn't be," Bell broke out. "She'd always be the same. Generous—warm-hearted—magnanimous."

Finch looked at him enquiringly.

"It's Patience Vaughan I'm thinking of," said Bell in a low voice. "She's never out of my thoughts."

"Patience! Well, I am surprised."

"I don't wonder. You are surprised that I should have the nerve."

"Not at all. I'm surprised because I hadn't known you were going about together—spending much time together."

"We haven't. But—what time we have spent together—I can't tell you how precious it's been to me. I"—the colour rose in his small face—"think she likes me."

"You know of her engagement to young Green?"

"Yes—I hated that fellow," said Bell mildly. "My opinion of myself is not high, but I do feel that I am a better man than he. If I had Patience by my side I might make a success of my life." He jumped up and stood facing Finch in sudden excitement. "You know, my publisher thinks well of my novel. He's placed it with a publishing house in the States. . . . I came to you because I want to ask you if you honestly think I have a right to let Patience know I love her."

"I think you are quite justified, Humphrey, and I wish you all the luck in the world. It would be fun having you for a nephew."

Bell left, striding purposefully to seek out his beloved. An hour later he returned, leading Patience by the hand. His silvery fair hair was standing on end, his harebell-blue eyes were dancing in triumph.

"I did it," he cried. "I did it and she said yes! What do you think of that?"

Patience added, in her soft contralto voice, "It was the strangest proposal you can imagine. He came up to me where

I was plaiting a pony's forelock and he said, right out of the blue, 'I guess you could hardly do worse for yourself than to marry me.'"

"Wonderful!" cried Finch. "No need to ask what you said."

"May I tell him?" Bell delightedly asked of Patience.

"Go ahead," she said, still holding his hand.

"She said, 'The worst with you would be better than the best with any other man.'"

"I had to get him out of his inferiority complex," said Patience.

Finch was genuinely happy for them. The three sat talking over plans for the future. Patience soon made it clear that she did not want a long engagement. They would get rid of the Chases, prepare the small house for their own occupation, get married and move in.

"So, after all," she said, "I shall not be coming to live with you, Uncle Finch. There'll just be Mummy. She is so looking forward to coming here. When do you think you will be ready for her?"

"Quite soon," he answered easily, then added in a somewhat lugubrious tone, "It'll be fun."

The telephone rang. When Finch answered it, Piers's voice demanded, "Is Patience there?"

"Yes."

"Well, I'd like to know why she doesn't come to feed the sick calf."

"Listen, Piers—the girl has just got engaged."

"Again! Well, I'll be damned! To whom?"

"To Humphrey Bell."

"That lily-livered bird!"

"He is a particularly nice fellow. For my part, I'm very well pleased."

"This calf"—Piers spoke emphatically—"is a valuable one. It's sick. It won't take its food from anyone but Patience. It loves her."

"So does Bell and not with calf-love."

"Send her to the phone."

Obediently Finch returned to the engaged pair. They were holding hands. An aura of bliss surrounded them.

But when Patience, in deep concern for the calf, had run off, Bell turned to Finch and said, "You know, I don't think this should be allowed to go on. This engagement, I mean."

"B-but, Humphrey," stammered Finch, "you—both of you looked so happy. I thought——"

"So did I."

"Then what's happened?"

"Nothing. Nothing new. But—I can't help thinking. Well, a novelist—a story-writer—what's he got to offer a girl? Besides—look at me! Why, I'm almost an albino! If only I might have looked like your brother, Wakefield! Tall and dark, and what a profile, and what eyes!"

"Look here, Humphrey, I'm willing to bet that if Patience had the power she wouldn't alter one feature of you, least of all your creative ability. She's very proud of you as an artist."

Reassured, in spite of himself, Humphrey Bell departed, the felicity of the day almost overpowering him.

Left alone, Finch sat for a while at the piano playing a little secret air that might have sounded meaningless to a listener but to Finch was full of a subtle significance. Over and over he played it, till at last it merged into the whisper of the leaves, the song of the locusts that came through the open window.

Then he rose and went outdoors. He stood enjoying the sight of his little ivory-coloured house set so elegantly against the vivid hues of the autumn foliage. It suited him perfectly. He revelled in the delicious monotony of his days. In the fall of the year he usually faced a long series of concert engagements, but this year he was free. He was his own man.

He went through the gate at the end of his vegetable garden and into the grounds of Jalna. He passed the two bungalows, built by the former owner of his house, which were occupied by the families of men who worked in the Jalna stables. He passed the stables. He followed the path through the orchards, stopping long enough to put a ruddy apple into each of his jacket pockets. He crossed the fields, where a mist of Michaelmas daisies surrendered to the bright blaze of goldenrod and black-eyed Susan. A flock of tiny birds were twittering the forecast of their southward flight. He climbed the gate on the side road where the church was, and there, coming out of the church, was the very man he wanted to see—the Rector, Mr Fennel.

Mr Fennel always looked the same—solid, benign, as much a part of the church as its steeple. He had talents which might well have advanced him to a position of some importance, but he was quite without ambition and found all the excitement his nature craved in this backwater. He had been a widower for two years.

"Good afternoon, Finch," he called out genially. "What wonderful weather after all the rain! Are you going anywhere in particular or would you like to come and take tea with me?"

"There is nothing I'd like so well," said Finch.

"Of course, you have heard the news," said Mr Fennel.

"I have, and very pleased I am. Humphrey needs a wife like Patience to bring him out."

"A dear sweet girl," said Mr Fennel.

"She ought to be, with the mother she has."

"What a woman!" Mr Fennel's face glowed. "What a tower of strength she has been to me through the years! Never too busy to help with the church work. Always able to enlist the help of even the most tepid members of the congregation. She has a wonderful talent for getting the best out of people."

Mr Fennel opened the low gate that Finch had so often swung on as a small boy, and they passed into the garden of the Rectory.

"I suppose it means a great deal," said Finch, "for a man in your position to have the right sort of wife."

"It does indeed." Mr Fennel drew a deep sigh. "I sorely miss my own dear wife."

In the comfortable dining room the Rector's housekeeper had high tea awaiting him: thick bread and butter, two poached eggs, a cottage cheese, maple syrup and a johnny-cake, crisp-crusted and hot from the oven. Certainly the man appeared to be well looked after.

"You must have these eggs," said Mr Fennel. "And my housekeeper will do others for me."

"I couldn't possibly. I've promised to go to Jalna for dinner. But I'd like some johnny-cake. It's ages since I have tasted it." He took a square of it and drowned it in maple syrup.

Over the second cup of tea Finch remarked, "Perhaps you may marry again some time, sir."

"Never, never." The Rector spoke in fervent denial; a little later he leaned back in his chair and gave Finch an almost coy look. "I'm too old," he said. "Don't you think I'm too old?"

Finch stared his denial of this. "Too old? Not at all. In fact, if you are getting on a bit there's all the more reason.

A wife—of the right sort—would be of enormous help to you. In your work. In companionship."

"I have lived like this," said the Rector, "for two years and three months."

"Indeed, so you have." Finch's expressive eyes gave him a look of tender pity. He repeated, "Two years and three months."

It was a long while since the Rector had felt so sorry for himself.

"There's nothing so comforting as a sweet wife in one's house," said Finch.

"And you are a widower yourself." Mr Fennel beamed in sympathy. He quite forgot that Finch had been divorced for some time before his wife's death. "Ah, my boy, you should marry again."

"Set me the good example," laughed Finch.

"It's a new thought to me. A quite staggering thought. But I acknowledge that I sometimes do feel lonely."

"That's bad for you. Very bad. It's bad for anyone." Finch had become deeply serious. "The one I feel sorriest for," he went on, "is Meg. Often I find her quite depressed from loneliness. She's such a dear—not at all given to self-pity, but it will be still lonelier for her."

"But she tells me she is to live with you."

"That's true. She is—but——" Now Finch looked downcast indeed. "I'm afraid that's not going to make things much happier for her. Between you and me I'm not easy to get on with. Artistic temperament, you know. Up in the clouds or down in the depths. And sometimes I'm irritable, I know. I try to control it, but I'm not able to. Sometimes I play the piano for five hours a day. Sometimes it's modern music, with the loud pedal down. Do you like modern music?"

"I loathe it," said Mr Fennel.

"So does Meggie."

"Hmph. It doesn't sound very pleasant for your sister."

"Well," said Finch, "I'm perhaps picturing myself worse than I am. And Meg is so sweet-tempered, we are bound to get on."

"I've always greatly admired her."

"And she you."

At this Mr Fennel appeared lost in thought.

On the way home Finch's spirits were strangely exhilarated.

He threw back his head and took deep breaths of the autumn-scented air. He did not trouble to open the five-barred gate but vaulted over it. He picked a little flower and put it in his buttonhole. When he reached home he sat down at the piano and played the same mysterious little tune which he had invented earlier in the day.

21

WEDDING BELLS AND PLIGHTED TROTH

A FORTNIGHT LATER, when the family were collected at Jalna for Sunday lunch, Meg took up a position of importance in the wing chair in which her grandmother had always sat. She had herself ranged the other chairs in such a position that they appeared to be set for an audience. The first large fire of the season blazed on the hearth. Meg wore an attractive black and white dress and had had her hair done at the hairdresser's.

Renny gave her an admiring look from where he sat, with his coffee-cup in his hand. "You look nice," he said, "very nice indeed. Is that a new dress?"

"It is, and the first new dress I've bought in ages."

"It's very becoming. You look ten years younger in it. Don't you think so, Alayne?"

"I do indeed. There's something very enlivening in a new dress."

Somehow the adjective did not quite please Meg. She remarked, "Then you should be continually enlivened. You get so many."

"Me?" cried Alayne. "No woman could buy fewer clothes than I and look respectable."

"What about me?" exclaimed Pheasant. "I have had only one new dress in a year. The one Maurice bought me."

"You wear slacks and riding breeches so much of the time," said Alayne. "And look so well in them."

Meg now waved this discussion aside with a gesture of her plump hand. "I set out," she said, "to decide what sort of wedding Patience is to have."

But Renny had sprung up, caught her hand in his and was examining it. "Where is your wedding ring?" he demanded.

"That?" she murmured absently. "I'll explain later.

First I think we should decide about Patience's wedding—whether it is to be formal or small and just the family."

"I should think Patience is the one to decide that," said Christian.

"Patience," said that girl's mother, "will be glad to do what we decide on."

"The quieter the better so far as I am concerned," said Patience.

"I don't agree," said Renny. "I think we should make a splash of it. You are the first girl of the family to marry."

"With Adeline it would be different," said Meg. "Adcline is the only daughter of the eldest son. If Adeline's bridegroom had been the one we expected him to be"—tactfully she omitted mentioning Fitzturgis's name— "he was a man whose appearance would well become a formal ceremony; but Humphrey—though he is a nice-looking young man and I like him immensely, and even though blondness is so fashionable—he has an appearance which, it seems to me, goes better with a quiet ceremony. Patience and I will be glad to know what you all think."

"Certainly a quiet wedding would save money," said Piers, with a wink at Finch.

"Money is no object," said Meg, looking noble.

"Money no object!" Piers roared with laughter.

Meg gave him a look of sorrow rather than anger. "How you spoil things, Piers, by your strange insinuations! Everybody knows that I would gladly spend my last dollar to give my daughter a showy wedding if she wanted it."

"These ostentatious modern weddings," said Alayne, "seem to me in rather bad taste when the young couple are probably going to creep into a couple of rooms and eat out of tins."

"I think," said Finch, "that as Patience wants a quiet wedding she should have one, but I should like to see her in a pretty wedding dress and veil."

"I agree," said Mauricc, and other assenting voices were added to his.

"Shall we call it settled then?" asked Meg. "Still," she hesitated, "is it not possible that Patience, being a largish girl, would, in bridal array, rather overshadow Humphrey?"

" 'A man's a man for a' that,' " said Renny.

"What will Humphrey wear?" asked Archer.

"He'll hire a morning suit," said Patience.

"And shall you hire your outfit?"

"No. Mine must be bought."

"And you'll have it on your hands for the rest of your days?"

"Yes."

"Mercy!" said Archer.

"I," said Renny, "shall buy the wedding dress and give the wedding reception here at Jalna."

Alayne tried to smile happily at this. Piers, with laughter in his eyes, was watching her.

Meg rose, went to Renny and kissed him on the forehead. "Thank you, dear brother," she said, then turned to Patience. "Thank Uncle Renny, dear. Give him a big hug and kiss."

Feeling like a five-year-old, Patience obediently bent over Renny. He reached out and took her on his knee. They kissed. "A long time," he said, "since I have dandled Patience. And what a solid girl! Lord, I'll bet you weigh more than Humphrey."

Meg beamed on the two of them. "Now," she said, "I have something startling to tell you, so hold yourselves ready for a surprise."

All faces were turned toward her. She blushed in true Victorian fashion. "It's about the Rector and me. We're going . . . we've decided . . . oh, really I can't tell you. . . . Can't you guess?"

Either they could not or would not. "Out with it," Renny ordered her. "We can't endure this suspense."

"Mr Fennel and I are going to marry."

If Meg had wanted to create a sensation she had her wish.

"I'm delighted," said Alayne. "I think it's a splendid idea." She also had a smile of congratulation for Finch.

"Splendid," said Piers. "Which of you thought of it first?"

"I'm sure you'll be very happy," from Pheasant.

"You're a perfect wife for a clergyman," added Finch. He went to her and hugged her, thinking what a success he would have been in the diplomatic service.

The younger members of the family were astonished and a little embarrassed by this venture into the realm of love and marriage which they considered their own.

Renny, one arm encircling Patience, held out the other to Meg. "Come and sit on my other knee," he said. "I dote on you both."

Meg came at once and plumped herself on his other knee. He clasped and kissed her, but after a few moments of this double weight he pushed them from him, exclaiming:

"Poor little Humphrey! Poor old Fennel! Upon my word, they'll need all their strength."

"There's nothing so nice"—Piers showed his white teeth, laughing—"as a little light wife to sit on a fellow's knee when he has only one leg."

"I have a little light wife," said Renny, stretching out a yearning hand toward Alayne. "A lively little light wife."

Alayne gave him a repressive look. Whereupon with dignity he remarked that the health of the prospective brides must be drunk. "Archer," he told his son, "go to the dining room and bring the tallest decanter—the one with the chipped stopper—and enough glasses for everyone. This is a great occasion." Archer went.

"What about your house, Meg?" asked Piers.

She gave a complacent sigh. "It all works out so beautifully. Humphrey and Patience will want his house for themselves. The Chases are going to rent my house furnished. I, of course, will move into the Rectory."

"Splendid," exclaimed Renny. "I'll wager that the dear old Rector is happy. It will seem funny, Meg, to see you with a husband wearing a beard."

"Why does Mr Fennel wear a beard?" asked Adeline.

"As a very young man he went to the far north as a missionary," answered Meg, "and grew it to protect his throat. Ever since he has clung to it."

"A strange thing to cling to," observed Christian.

"I don't agree," said Pheasant. "I think that clinging to a beard is quite understandable."

"I'll grow one," declared Piers.

Meg folded her arms and looked as firm as she was able, considering the soft contours of her face. "I have told Rupert that I cannot marry a man with a beard."

Everyone looked astonished. Piers asked, "What is he going to do about it?"

"He is going to cut it off."

She spoke so calmly, yet there was almost consternation in the room.

"I thought the man had more character," said Piers sadly.

"He fondled it in church with a pensive air," observed Finch.

"It shows," said Renny, "how badly he wants her when he will sacrifice his beard."

"I wonder," said Pheasant, "how Mr Fennel came to be named Rupert—it's a lovely name."

Meg beamed. "His father was a missionary in Prince Rupert's Land. It was named after Prince Rupert, and the parents liked the name so well they gave it to their son."

Archer now returned with the decanter of sherry and the glasses on a large silver tray.

"Archie," said his father, "come and congratulate your Aunty Meg."

"Mercy!" said Archer. He went and shook hands with Meg, who drew him into her arms and gave him a tender kiss.

At this time Humphrey Bell arrived for lunch. Glasses were filled and a health drunk to the prospective brides and bridegroom. The family circle opened to admit Bell, and shyly he took his place in it. He looked singularly happy. Yet when the lively meal was over he drew Patience aside into the library and said:

"There's still time for you to get out of this engagement, Patience dear, if you want to."

"Do you want to get out of it, Humphrey?"

"Never. But I thought . . . I wondered if you . . ."

"Oh, dearest—just to have you here at Jalna—as one of us—to know that we belong to each other—makes me so happy." She took his hand and raised it to her cheek.

In fact all the family liked Humphrey Bell. In his unostentatious way he became one of them, as Fitzturgis, so strongly individualistic, failing in his efforts to fit a square peg into a round hole, could never have done. So much had been expected of Fitzturgis. Bell was looked on as a sweet-tempered, rather lovable oddity who possibly had it in him to write something that would add lustre to his name.

Less than a week later Mr Fennel appeared with shaven face. Renny, walking on the country road, met him face to face and did not recognize him. They passed, then Mr Fennel turned and called after Renny in a high falsetto voice quite unlike his own, "Pardon me, sir, but can you tell me if I am on the road that leads to St John's Church?"

Renny wheeled and strode back to him. "You are going in the opposite direction," he said. "You must . . ." Then his voice faltered; he stared and broke out, "Mr Fennel—you—without a beard! I never believed you'd do it. By Judas, you look wonderful!"

"You think it's an improvement?" asked the Rector, embarrassed yet rather pleased with himself.

Renny viewed him full face, then in profile. "You look nothing short of a bishop," he declared, "and if they don't make you one after this, I miss my guess."

"My dear fellow," laughed Mr Fennel, then added seriously, "The difficulty is appearing before the congregation on Sunday morning."

"I'll tell you what. I'll grow a beard that will take their mind off you. Mine would be fiery red, I'll wager."

In truth the congregation were almost as surprised by the disappearance of the Rector's beard as they were by the announcement of his engagement to Meg. It was universally agreed that both changes were for the better. Meg was looked upon as the perfect wife for a clergyman.

It was decided that Patience's marriage to Bell should take place in December, and that of Meg to the Rector early in the spring. Someone had suggested a double wedding, but Meg declared it would take her all the winter to prepare her house for the removal and the letting. In the meantime the young couple were to live with her. Often she condoled with Finch for having failed him.

This autumn was a successful one for Renny. East Wind more than lived up to the high hopes for him. He was not a temperamental horse. The confusion of a bad start did not trouble him. A piece of paper blown across his path did not cause him to swerve. Straight ahead, in a glory of speed, seeming to enjoy it, he won race after race. In the most important race of the season he defeated the favourite. Renny took him to Kentucky and he was victorious in a great race there. All this good luck, to him who had so often experienced the reverse, put Renny into high good spirits.

Adeline accompanied him on these occasions. He was delighted to have her with him, to be able to take her to the sort of hotels he considered suitable for his daughter. He devoted himself to her—to charm her into the obliterating of Fitzturgis from her mind. Sometimes he succeeded, but there were times when that scene by the lake rose before her with tragic distinctness and she would hear herself give a little moan of pain. Strangely the wild anger she had felt slept in her breast and only the pain was awake, ready still to stir. Once, in the dining room of an hotel, she glimpsed a face that set her pulses thumping. She could not swallow, she could not speak, but sat staring transfixed. Then the man, as though he were conscious of her eyes on him, turned and looked at her. It was a quite different face, not comparable to his in fineness or attraction, she thought, and realized in herself both disappointment and relief. It came to her as a shock, filling her with wonder, for she had never yet analysed her emotions, that if the man had been Fitzturgis she would have sprung from her seat, gone to him, forgiven him. Yet the idea of writing to him, of making an effort to heal the breach between them, never entered her mind. She had sent him off, she was done with him. He had not, since leaving, written to her. Surely if he had loved her deeply he would have written, begged for forgiveness. She had not, in truth, expected a letter from him.

When the time for the wedding of Patience and Bell drew near Meg asked her daughter whether Roma was to be invited.

"No," Patience said firmly. "I don't want her at my wedding."

"But we cannot treat Roma like that. It would be too unkind and would look so small-minded to the rest of the family and very strange to our friends. You should be grateful to her, dear, for getting Norman out of the way to make room for Humphrey."

"I hadn't thought of that. . . . If you think she should be invited, let's do it."

Roma was invited, and Roma came, bringing with her a handsome New York handbag as a present to Patience. Somehow the family had expected her to be different, to have about her the air of the great metropolis. They were prepared to see her elegantly trigged out in expensive clothes. They felt sure that she would be foolishly extravagant with the legacy from Nicholas.

But Roma looked exactly the same. She went up to her old bedroom at Meg's, hung up her things in the clothes cupboard, hummed a little tune, just as though she had never been away.

She was charming to Humphrey, was pleasant to everyone, though a little pensive in the presence of Adeline, a little puzzled, as though she wondered why Adeline treated her with such coldness.

Adeline was bridesmaid to Patience, little Mary was flower-girl. Renny gave the bride away. White chrysanthemums decorated the church, which was filled not only by the guests but by farmers and the working people of the neighbourhood, for everyone liked Patience. Mr Fennel, clean-shaven, looked so different from the Rector of old that Pheasant almost questioned whether the ceremony were legal. Humphrey was so nervous that he persisted in trying to place the ring on the wrong finger. But finally the two were united and the bride-groom kissed the bride with a strange gaiety, as though to imply that they were now in for it and that, on his part, he had cast humility to the winds. As for little Mary, who had so valiantly led the procession, followed by Adeline, in a primrose-yellow dress, then by the bride on Renny's arm, little Mary bent her golden head over her basket of flowers and shed an unseen tear or two. But, if her tears were unseen, certainly Meg's were not. No Victorian mother ever wept more feelingly over the loss of a daughter. Yet Patience was marrying a man whom Meg liked, and the pair would live within a stone's throw of the Rectory.

On the way to Jalna after the ceremony Renny remarked to Meg, for they were driving in the same car, "I hope that when your time comes you'll not disgrace us all by blubbering throughout the service."

"It will be an entirely different thing," she cried hotly. "Being married oneself is not like losing one's only daughter. And besides, when I saw Rupert"—she now called the Rector Rupert—"standing there, looking so beautiful in his clean surplice and his clean-shaven face, and realized how soon . . ." She began again to weep.

"Do you mean," he said, "you were thinking how soon the surplice would get soiled and how soon the Rector will grow another beard? For he can, you know, and probably will, as soon as you're married."

"Never. I shall never let him!"

They were now turning into the driveway. From other cars people began pouring into the house. A contingent of Humphrey's relations had arrived from New Brunswick. One and all thought his bride an attractive girl, and several of them wondered what she saw in him.

Wakefield had been unable to come to the wedding as he was on a tour through the United States in a successful play. He was playing male lead to an established actress. His own position in the theatre seemed secured. He sent one of the most admired presents received by the pair and a telegram so amusing that when it was read aloud the guests broke into genuine applause. The wedding was indeed a happy occasion. Meg dried her tears, and she and the Rector, standing side by side, for their engagement had been announced, were almost as much congratulated as the bride and groom. Renny, as the bride's guardian, made a lively and pungent speech. Referring to the bride's father as his dearest friend, he all but brought Meg to the point of tears again, but in consideration for the Rector she restrained them. Mr Fennel spoke felicitously, recalling how he had baptized Patience, who had not once cried; how he had prepared her for confirmation, performed the ceremony at her wedding. He even hinted, amid great applause, that he was soon to take on a new relationship toward her. Yet it was Maurice, as best man, who made the best speech. None of the family had believed it was in him to make such a speech—so warm, so eloquent, so poetic. Pheasant was so proud of him that she could scarcely restrain herself from open demonstration of her pride and tenderness. His brothers (for it was the first day of the Christmas holidays and Christian and Philip were present) were proud of him. Piers was proud of him.

Adeline said to him at the first opportunity, "You were splendid, Mooey. When I was listening to you I felt that you could do anything you wanted—if you chose to try."

"I could do anything with you beside me." He spoke close to her ear because of the din of talk. His cheek touched the fine hair at the temple.

The bridegroom also spoke. With literary care he had composed his speech. He had carefully memorized it, so there should be no haltings, no stammerings—and there were not. However, he uttered the speech in so low a tone that it was practically inaudible, yet everybody was so in sympathy with him that when he smiled at a little witticism he had made they all smiled too.

Maurice had been firm in his promise not to drink—that

is, up to this day he had been firm. But there were healths to drink and champagne to drink them in. Flushed, laughing, happy in his success as a speaker, happier still in Adeline's praise, he was carried away, his resolve melted. By the time the married pair had driven off in a car stormed by confetti he was uncertain in everything he said or did. Only one certainty was left him and that was that he must leave before Adeline noticed his condition. He saw Finch and went to him.

"Uncle Finch," he said, "I want to spend the night with you. I c-can't go home. Do you mind?"

"Of course, old man—I'll be glad to have you. I'll bring round my car and take you over whenever you like. What about going up to my old room here and resting for a bit?"

Maurice gave a dazed laugh. "Two flights of stairs! I couldn't do it. For God's sake take me now."

Piers strolled up. He looked his son over.

"Tight, eh?" he remarked, not unsympathetically.

"He thinks," said Finch, "he'd like to spend the night with me."

"Good idea. Get him out of the way before his mother sees him."

Maurice stood, swaying a little, a troubled smile on his face. Piers took his arm and walked beside him, as though in confidential conversation, to the porch.

"Explain to Aunt Alayne," said Maurice. "Tell her I have a headache."

"I will."

Finch was in his car on the drive. Piers said to him, as Maurice sank into the back seat. "Make him go to bed. Don't let him drink any more." He added in a lower tone, "Damned good speech he made, wasn't it?"

Adeline had not seen the departure. At that moment Archer was asking her, under cover of the babble of voices, "I wonder why there are so many flowers and so much ceremony and, after that, eating and drinking, both at funerals and weddings."

"I've never thought about it."

"I guess——" His eyes did not leave her face. He seemed to be watching for the effect of his words. "I guess it's to hide what's really going on."

"You," she told him, "should always wear a wreath of flowers on your head—to hide what's going on in it."

Alayne was passing, and, seeing them apparently engaged

in a pleasant interchange, asked, "Enjoying yourselves, darlings?"

"Oh yes, Mummy," they both agreed.

Dennis, in his best dark-blue suit and white shirt, had, as so often, been hovering near Finch, had heard him agree to Maurice's spending the night with him. He did not hesitate. He edged his way past the wedding guests, slipped through the front door, then ran across the snowy lawn, through the little gate and down into the ravine. It was not very dark down there, for there were many stars shining between the branches. Yet Dennis was very much afraid. He ran so fast that his heart became like a live thing struggling to get out between his ribs. He kept up his courage by saying over and over, "I'll get there first—see if I don't!"

At last he could see the house and the lights in the music room. There was as yet no sound of the car. He went into the hall, taking care to wipe the snow off his feet on the mat. He tore off his clothes and, naked but for his little woollen under-vest, got into bed between the cold sheets. He heard Finch and Maurice coming in at the door.

"I'm going to put you right into bed, Maurice," Finch was saying. "Then I must go back to the party."

"Awright," came docilely from Maurice.

They came into the bedroom. Dennis kept his eyes tight shut.

"W-why," said Maurice, "there's your boy in the bed."

Finch leant over Dennis. "Why are you here?" he asked. "And so early to bed?"

"I was tired. I thought of my own bed and I came to it."

"S-splendid," Maurice said, smiling down at Dennis. "I'll shleep on couch." He added, in what he believed to be an undertone, "Sweet lil boy . . . how nice he looks lying there."

Dennis smiled up at him, very pleased with himself.

"Dennis can sleep on the couch," said Finch. "I'll give you pyjamas . . . Lord, I must get back to the party."

But Maurice insisted on leaving Dennis in possession. When Finch had established him on the couch in the music room and gone off in his car, Dennis could hear him singing softly to himself in a pleasing baritone:

"*She is far from the land where her young hero sleeps.*"

After a while he called out, "Dennis! Are you awake?"

"Yes, Maurice."

"Do you think you could get me a drink? I'm not feeling well . . . shouldn't risk walking . . . too damn dizzy."

"A drink of water?"

"No. . . . Something out of the decanter on sideboard."

"I'm afraid I couldn't."

"Awright, Dennis. . . . Doesn't matter."

After that there was silence.

22

MEG MARRIED

EARLY IN the New Year Maurice returned to Ireland and Christian accompanied him. He was to remain with him till spring. He then was to go to the Slade School of Fine Arts in London. When he left Ireland, Pheasant was to make her long-promised visit to Maurice, taking little Mary with her. Though Maurice had—with the exception of his lapse at the time of the wedding—shown real firmness in his resolve to avoid drinking, Piers and Pheasant felt that it would be reckless to allow him to return alone.

At the time of saying goodbye Maurice took Adeline's hands in both of his. "Remember," he said, "that I have not given up hope."

Her hands in his did not relax. "I shall not marry anyone. I can be happy without that. I don't want it—not now."

"You say that, but you'll change your mind. Adeline, you can't make me believe that a love like mine won't beget love. It can't just perish."

"I've seen love perish."

"Not my sort." He tried to draw her to him. "A kiss," he pleaded, "a real kiss—not just a peck, sweetheart."

She kissed him, taking the initiative in almost aggressive consent. "There," she said. "Now, goodbye."

She was relieved when he was gone. Yet strangely she missed him. Sometimes she pictured him and Christian at Glengorman. Christian sent her a sketch he had made of Maurice—an excellent likeness—and this she pinned up in her bedroom.

The winter passed, quickly it seemed, in its first months, then slowly, as March absent-mindedly still wrapped itself in garments of ice and snow. But at the end a heavy rain came and warm spring air, and in the morning mail the collected edition of Eden's poems. The three slender volumes made a sizeable book when bound together, with an introduction by a well-known American critic. The binding was a charming shade of blue, with silver lettering. The frontispiece was a portrait of Eden. He looked ready for a long and happy life.

Renny, who found the book on the desk in his office in the stables, where it had been brought by Wright from the post, examined it with pride, the lines about his lips and eyes intent. Through the open door he saw Wright passing and called out to him. "Wright—come in here for a minute."

Wright entered. "Yes, sir." He looked at the book in Renny's hands.

"Wright," said Renny, "this is the collected poems of my brother Eden. You remember how he was always writing verses."

"I do indeed, sir. Well . . . that's wonderful . . . and so long after . . . I'll not touch it, as my hands aren't very clean. But—thanks for showing me."

"Look." Renny opened the book at the portrait. "A good likeness, eh?"

Here was something Wright could appreciate. "Gosh, sir," he exclaimed. "I've never seen a better likeness. It's as though he was in the room with us." Both men bent to examine the portrait.

"I used to think," Wright said, "it would have been better for him if he'd written less poetry and done more riding. He was a first-rate rider. Good hands and a good seat."

"Yes. I thought so many a time when he was ill."

"But—in that case—you'd never have had the book, sir."

"True."

"There's compensations, I always try to think."

Six copies of the book had been sent from the publisher. Renny went over in his mind the names of those to whom he would give them. It did not enter his mind that other copies might be bought. One for himself and his family. One for Meg and hers. One for Piers and his. One for Finch. One for Wakefield. One for Roma. She, of course, would have the royalties. These, he guessed, remembering Eden's other books of poetry, would not be large. He gave a grimace, half pride, half ruefulness, when he considered what a family of artists they were growing to be. Eden, Finch, Wake, Nook, and now here was Humphrey with his novel.

He walked across the squelchy fields, with crows flying overhead, to carry Meg's copy to her. She took it in her hands with an exclamation of delight, but when she opened it and saw Eden's picture she burst into tears.

"Oh, the poor dear boy," she sobbed. "To think that he had to die! And to suffer so long! My one consolation is that I did everything in my power to comfort him."

"You did indeed, Meggie. . . . Now, cheer up. Your wedding is coming soon. You have lots of pleasant things to think of."

She dried her eyes. "Already the presents are beginning to come. And the Bishop is to perform the ceremony. Rupert is so pleased."

"Splendid." He patted her plump back. Then he asked, "Meggie, why don't you dye your hair before the wedding?"

"Me dye my hair! Why, I've been grey for years and years. Why on earth should I dye my hair now?"

"Well, Rupert has shaved off his beard. Am I to call him Rupert, by the way?"

"It scarcely sounds respectful, but—I think he'd like it. I am sure he'd not like to see me with different hair. In fact he has more than once admired my hair. He says it sets off my fresh complexion."

"But how much better would red hair set it off. I say, Meg, I've read the advertisements for hair-tinting. I do wish you'd try red."

"Me with red hair! You're joking."

"No—I'm in dead earnest. I can just picture you and Rupert marching along the aisle to the strains of the Wedding March —he smooth-shaven, you red-haired."

"I'd break off the engagement first."

"Aunt Augusta dyed her hair, didn't she?"

"She did. A purplish black."

"Ah, but the new shades are different. How about blue?"

"I loathe blue hair. No, Renny—I refuse. You're wasting your breath."

At this moment Humphrey came into the room in a panic.

"Whatever is wrong, dear?" Meg asked him, as one would speak to a frightened child.

"A reporter," he said, breathing hard. "Come to interview me about my book."

"That just proves," she said soothingly, "how successful it is."

"But he's a reporter for an *American* magazine!"

"Better still. Humphrey, dear, it's splendid."

"But he will probably call me the undersized, thirty-three-year-old albino author. I won't see him . . . I won't . . . I won't. Tell him I'm having an attack of amnesia. Tell him I'm dead!"

"I'll see him for you," said Renny.

"Oh, thank you. Could you possibly pretend you're me?"

"Well . . . I'll think about it."

"Those fellows give you no time to think," said Humphrey Bell.

In Meg's pretty drawing room Renny found the personable young reporter, who asked with unconcealed surprise, "Mr Bell?"

Renny shyly bowed and offered him a limp hand.

"You have written a very unusual novel, Mr Bell."

"We think so," said Renny, looking at the young man's shoes.

"We?"

"My wife and I."

"I see." He was writing in a notebook. "Been married long?"

"Since last December. If you look out of that window you'll see my wife coming in at the gate."

"She looks very young."

"She is, but I don't mind."

"Mr Bell, would you tell me what influenced your choice of the theme of the story?"

"I don't know. It just came to me."

"I see." He was writing in his notebook. "It's very fine, I think, the way you have turned the struggles of pride and envy and passion into life in this book."

"Yes, isn't it?"

"You see, I've read the book."

"I'm glad to hear that."

The reporter grinned, then asked, "Have you read it, Colonel Whiteoak?"

Renny stared at him in amazement. "Why—I've tried to," he said, then demanded, "Who the devil do you think . . ."

The young man answered with a laugh, "I saw you ride in Madison Square Gardens several years ago. I recognized you as soon as you came into the room."

"Well, I'll be damned."

"That was a lovely horse and a grand performance you gave on it."

"Thanks. You like horses, eh? Now let me take you to my stables and I'll show you some very promising colts. . . ."

"I'd like very much to see them, but my job is to interview Mr Bell. Is he here?"

"He is, but he just can't stand interviews. He's a very nice fellow but shy, and he has a strange sort of idea that his manner of living is his own business.

"I'd ask no more than a quarter of an hour."

"There's not a chance of it. Better come straight to the stables with me."

It all ended by the young journalist's writing an article about the stables at Jalna. In Renny's office, over a drink, material for a lively interview was garnered.

With great speed the weeks flew to the time of Meg's marriage. The day came, in springtime warmth. Noah Binns was able to get as far as the church and sit on a bench directing young Chalk in the bell-ringing. Meg had carried spring flowers that morning and laid them on the graves of the departed Whiteoaks. The prettiest she laid on the graves of Eden and Nicholas.

The wedding was an impressive ceremony, for there was the Bishop, and there was Mr Fennel, looking like another bishop. There was Finch at the organ, for Miss Pink was down with 'flu—providentially, it seemed to Meg. There was Meg herself, in a lovely lavender silk dress and a tiny French hat. There was Renny, giving her away, and there was Rupert, taking her—to have and to hold till death did them part. There was the church packed with people, there was Jalna packed with people. Finally there were the happy couple setting out to fly to Victoria, where the Rector had a brother, an aunt aged ninety, three cousins, a niece and five nephews.

Roma regretted, she said, that because of a press of work she could not come to the wedding. She sent Meg a pretty handbag, the replica of the one she had sent Patience.

There was general rejoicing when Wakefield was able to be present. He was so attractive, so gay. These high spirits he took with him to Vaughanlands on the morning after the wedding. He had already inspected the house, found it admirable, sighed to think he never was long enough in one place to have a proper home. Yet soon he was cheerful again.

Finch, seated at the piano, sheets of music sprinkled with cigarette ash scattered over the floor, his jacket in a heap on the floor also, his hair on end, said, with a touch of his old manner toward a cocky younger brother, "Well, you look nice and sunshiny."

"And you look the perfect picture of genius at work. I'll not disturb you. I just dropped in to see how you are after the party."

Finch got to his feet and stretched. "Not feeling like work. I'm going to take a day off. Too much champagne."

Wakefield gave a sympathetic grunt, then said, "I met Dennis outside with your Great Dane. What a picture they made! I envy you that little boy, Finch. I shall never have a son."

A shadow fell on his face. The darkness of his hair, his eyes, his olive complexion, made the shadow more palpable.

"Why do you say that?" asked Finch, wondering if Wake were being melodramatic.

"Because I'm . . . living in a way . . ." He put his hand to his forehead.

Finch perceived something in Wakefield's face that made him ask, in eager sympathy, "What are you trying to tell me, Wake?"

"It's quite simply this. Molly Griffith and I are living together as man and wife."

"But . . ." stammered Finch, "I thought . . ."

"You thought we had given each other up—for ever. And so we had . . . till this happened."

Finch dropped into a chair, his face a picture of astonishment. "I'm flabbergasted," he said. "I looked on you two as adamant in your renunciation. I admired you for it, but—I wondered how you could do it. I guessed what it had cost you."

Wakefield halted in his nervous pacing of the room. "No one could imagine . . . not unless they had gone through it. There we were, in the same company, acting together, sometimes passionate love scenes, and . . . all the while subduing our own feelings . . . crushing them under. Sometimes we joined other companies. Then it was even worse . . . the longing to be together."

"But always you resisted?"

"Together or apart we always resisted."

"You know, Wake, you deserve wings and a halo."

"I have something better. I have Molly."

"Tell me how it happened—if you don't mind."

"That's what I came for. I wanted you to know and for a special reason." He sat down close to Finch. Finch felt that Wakefield was aiming some disclosure directly at him, but Wakefield went on, as though completely self-absorbed. "One day I met Fitzturgis face to face. We chatted for a bit. I was feeling sort of down. I asked him to have lunch with me and he seemed pleased."

"What is he doing?"

"Well, he didn't last long in the advertising business. I never expected he would. Now he's got a job in the British Consulate—much more in his line."

"Did he . . . speak of his sister?"

"He did indeed. I'm coming to that later. Well, the upshot of this meeting was that he came to see the play, and backstage afterwards. I invited him to my lodgings. We had a long talk. I can't think of another man I've been so drawn to. It ended by my telling him about Molly and me."

"Good Lord, I don't see how you could!"

"I wanted to. I had not talked of us before . . . to any outsider, and it was a relief and . . . he was so sympathetic. I'm sorry that Adeline is not going to marry him."

"I'm not," Finch said stubbornly, then asked, "What reason did you give him for a marriage between you and Molly not being legal?"

"I told him that we are connected—not closely—no closer to my mind than first cousins—but that legal marriage is not possible. I told him that during all the years we'd loved each other neither of us had any attachment to anyone else. We'd been virtuous. We'd never lived together. Well, Finch, he gave me a sombre look—a penetrating look—and he asked, 'Has this virtue made you happy? Has it been its own reward?' And I had to answer that we'd been wretchedly unhappy. Then he asked, 'Why can't you make a complete break—have done with the ordeal?' And I said we'd never give up our love. That set him off. Somehow he convinced me that we were fools to throw away our chances of a happy life because of a legal quibble or some worn-out rule of the Church. He's some years younger than I, but he is more worldly. Perhaps you'd call him hedonistic. Anyhow, I took his advice. Molly was eager to take it."

"Yet once she was as ready as you to abide by the rules."

"She was. But now"—Wakefield gave a little laugh—"our rule is—love and be happy. We've got a nice little apartment near the Park. Will you come and see us before we go back to London?"

Finch reached out to grasp Wake's hand. "I will indeed."

"I haven't told Renny yet, but I shall today."

"Gosh, I wonder how he'll take it."

"I can't imagine. Anyhow—it's done, and we're happy. Completely basking in the sunshine of our new life."

"Yet you looked sad when you spoke of never having a son. That rather surprised me."

"One can't have everything, I suppose, but I am fond of children." He was thoughtful for a space, then he said, "I've seen Fitzturgis a number of times since those first meetings. I've met his mother. He and Sylvia live with her. She's a dear but rather garrulous."

"That sister of Fitzturgis's—how is she?"

"Very well. She has a job, modelling clothes. Molly and I went to one of the spring exhibitions. Sylvia looked lovely—a figure like a sylph, though a bit too thin."

There was a pregnant silence between them, then Wakefield said, "Fitzturgis has told me about you and Sylvia."

"She'd not thank him for that. I think it was brutal."

"He's been a good brother to her. I've never seen a brother and sister so devoted. Finch! I can't believe you will let her affair with Galbraith keep you permanently apart."

"My God, that fellow told you everything!"

"Only because he thinks it might have gone differently if she'd come to you herself. You're not the man I think you are if you have been able to put her out of your mind so easily."

"*Easily!*" echoed Finch with violence. "*Easily!* Look here, Wake, I refuse to talk about this. It's all over between Sylvia and me. It was a flare-up—a brief passion—it's left me unmoved." As he said this he trembled from head to foot. Drops of sweat showed on his forehead.

A step was heard in the porch. Renny came in, followed by the Great Dane.

"Hullo," he said. "Recovering from the party? By Judas, Finch, you look all in."

"I'm all right," muttered Finch.

Wakefield stood very straight in front of Renny. "I've something to tell you," he said. Then hurried on, looking right into his elder's eyes. "It's this: Molly Griffith and I are living together—as man and wife, you understand. Nothing you or any living person can say will dissuade me. Our union is a *fait accompli* . . . I want you to understand and sympathize. If you don't—well, I'm sorry, but—nothing can change us."

As he talked the colour left his face. He was white and tense. Renny's weather-beaten face, on the contrary, deepened in colour. He stared in surprise, then put up his hand and stroked an eyebrow in embarrassment.

"Ah . . ." he said, "so." And after a little he repeated—"Ah . . . so . . . yes, I see." He looked at the scattered sheets of music as though for inspiration. "Well, that's as it may be," he went on. "We all have to compromise, as it were. . . . Has Finch told you he has written a piano concerto? It's good, I can tell you. He's a bit of a genius, this fellow. Look here, Dennis"—for the little boy now came into the room—"tell Uncle Wake what the movements are."

"First movement: allegro spiritoso; second movement: adagio; third movement: minuet and trio; finale: presto," rattled off the little boy with surprising glibness, while Finch regarded him in pessimistic wonder.

"Get Finch to play it for you, Wake," said Renny. "You'll love it. . . . Isn't this a picturesque little house he has built!" It was the first time Renny had deigned to praise Finch's house, but he now ran his hand across the door nearest him and praised the quality and finish of the wood.

Dennis and the Great Dane were looking up at him expectantly. "This boy," Renny remarked to Wakefield, "was given Finch by a woman who loved him too well. This dog was given him by one who loved him not enough. I wonder what the next one will give him. . . . Well," he added thoughtfully, "that's as it may be. . . . Dennis, do you want to come with me and see a lovely pair of twin lambs?"

"Oh yes," cried Dennis. "Let's go now!"

Dog, boy and man left with one accord. Finch and Wakefield saw them climb into Renny's mud-splashed car—Dennis in the front seat beside Renny, the Great Dane occupying the rear seat.

There was silence for a moment after the sound of the departing car, then Wakefield said, "He took it pretty well, didn't he?"

Finch's only answer was an hysterical laugh. He laughed till there were tears in his eyes. Blinking them away, he said seriously, "Tell me more about the Fitzturgis family."

"Well," said Wakefield, "one thing I can tell you is that our little Roma is hot in pursuit of Maitland."

"Ah . . . so," murmured Finch, in very poor imitation of Renny. "That's as it may be. . . . But . . . actually, the one I should like to hear about is Sylvia."

"She is a lovely girl, Finch," said Wakefield, "and, I believe, is very much in love with you."

23

THE SPRING MOVES ON

BEFORE THE Rector and Meg had returned from their honeymoon, Pheasant, taking little Mary with her, had set out for the long-promised visit to Ireland. It was planned that later Piers should follow her. The bequests from Nicholas had made so many pleasant things possible. Letters from Christian were reassuring on the subject of Maurice. It was seldom that Maurice drank more than was good for him—so seldom that this had ceased to be an anxiety. Christian himself was supremely content. Both sons were counting the days till Pheasant's arrival.

Piers was to spend the time of her absence at Jalna. Young Philip, when the holidays came, would be there also. By a miracle, it seemed, Alayne's domestic worries were solved. The winter had been a nightmare of makeshift. The daily help was erratic, to say the best of it. Adeline, though strong and willing, could scarcely be depended on. However, one propitious day a Dutch farmer and his wife were sent by an agency. The man intended to farm in Canada later on but first wanted to learn the methods of Canadian agriculture. The couple agreed to remain at Jalna for the season. The man was to help Piers on the farm, the wife to do the cooking. At the beginning Alayne hoped they would stay till the Wragges' return, but after a month of the Dutch couple's efficiency, cleanliness and energy she frequently wished she might keep them permanently.

But the felicity in the kitchen was a dim affair compared with the exultation in the stables. The high hopes of the horsy company of Renny, Wright, Crowdy, Chase and the trainer were filled to overflowing by the colt East Wind. In the spring races at the Woodbine blithely he blew past the winning-post a full length ahead of the favourite. Before the year was out he was to be a winner at Jamaica, New York and Maryland—earning for Renny almost a hundred thousand dollars.

"I don't want to crow over you, Alayne," Renny would exult, "but you must acknowledge that I used very good judgment in buying East Wind. Think what he's done for us."

"It's splendid," Alayne would admit, "but I do hope you will save what you have made and take no further risks."

"Trust me," he would say. "I will show both caution and enterprise—as I always have."

In June, when the freshness of early summer was brightly visible, even in so great a city as New York. Finch arrived there with the manuscript of his concerto to arrange for publication. One of the first things he did was to telephone Wakefield, who promptly invited him to lunch with himself and Molly. The two made a scene of blissful domesticity as together they prepared the lunch.

"It's glorious," Wakefield said, "to buy your food yourself and cook it yourself, after eating in restaurants."

"Who does the cooking?" asked Finch.

"Me," said Molly, her cheeks pink as she bent above a pan of sizzling sweetbreads.

"And she's really good at it." Wakefield's eyes joined in the praise of his lips. "But I make the salad."

It was a delicious meal and Finch did justice to it. Both Molly and Wakefield asked him many questions about his concerto, about his plans for the coming season, but neither could keep long from the subject that held their single-minded interest—the stage. They were in a new play, the scene of which was set in medieval Florence.

"You should see Molly in her costumes. It's her best part in New York, you know. You must come tonight. I'll get you a ticket."

"You should see Wake," said Molly. "He takes the part of a Spanish prince and looks it."

"Don't tell anyone," said Wakefield, "that I simply resemble my Irish relations."

They were so happy together Finch envied them—Molly with her sleek waves of golden-bronze hair, her daring, tilted profile, the golden freckles on her nose. The *picture* of what she was, the woman she was, showed in her face, as did her profession of acting. It was mobile, yet it was steady. To Finch it seemed the face of one who had been in flight but was now come to rest.

Before he left he asked, "What of your sisters, Molly?"

"Althea is here in New York, doing very well in commercial art. Garda is happily married and living in Detroit where her husband has something to do with motor cars. Gem—you remember Gem?"

"Who could forget her?"

"She married Tom Raikes, you know. They went back to Wales and she bought the house we used to live in. She has two children and is expecting a third."

"I hope she's happy."

"As happy as any woman living with Tom could be."

Finch longed to speak of Sylvia but could not find the words. He lingered, hoping they would do so, but neither mentioned her name. He left them, feeling oddly depressed. Did they avoid speaking of her because they thought Finch shrank from speaking of her? Or were they so selfishly absorbed by the fascination of their own life that they had no feeling for others?

In the afternoon he was free to wander in the streets. This was new to him because on other visits he had an engagement to face or was about to sail or had just arrived and was on his way somewhere else. The day was warm. On his return to his hotel he enjoyed a cool shower.

He was early at the theatre. There was a quite good audience. The play had been running for a week. Three seats next to his remained vacant till just before the curtain rose. Then their occupants filed in, disturbing those in the same row with them. The three, a man and two women, murmured an apology as they passed. Finch hated late-comers and gave their dark figures a surly look. The lights had gone down. The man seated himself in the middle. The woman next Finch dropped her programme. Both she and Finch bent to pick it up. Their hands touched. He saw her incline her head in thanks and felt somehow mollified.

The first act went well, though it was a little confusing. When the curtain fell the three late-comers bent to consult their programmes. Finch cast a glance at the woman on his left. He saw the close curling hair, the shapely nape. There was something familiar about her. She raised her head and he saw her profile. She did not yet see him. It was Sylvia. On her other side sat Fitzturgis, and beyond him Roma.

Finch's first thought was to escape. He could not meet her here, not in this way. But—if he left she would almost certainly see him go—see him running away from her. This was no chance encounter. Wakefield had arranged it. Did Sylvia possibly know that their seats were side by side? Did Fitzturgis know? But they did not glance at him. They, and Roma, appeared absorbed in each other.

After the second act came the intermission. Finch scarcely had known what was taking place on the stage during this act. He could give his mind to nothing but the fact of Sylvia's nearness. He felt isolated with her as he had felt isolated when he played the piano for her in his own house. At moments a strange happiness surged through him and he longed to turn to her.

When the lights came up and people were pouring into the aisles on their way to the foyer he remained in his seat, as though studying his programme, till the three had passed out. He watched them move along the aisle, Sylvia first, with her graceful walk, her lovely wan face and too slim body; Roma, round-cheeked, smiling up at Fitzturgis. When they were lost in the crowd Finch too went out but avoided them.

Wakefield had asked him to listen to the comments of people about him concerning the play, and more especially what might be said of himself or Molly. But it was impossible. Finch was conscious of nothing but Sylvia's nearness. He had thought he was finished with Sylvia, but now, in this crowded theatre, she was nearer to him than ever. Does anything in life ever end, he wondered. Sarah was dead, buried far away in California, yet he had not finished with her. Even at an hour such as this her pale face, her black hair appeared before him. . . . He was scarcely conscious of returning to his seat, but found himself in it. The three had not yet come back. He thrust the thought of Sarah from him. She was dead and should have remained dead, not come back to force her cold presence on him.

He kept his head bent, reading the advertisements in his programme. Roma was pressing past his knees. His little niece so near to him. Her touch made her seem a child again. Her head was bent, as she peered into his face. "Uncle Finch!" she was saying. "What a surprise!"

"Roma." He took her hand in his. His heart warmed to her.

"Look, Mait," she said, over her shoulder. "See who's here."

Fitzturgis smiled down at Finch but firmly propelled Roma toward her seat. The lights were going down. He had a brief glimpse of Sylvia's face. Then she was sitting beside him in the dimness. He had seen, too, that she had made an attempt to change places with Roma, had heard Fitzturgis say in a low voice, "Sit down—sit down."

The voices of the actors came loudly, meaningless, from the stage. There all was brightness, colour, movement. Here, the four whose lives were so interwoven mingled in a new pattern; here was darkness, isolation. Finch could see the paleness of Sylvia's arms meeting in her tensely clasped hands. He remembered, he lived again, those hours at night when he had played to her, when their newly born love had been the theme of all he played. He was tremulous in that recollection, shaken by the thought that he had let her go—no, not that—had driven her out of his life.

What if now she would refuse to enter it again?

Her face was turned away. She was not looking at the stage but appeared to be studying her brother's profile. The play had ceased to have any meaning for them. They might have been sleep-walkers for all the meaning the play had. Yet now on the stage was Wakefield uttering words of impassioned love.

"My life is yours. . . . Do with it what you will. . . . Forgive me if I cannot make myself worthy of you. . . . It will not be for lack of trying. Oh, my beloved. . . ."

High-flown words, but Finch made them speak for him. He laid his hand on Sylvia's arm. She did not move. She was now looking at the stage, as though rapt. Finch slid his hand along her arm till her hand was reached. Their two hands lay together like the hands of sleepers dreaming the same dream.

His hand folded itself about hers. With all his skill as a musician he sought to give her the message which later his lips would give. She understood. Her fingers closed on his. He raised her hand to his breast.

A good moment had come in the play. There was loud applause.

Pastoral 70p

A magnificent story of a tortured love affair set against the intensely charged atmosphere of an RAF bomber station.

Marazan 75p

The first of Nevil Shute's many brilliant novels – a story of prison escape, murder and smuggling.

Round the Bend 80p

'A flight of fictional magic that is lovely to witness and enchanting to experience' NEW YORK HERALD TRIBUNE

Lonely Road 70p

A compelling and intriguing story that blends a haunting romance with the sustained suspense of a gun-running drama.

Slide Rule 60p

Nevil Shute's fascinating autobiography, the life of a writer and engineer.

In the Wet 70p

Fascinating and richly dramatic, a tale of tomorrow, as foretold by a remarkable old man dying in the flooded Queensland bush.

Trustee from the Toolroom 75p

A shy engineer's odyssey in search of his niece's birthright.

Hugh Walpole

Rogue Herries £1·25

The history of a divided family that mirrors eighteenth-century England – magnificent fiction set against the wild and beautiful scenery of the Lake District, crowded with fairs, revels, witches, murder, strolling players and Jacobite agents. Dominating all is proud, intolerant Francis Herries – the dark Angel of Borrowdale – who despised his wife and sold his mistress at a public fair, yet came to love sixteen-year-old Mirabell Starr above life itself . . .

Judith Paris 90p

The most delightful of Hugh Walpole's heroines, Judith, tempestuous daughter of Rogue Herries, is torn between ambition and her longing for the wild beauty of Cumberland. Never one to think of the consequences, Judith, loving as fiercely as she hates, knows passion, tragedy and triumph, and finds in her son Adam her past, her future and her destiny.

The Fortress 95p

Walter Herries swore he would destroy everyone in Fell House: Judith Paris knew she alone could foil him . . . This compelling novel traces the wildly fluctuating fortunes of the Herries family through fifty momentous years, up to Queen Victoria's coronation. Dark, violent and passionate, the story yet glows with excitement and the fullness of life amid the unchanging countryside that all the Herries so loved.

Vanessa £1·25

Everyone said that Benjie was no good . . . At fifteen, Vanessa had Benjie in her blood: she would never betray him. This absorbing novel portrays the lives of successive generations of Herries – from the triumph of Judith Paris's hundredth birthday in the 1870s to the disillusionment of the 1930s. The author's understanding of love is matched by his masterly descriptions of the wild Cumberland countryside – where the past was never dead and the spirit of Rogue Herries lived on . . .

Susan Howatch

Cashelmara £1·75

A glorious, full-blooded novel which centres on Cashelmara, a coldly beautiful Georgian house in Galway, ancestral home of Edward de Salis.

The fast-moving plot follows the turbulent fortunes of an aristocratic Victorian family through half a century of furious encounters, ill-advised liaisons and bitter-sweet interludes of love.

'Another blockbuster from Susan Howatch' SUNDAY TIMES

The Waiting Sands 60p

Six people are gathered to celebrate Decima Mannering's twenty-first birthday in her isolated Scottish castle. Rachel Lord, summoned urgently by Decima, finds the house filled with unbearable tension . . . There would be six guests – would death be the host?

Call in the Night 60p

Claire Sullivan comes halfway round the world to answer a desperate cry for help from her sister, Gina. But when she arrives in Paris, Gina has disappeared. Her trail leads her to Garth, who is unconcerned about Gina, but very interested in Claire . . . But what is the terrible secret he is trying to hide?

The Dark Shore 60p

Sarah Hamilton, the second wife of the enigmatic Jon Towers, comes to the Cornish farmhouse where his first wife had mysteriously died . . . Everyone said it was an accident. But why did everyone who had been together that fatal weekend gather again? On the stark, romantic cliffs, Sarah's dreams become nightmares as the past looms over the future.